WHAT
LIES
HIDDEN

FRAN McDONNELL

POOLBEG

This book is a work of fiction. The names, characters, places, businesses,
organisations and incidents portrayed in it are either the product of the author's
imagination or are used fictitiously. Any resemblance to actual persons,
living or dead, events or locales is entirely coincidental.

Published 2020
by Poolbeg Press Ltd.
123 Grange Hill, Baldoyle,
Dublin 13, Ireland
Email: poolbeg@poolbeg.com

ISBN 978178199-724-6

www.poolbeg.com

About the author

Fran McDonnell was born and raised in Newry, County Down. She has a degree in Nursing and worked as a nurse in England. She also has a Master's in Women's Studies. After travelling, Fran did a Diploma in Kinesiology and set up her kinesiology clinic in Limerick city. She lives in County Tipperary where she grows vegetables and enjoys watching beautiful sunsets.

What Lies Hidden is her debut novel.

Acknowledgements

Thank you to Paula Campbell at Poolbeg Press for believing in my book and for the attention and enthusiasm she gave to every aspect of the process. Thanks also to Gaye Shortland for her insight, finesse and commitment which polished what I wrote into this form.

Anne said I should do something creative with my time during my recovery and this is it. Thanks also for reading it, Anne, and for the feedback.

I want to thank my beta readers, my mum, my sister, my dad, my brother and his wife and my cousins. Your encouragement and feedback made me believe that this book was worth working on. A special thanks goes to my nephew Liam McDonnell, my alpha-beta reader. He maintained that this book could get published from early on and without his insistence that I persevere I would have given up. Thanks also to my mum who has read every word of every draft and painstakingly given me feedback. We did it, Mum.

Words seem so inadequate to convey the depth of gratitude I feel to the nurses and doctors of University Hospital Limerick who looked after me during my cancer treatment. Your kindness and care were out of this world. Thanks also to the staff of the Cancer Support Unit – you were a real comfort to me in those difficult times.

Thank you to all my friends who rallied around and took me to chemo, cooked for me, shopped for me, drove me around and generally got me through what had to be faced. They sent cards, prayed, lit candles and texted until I felt that I was wrapped in a net of love and care and support.

Thank you to Anne Marie who sent me pictures of rainbows to keep my spirits up. Thanks especially to Nuala and Denise who were with me for every important appointment, helping me cope with what I heard. Thank you to my family who were with me through the pain and who celebrate with me now. I love you.

For my family, friends and carers. Without your love, support and care I wouldn't be here.

Chapter 1

Monday 21st May 2018

Isobel McKenzie stopped walking and placed one hand on her hip. "Are you here to make sure I get on the plane?"

A step later her escort stopped too. The stream of people behind them flowed out around the sudden obstruction.

"I thought –"

"You thought I might chicken out."

A young girl slowed, interested in this unfolding drama but her mother, oblivious, pulled her on impatiently before she heard the reply.

"I thought you might be nervous and appreciate the support."

Isobel swallowed the lump that rose in her throat. Dave touched her arm and turned her towards a café. Isobel found a table, wiped her eyes and took some deep breaths. She watched her older brother as he busied himself getting coffee. There were only three years between them and, while that made him only forty-two, he seemed older. His six-foot-two frame was straight and imposing and his dark hair had only a smattering of grey at the temples. Isobel was a whole foot shorter and was inclined to curves. Her hair was dark but now sported an ash front.

1

Dave brought the coffees back to the table.

"I'm sorry," Isobel said. "I am nervous. Very."

Dave nodded. "I encouraged you to take this trip. Peter is a good guy. I've known him a long time. I trust him. He asked for your help and since you're not working at the moment . . ."

Isobel played with her spoon. "Maybe I won't be able to help him."

"Maybe not." He shrugged. "Look – he wants your opinion on a case. He obviously thinks you might see something that he's missing. If you can't see anything, fine, he gets his mind put to rest and you get a couple of days in London. How bad is that?" He relaxed back in his chair.

Isobel shrugged. In the face of such logic there was no room for anxiety and doubt. She wrinkled her brow. "I know you've been worried about me but I just need some space, some time out."

Dave leant forward. "I understand, but I thought this trip could help you remember some of who you are, what you can do, what you could do again – that's all." Sensing her withdrawal, he sat back again.

Isobel took a deep breath, exhaled and then nodded.

Dave reached out and squeezed her hand. "It's only a few days in London. It might help you."

"I've never consulted on a legal case before. What can someone who listens to people's problems do on a legal case?"

"I don't know."

Isobel raised an eyebrow.

"Remember, Peter knows you from college," he said. "He knows that you studied psychology and he asked me a lot of questions about the other things you've done. I told him about your work with addiction, with couples

2

separating, divorcing and getting back together and with all sorts of abuse. Obviously he wouldn't tell me about the case, but he said he wanted an outside opinion from someone who knew people, not a legal one." He frowned. "I don't think he's done this before either."

Isobel made a face, then sipped her coffee.

He hurried on. "And, I think he wanted someone he could trust because he's in uncharted territory too. Your qualifications as a psychotherapist speak for themselves but I think it's really your experience that interests him."

Isobel nodded. "We'll see."

"Hopefully it won't be too taxing. Make sure you rest."

She grinned. "Stop fussing. I'm going to mind myself."

Dave stood up. "We'd better get you through security or you're going to miss your flight. Ready?"

Isobel nodded.

"Let's get you airborne then."

Just over an hour later Isobel landed in Heathrow. It was a simple matter to get the shuttle from the airport and the Tube to Hammersmith where she checked into her accommodation. As part of her consultancy expenses, Peter had offered to book her a room in a hotel convenient to his office but she preferred to stay in the Temple Lodge Club where she had stayed before. She loved this place. It was like an oasis in the middle of London, with organic food and cotton sheets and a marvellous vegetarian restaurant at the bottom of the garden. She had always felt comfortable here and this familiarity might make these next few days and this new assignment more manageable.

She unpacked and, since she was here working, changed into a pair of black trousers, a blouse and a jacket. She grinned at herself in the mirror. Now she looked like a professional. Whatever help Peter expected with this case she could fake it until she made it. She straightened her collar, squared her shoulders and, with a last encouraging look at herself, she set off.

She walked to Hammersmith Tube station. She looked at the Tube map, at the different-coloured lines, all of them different paths, different journeys. Her life had had a few line-switches recently and that had been very challenging and stressful. For the city she needed the District line. It was green – maybe that was a good omen that things were moving forward.

Chapter 2

The office on Queen Street was a very impressive concrete and glass edifice. An efficient lady at the reception desk directed Isobel to the third floor. Stepping out of the lift, she saw more glass doors ahead which led through to an open area where two women were sitting at desks typing. They both looked up – a lady with white hair who after a cursory glance resumed typing, and a younger blonde woman.

Isobel smiled slightly. "I'm here to see Peter Wright."

"Isobel McKenzie?" said the blonde, getting to her feet. Isobel nodded.

"I'm Patricia, Peter's secretary."

She was taller than Isobel, about five foot six, and slim. She gave off a general aura of being efficient and capable.

"Peter is expecting you. Please come this way."

As Isobel followed her down the corridor, she turned and said, "Was your flight all right?"

"Yes, thank you."

"Here we are." Patricia swung the door open and ushered Isobel in. "Ms McKenzie," she said then withdrew, closing the door.

The room was not huge, about the size of an average

sitting room, with a desk facing the door. Behind the desk was a window letting in as much light as the buildings around allowed. There were two chairs for clients, filing cabinets lined up on the righthand side and above them shelves of what looked like legal reference books.

The man at the desk rose. Peter Wright was tall, six foot, with short blond hair and tanned. He held himself with an easy confidence yet Isobel detected a level of stress and uncertainty beneath his urbane manner. He stepped out from behind the desk and held out his hand. Isobel extended hers and found it cupped in both of his.

"Isobel, thank you so much for coming. I realise that this has all happened rather fast."

"Yes."

"Sit down, sit down."

The chair was surprisingly comfortable.

Peter hesitated and then sat back behind the desk. "I remember you from when I was at college. I think we met a handful of times when I was out with Dave."

Isobel nodded. "I remember you too."

"I know you're on a sabbatical at the moment, so I appreciate you taking the time to help me with my case."

Isobel inclined her head. "I'm not sure what kind of help I can give you."

"Well, your experience would lead me to believe that you can."

Isobel raised an eyebrow. "Dave was a bit mysterious about it all."

"Dave doesn't know anything." Peter pushed forward in his chair, leaning his arms on the desk.

Isobel sat back in her chair.

Peter waited and when the silence lengthened he broke

eye contact and stood up. He put his hands in his pockets and paced behind the desk.

"I find myself in an unusual position." He paused and looked at Isobel.

She maintained eye contact.

Peter resumed pacing. "I think there's a problem with one of my cases – but there may not be. I suspect something is going on but it's not obvious and I need someone who can see beyond the nose on her face."

Isobel said nothing. The silence lengthened.

Peter sat down, rubbing his hands down his face. "You probably already think I'm crazy, bringing you to London to talk to you." He paused but Isobel stayed silent. "I just thought that with your experience you might give me a second opinion."

"Why not ask one of your people from here?"

Peter pursed his lips. "On the surface the case is fine." He hesitated. "What I feel is a hunch."

"So you prefer not to deal with one of your professional colleagues and instead use an old acquaintance."

"Something like that."

"Obviously this case has got under your skin."

Peter looked away and then nodded. "I've been a divorce solicitor for twelve years. Something feels off about this case."

Isobel rubbed her lips, her forehead wrinkled. "Under your skin to the point that you flew me in from Ireland."

He looked at the desk, then at his hands. "Maybe I am overly involved but I'm concerned that I'm doing the right thing, for me and for everyone." He lifted his head then and met her gaze.

"I've been on sabbatical for a year and a half now."

"I know."

"Maybe my skills won't be up to the task, maybe I'm out of practice."

"Your experiences with addiction, with couples separating – you can't lose that – and I want the benefit of it."

Isobel pursed her lips. He seemed a harmless guy, kind almost, and it was hard not to be softened by his genuineness. She could feel a war inside. Did she really want to get involved? At the same time, she had to confess that she was intrigued – and, he was just asking for an opinion on what was going on – how big a deal was that? The latter side won.

"Why don't you tell me about it?"

"As I'm requesting your services, I can cover you under client privilege."

Isobel nodded and, when the pause was extended, she said, "Let's hear it."

Peter's eyes moved from her face to the wall. "It all started with a new client, Anne Banks. She made an appointment and arrived with her husband, Thomas, to get a divorce. They said that it was amicable, and so all they needed was a solicitor for her – he had one, and they had already agreed on terms that they were both happy with. Unusual."

"In what way?"

"Well, normally we have to help the couple reach an agreement. We started going through the terms of the divorce. He was getting sole custody of their nine-year-old son, Tommy, uncontested, and she would have visitation which they would organise themselves. He was also getting their home so that their son could stay in familiar surroundings. There was to be no payment to her in terms of alimony. She was getting nothing."

"And, you queried that, naturally."

"Yes, and they assured me that her soon-to-be-ex-husband would pay for her rental flat, and later purchase a home for her, but that was not to be in the papers. Likewise future visitation with her son was to be agreed verbally and not mentioned in the divorce agreement."

"So how come he was getting everything?"

"I asked that and they explained that Anne, my client, was an alcoholic who had just finished rehab recently. They felt that he should be in charge of their money in case she started drinking again. In terms of Tommy, their son, and seeing him, it depended on her sobriety."

"Is that not normal? If she has a huge problem with alcohol then that might not be safe for her son."

"Yes, but usually there is provision made for visits when sober, or supervised visits. This mother has not seen her child for three months. According to her she's getting sober and dealing with her guilt and shame. She is going to see him but not yet. But there's no legal protection for her. I asked how bad things had got and Anne said her drinking had wrecked their marriage and she needed time to get herself sober and back on her feet. Of course I understand all of this but to get nothing formally agreed on to protect her future seems a bit much and also I'm concerned about her son not seeing her, when she is sober."

"But, realistically, what can you do? The decision on all of these things is up to the couple."

"Yes."

"So what's the problem? Are these two people not being responsible and doing their best to negotiate a divorce and protect their son?"

"Yes, but . . . I asked to confer with Anne privately and they declined politely. They maintain that they are a family

9

who are going through a divorce but they know how to work things out and they just want the legalities sorted. Essentially, I am only there to sign as her solicitor. They want to do this as soon as possible. They gave me their documentation – birth certificates, their marriage certificate – and we have an appointment next week on Wednesday. But I'm concerned that this is not in my client's best interests, despite what they say. This doesn't feel right to me and I can't get it out of my head." He paused. "With all of your experience, I thought if you met them you could see if anything struck you about the situation."

Isobel looked at him speculatively. She could feel her old training coming back. She felt Peter's tension when he'd spoken about the mother working on her relationship with her son was personal. There was something there and the problem was that it could be clouding his judgement. Maybe what was driving him mad wasn't the case but something personal the case was reminding him of?

She decided to take a chance. "So what happened with your mother?" she asked, looking him in the eye.

His eyes widened then showed a deep emptiness. Within a second it was gone. A flush appeared on his cheeks, his chin rose and his jaw tightened.

Isobel waited.

"I don't think my personal life is pertinent to the situation," he said.

"You want my opinion, and then when I ask about something that may be affecting your perception of the case, you're closing down on me?"

She leant on the table and stood up.

Scrambling to his feet, Peter reached out to her, "Please," he said. "Hold on."

Isobel paused, meeting his eye. Then she sat down slowly and waited.

Peter looked down, inhaled deeply, and then met her gaze. "Yes, my mum was an alcoholic. Yes, she left me. No, I didn't see her again."

She relaxed back into the chair, resting her hands on her thighs. "You know what I'm going to say."

"Yes." He swallowed. "How did you know?"

Isobel shrugged. "Experience, as you said. And instinct."

Seconds passed.

Then she said, "That is why you brought me here."

"Not to pry into my background."

Isobel shook her head and stood again.

Peter's eyes never left hers. "I'm not imagining something because of what happened to me."

"Peter, we all do. Our perception of everything is coloured by our experiences, and you're the same as the rest of us."

"That may be true."

"*Is* true."

"But, *honestly*, I do believe there's a problem. Do you think I would have gone to all the trouble of bringing you over, if I wasn't genuinely worried? Yes, I have a past but maybe that's one of the things that has enabled me to sense that something is off here."

"Peter –"

"Maybe it is my stuff, or maybe there is something going on. Please, I need to know, one way or the other. You're here, please see this through."

Isobel dropped back into the chair.

"Have you seen a therapist about your mother deserting you?" she asked.

"No."

"You need to." Leaning forward, her hand on her forehead, she said, "I'm really uncomfortable with this. Maybe I'm doing you more harm than good by going along with it."

He shook his head. "I need to know one way or the other. You will be helping me."

Isobel looked at him, her mind miles away. "How are you going to organise for this couple to meet me?"

"That's my problem." For the first time his face relaxed. "Does that mean you'll do it?"

Isobel felt his relief and pursed her lips. "OK, here's the deal. If you promise to go to a therapist and have six meetings with her about what happened with your mother, I will see this couple. Irrespective of what I find, you have to do this, and I want your word."

Peter blinked a number of times. "OK."

"You'll get an appointment for this week?"

Peter nodded and stood up. "So we have a deal then?"

Isobel stood too. "We have a deal."

They shook hands.

Peter grinned. "Now, to have you meet this couple we're going to need some help." He left the room.

Alone briefly, Isobel rolled her shoulders and wondered if she was doing the right thing. It already had become more complicated than she'd expected.

Peter reappeared with the blonde lady. "You have already met Patricia. She's been my secretary for five years. She knows all about my concerns and is going to help us tomorrow."

Patricia smiled warmly at Peter and made herself comfortable in the other chair.

While she appeared friendly, Isobel could detect a wariness towards her.

"So what's the plan?" she queried, sitting back to listen and absorb, her eyes moving from Peter to Patricia.

"Basically I've told my client, Anne Banks, that Patricia inadvertently shredded the contract she signed with me and that I need her to come in and sign another one. The story is that Patricia has been really stressed about her child's health – frequent asthmatic attacks – and that's why she's been distracted and making errors. I've apologised profusely and grovelled and, I think, persuaded her that a genuine mistake has ensued. They're coming at lunchtime tomorrow to re-sign the contract. Patricia will stay out of the office and you'll be here as an old friend of mine who's stepped in to help me while my secretary sorts out her home life. We get the contract re-signed and while we're doing that you can assess this couple. Patricia has typed out another document and has everything ready to go."

Isobel pursed her lips, feeling the anxiety in her stomach.

Peter hurried on. "Look, Isobel. Just do what you do and give me your impressions. If everything seems OK, I can resign myself to doing my job, knowing that I did my best. Final contracts are being prepared and will be ready next week as we had arranged."

"So, if there is a problem, there isn't much time to do anything?"

"Right – if there is something going on, time will be of the essence."

Isobel pursed her lips. "I might say something that a legal secretary wouldn't."

"That's why I've described you as a friend, not a professional."

13

"You seem to have covered most bases." She turned to Patricia. "*Do* you have children, Patricia?"

Patricia, who had listened attentively, laughed musically. "No children."

As she spoke Isobel noticed her quickly glance at Peter.

"What time do you want me here, Peter?" Isobel asked.

"Anne is coming in at a quarter past one, so you need to be ready for then."

"So we're good to go."

"I think so."

Isobel nodded and rose to leave. "OK. I'll see you tomorrow."

He rose and they shook hands. "Thanks again, Isobel. I really appreciate this."

"Don't forget our agreement."

Patricia frowned and shifted in her seat. No one enlightened her and she stood up. "Good luck."

"You too," Isobel said and left.

There was no one in reception and, glancing at her watch, she realised it was six o'clock. Time had flown.

Isobel sat on the Tube, checking off the stops to Hammersmith. Her life had been like that for the past eighteen months, a route she had to follow that was laid out for her until she reached a destination, the end of treatment. She was nervous about tomorrow and felt tired. It had been a long time since she had worked and today had been a challenge. She didn't really feel like herself, or not like her old self anyway. To borrow a line from the movie *Hitch,* 'Who she was, was a fluid concept right now'.

Back in her room, she pulled out her case and unpacked her two wigs. It was a year since she had worn them. The silver-white one which had made her feel a bit sophisticated and the brunette one that was more relaxed. Trying them both on, she decided that she would wear the silver one.

Her mobile rang and she knew it was going to be Dave.

"How did your first day as a consultant go?"

"I'm not a consultant."

"You're consulting with Peter on this case, giving him the benefit of your experience and expertise."

Isobel laughed.

"Peter was on the phone to me earlier, telling me that you'd given him a hard time –"

"I didn't –"

"He was very impressed. He said you challenged him about something related to the case and you were spot on."

She was relieved to hear that. "Well, that's good."

"It's certainly a good start."

"We'll just have to see how tomorrow goes."

"Good luck."

"Bye."

No doubt Dave would be on the phone to the whole family now, letting them know that she was working. Isobel let it go – there was no point trying to dampen their delight. She collapsed into bed. It had been a long day.

Chapter 3

Tuesday 22nd May

By eleven o'clock the next morning Isobel was dressed in a black skirt, white blouse and grey jacket – more consultant clothes. She carefully arranged the silver wig to cover her hair, put on a little neutral make-up and added her glasses.

Her journey took over an hour and she walked slowly the last bit of the way, arriving in the reception of the office at a quarter to one.

Patricia looked up as she entered. "Hello, can I help you?"

Isobel almost laughed out loud. "Yes, I was hoping to have a quick word with Peter Wright – I'm an old friend of his."

At the sound of her voice, Patricia started but quickly covered it up. "I'll let him know you're here."

The white-haired Mrs Brown looked up with interest. Isobel turned to the wall paintings behind her, preventing any conversation. Mrs Brown resumed typing.

Peter came out to reception.

When Isobel turned he looked at her blankly.

"Hi, Peter. I hope this is an OK time to call."

Peter's eyes opened wide. "Yes, yes."

Isobel quickly added, "Sorry to surprise you but I hoped that you would be free at lunchtime."

Peter, smiling now, said, "Good to see you. Come in, come in." Turning to Patricia, he said, "Why don't you two head on to lunch? There are no meetings now until mid-afternoon so there's no need to rush back."

"Great, thanks." Patricia turned to Mrs Brown. "We don't often get an opportunity like this, so let's make the most of it."

"Let's," said Mrs Brown with a smile as she got to her feet.

Patricia quickly shepherded Mrs Brown out of the office, suggesting places for them to go to have their long lunch.

Isobel belatedly wondered if they were doing anything illegal. Hopefully Peter, the solicitor, was keeping them on the right side of the law. She followed him into his office.

Peter laughed and handed her the contract that Patricia had prepared to be re-signed. "God, I didn't recognise you."

"I just thought this might help me carry off the role better."

"Where did you get the wig at such short notice?"

Isobel shrugged her shoulders, "Oh, it was something I was doing last year."

"An acting job?"

Isobel looked pointedly at the documents, turning the pages. "Something like that."

Familiarising herself with the contract, Isobel realised that Patricia had left small pieces of bright Post-It paper stuck to the relevant pages where signatures were needed. She was certainly efficient.

Peter instructed her on what to say to the couple on arrival and then said, "Now you're ready to meet Anne and Thomas Banks."

17

Isobel nodded and, taking a deep breath, went out and took her place at Patricia's desk in reception. She checked the documents again and made sure that she had a pen ready.

She'd not been seated long when she heard the lift door open. Coming towards her were a man and woman. The woman – Mrs Banks, she presumed – was about 5 foot 7 inches tall, slim, with long blonde hair, and she was beautiful. She appeared poised and confident but distant. The man beside her, standing about 6 foot 2 inches and broad-shouldered, was sallow-complexioned with dark-brown hair and eyes. He moved with an easy grace and seemed very self-assured. Isobel suspected that he was very aware of his impact on others. They were a very attractive couple.

Standing up, Isobel assumed her role.

"Mrs Banks," she said, coming around the desk and shaking the woman's hand, "Thank you so much for coming. I really appreciate your understanding and help in this matter. Patricia was so upset about the mistake she made and afraid of losing her job, so thank you for solving the problem at this stressful time for her. Her son is still not very well but we're hoping that he'll turn the corner in the next few days."

Anne Banks withdrew her hand and flexed her lips in what could be described as a smile.

Mr Banks stepped forward, extending his hand. "Thomas Banks." His hand was warm and soft. He held Isobel's hand gently as he continued. "We hope so too. Having a son ourselves, we understand the stress involved when a child is sick. Hopefully he'll improve soon." He turned slightly to his wife. "Thankfully, whenever our Tommy was sick Anne was there to mind him. It makes such a difference. Of course, with the stress of a sick child,

18

we can all make a mistake. And Peter says that coming in today will expedite things and hopefully there'll be no further delays." At this he smiled, flashing white teeth.

Isobel could feel the power of his charm and his persuasiveness. He still had hold of her hand and she gently extracted it.

Rehearsing the lines Peter had fed her, she said, "The final documents are being drawn up and should be ready next Wednesday as arranged. This seemed the easiest way to remedy the mistake and ensure that nothing holds up the final signing."

"Excellent."

Peter appeared at the door of his office and Thomas Banks, with a small nod, made his way towards him.

Isobel moved towards Anne Banks and said with a smile, "What age is your son?"

"Nine."

"Ah, getting big now!"

"Yes, he is."

"Was he sick much when he was younger?"

"No, not really."

Isobel waited, still looking attentively at her.

"As Thomas said, I was always there for him," the woman said.

"This must be a very difficult time for you."

Anne Banks turned away, saying brusquely, "It is. I'm finding it all upsetting and I just want to get the paperwork done."

Isobel was startled but quickly pulled her face into an inscrutable mask.

Thomas Banks came back and, taking his wife by the arm, escorted her into Peter's office.

Isobel followed them in.

They seated themselves across the desk from Peter.

"Yes," said Thomas. "It's been a trying few months, hasn't it, Anne?" He looked at her. "We just want to get things in order so we can move on with our lives and do our best for Tommy."

She nodded quickly. "Yes, as best we can."

Isobel opened the documents at the first page requiring a signature and handed over the pen. Anne paused and then, collecting herself, studiously scribed her name. Isobel turned to the page for the next signature. Anne took her time signing.

Thomas stood up immediately it was done. "So everything is in order again and we can proceed?"

"Yes," said Peter, getting to his feet.

"Great. Please pass our best wishes for her son on to your secretary."

"Of course."

"See you next week." He shepherded Anne towards the door.

Isobel hurried forward in her secretarial role, to escort them out. In the outer office they left with a brief goodbye and she returned to Peter's office.

It had all taken fifteen minutes.

Peter was sitting behind his desk again. "Not much time for you to decide. What do you think?"

Isobel looked at him and was silent, pursing her lips. What was going on?

Like a good lawyer Peter was comfortable with the silence. So many people were not, and ended up speaking, often revealing information they regretted.

Isobel took a deep breath and said, "I'll let you know

later. Perhaps we could meet after work. I'll reflect on it this afternoon." She paused, wrinkling her forehead, "Could give me their addresses?"

Peter frowned. "What for?"

"I want to go and have a look at where they lived before and where Anne lives now. I might get a better feel for things. It might help me clarify my thinking."

"Don't let them see you in case they recognise you."

Isobel pulled off the wig. "I won't."

Peter grinned. He wrote down the addresses. "I didn't want to influence your assessment before you met them but now let me tell you what I wondered about, or was concerned about –"

"After work, Peter. I haven't made up my mind yet so don't influence me now. Let's meet this evening. You can tell me what you're worried about then and I'll give you my impressions, my assessment. We can brainstorm."

Peter nodded. "I'll get Patricia to come too. Let's meet at about eight o'clock. Would my flat be OK with you as this is all confidential and at least there we will have some privacy?"

"Sure. Give me your address as well."

"We can order a takeaway and chat."

"See you then."

Isobel took her stuff and left. She went to the toilets and folded her silver wig into a plastic bag for protection and put it in her floppy handbag. Not being comfortable in formal clothes, she'd brought a bright-pink cardigan with her to wear on the way home. She removed her jacket and shrugged her way into the cardigan, placing her jacket also in her large bag. Finally she took off her glasses and surveyed herself in the mirror. She smiled, the dimple in her left cheek flashing into existence and the fine lines around her wide-set brown eyes showing the depth of habitude. With her now short, dark, highlighted hair and more casual attire she looked different. She knew her accent might give her away if she bumped into the Banks but she wasn't intending to do that and after all London was full of Irish people.

Isobel had some impressions from the meeting even though it had been short. Giving her assessment of people, especially if Peter was going to use it in his work, was important and really she needed more information, so it was time for some reconnaissance.

Chapter 4

Isobel walked past the address given for Mrs Banks. It was a flat above a clothes shop, not far from Kensington High Street. It was a comfortable-looking building in red brick with large windows.

Wandering down the street she saw there was a grocery shop at the corner. It seemed to be well stocked and even had a noticeboard with information about local people offering babysitting, exercise classes and AA meetings in the area.

Buying a bottle of water, Isobel did her best to engage the shop assistant in conversation.

"A friend of mine lives near here," she said, as casually as she could. "A tall lady with blonde hair, a Mrs Banks. Do you know her?"

"No," was the monosyllabic answer.

End of discussion.

Isobel walked back outside and headed down the other side of the street. Obliquely across from Mrs Bank's flat there was a café and she decided to go in and have some lunch. It was around three o'clock so she got a salad sandwich and sat down at the window table. While she ate she jotted down in her notebook the key impressions that had struck her during the meeting earlier. Gazing at the building across the road, she tried to decide what to do.

In the end the only thing she could come up with was to talk to the lady in the clothes shop and see what she could find out. Finishing her lunch, she crossed the road and entered the shop. As she did a bell tingled and a dark-haired glamorous woman of about sixty looked up. Her face was narrow with high cheekbones and her eyes were bright. This was a woman who was perceptive and would be hard to fool.

Based on the premise that most people are helpful if you ask, Isobel said, "I was wondering if you could help me?"

Politely the older woman inclined her head.

"I've noticed a woman walking around who maybe lives near here. She's about five foot seven with lovely blonde hair and is a beautiful dresser. I really admire how well she looks and dresses and –"

The woman lifted an eyebrow as she openly surveyed Isobel's height and shape.

"Oh, it's not for me!" said Isobel. "A friend of mine is a similar size and shape to the lady I described, and she's been going through a rough time and I thought a makeover, a change of style, might help her."

She paused, wondering where this elaborate story sprang from and also if she had gone too far.

"Oh, that will be Mrs Banks. She's beautiful, isn't she? And, funnily enough, not that interested in clothes."

Isobel affected a surprised but interested demeanour and, knowing that most people feel responsible for a silence and rush to fill it, she waited for her advisor to go on.

"She came in one day and wandered round and you

would think, looking so well, that she would know what to go for – but she was lost. In the end she showed me a photograph of herself and her husband all dressed for a night out and asked me if I could advise her on something more dramatic than the more conservative things she had for everyday wear, something in a similar style to the evening dress. At the time I had nothing suitable but I said I would order some things in for her."

"It sounds like you're her stylist and personal shopper now, helping her with dress choices and styles?"

The lady smiled and leant forward. "You wouldn't believe how much of that I do."

Isobel frowned and waited.

"More and more people come in now with pictures of celebrities in outfits or Kate Middleton at a function and want something similar. They all just show me a photo on their phone."

"How do you keep track of the different people and their size and style and colour?"

"Oh, I use my phone too. Sometimes I can bring up images of other dresses to show them. It's very handy."

Isobel hoped that she wasn't pushing too hard now. "Could you show me the sort of thing that would suit that lady I mentioned . . . and hopefully my friend too."

"Well, like most people she texted me a photo. In fact, she only sent one – most people want to send a number."

With some deft swishes on her phone she proffered it to Isobel.

"What a lovely couple!"

"That's what I thought but unfortunately they're getting divorced."

"You certainly couldn't tell from the picture."

"No, and she said it was very recent."

"Really? That dress is gorgeous on her. Have you been able to find similar things for daywear then?"

"Yes, a similar shape which flatters her figure."

"I do think my friend would look good in this sort of style."

"The new stock should be here later this week." The assistant paused expectantly.

Isobel thought quickly. A photo of Anne Banks would be handy but she hadn't thought to get one earlier.

"Perhaps I could have a copy of the photo?" she said. "Just to show my friend what I'm suggesting for her and how well she could look?"

No reaction, no response.

"And when the stock comes in we could come back . . ." She tailed off then and waited, looking as innocent as possible, despite her lies.

The dress advisor looked at her speculatively and then conceded, "Well, that photo was taken at some event they were at so it's probably on the internet. I suppose it would be OK to let you have it."

"Thank you so much!" Isobel made a mental note to get Patricia to see if either Mr or Mrs Banks had an online presence with more photos.

Quickly, the photo was texted to Isobel's phone.

"That delivery will be in this Friday. Hopefully you can come back with your friend at the weekend."

"Yes, hopefully."

On this mutually beneficial note Isobel took her leave.

Isobel's next port of call was the family home in Wimbledon. At the nearby Tube station she got a taxi and asked to be driven past the Banks' address. "I'm looking for a house and my friend thought that this one, or something similar, might float my boat – apparently it's beautiful."

"I think you're wasting your time, but I'll take you."

"Why?"

"You'll see."

"*Er*, thank you." Maybe she'd pushed it too much with the beautiful house story.

She looked out the window as she travelled through the busy streets of London. There were so many people, all so busy, all going somewhere, such a contrast to the inactivity she had become used to. She could feel a tension in her stomach just being around all of this activity.

Before long the taxi driver pulled up at an address.

"That's it there, love. I reckon she was taking the piss."

Isobel looked at the elaborate gates and high walls and the hint of a rooftop. No wonder he'd been dubious about her story.

Isobel laughed. "I think you're right but since I'm here I'm going to explore the area. Maybe I can find something and have the last laugh. Just drop me further up."

Isobel walked back past the Banks' property. The gate was solid metal and had a see-through panel high up. Standing on tiptoe, she could see that the garden was sizeable and the house detached. This was a very affluent area and each property was unique. Isobel was perturbed. Surely in this amicable agreement Mrs Banks could move to a house nearby rather than rent a flat? Maybe the rental was a temporary step until they decided where was best for her to live or something suitable came up.

She decided to call on the neighbours and see if she could glean any information.

The house next door appeared more accessible, with lower walls and gate and an abundance of flowers which softened it. There was a silver car parked in the drive and Isobel hoped that meant that there was someone at home. While she waited for the door to be answered she admired the roses in bloom, wafting a delicate fragrance into the air. Planters with a profusion of violas, pansies and petunias abounded, making a rainbow of colour and giving a cheerful look to the front. An orchestra of insects gave a steady hum as they danced amongst the flowers.

Hearing the door open, she turned around to face the short, white-haired lady framed in the doorway. She was maybe seventy but her spritely welcome gave the impression of someone younger. Her eyes were direct and Isobel suspected that her diminutive stature was matched with a formidable intelligence.

Filled with genuine enthusiasm, Isobel said, "Oh, your flowers are beautiful!"

Immediately the older lady smiled back at her. "Thank you." She waited with her hand on the door surround.

Isobel decided to take a risk based on a shared love of flowers. She knew also that sometimes you had to give a little bit of information to get some.

"Hi, my name is Isobel McKenzie. I'm a friend of Anne's." She smiled. "From Ireland."

"I gathered as much from your accent."

Isobel could feel her smile faltering. "I've been concerned about her and her husband and son. I know she's moved out and I'm worried about how she's doing, how they're all doing really." She winced.

"I haven't seen you around before visiting Anne . . ."

Isobel grimaced. "No, you wouldn't have."

"But then they never were fond of visitors."

Isobel smiled. "No, they weren't." She tried again. "I've spoken to Anne very recently and while she has told me all about the divorce and her problems –" she made a face, "I saw her yesterday and I find myself very concerned . . ." She could feel a real lump in her throat and she gave a wobbly smile. "I'm sorry, I'm probably not making much sense . . . you see, I was in London for some business and, after seeing Anne and feeling worried, I thought that if I spoke to someone else who knew her it might reassure me . . . I'm not just being nosy . . . I'm genuinely concerned."

There was a silence as the older lady regarded her.

Isobel shook her head. "I'm sorry, this was a bad idea. I'll just go. Please forgive me for disturbing you – and please don't mention to Anne that I called as it would only upset her. It was silly of me." She turned to leave.

"Wait!"

Isobel turned back.

"You're a friend of Anne's?"

"Yes." Isobel wondered how far she could stretch the truth.

"And you're worried about her?"

"Yes. I suppose I thought if I talked to someone who knew her on a more daily basis, not just from the phone or Skype, and who might understand her better, that it might help me when I'm talking to her . . ." And that was literally the truth, Isobel thought.

With a small nod the older woman gestured to her to come in.

"I'm Grace Allen and I'm worried too."

Isobel stepped in, feeling a mixture of anxiety and relief.

Turning, Grace Allen led the way down the hall into a big and bright kitchen at the back of the house with open doors to a sunroom. The view of the back garden was stunning, with more colourful flowers and shrubs and an area for growing vegetables in beautifully raised beds.

Isobel crossed to the windows of the sunroom, absorbing the wonder of the garden. "Oh, *wow*! This is amazing. I am so jealous. My garden never looks as tidy as this."

Grace smiled as she poured water from a jug with floating mint and lemon. She handed Isobel a glass and gestured for her to sit down.

Isobel suspected that she had struck gold – a precise lady who was lonely and therefore eager to talk and, if she was to be believed, was worried too.

Grace stared into the distance and then she straightened her shoulders,

"I first met Anne Banks ten years ago when they bought next door. I'm old-fashioned so I called over to meet them and take them an apple tart I'd baked. Anne invited me in. We had a cup of tea and some tart and chatted. She was unpacking and was all excited, telling me about her wonderful husband, their honeymoon and how happy she was. Then we heard the door opening and Anne suddenly jumped up and ran out into the hall. I was surprised. I heard some whispers and then her husband came in with Anne beside him. She seemed different. She was all apologetic, explaining that we'd lost track of time and so the dinner wasn't ready. It could've just been a new wife fussing about housework, but I was a bit uncomfortable. I left shortly after that and the next day I bumped into her as she was coming back from the shops.

She set down her bags to say hello and we chatted briefly and when she picked them up again she winced. I asked her if she was in pain and she passed it off as having hurt her back, lifting boxes. She was a different woman from the open chatty one I had met the day before. I asked if she was all right and she told me that she was tired from all the unpacking. A week later I called over but she was on her way out. I tried a couple of times more but she was always busy or there was something on. I was never in the house again."

"Never?"

"Never. Oh, I bumped into her sometimes at the shops and, would you believe, we even used to go for coffee? She chatted away about the house and decorating."

"So she was happy to meet if it was elsewhere?"

"Yes, in fact I would say that she was lonely and was glad to have some company. Very soon she fell pregnant and she talked openly and excitedly about being a parent, about motherhood. I'm a retired social worker so she was keen for me to tell her anything that would help her to be a good mother. But she never said anything about her marriage or about Thomas."

"Did you ask?"

"Of course I did. Initially I asked too many questions and she just used to say, 'Oh, let's talk about ourselves not men.' After a while I realised that I learned more if I slipped in subtle questions like, 'Is Thomas pleased about the baby?'. She might let something slip then but never if I asked directly about him. The conversations she was having with me were the ones you have with your girlfriends, or family. She wouldn't plan any coffees with me but if we bumped into each other she would have one.

31

She seemed so lonely that I used to pretend to bump into her." She paused. "When she had the baby she was ecstatic. I decided to call to the house and deliver a present. She chatted on the front doorstep, thanking me and saying how happy she was but she didn't ask me in. I got the message. I was welcome but not inside."

"How odd."

Grace nodded. "Her mother and sister did come when the baby was born. They stayed in a hotel nearby for a few days. I happened to see them all when they were having coffee in the shopping centre nearby. I stopped to say hello. Eventually Anne went to the mothers' room to change little Tommy's nappy and her sister told me that she was worried, that they never got to see her, and that Anne had changed. At a later stage I asked Anne about her family and she said that they weren't close and so she didn't see them very often."

Isobel frowned.

Grace nodded. "I know, but families are complicated and it is hard to know what is really going on."

Isobel raised her eyebrows and almost smiled. "Ain't that the truth?"

Grace gave a half-smile. "When Tommy was about ten months old I saw her out in the front garden. I was walking past and the gates were open. I called out and when she turned I saw that she had a black eye. Needless to say, I enquired about it and she said that she'd banged into an open kitchen cupboard. Well, that's such a cliché, so eventually one day when I'd bumped into her in town and we were having coffee I asked her outright if she was being beaten or bullied."

Isobel leant forward. "What did she say?"

Grace shrugged. "She denied any problems and was shocked that I would even think of asking her that. Oh, she still met me and talked about Tommy, but she wouldn't hear a word against Thomas. In fact she went out of her way to drop in facts that showed how good to her he was. In the end I wondered if I was imagining the few things I'd seen or if I had been misinterpreting them. Sometimes, when you're too long on a job like mine, you start seeing problems everywhere. But, on the other hand, there was a child involved and so one last time, when Tommy was older, I did bring the subject round to Thomas and how he treated her and asked if he was ever controlling or – well, I didn't get any further. Anne was so upset that I could even suggest such a thing. That kind of put the tin lid on it. She just avoided me after that or kept things to a minimum."

Isobel chewed her lip.

"Over the years, Thomas always saluted me and was pleasant but somehow always made it clear that I should keep my distance. He was never rude, just unwelcoming. In the end I accepted that they were very private people. Then, out of the blue, a few months ago, he arrived at my door one evening. He asked if he could talk to me and seemed agitated and upset. Needless to say, I said yes and invited him in. That night he confided that Anne had a secret drink problem that he'd just found out about. He claimed that sometimes she had bruises and when he'd ask she'd say she'd bumped into things but he now realised that it happened when she was drunk. He said that he'd thought she was happy and she seemed to be functioning, but that actually during the day when Tommy was at school she drank. She drank vodka so he had never smelt anything. The school isn't far away so she walked round to pick up Tommy. She wasn't aggressive or falling-down drunk, but her drinking was escalating and she was more and more depressed. He had noticed that and so he came home from work early, because he was concerned, and that's when he found Anne at lunchtime, passed out on the sofa, with the vodka bottle on the floor. Apparently this was her pattern, to drink all morning, then sleep it off and so be hungover collecting Tommy."

"Were you shocked?"

"Well, yes, I was. All along I wondered if he was off in some way and suddenly here I was hearing that Anne was the one who had been causing problems. He said that they rowed for weeks but eventually they both admitted that there was a problem and he persuaded Anne to go into rehab for a month. Apparently she did well there but their marriage had been badly damaged and Thomas felt that he just couldn't cope with things any more. When she left rehab she moved into a flat so she could have the space and time to focus on her recovery. Thomas said they were going to divorce as he'd had enough. Anne was going to aftercare and AA meetings but, as far as he knew, it was going to take time. He said that at the moment Tommy wasn't seeing her but hopefully, in the future, Anne would be ready and able for that." She paused.

Isobel nodded and waited.

Grace took a deep breath. "Well, the first thing I said was that Tommy must miss his mum because they were always so close. Thomas got upset and said he was very worried about Tommy and how he'd been affected by Anne and her drinking. He said they were giving Anne a chance to get sober and find her feet and then they were hoping to have visits so that Tommy could get used to the new arrangement."

Isobel said, "So they're making plans for the future and are trying to balance everything."

Grace made a face. "Maybe."

"Go on."

Grace took another deep breath. "All I know is that Anne was devoted to Tommy. Even if she was an alcoholic she would want to see her son and, to be honest, he would want to see her. I said as much to Thomas."

Isobel leant forward again. "What did he say?"

"He said that he and Anne were taking advice from the workers in aftercare and that they were doing everything they could to make this work for Tommy. In the end I said that seeing his mother was the best thing for him. Thomas agreed but said that unfortunately it couldn't happen just yet and he was doing his best to get everything right for everyone. He left shortly after that. I haven't seen Anne. How was she when you saw her?"

Isobel chewed her lip. "She was disinclined to talk, not even about Tommy. She seems very focused on getting her divorce sorted and has some future plans to see Tommy. She is sober and looking well. To be honest, I found it hard to know how she is . . . inside."

There was a lengthening silence.

Then Grace rubbed her hands together. "I'm worried about Tommy. But if Thomas and Anne have agreed a plan and are getting help, what can I do? Thomas seems to be managing. He leaves Tommy to school. After school Tommy goes to an afterschool club and then Thomas comes home from work earlier to mind him."

"I see. It's all been a bit of a shock to you?"

"Yes."

"Is there anyone else I could talk to who knew Anne well?"

Grace tapped her fingers against her lips. "As I said, she never had that many friends but she did look after herself. I remember her mentioning her hairdresser in particular. The saloon is on the main street – Brushstrokes. I don't remember the stylist's name. Oh, and you could try the beautician. Anne used to get her nails done regularly. It's also on the main street, the place with the pink sign – I don't remember the name."

"Thank you, Grace, for being so honest. I really just want to help."

Grace looked down at her hands clasped on her lap. "I believe that. I suppose I just feel bad that I didn't help Anne, that I didn't realise she was struggling and was turning to alcohol." She looked up at Isobel with eyes shimmering with tears.

Isobel reached out and squeezed her hand. "You did what you could."

Grace nodded. "Talking to you, I realise how upset I am about everything."

"It is upsetting. But I think you'll feel better having talked to someone about it all."

"I hope so."

"I'd better go." Isobel got to her feet.

Grace stood too. "If you see Anne please tell her that I was asking for her."

Isobel nodded, not trusting herself to answer that. She reached into her bag and pulled out a pen and scrap of paper. "Here is my mobile number. If you think of anything else or if you want to talk, give me a ring."

"I will, Isobel. Thank you for listening."

"Thank you for confiding in me. But, Grace, should you see Anne, please don't tell her that I talked to you. I'm only trying to help, and I don't want her to misunderstand and think that I'm going behind her back. Is that all right?"

"Of course. I won't say a word."

As she made her way out of the drive, Isobel wondered why she had given Grace her mobile number. She would be back in Ireland soon and miles away from the drama of the Banks marriage.

Chapter 5

Out on the street once again Isobel glanced at her watch: four thirty. She should have time to get to the hairdresser's before it closed. As she walked along the street she noticed that the beauticians did indeed have a pink sign saying *'Ladies Made'*. Isobel kept walking, looking for Brushstrokes. As she approached, she could see through the window that there was a counter inside with a receptionist.

Isobel swung open the door, a bright smile on her face.

"Hi, my name is Isobel. A friend of mine, Anne Banks, who lives near here, recommended her hairdresser and I'm sorry but I just can't think of the name she told me. I was wondering if I could see her?"

The receptionist, a rather dapper man, tall with black hair, smiled. "Let me see," he tapped on the computer facing him. "Oh yes, Tanya is her usual colourist and Aaron cuts her hair. Which are you looking for – a cut or a colour – or maybe both?"

"Oh. I'm not sure. We talked about so many things I can hardly remember which she was particularly suggesting. I do remember that Anne is a regular with this person and has been for some time. Anne was sure that they could help me with my look." She laughed and fluffed up her hair.

He tapped on the computer keys a bit more. "Well, of the two, Aaron is here the longest and he's a great cutter, so I imagine it's Aaron."

"Is he here now? Perhaps I could have a quick word?"

"He's gone for the evening and he's off tomorrow, and he's also very booked up for the rest of the week."

"Oh no! Couldn't he squeeze me in at the end of the day? Thursday or Friday?"

"No, I'm afraid. He's working right up to closing time each day, six o'clock on Thursday and eight on Friday."

"Oh. Why don't you give me your card and I can always ring and make an appointment for next week when I see how my schedule is?"

"Certainly. That would be excellent."

It was a shame. Isobel knew that a hairdresser could be like a confessor – they heard everything, especially if you'd been going to the same one for a while.

Having had no success at the hair saloon, she made her way to the beautician's. Using the same routine she asked the receptionist for the person who took care of Mrs Banks' nails. Luckily Sharon was available for a manicure. In fact, Isobel's nails had got quite brittle from the chemo so she was glad to settle down for a manicure and a chat.

Sharon turned out to be about thirty, with long blonde hair and the heavily made-up face of someone very familiar with cosmetics. However, her smile was welcoming and her greeting showed her to be open and warm.

Isobel picked out a colour for the shellac nails and got ready to go fishing for information.

In the end it turned out to be relatively easy. Isobel

mentioned that Anne had recommended Sharon which created a sense of relationship and then hesitantly she added that she hadn't seen that much of Anne recently. Immediately Sharon jumped in.

"No, I haven't either and she used to come in every two weeks for her nails and every month for a leg-wax. She was one of my regulars, a lovely lady." Sharon studied Isobel's nails, eyes only on her work.

Isobel said nothing, realising that Sharon was used to chatting as she worked and would probably get into a flow.

"Anne talked non-stop about Tommy, her little boy. I have a little boy too. He's four and we were always discussing the best way to be a good mother. To be honest, she was really helpful to me. Brandon, my little one, hardly slept for the first ten months. I was back at work and I was so tired. Anne was great, she used to bring me in information she'd found for me. That year was so hard. I wouldn't have got through it without her help." Sharon paused and looked up at Isobel. "She told me about someone she knew, their child wasn't sleeping, was crying all the time, just like my Brandon. It turned out that the little one couldn't tolerate the regular baby formula. When they switched to goat's milk everything changed for them. She wanted me to try it because she knew I was at the end of my tether." Sharon had forgotten about Isobel's nails, lost in her story. "It's more expensive but she brought me in one of the big containers because it made such a difference with this other baby. It worked a treat. Two days and no more colic – just sleep for him and me. Well, Brandon never looked back. You should see him now, as healthy as a horse!"

Sharon gave a little start and resumed her buffing. Isobel made gentle murmuring noises. Sharon continued her monologue.

"Anne knew that money was tight so, when she came to get her nails done, she brought me a container of goat's milk formula every time until Brandon got too big. She was amazing, so concerned and generous. I couldn't have got through that year without her."

"That was kind of her."

"Yes."

Sharon had started to apply the colour.

"How long is it since Anne was in?" Isobel asked.

Sharon paused to consider then resumed her task. "She stopped coming in maybe three or four months ago. You're her friend – will you tell her I miss seeing her? I know she's a client but I kind of thought of her as a friend."

Isobel debated what to say. What was confidential and what was general information in the public domain? Reassuring herself that what Grace had shared with her was public and had come directly from Mr Banks, she said, "Anne's neighbour told me that Anne is an alcoholic and has been to rehab. She and Mr Banks are getting a divorce and it seems that she's not seeing Tommy at the moment until she has completely recovered."

Sharon stopped her work on the nails and stared.

Isobel bit her lip. She realised that she had slipped up. If she really was a friend of Anne's, she should have known all of this directly. She felt annoyed at herself for not planning her back story more thoroughly.

"I don't believe it. I just don't believe it."

Isobel swallowed noisily but, before she could say anything, Sharon continued.

"*No way*. My mother was an alcoholic and, believe me, I know the signs and Anne didn't have them."

"It seems Anne was a secret drinker, when Tommy was at school. You don't think that maybe she just fooled you, that she was clever?"

"*No way*."

Isobel knew there was more than a grain of truth in what Sharon was saying. The hardest people to fool were the children of alcoholics because they'd seen it all before, experienced all the dodges. But, on the other hand, Sharon didn't live with Anne and she couldn't know all that went on. Hiding drinking was a skill most addicts developed.

"Anne loved Tommy," Sharon said. "She wouldn't do this to him. She just couldn't and no matter what happened, no matter what she'd done, she would always want to spend as much time as possible with him." Sharon's hands were still, her eyes focused on the wall but seeing another time. "Mind you, she never mentioned her husband. She never said anything bad, but she never said anything good either. He just didn't figure. I asked her about that once. All she said was that sometimes marriages were not all they seemed – and that was it. She never spoke about him again to me. She just changed the subject if I brought him up."

Sharon studied the nails once again and continued with the painting and drying. There was silence now as they both thought about all that had been said.

As she finished, Sharon grasped Isobel's hand. "When you see Anne, will you tell her I was asking for her? She helped me so much. If there is anything I can do to help her, I will." Her eyes filled with tears. "She saved my life. She cared about me and Brandon. Tell her not to forget us." She shook her head. "I find all of this so hard to believe."

Isobel squeezed Sharon's hand. "I'm sure Anne will be in touch when things settle down. I'm sorry if I upset you by telling you."

Sharon shook her head and, with a sad smile, led Isobel to reception.

"I'll give you my number," Isobel said. "If you think of anything else that would help me understand, and help Anne, would you please let me know?"

Sharon nodded. "I will. And don't forget to tell her I was asking for her."

As Isobel walked out into the street, she wondered what Anne Banks would make of her mysterious friend Isobel McKenzie if she decided to reconnect with her old acquaintances. Thank God Peter hadn't introduced her to the Banks by name in the office. Isobel glanced at her watch. It was six o'clock and she needed to collect her thoughts before she gave her report to Peter.

Chapter 6

Isobel arrived at Peter's flat shortly before eight. He'd phoned her half an hour before to ask for her order of Indian food. Patricia arrived a few minutes later with the food. Peter had plates and cutlery laid on the coffee table in the sitting room so they could eat there.

Peter and Patricia tucked in enthusiastically, but Isobel felt tense and, despite having been hungry earlier, she had lost her appetite.

"Well, what do you think?" Peter asked. "Is there something going on?"

Isobel had spent nearly an hour making notes on the meeting with the Banks and the other people she had talked to and then summarising them, but she spoke from memory.

"I have two areas of concern."

Peter stopped eating. "Go on."

"My first concern is that Mr and Mrs Banks don't have any emotional tension between them."

"What does that mean?"

Isobel blew out through her lips. "Normally when people are in relationship, any relationship, there's an atmosphere between them that you can feel. It's also

44

observable in how they relate to each other, or you can hear it in the tone of voice they use with one another."

Peter frowned.

"Patricia and Mrs Brown work together – they have an atmosphere," Isobel said.

Patricia laughed. "Yes, she disapproves of me."

Isobel grinned. "You and Patricia work together and you have an atmosphere."

Patricia blushed.

Isobel rubbed her hand on her forehead and hurried on. "Obviously, a marriage relationship has a very strong atmosphere, good or bad. So when a couple have reached the point where they're going to divorce, they have a really palpable atmosphere. It could be anger, betrayal, hurt, hatred, indifference, fear. Whatever has brought them to the point of needing to divorce leaves an emotional charge, a residue, with the couple, and even if they have agreed equable terms there's still that residual emotional charge that you can feel, or observe, or hear in how they relate to each other. My concern is that I couldn't feel an emotional charge. Over time as people heal after a divorce it dissipates but initially it's usually very strong. This divorce is happening now, a lot has gone on and I can't feel any of that charge with this couple – it's just not there."

"I've never heard of this," Peter said.

Isobel shifted in her seat. "You won't have. This is my way of putting my impressions into words."

"But what does this impression mean?"

Isobel could feel herself shrinking inside but he'd asked for her opinion and she was going to follow through. This is what she did with her clients, with the couples she worked with – she helped them understand what was between them and hopefully helped them heal it. She felt her shoulders tensing. This was what he had employed her for. Just because he mightn't like what he was hearing, well, that wasn't her problem.

Peter frowned at her then looked at Patricia and back to Isobel.

"The second thing I'm concerned about is that Tommy isn't seeing his mother. When I talked to Anne today she seemed a bit distant from Tommy. Most people want to tell you about their children. She didn't. Thomas talked more about kids and Tommy than she did. That could be because she's in pain. All that Anne Banks is going through, alcoholism, divorcing, just getting out of rehab, moving out of her home, living in a new place, not living with her child, that's a lot. Any, and all of these events, are hugely emotional and challenging. My previous experience with people just out of rehab, just starting a programme, is that they're very vulnerable, upset, overwhelmed and emotional. I suppose I'm concerned that Mrs Banks isn't more upset. Maybe she's on tablets, maybe that's dampening her mood, but I am concerned about this and how this might impact on her relationship with Tommy."

"So you agree with me that there's something going on, that I'm not imagining it and my past isn't causing me to make up problems?"

"Tell me what has crossed your mind, what your concerns were."

Peter put down his fork. "I'm wondering if she's a victim of spousal abuse who's being robbed of her assets and is too afraid, or too intimidated, to say it. If that's the case I can't be a party to that. If she's in danger I'm not colluding with that."

Isobel made a face. "You're not the only one who thinks that is a possibility. Let me share the conversations I had this afternoon."

Peter raised his eyebrows and looked intently at her.

"Her neighbour, Grace, is concerned. Her background is as a social worker and she told me that when she met the Banks ten years ago she'd originally been concerned that Mr Banks might be abusive. The evidence was thin, as it often is in situations like that, but there were some bruises, a change in personality, extreme privacy issues, all of which are possible indications in abuse cases. She did ask Anne directly about abuse but Anne denied it, although that again often happens. Grace was really blindsided by the revelation of Mrs Banks as a secret drinker. But then again, that's also frequently the case. She seemed very certain of Anne's devotion to Tommy and is concerned about their lack of contact."

Peter and Patricia were both staring, food forgotten.

"In addition, Sharon, the woman who has done Anne's nails every two weeks for years, is convinced that she is not a drinker. She describes her as a woman who is devoted to Tommy – a very good mother. Anne Banks actually helped Sharon when she had a new baby and was having problems."

"That's most surprising," said Peter.

The silence stretched.

Isobel rubbed her face with her hands. "I agree that there is something not right but I'm not sure if him being controlling and abusive fits with how they were at the office."

"So you don't think there is abuse there?"

Isobel shrugged. "No, there may be and what I heard

today supports that possibility – but I feel there is still something I'm not seeing."

"So you agree there is something off in the situation?"

"God, yes – alcoholism, divorce, a child not seeing his mother. I think you're right to be concerned about Anne's unfavourable agreement and I feel we don't have all the answers as to what is going on. But I'm sorry – I can't put my finger on what is still bothering me."

"Well, what you have found out at least means that I need to talk to Anne again."

Isobel nodded, suddenly feeling exhausted. "Yes. I don't know what else I can tell you." She stood up. "I'm sorry – I'm really very tired. It's been quite a day. I must go."

Peter and Patricia stood and accompanied her to the door.

"Thank you, Isobel," said Peter. "I really do appreciate you taking time off from your sabbatical to help with this. At least now I can ask Anne some questions and see what she says. Have a safe trip back to Ireland – and I'll talk to you then."

"Goodbye. I hope what I've done will be of use – sorry it's been so inconclusive."

Isobel gave both Peter and Patricia a gentle hug and left.

On the journey back to Hammersmith those questions dominated her mind, chief among them being: why was there no emotional atmosphere? Peter might be right that there was something going on here, and that it could be spousal control and abuse. But something else was still bothering her and she hadn't been able to put it into words. She needed to clear her head. This trip, rather than giving her confidence and adventure, had actually really upset her.

Isobel's sleep was fitful that night. She dreamt she was walking in a street, then a garden and then a forest and each time there was someone just out of sight. There was no feeling of threat, rather it was a feeling of someone waiting for her to become aware of them, to look further, to search for them, to see just a little bit further.

Chapter 7

Wednesday 23rd May

Isobel arrived home to Ballycastle, emptied her case, let the family know that she was back and then headed for the beach. She pounded across the mile of sand towards the cliff of Fairhead which stood dramatic and proud. It looked like a forehead. Isobel wished her head was as resolute and sure. She climbed over the Pan's rocks and found the Devil's Churn, a hole in the rocks where the water surged up as the tide came in. On the stones around this opening there were, according to local tales, seven faces on the rocks. Isobel had only ever found three of them, and that was as a ten-year-old, thirty years ago. Today, however, she couldn't see any, reminding her that there was still something going on with the Banks that she felt was eluding her. Her own past experiences told her that feelings like this were important and often led to insights – but at the moment there was no clarity coming. Her eyes filled with tears of frustration and inadequacy. Maybe if she was well and wasn't so rusty she would be clearer and quicker. Rather than this trip and job giving her confidence, it had made her feel inadequate.

When the tears had passed she sat on, listening to the

advance and retreat of the sea, no longer searching but resting, almost lulled by the repetitive sound. Moving eventually, she walked over the rocks to stand closer to the edge. Suddenly, she saw on the rock ahead of her the clear image of a face.

Isobel grinned then stood still. Maybe it was the same with regard to the Banks. She needed to reboot and keep looking, maybe in a different place, a different way – extend the search.

She walked back across the beach, her feet moving slowly over the sand, matching her reflective mood.

Dave was waiting for her outside her front door. "How did it go?"

"All right."

"Peter told me he was grateful that you came over."

Isobel made a face and opened the door, leading the way inside.

"What's on your mind?" he said.

"I think I ran away."

"But I encouraged you to go. I thought it would help. Sorry."

Isobel touched his arm. "No, I mean I think I ran back home. Instead of waiting to get full clarity on the situation, I just bailed."

"No, Peter said you helped. He is clear about what he can do now, he says."

Isobel grimaced. "I don't think it's at all clear."

"Well, clearer then – and Peter's happy – so what more can you do?."

"Dave, I'm thinking of going back tomorrow if I can get a flight."

51

"*What?*" He stood back, aghast. "For goodness' sake, why? What can you do if you go back that you didn't do this time?"

"I can do some more digging and maybe –"

"Three flights in a few days, after months of taking care of yourself – you're going to wear yourself out on a wild goose chase." Dave paced up and down.

"No." Isobel laid a hand on his arm and looked into his eyes. "It's not a wild goose chase. There is something we are missing. I can feel it. I've no proof but, just like Peter did, I can sense something."

"Like what?"

Isobel spread her hands and shrugged her shoulders. "I don't know. I have no facts to prove it but there is something wrong."

Dave looked at her, frowning.

"I'm going to finish what I started, Dave. I'm going to chat to more people and see if I can find out where this sense of discomfort is coming from. Let's call Peter so I can talk to him."

In the end they set up a Skype call with Peter and Patricia at the office.

"Peter, have you done anything about the Banks?"

"No, not yet. I was busy today and didn't get round to contacting Anne."

"Good, can I ask you a few more questions?"

"Sure, anything that might help."

"Right – did Anne Banks seem afraid of Thomas, to you?"

Peter scrunched up his face. "Well, not really, but that doesn't mean she isn't."

Isobel nodded. "Setting aside the fact that it resonates

personally for you, why do you think, of all your cases, that this one has got to you?"

"Now that is a good question."

Isobel grinned. "I think so too. So tell me the answer."

Peter spoke slowly as his thoughts coalesced. "Well, usually a mediated settlement is negotiated to ensure the best outcome for the children, or in this case the child. And, I suppose, with the Banks, it just feels as if this divorce settlement is not about Tommy and what's best for him, but about Thomas getting everything."

There was a tense silence.

"Exactly, a good summation."

"Yes, I think that is it. It feels as if Thomas Banks is in charge of everything and maybe that's why I'm worried about coercive control. It feels like he's pulling all the strings."

"Have you ever spoken to Anne alone?"

"No, but I intend to, to satisfy myself as to whether there is coercion. I realise that Anne may not tell me, she might be too afraid."

"Look, Peter, I am concerned. There is something strange going on between that couple but I'm not convinced that it is coercive control or spousal abuse."

"Is this back to the emotional atmosphere?"

Isobel made a face.

"So what do we do?" he asked.

"We need more information and I'm thinking of coming back tomorrow to see what I can find out for you."

"I couldn't ask you to do that."

"You're not – I'm volunteering."

"Where would you start?"

"Maybe go and talk to her family. That would help me build up a picture of Anne which might clarify what is going on. Do you have an address?"

"Yes, it was on the marriage certificate. Her father is dead but her mother, as far as I know, still lives in the same house. It's in Petersfield."

"How far away is that?"

"About an hour and a half on the train."

Patricia said, "I'm bringing up flights now. There's a seat on the morning flight at ten to eight from Belfast city airport landing in Heathrow at twenty past ten."

"That sounds good."

"You could stay with me this time, Isobel," Patricia said. "I've a sofa bed that's really comfortable. It might make things easier for you."

Isobel tensed but knew that this was practical. "Thank you."

"I could organise a rental car for you to collect in the airport – then you could go straight on to Petersfield."

"Good idea," Isobel said.

"Patricia is great at organizing. I would be lost without her."

Patricia blushed and lowered her head. She saw Isobel watching her and flushed more darkly. "Give me your phone number and I'll text you my address," she said, "and if you send your email address then I can forward you the bookings for the flight and the car."

Isobel met Peter's eyes. "So, we find out as much as we can as quickly as possible."

He nodded. "Yes, the more information I have before I speak to Anne the better – otherwise it's likely she'll say no there's no coercion and then asking would be just a tick-box exercise."

"How long until the divorce papers are signed? You

were planning for next week, Wednesday, weren't you?"

"Yes," Patricia said.

"There are a couple of other places where we can get information," Isobel said. "Firstly, the school – they'll have known Anne and they may also be able to tell us if Tommy has changed. Tommy has been dealing with an alcoholic mother and that may have shown up in his behaviour. It would be good to know if they noticed anything or were concerned. Obviously, because of confidentiality, they won't want to talk so it's probably more in the line of gossip that we would hear anything. I'm wondering if you and I could do that, Patricia? Perhaps you could pose as a prospective parent with a child Tommy's age?" Isobel grinned. "You know, your asthmatic son who is now miraculously better and maybe about to change schools due to problems brought on by a father who is drinking and who has now left the family home?"

Patricia laughed. "My poor son has had so much to deal with!"

"Exactly. I can be your supportive friend. You could always say that you met Anne some time back and she recommended the school. Basically, a fishing expedition but, you never know, we might be able to pick up something from someone. You could ask for a tour, you get the general idea?"

Patricia was nodding enthusiastically, her eyes bright. "What are we going to do about my work?" she asked, looking at Peter.

Peter frowned. "I'm already putting the company in a difficult position with this and I don't want you to jeopardise your job as well, Patricia."

Patricia shook her head. "I know. I'll tell them that I

have to go to the dentist and am taking a half day, always assuming that the school will agree to see me."

"If you're sure," Peter said.

"One hundred per cent. I'll check with the school first thing. Perhaps Friday afternoon is a good option to suggest. I can angle for it, saying it's the easiest time for me to get off work and that I'm very worried about my son and keen to find an alternative for him. If they agree then I'll start the toothache story on Thursday afternoon."

Isobel nodded, satisfied. It seemed clear that Patricia was relishing the challenge of what they were doing, not to mention enjoying spending more time with Peter, outside of the office.

"There are a few other possibilities," she said. "I could talk to Aaron, Anne's hairdresser – I really wanted to do that last time but he wasn't there that day. I'm going to call at close of business on Thursday or Friday and see if I can have a private chat with him, maybe hear some gossip. Perhaps over a drink. I think a glass of wine might create a cosy confiding atmosphere. The only other place I can think of is the rehab centre. Again, we might not get much because of confidentiality but I would like to see the place and get a feel for it. Do you know which place Anne went to?"

"Yes," Peter said. "I made a note of it."

"It's not too far from Petersfield actually," said Patricia.

"Maybe I can take it in when I'm down there then. So I guess I'll see you tomorrow evening when I get back from Petersfield."

"Thanks, Isobel," Peter said. "I feel better knowing that we're doing our best to find the truth."

"Me too. Bye."

Dave was waiting in the kitchen for her. "Well?"

"I'm on the early flight in the morning from Belfast –"

"Isobel –"

"I have a one-way ticket. I'm going to do a bit more research and then I'll be home. It'll only take a few days. I'll probably be home at the weekend."

"But –"

"Dave, I feel better already. I'm doing the right thing here."

He sighed. "OK. Keep in touch."

She smiled. "I will."

Lying in bed, Isobel let her mind wander over what she'd heard. This was when she had her best ideas – when her mind was jumping from subject to subject, event to event, free-associating. Then, unexpectedly, as if her brain had been working on it, suddenly it could put the pieces together and see a picture.

Years ago she had read a book called *Blink* by Malcolm Gladwell. In it, an expert came to the Metropolitan Museum, looked at a new acquisition and, despite the carbon-dating tests that had been done, knew it was a fake. In a way, Peter had picked her for the same sort of reason. She didn't know what was wrong yet, but she knew that there was something off. Hopefully, over the next few days, she was going to find out what.

Chapter 8

Thursday 24th May

Isobel was driving out of Heathrow Airport car rental at midday in a black Nissan Micra with a satnav. Patricia, efficient as ever, had emailed a copy of the marriage certificate. Anne Banks, née Graham, even though she lived in London had got married in a little church near home in Petersfield. Her father was listed as deceased at the time of her wedding as was Thomas's father. The witnesses were recorded as being Claire Graham, a relative, maybe a sister or cousin of Anne's and Brian Poole, presumably known to the groom. Isobel planned to speak to Mrs Graham and Claire if she lived nearby.

When the satnav told her that she had arrived, she was looking at a terraced house on the outskirts of Petersfield. There was a central green and around that a semi-circle of twenty houses. Donna Graham's house was Number 12. It had a small garden in front with beautiful roses which surprisingly, and not so commonly, gave off a delicate perfume. The front door was painted a strong green with a shiny brass knocker.

As Isobel waited on the doorstep, she realised that she was nervous.

The door swung open, revealing a woman, tall and willowy with blonde hair now silver pulled back in a loose chignon.

This was definitely Anne's mother.

"Hello?"

It was a question.

Isobel smiled. "Hi, I'm Isobel McKenzie."

"If you're selling something I'm not interested."

Isobel had heard the expression 'a face like she was sucking a lemon' but had never witnessed it until now. She took a steadying breath.

"I'm a friend of Anne's. She mentioned growing up here a number of times." She hurried on. "I'm sorry, I just passed the road end and saw the sign and recognised it and on the spur of the moment decided to call."

Mrs Graham flexed her facial muscles in what might pass for a smile, opening the door slightly wider. "Have you seen her recently?"

"Only briefly, the other day, but we didn't have time to talk much. I do know that things aren't so good with her . . ." Isobel paused, allowing a silence.

Mrs Graham rushed in to fill it. "I know. Poor Thomas has had a lot to put up with – me too, if the truth be known."

Isobel struggled to keep her face neutral. "It's all so upsetting."

Mrs Graham swung the door open wider. "It's almost too much for a poor mother to bear. Come in, come in."

Isobel followed Mrs Graham down the narrow hall, past a sitting room to the kitchen at the back. She took a seat at the table while Mrs Graham busied herself filling the kettle and readying cups and a teapot.

"Such an ungrateful girl! I can't believe it – divorcing poor Thomas. I know he thinks it's for the best and he has been through the mill, but I was hoping that she would get herself sorted in that rehab place and that they could stay together."

"Did you know Anne was drinking, Mrs Graham?"

"Call me Donna. No, not until recently. Did you?"

Isobel shook her head. "Only recently. How long was that going on, do you know?"

"Well, it's hard for me to say." Donna played with her teaspoon. "As you probably know, Anne stopped associating with her family –" She paused.

Isobel, guessing that she didn't like being seen in a negative light, said, "Oh no, I didn't know that."

"Oh, I thought she would have told all her friends how bad I was. I'm glad she didn't. I was widowed when the girls were young – eight and six." Donna wet the tea and, setting it on a tea stand, sat down at the table. "I did my best to manage on my own but it was really hard. When Anne was seventeen and started dating Brian Poole, I thought she would settle down and marry him."

Isobel bit her lip to stop herself exclaiming in surprise. After a moment she smiled at Donna and nodded, her mind racing.

Donna poured the tea and moved the milk jug and sugar closer to Isobel. "Brian was a nice enough boy, but I was delighted when she left him and decided to move to London. I never got the chance to do those exciting things. She worked in London for a few years, coming home less and less and then she rang and said that she wanted to bring down her new boyfriend. Thomas is great, so kind, so successful, so good-looking, the sort of man you could depend on. Anne got married here. In fact, Brian was Thomas's best man."

"Was that not a bit unusual, having an ex-boyfriend for the best man?"

"I thought Anne would have told you all of this."

"No, she never mentioned dating Brian. How did he end up as the best man?"

"Thomas's friend couldn't make it at the last minute – a family emergency – and, as Thomas said, at least Brian knew Anne and he was available."

Isobel sipped her tea and said nothing.

"After they got married Thomas bought that lovely big house in Wimbledon. Oh, in the early days we were up a few times, but she was always so busy decorating and cooking and cleaning. Then she got pregnant and we saw even less of her. We went up once and she had a black eye."

"Did you ask Anne about it?"

"Of course. She said she'd walked into a door and that, with the baby, she was bruising easily and tender all over. Of course, Thomas says now that she could have been drinking even then. He used to find bruises too and that's what she used to tell him, that she had banged into a cupboard or something. Thomas was great, so protective of her, so attentive. A few weeks later she rang and rowed with me for even asking her about the bruise. She said I was against Thomas and she didn't want to see me again. I rang a few times. I apologised. I spoke to Thomas and he was fine with me but she just took against me then. Thomas eventually rang a few months later and said that he'd been trying to get her to forgive me and move on but that she wouldn't listen. He said he would keep trying. I think now that it must have been the drink affecting her."

"No doubt." Isobel nodded.

"After that he would ring every three months or so and let me know that Tommy was OK, but Anne, well, she just wouldn't relent. Thomas said that she'd changed. He worried that it might be post-natal depression but she wouldn't go to the doctor and wouldn't go for therapy. He tried everything. Every now and again he arranged to meet me so that I could see Tommy. In the end he had to tell Anne he was doing that because, as Tommy got older, he didn't want him to have to lie. But in all that time she never forgave me. I went to London, to the house, a few times but she refused to see me. Thomas called a few months ago and said that he was more worried than usual. He said that she was more erratic and wondered if she had been in touch with me. Of course she hadn't. I offered to go up but he said that would only make things worse. He said he'd discovered that Anne was drinking secretly and had been for some time. He was distraught on the phone. That time when she had the black eye – Thomas thought it went back to before then, that the black eye was from a drunken fall. He was so upset that he'd missed all the signs. He cried on the phone, saying that since there were no alcoholics in his family he just didn't know what to look for. He was trying to persuade her to go to rehab. He rang again a while later to say that he'd talked her into going to rehab for a month."

"Did you go up to the rehab for any of the family days?"

"Well, of course I asked but he said no, not at the moment, but that he would let me know when I could. Anne probably didn't want to deal with all that. I really hoped that the rehab would sort everything out. Unfortunately, when Anne came out of rehab she wanted to stay on her own and focus on being sober. Thomas was upset. A month later he rang to say that they were getting a divorce. He was sad but understood what Anne was saying, that this would be the best for Tommy, for now. She still doesn't want to see me, and I have to respect that as she's going through such a hard time. I'm just so glad that Thomas keeps in touch. At the moment Tommy has a lot to deal with but Thomas says hopefully when things settle down I will get to see him."

For a little while neither of them spoke.

Then Isobel said, "Have you ever seen Anne drunk? I'm a bit like Thomas – I didn't notice so I'm really upset by the whole thing."

"Well, she drank a bit when she reached eighteen but no worse than her friends. Then when she moved to London I just wouldn't know. Thomas said that in the rehab centre he learned all about how deceptive someone drinking can be."

"By any chance did Anne's dad drink?"

"Certainly not!"

"I'm sorry. I didn't mean to offend you."

"Her father was a handful, all right, but drink wasn't his problem."

"Oh, I'm sorry to hear that. Were things difficult for you?"

Donna inhaled sharply and a myriad of emotions played across her face. Then she burst into tears.

For a moment Isobel just sat there, then she reached across the table and touched Donna's arm gently. The crying showed no signs of abating so she murmured softly, "I know, I know."

Gradually the sobbing tapered off and Isobel handed

Donna a tissue. Nodding her thanks, she mopped up her tears.

Isobel got up and put the kettle on again. She made a fresh pot of tea and settled back at the table.

Donna said, "Anne's problems have just made me think of the hard times I had myself."

"Of course, of course . . . how were things difficult for you?"

"Well, I was very young when I fell in love with Anne's dad, Harry. He was a real charmer, very attractive. We married quickly and I was pregnant within a few months – and then it started. I had a lot of morning sickness so I wasn't waiting on him hand and foot ..." Donna's eyes filled again with tears, "and he hit me." She covered her face with her hands. "I was three months pregnant and he hit me. Oh, of course he apologised. He told me it was stress from trying to provide financially because we were having a baby. He promised it would never happen again and I believed him. I forgave him, we made up. But by the time I was going to deliver Anne I was used to getting a punch. At the start it was a black eye but he soon got clever and started only leaving marks where no one else would see them." She shook her head, her eyes on the tabletop. "No one knew. On the outside he was Mister Charm, everyone loved him and thought I was lucky. After Anne was born things were a bit easier for a while. Then I got pregnant again with Claire, Anne's sister, and it was worse than the first time. He beat me up at eight months pregnant and I went into an early labour. Thankfully, Claire was OK." Donna looked into Isobel's eyes. "I didn't know what to do. I had two young children, no job and nowhere to go. He never touched the children but it became a more and more regular thing with me. I was depressed and then one day, unexpectedly, he was killed in a car crash coming home from work. A lorry skidded in the rain and hit his car. A random act of God and I was free. Anne was eight when that happened and Claire six. I raised them myself and we managed well. The three of us were close, we got on and we talked." Donna hesitated. "But never about how their father behaved with me. Anne never asked so I hoped she'd forgotten and I prayed that Claire was too young to understand. I decided that I wasn't bringing another man into their world. I believed that we could be happy, the three of us, and we were until ..." Donna paused. "That's why, when I saw Anne's black eye, I jumped to the wrong conclusion. Thankfully Thomas understood why I made that mistake and forgave me. Anne never did. I think now that maybe she pushed me away as part of her drinking."

"So you think Anne's drinking has been the problem? You don't think that Thomas could be hitting Anne or bullying her?"

"No, not at all. I had my concerns but they were unfounded. That was just me being paranoid. Thomas is great. It's Anne's drinking that has ruined things for them."

"Donna, thank you for talking to me. I want things to work out for Anne and Tommy – for her to be happy –"

"And Thomas," Donna cut in.

Isobel started a little. "Yes, of course – but I suppose Anne seems to be losing everything and I'm just concerned about her. She hasn't seen Tommy for a while and I'm sure that's hard for both of them."

Donna's eyes welled up. "How is he? Have you seen him?"

"No, I'm sorry. I haven't seen him."

"Thomas is doing his best to protect him but …"

"Anne has been so busy with her recovery that I haven't had a chance to see her and Tommy. Apart from meeting her just briefly the other day." Isobel got to her feet. "Well, Donna, I'd better be off. Thank you so much for seeing me. I was hoping to catch up with Claire as well. In the past Anne talked about the three of you so much that I thought I would say hello. Where did Claire move to?"

"Claire has a restaurant, called 'Roasted', here in town," Donna said. "It's very good and very popular. Anne isn't speaking to Claire either. They fell out over Thomas. Claire took a real dislike to him. Despite Anne denying it, Claire believed that Thomas was hitting Anne and nothing would persuade her otherwise. I think she sees trouble everywhere, that girl."

At the front door, Isobel turned and said, "Thank you so much for the tea and the chat, Donna. Please don't mention to Anne or Thomas that I've called. I don't want them to think … well, they might think I was talking about them behind their backs … I mean, they both must feel vulnerable at the moment … I'm sure you understand …"

"Of course I do. I wouldn't want them to think that either." Donna smiled. "Gosh, I did go on so. I haven't talked about any of that in years and once I started I couldn't stop."

Isobel smiled. "I learned a lot from you."

She wondered at the nature of relationships and allegiances.

Chapter 9

Isobel drove into Petersfield and parked in the car park at Waitrose. She used Google Maps and waited for directions. The restaurant was a five-minute walk away. Isobel glanced at her watch – it was three thirty. Hopefully, Claire would be at work and not too busy. Roasted was a glass-windowed delicatessen, with a restaurant behind. There were people sitting at tables, chatting happily.

Isobel found a table in a quieter area and ordered a scone and coffee from the waitress.

"Is Claire Graham, the owner, here today?" Isobel enquired.

"Yes. Is there a problem with anything?"

Isobel smiled. "No, no, not at all. It's a personal matter. I wonder would you see if she could talk to me?"

Within minutes a tall, blonde, beautifully dressed woman was walking towards her. Isobel didn't need to be an expert in genetics know that this was Claire.

"Were you asking for me?" Claire seemed polite but distant, reserved.

"Yes. I know Anne and since I was in the area I thought I would just pop into your restaurant and say hello."

Claire raised an eyebrow. The silence stretched. "Do you know Thomas as well?"

Isobel hesitated. "I've met him briefly once but I can't say that I know him."

More silence.

Then Isobel said, "I know things aren't great for Anne at the moment –"

"Well, at least she's away from that man, but unfortunately Tommy isn't."

Ah, thought Isobel, it's safe to be more direct with this woman.

"My main concern is ensuring the best outcome for Anne and Tommy," she said. "I'm trying to find out more about what is going on with a view to helping and I would really appreciate it if you would be honest with me."

Claire just looked at her.

Isobel continued, "Please trust me and tell me as much as you can. I promise I will do everything possible to help."

Claire's eyes filled with tears and she nodded. "Come with me." She led Isobel through a door marked staff only into an office. She sat down behind the desk and Isobel took the chair opposite her.

"Tell me about Anne and Thomas," Isobel said.

Claire wiped her eyes with her fingers. "She should never have married him." She put her hand over her eyes and took a deep breath before looking at Isobel again. "I never liked Thomas Banks. When Anne was at school, at about seventeen she started dating Brian Poole. He was her first boyfriend. They were a couple for about eight months. Brian was mad about her. I think he saw them married and living here in Petersfield. Anne finished her A levels and went on holiday to the Isle of Man with some of her friends and when she came back she decided to head off to London with one of the girls. She finished with Brian and moved to London. She said she was too young and didn't want to be tied down. I think she and Brian kept in touch a bit and they used to have coffee sometimes when she was home." She sighed. "When Anne was about twenty-five she came home for the weekend, saying that she had met this amazing guy, Thomas. He had swept her off her feet, meals out, flowers, presents. She was head over heels. She seemed happy so I was glad for her. Within six months she was telling me that they wanted to get married. It sounded a bit quick and I was disturbed by that. I pressed her to let me meet him and we arranged for them to come down to Petersfield for the day. From the moment I met him I had concerns. Oh, he did his best to charm me, but I guess what upset me was how Anne changed when she was with him."

Isobel raised an eyebrow in question.

"Anne was always full of fun but with him she seemed uptight, quiet, restrained, not herself. She was trying to be too perfect." Claire looked pensive. "And, the day they were down something happened when we were having lunch that really cemented it for me. The waitress splashed some gravy on the table as she set down the plate and Thomas lost it. He called her a 'stupid bitch'." She shivered. "Anne covered it over quickly, jumped up, wiped up the spillage with her napkin and said it was fine and didn't matter. I saw his face though. He was raging. As Anne fussed he seemed to steady himself and realise where he was. Then he turned on the charm and had the waitress eating out of his hand in a minute. I could see Anne just sighing in relief. For the rest of the afternoon she draped herself around him like an adoring partner but I thought it was also to keep him in check."

"I see." That pattern of behaviour was all too familiar to Isobel.

"I was so upset about how he spoke to the waitress. When he called her that name it was in a murderous tone. I was sitting opposite him and for a second I saw what he was really like. He saw me staring and the look he gave me was so cold. Of course, I spoke to Anne about what happened. It was on the phone because he made sure that I never got a chance for the rest of that day – in fact, they left early because of an 'emergency at his work'." She made air quotes. "By the time I got to speak to her it was the next day and he had done a number on her. She said that Thomas was afraid that I didn't like him. I mentioned what had happened with the waitress and she said that Thomas was extremely stressed that day because he was meeting me and Mum and had overreacted because of that. She said I didn't know him, that he was a gentle, caring man and that I had misinterpreted things. It was one event, my sister was happy and I told myself I was overreacting." She paused.

"And then?"

"Within a month they were engaged. Thomas wanted to get married in London but Anne held out for a small wedding at home. He was as good as gold. The next time I met him he talked about what had happened with the waitress and explained his nerves and did everything he could to smooth it over. I suppose I gave him the benefit of the doubt. The wedding was three months later. Anne was so busy with work and organising everything that we saw her only briefly. There was never much of a chance to talk. She was thrilled to be getting married. Thomas bought that beautiful house in Wimbledon. They were moving in shortly after the wedding and she was thinking about paint and furniture."

"How did Brian, Anne's ex-boyfriend, end up as the best man? Did he know Thomas?"

"No. That was a bit strange. One of the times they were down about the wedding they bumped into Brian. I imagine the only thing the men had in common was that they both wanted to marry Anne. Thomas's parents are dead and he has no siblings. One of his friends was going to be best man but at the last minute there was some family emergency and he couldn't come and none of his other friends were available. He told Anne that he wanted a best man that at least one of them knew, so he asked Brian."

"Why did Brian do it?"

"Oh, I'm sure he didn't want to, but Anne asked him. She probably begged him because Thomas wanted him, and Brian couldn't refuse Anne. Brian told me later that day that after the ceremony Thomas went up to him and told him that Anne was now his. Brian said he gloated and made it clear that Brian was to stay out of their lives."

"Where's Brian now?"

"He still lives here in the village. I don't see much of him. He's a bit intense. I think he still carries a torch for Anne." Claire took a deep breath, "Then, when Anne became pregnant she gave up work to prepare for motherhood. We were excited too. I wanted to help and support Anne but we saw less and less of her. She was busy with her new life or out with Thomas. Obviously we saw Tommy when he was born. Anne was tired then and a bit overwhelmed and she kept putting us off when we wanted to visit, saying she just wanted to get used to her new role as a mother. We did go to London for the christening. When we visited Anne had a bruise."

"Did you talk to her about it?"

"Yes, I asked her about it, but she denied that Thomas had hit her. Well, that just confirmed for me my earlier doubts. In my heart I felt that Thomas was hitting her, controlling her and that she was afraid of him. Basically my sister, like my mother, had married an abuser." Claire looked into Isobel's eyes. "I got caught too, but younger, and I didn't marry the man. I was dating him and he beat me up. I went for help then. I had counselling. I talked about my childhood. Of course, Mum wants to pretend that I was too young to know what was happening but I did. Through all the help I learned the signs to look for: the push for early involvement, the control, the isolation, the hypersensitivity, making others responsible for feelings, rigid gender-role behaviour, verbal abuse, mood swings, battering."

"And you saw all of these present with Anne and Thomas?"

"Yes. I was really worried about Anne, worried that she was making the same mistake that I had. I decided to go up and see her and talk to her about our dad and about my experiences. I didn't tell her I was coming because she would have made some excuse and put me off. I just arrived. She was terrified. I suggested going to a little café, out of the house, as she seemed frightened that Thomas would find out. We spent a couple of hours chatting. I told her about Dad, my ex-boyfriend and how I saw Thomas behaving. She cried."

Tears started to run down Claire's face but she seemed oblivious.

"I asked her if Thomas was hitting her. She nodded. I told her that she could leave, that I would help her. She just shook her head and whispered that nobody could help her. She was terrified. Then her phone rang. She looked at it and I knew by her face that it was Thomas. She answered immediately and explained that she had come for coffee in town. In a second she was jumping up, gathering her stuff and getting ready to leave. She said she had to go and that she wasn't going to tell him that I'd visited." She paused and drew a deep breath. "A week later she rang me and started a fight with me about how I was trying to destroy her marriage by badmouthing her husband. I reminded her that she had told me that Thomas had hit her. She said that she only said that to make me feel better about what had happened to me. She said that she never wanted to see me again. If I came near her she was going to get a solicitor to issue a barring order. I felt that Thomas was behind all of this, maybe even listening to the conversation and orchestrating it, making sure that Anne was cut off from any help. A week later a letter arrived from their solicitor threatening legal action. I didn't know what to do. They changed their phone numbers. I sent some letters but they were returned unopened. Once, I even waited outside the school where Tommy was. I managed to speak to Anne as she was collecting Tommy. She basically begged me to leave her alone, that I was causing trouble for her and Tommy."

Claire paused and looked in anguish at Isobel.

"And did you?" Isobel prompted.

Claire whispered, "I didn't know what to do for the best. In the end all I could say was 'Never forget that I will help you'. I did speak to a solicitor myself. He basically pointed out that unless Anne was prepared to make statements about what was going on, there was nothing I could do. In the end I prayed, that seemed all that was left. Then, I heard from Mum about the divorce and Anne's drinking."

"Were you surprised? Had Anne always been a drinker?"

"Well, she liked to have a good time as much as anyone when we were younger. Obviously I haven't been around much so I don't know about more recently. To be honest, I thought she'd found a way out at last and I was delighted."

"What do you mean?" Isobel asked, puzzled.

"Well, I always thought that Thomas would be a man who wouldn't let go and I thought Anne had figured out a strategy where he would be happy to get divorced. I thought the drinking was serving that purpose. I was afraid to mess things up for her so I didn't get in touch. But as soon as everything is finalised I plan to see her. I'm not happy about Thomas having Tommy at the moment. I'm a bit confused about what Anne is doing in that respect. Maybe this is the only way she can get the divorce and, when things have settled and Anne has shown that she has been sober, she can have more and more time with Tommy. Hopefully eventually Tommy can live with her."

"So you think that the real problem is spousal abuse rather than Anne's drinking?"

"Living with that man would have driven anyone to drink. So what if she drinks? From what I hear, Anne is sober now and she isn't living with him. I call that progress. I think she's better off. And hopefully when she is on her feet she can see more of Tommy."

Isobel twitched in her seat. "Claire, no one else seems to feel that there's abuse here. If anything Thomas seems to be doing his best for Anne and Tommy."

"So he has you fooled as well. You've no idea who you're dealing with. He has my mother convinced that he's the good guy and that Anne is a bitch – I mean, her own mother! Mind you, my mother doesn't have the sense she was born with and she was always a sucker for a charming man – first my father and now Thomas."

Isobel rubbed her hands over her face. "So you think that Anne found the one thing, her drinking, that would cause Thomas to divorce her?"

"Yes – he would hate to have a wife doing that, being messy. Look how good he looks in all of this. He needs to always look good. He's a narcissist. So I think when Anne gets her divorce and when she has been sober a while she can petition the court again to get visitation – and eventual custody. She just has to play by Thomas's rules to get out of the marriage. And she feels secure in the belief that Thomas would never touch his son and heir."

"So you think that Anne is faking an addiction to get out of her marriage?" Isobel put her head in her hands. "Claire –"

"I know, I know, I sound crazy."

Isobel winced. "Not crazy – maybe a bit fixated –"

"I don't care what you think. When Anne gets away she'll tell you all about what's been going on. It won't be long now. She said she had a plan. I have to be patient so that I don't mess things up for her. She'll contact me again soon."

"Again?" Isobel asked softly.

Claire put her hand over her mouth, her breath catching in her throat. She peered at Isobel. Neither of them spoke, neither moved.

Taking a gentle breath, Isobel said, "Claire, I'm not actually a personal friend of Anne's. Her solicitor has brought me in to consult on the case because he's concerned that there's something off about the divorce."

"Oh, no!" said Claire, aghast. "You're going to wreck Anne's plan!"

"Not at all. Neither Anne nor Thomas knows that I'm talking to people. Anne's solicitor has done this because he was concerned that her rights were not being protected and that was a worry for him. My job is just to clarify what is going on. He doesn't want to disrupt the process, just to be clear that it is in everyone's best interests. Please believe me, we only want to help."

Claire frowned, then after a few seconds she said, "All right, I'll tell you what happened. From what I've told you, you can see that Anne and I weren't in touch much over the years. Then, about three or four months ago I got a letter from her. In it she said that she had a plan. She couldn't give me details because that would put me in danger and maybe jeopardise the outcome – but as soon as everything was sorted she would be in touch. In the meantime, I was to tell no one that she had written to me and I was just to play dumb. I don't even know if I'm making a mistake in telling you this."

"Did she say anything about Thomas abusing her?"

"No, no – but don't you see that's why she wrote to me? Because she knew what I believed about her marriage and this was her way of alerting me that she was ready to do something about it. To be honest, I thought that she was going to run away. She knew Thomas would come to me and Mum first, thinking we would know where she was, and this was her way of warning me. I never mentioned the letter to anyone." She covered her face with her hands. "I'm only telling you because it seems to be taking so long and, maybe, if you're in contact with Anne, you can quietly find out if things are working out for her. And, I'm still concerned about Tommy."

Claire bowed her head. Isobel leaned across the table and touched her shoulder. They sat silently for a few more minutes and then Claire lifted her head, wiping her eyes with her fingers.

Isobel looked into her eyes. "I'm on Anne and Tommy's side. I promise you that I will do everything that I can."

Claire nodded.

"Can you tell me where Brian Poole lives or works or his phone number?" Isobel asked. "I'd like to talk to him about Thomas – to get his impressions." She could see Claire about to make an excuse so she hurried on. "I want to get all the information that I can. It helps me be clearer about what's going on and what's the best, and safest way, to move forward."

Claire nodded, and opened one of the drawers in her desk. She pulled out an address book and copied an address onto a piece of paper.

Isobel then exchanged numbers with her, exhorting her to make contact if she thought of anything else or heard from Anne.

Chapter 10

Isobel put Brian Poole's address into her satnav and drove to his home. It was on the outskirts of Petersfield. There was no car in the drive. It looked like he was at work. She decided to go for dinner and maybe take a walk. Her mind was reeling from all that she'd heard. It was seven o'clock when she called back at the house. This time there was a van in the driveway.

Brian Poole proved to be an enigma. He was six foot tall, with brown curly hair and blue eyes. His face wore the colour of someone who spends a lot of time outside. His initial greeting as he swung open the door was pleasant, his smile warm.

"Hi, I'm a friend of Anne Banks. I was wondering if . . ."

His face became shuttered. "No. I'm on my way out. I can't talk now." He started to close the door.

"Claire told me where you lived."

He paused. "You know Claire?"

"Yes, I've just come from her. We spent the afternoon chatting. She said that you were close to Anne."

"Was – past tense."

"I was hoping that you would talk to me about her."

"Why?"

"Well, I'm concerned about her and –"

"I'm going to phone Claire and check up on you." Brian closed the door.

Isobel bit her lip. Claire wasn't wrong – this man was intense and a bit strange. Why so paranoid? She realised that she was nervous. Quickly she took out her phone.

Patricia answered almost immediately. "Hi, when are you getting here? I was going to get pizza –"

"Patricia, listen. I'm about to talk to Brian Poole."

"The best man?"

"Yes, yes. I'm a bit nervous. Here's the address. If I don't call in an hour, ring me."

"Jesus, what are you getting yourself into?"

"Nothing, nothing. This is just to make me feel better." Isobel heard footsteps in the hall.

"Are you sure?"

"Yes, yes. I'm fine. Just ring me in an hour. I've got to go."

Brian swung the door open again. "I'm only talking to you because of Claire. Come on in."

The hallway had honey-coloured wooden floors. The wallpaper was of trees. It was like walking into a forest. The stairs rose ahead, beautifully varnished with wooden knots on every step. The sitting room was off to the left with the floor there just as beautiful.

Isobel perched on one of the chairs. Brian filled the other one.

"So what do you want? Claire said that you knew Anne and cared about her."

"Yes, I'm working for Anne's divorce solicitor. I'm checking up on some background to make sure that everything is in order."

With a jerk of his head, Brian said, "This is the first sensible thing Anne has done, get a divorce."

"You don't like Thomas?"

"That obvious, eh?" Then silence.

"Why not?"

Brian looked at her. Isobel returned his gaze steadily, not challenging him but open, attentive.

After a minute he said, "What do you want me to say? That he stole my girl, he did – that he turned her head, he did – that she is the love of my life and that I've never got over her, she is, I haven't. So, I don't see her. He asked me to be his best man, I refused. Then Anne asked, said his friends couldn't get away from work. I agreed for Anne, more fool I. He rubbed my nose in it. Said he was the better man and warned me off. The first few times Anne came to visit her mum she rang and we had coffee together but I had to stop meeting her. It was just like salt in an open wound."

"Did you know that Anne had been drinking?"

"I don't know anything about what she's been doing. I told you, I keep away."

"Did you know that Anne was getting a divorce?"

"I saw Claire one day and she mentioned it. It's none of my business anymore."

Isobel leant forward in her chair. "But this is the love of your life, and she may be free again."

He met her gaze. "She'll never be free of that man." He looked down at his hands.

Isobel pursed her lips pensively and kept her gaze on Brian.

Sensing her regard, he looked up. "I haven't seen Anne

in years. I know nothing about her life. I'm surprised she's getting divorced but that's mainly because I never thought Thomas would let her go but, if that is what they're doing, fine. It's none of my business. I'll believe it when I see it. What do you want from me?"

"Claire believes that Thomas is a bully, violent maybe. Do you know anything about that?"

"No. It doesn't surprise me, but I don't know anything about it."

"Anne's an alcoholic and has been to rehab. Do you know anything about that?"

"Again, I'm telling you that I know nothing about what's going on. I haven't seen Anne in years!" Brian's voice was raised now.

Isobel shifted in her chair. "I wonder if I could use your bathroom?"

Brian frowned but stood up, opening the door into the hallway. "Up the stairs, to the left."

Isobel stood up. Entering the hall she gently closed the sitting-room door and made her way upstairs. Thankfully there were carpets upstairs to muffle any noise and she had flat shoes. She looked quickly into the bathroom: one toothbrush. Opening the bathroom cabinet she saw some shaving foam, a razor, aftershave and a bottle of perfume – Coco Mademoiselle – maybe Brian had a girlfriend. Moving back out of the bathroom, she closed the bathroom door noisily, then very gently opened one of the other two doors upstairs.

The first door opened into a boxroom. There was a desk with a laptop, a filing cabinet, a calendar up on the wall and a cork board. Knowing she had very little time, Isobel scanned the room. The calendar was Brian's life planner. There were the names of woods and gardens listed and hours of work. It looked as if it had been quiet in the first few months of the year, apart from a weekend in London. A weekend in Glasgow in March was also marked. There was another weekend in Glasgow in October with a question mark. Obviously that was his favourite place to go – maybe he had family there.

The cork board had tickets for a local play pinned to it along with numbers for plumbers, carpenters and other handymen, some fliers for counselling and for Adapt house, a woman's shelter. Brian was obviously quite community-minded.

Moving back into the corridor she entered the second room, Brian's bedroom. It was very tidy, the furniture was wooden and the colours masculine. The only relief from austerity was two silver photo frames. One showed a young couple dressed in formal attire. Isobel picked it up. It was Brian and Anne, very young. It must have been a school formal or something.

The second picture looked familiar. It was of a blonde woman beautifully attired in a black dress. This was the same picture of Anne Banks that the lady in the clothing store had given her. But Thomas Banks was not in this picture. As the lady had said, it must have been on the internet – or perhaps in a local paper? Wherever Brian got it, he had photoshopped Thomas out of the picture. It seemed he was obsessed with Anne Banks.

Realising she needed to hurry, Isobel quietly made her way out of the bedroom, opened the bathroom door quietly, flushed the loo, splashed her hands and then noisily closed the bathroom door and came down the stairs.

"Are you OK?" Brian asked.

Isobel smiled. "Yes. Thank you for talking to me. Goodbye."

She drove quickly away and pulled into a pub car park.

Patricia answered on the first ring. "Thank God. I've been so worried. Are you OK?"

"Sorry, Patricia. I didn't mean to worry you. I suddenly got a bit nervous and I just wanted you to know where I was."

Peter's voice came over the speaker. "Isobel, don't do anything like that again. We were worried sick."

"I'm sorry, I'm sorry. I was probably overreacting."

Peter said, "You're all right, that's the main thing. How did it go?"

"Fine, fine. Brian Poole, the best man, is an old boyfriend of Anne's and is still carrying a torch for her. He has two photos of her in his bedroom."

"Isobel, what were you doing in his bedroom?" Patricia said.

"Oh, I pretended to go to the bathroom. He didn't know. Patricia, I'm going to send you the photo. Will you check Anne and Thomas's online accounts and see if you can find that picture? Also see if it's in a local paper, or webpage for the event. It's the same photo as I was shown before, but Brian Poole has photoshopped Thomas out of the picture."

"That seems a bit extreme," Peter said.

"Exactly," said Isobel. "He says he hasn't seen Anne and knows nothing about her present life, yet he has a recent photo of her."

"I'll check it out."

"How are things with you – anything new?"

"I'm going to the school to talk to the principal at half past two tomorrow."

Isobel laughed. "How's the toothache?"

"It was terrible today so no work tomorrow while I get it sorted. Oh, and I made an appointment with a Mr Byrne for you tomorrow at the rehab centre for ten o'clock – you said that you wanted to see it."

"Great, Patricia. I should probably stay here tonight then, find a room in a pub or a hotel and go on to the rehab in the morning."

"I thought you might say that so I found out that there's a room available at a hotel in town. The car is fine for tomorrow too."

"You're way ahead of me."

"I told you she was a star," Peter said.

Isobel raised her eyebrows and was glad they couldn't see her. "I'll phone you tomorrow after the centre. I should have time to get back for our school trip."

"Yeah, I would prefer if you were with me."

"I'll do my best. Bye."

Isobel was delighted to get to the hotel. She ran a bath, got in and tried to relax. All of the conversations had taxed her and continued to run through her head, even after she got to bed. There were two different versions of the Banks marriage: one where Anne was the problem, drinking, falling, banging into things and Thomas was the good guy trying to maintain things – and the other where he was the bad guy, controlling, abusing, bullying and Anne was his victim. Different stories, different viewpoints of what was going on. What was the truth? Did Anne Banks need help? Or was the divorce the best thing to happen for this couple and they should let them get on with it?

Eventually, she drifted into sleep. She dreamt she was searching for something, something precious and shiny. She met a man who smiled and seemed helpful but as she looked at him his face became warped and threatening and blood dripped from his hands. She stirred and turned over only to plunge into a new world. She was in a house that was large with beautiful furnishings. She walked through the house. When she sat on the gold armchair it gradually deteriorated into a dirty, tarnished chair that fell apart. She stood up and moved into the next room. The walls were covered in William Morris wallpaper but when she touched it, it turned mouldy and black. She touched a picture and it too became rotten. Isobel ran from room to room but everywhere what initially appeared beautiful disintegrated.

She woke at five o'clock, short of breath and anxious. She got up and had a drink of water before turning over again to sleep. This time she found herself dressed in a red cape. She was walking through a forest which was dark, and she felt scared. Eventually a house appeared and she ran to it. Once inside she moved from room to room looking for someone. In the bedroom there was a person in bed who smiled and reached out a hand to her. Isobel moved closer. Suddenly the smile changed into big white teeth with blood dripping from them and arms reached out to grab her.

When she woke again, Isobel was glad to get up.

Chapter 11

Friday 25th May

By nine o'clock Isobel was on the road to the rehab centre. She wasn't hopeful that she would learn anything specific about Anne but it would be interesting to see the place where she had spent four weeks. The centre was on the outskirts of a town. It was an old Georgian estate house with graceful windows, in its own substantial grounds. The entrance was a long drive bordered by grass, so that visitors could see and admire the gardens. There was a vegetable garden, large greenhouses and a polytunnel. Dividing the areas were hedges and flower beds and what appeared to be a low-walled maze or labyrinth. There were some parking spaces at the front and Isobel pulled up there.

The front door was double width and open, revealing an inner access door. Inside there was a big, high-ceilinged hall where there was a reception desk. Everything looked very clean and Isobel thought opulent. Behind the reception desk was a bespectacled thirty-something woman who was dressed in a severe black suit and white blouse. Isobel introduced herself and was shown to a sitting room to wait. Mr Byrne, it seemed, was running late.

Isobel waited half an hour before anyone joined her. She flicked through some magazines but gradually realised how nervous she was. When Patricia made the appointment she hadn't stated the nature of her business. Now, sitting here, Isobel wondered if that might be to her advantage. Rather than ask about Anne and meet the predictable barrier of confidentiality, maybe there was another way. There was no further time to plan as the door opened and a dapper little man entered. He was around five foot five, slim, with dark, Isobel was sure dyed, hair and a moustache. His movements were precise almost formal, Hercule Poirot to a 'T'. Isobel suspected that just as his physical attire was important to him so was what others thought of him.

He gave a fake smile. "I'm Mr Byrne, sorry to keep you waiting."

Isobel reached out her hand. "Hello. Isobel McKenzie."

Mr Byrne gave it a lukewarm shake.

"Thank you so much for seeing me, Mr Byrne. I'm at my wit's end. My sister is in a terrible way and I'm desperate to find somewhere that can help her. This is the first lifeline I feel there's been in a long time." Isobel pulled out a tissue and dabbed her eyes with it.

Mr Byrne steered Isobel to a chair and then sat down himself. "Ms Mckenzie, only your sister can admit herself here. There is nothing you can do to make her come. Unless she wants to help herself nothing is going to happen. We cannot be a lifeline if someone doesn't want to be saved."

"Oh, of course you're right. It is just that I've been talking to Anne Banks and she told me about being here and how it had helped her stop drinking. She raved about the place and I just thought, with such a strong recommendation, that this was the place that could do the same for my sister."

Mr Byrne straightened his tie. "Well, we have success with many people and I'm delighted that someone is recommending us."

"The issues Anne told me about and those my sister is facing are very similar – that's why I was so keen to come – I hoped that knowing about Anne's success my sister would be more inclined to give this a chance."

"I cannot comment on individual cases obviously. Your sister would need to speak to one of our counsellors and be assessed for her suitability for our programme. Only after that could we even consider arranging admission."

"I'm trying to find a place where the needs of an alcoholic with young children are catered for."

"Our job is to get the person dry, help them understand what's been happening, give them coping skills, a programme to follow and put them in touch with a support network. We do speak to family but it's dependent on each case and our job is not to sort out the person's life but to give them the skills to do so."

"Do you make recommendations about how someone should proceed in repairing their relationship with their children?"

"That's a very specific question. In all cases we want the person to make amends with the people they've hurt. Obviously, with their children we would be supporting the building of a stronger, more honest relationship, but our primary focus is getting the alcoholic to stop drinking. More in-depth relationship-building may need a counsellor's ongoing support when the person leaves here."

"Do you make recommendations about things like that?" Isobel pressed.

"Not generally, unless there's a specific need. The children in the relationship are not under our care. We recommend, assist our clients, look for obvious dangers if there are any but we're here to treat addiction and to get the addicted person sober. That's a difficult thing to do and can take more than one attempt."

Isobel nodded. As Mr Byrne talked she'd realised that there would be a limit to what he would know about Tommy. She asked, "Is it possible to see around?"

Mr Byrne shook his head. "No, not today. We have open days when you can come to see the facility. The anonymity of our clients is sacrosanct. Tours are well organised so that no one meets any clients." As if reminded of time he glanced at his watch and stood up briskly. "The next open day is the first Saturday of the month, as usual. You and your sister are welcome to come. I'll give you information on the procedure she needs to follow to get a place here. Tell her to contact us if she is interested in our programme."

Isobel remained seated. "Fine – but, when someone leaves here, what follow-up services are in place or what is recommended?"

Mr Byrne sat down again. "There's a choice between an after-care programme which we run or they can return to a counsellor they were already seeing. We advise either of these options and of course the choice is up to the client. They also have AA meetings. We recommend ninety meetings in ninety days when they leave here."

"What happens if someone doesn't do these things?"

"Sadly, some people choose not to. Unfortunately that

often is a precursor to their drinking again. Getting sober and staying sober takes a lot of work and most people need all the support they can get and even then it's difficult."

Isobel smiled and stood up. "Thank you, Mr Byrne. I feel I've a better understanding of things now."

"My pleasure, Ms Mckenzie, and I wish your sister success in her sobriety."

Isobel made her way to her car and sat at the wheel. She felt guilty. Anne Banks had a lot to deal with in her addiction. Isobel put her head in her hands and let the emotions wash over her. Was she doing more harm than good here? Her fears mounted and she took a few deep breaths. As she calmed, her brain kicked in and she realised that the things Claire had told her meant that she needed to check everything out.

She scrolled through her contact list and found an old friend's number. As always Niamh was quick to answer, her musical Cork accent soon singing over the airwaves.

"Niamh, I have a bit of a situation here and I need your expertise to clarify a few things."

"No problem."

"If a mother was reluctant to meet up with her child post-rehab, what could her counsellor or aftercare worker do?"

"How old is the child?"

"Nine."

"That's unusual. For a variety of reasons, it's more typical for a mother to have a problem with meeting a teenage child. Well, they could continuously encourage her to re-establish a relationship with her child, pointing out that this was a vital relationship in her life and especially in the child's. All they could do is suggest, encourage, support."

"If the mother felt that her guilt and shame were so great that she couldn't meet her child, would that be OK?"

"If it were me, I would be pointing out to her that seeing her child would reduce that guilt."

"But if the mother was getting panic attacks at the thought of dealing with this?"

"If it were me, I would work with that and give her some time, but I would point out that those feelings were only going to escalate until she took that step." She paused. "Tell me, is there any evidence that she has abused the child?"

"No, but she is very reluctant to meet up with her son now that she is sober."

"Well, for a while I would give her some space to deal with some of the issues but honestly I would always be pushing for contact."

Isobel nodded as she listened. "Thanks, Niamh. I'll be in touch soon."

"Mind yourself."

Isobel sat for another minute and then rang Patricia.

"Hi, any news on the photo?"

"No papers ran this photo. I've checked Anne and Thomas's Facebook pages – nothing. And I've done a search of the web for images and again nothing."

"So, what does that mean?"

"Isobel, do you have a Facebook account, Instagram, do you post photos of yourself online?"

"No."

"Well, neither do Anne and Thomas Banks. They're kind of like you, in that they have no obvious presence on the web. You actually do because other people have put up photos with you in them – there are only a few but I could find them. All I could find of the Banks is a photo from nearly ten years ago for Thomas Banks out on a work do and nothing for Anne, and definitely not that photo of the two of them."

"So this seems to be a private photo not in the public domain."

"Yes."

"How did Brian Poole get it then?"

"That's the million-dollar question. How did you get on at rehab?"

Isobel laughed. "Not so good. I didn't really learn much except that Anne would be encouraged strongly to see Tommy."

"Which is common sense?"

"Yes, so why has it not happened yet? What's the problem?"

"It seems strange."

"It does, doesn't it?" said Isobel. "Despite everything the Banks say about thinking of Tommy, the one thing that seems a priority they're not doing."

"Well, maybe something we find out at the school will help."

"I'm on my way back to London now. I'll drop off the car and meet you at the school."

"Great."

"Are you nervous about today?"

"Yes."

"You're going to be fine, Patricia. Remember, this is us trying to make sure that Tommy is doing OK. Keep that in your mind – that makes it easier."

"Thanks."

"See you soon."

Chapter 12

When Isobel arrived at the school she found Patricia pacing up and down in the car park.

"Oh my God, I've the worst case of butterflies in my stomach that I've ever had!"

Isobel laughed.

"It's not funny."

"It could be worse – you could have diarrhoea," Isobel tilted her head, "or a toothache."

Patricia grinned.

"Do you have a friend or a family member who has a child of around nine?" Isobel said.

Patricia looked puzzled. "Yes, my friend has a nine-year-old called Luke."

"Do you spend time with Luke?"

"Yes, I do."

Isobel spun her hands round each other and nodded pointedly at Patricia to keep talking.

"We go to the park, swimming ..." said Patricia.

"So, use those memories and experiences. In fact, your son is called Luke too. Just model him on the Luke you know."

Patricia grinned. "He's great and getting so big and tall."

"That's the spirit. You sound like a doting mum. You're taking to this like a duck to water."

"Maybe you're right. It certainly beats typing and answering the phone. This is far more exciting."

"Exciting, not scary, just like a roller coaster. Maybe you're developing a taste for intrigue."

Patricia straightened her shoulders. "I'm ready to find a school for Luke."

It was half past two when the secretary showed them into the headmistress's office.

Mrs Winter was in her middle thirties. She was dressed in a very professional and expensive-looking pale-grey suit with a baby-blue blouse. Her black hair was pulled back into a loose chignon and her make-up was natural and well applied. She was the epitome of sophistication and professionalism.

"I'm so grateful to you for seeing me, Mrs Winter, and at such short notice," Patricia said.

"Not at all."

"As I mentioned on the phone we're relocating to the area and a friend told me about this school and recommended it, given my situation."

"How old is your son?"

"Luke is nine. Based on the good things I've heard, I was hoping you would have a place for him here."

"Well, we are a private school so we can normally oblige. And there are places in the classroom for a child of that age. When are you moving?"

"It's happening imminently. Before I finalise things, I need to be sure that Luke has a school to go to and that his needs will be met in the school he's transferring to."

"Your son has special needs?"

"Of a sort."

Mrs Winter inclined her head.

"Let me be frank with you," said Patricia. "My husband is an alcoholic and in the last few months the situation at home has become intolerable. My son and I are moving here to make a new start where we have friends around us." She gestured towards Isobel. "I'm concerned that Luke will get all the support he needs at this difficult time. I want to be sure that he'll be understood and that you will keep me closely appraised of any concerns you might have. Naturally, I'll be organizing extra support for him myself, but I feel that schools play an important role in a child's life and their input or lack thereof can have a huge impact."

Mrs Winter shifted in her seat, straightening her back. "I agree and here at this school we're very committed to supporting our children, educationally and with all the challenges that life now throws at them."

"From your experience, what help is Luke most likely to need? What should I look for? I'm new to dealing with all of this but I'm sure you've dealt with children going through something like this many times and have a lot of insights and experience." Patricia bit her lip.

Mrs Winter relaxed slightly. "Of course we have. Every child is different but we have experience. In fact, at the moment one of the boys of Luke's age is going through a similar thing – only it's his mother who's an alcoholic."

Patricia kept her face neutral and inclined her head.

"But he's doing well, thank goodness," said Mrs Winter.

"I noticed a change in my son's behaviour as his father got more out of control in his drinking. I'm afraid –" Patricia broke off, lowered her head and covered her eyes with a hand.

Isobel found a tissue in her handbag and passed it to Patricia. "I'm sure any child would change in a situation like that," she said, placing a comforting hand on Patricia's shoulder. "Luke is going to be all right. You're doing your best, Patricia, you'll get him through this. I'm sure Mrs Winter agrees that any child would be changed, that that's a normal reaction to what's happening." She looked at Mrs Winter in appeal.

Mrs Winter rested her arms on the desk. "Mrs King, changes in behaviour are to be expected – but rest assured we can help your son."

Patricia raised her head, dabbing her eyes with the tissue. "Thank you, Mrs Winter."

"As I said, every child is different. For example, in the case I mentioned it's only very recently that we've noticed a change in the child. Apparently, the drinking was going on for some time, secretly. It may have been years but the mother was always at the gate to collect the boy and they seemed to be very close. Thankfully, as things escalated the father realised what was happening. Really, it's only since this has come to light that the lad has been affected. He's lucky that his father is so supportive and aware. He's doing everything to make this work for his son while the mother sorts herself out. Does your son see much of his father?"

"Not at the moment," said Patricia. "Things need to settle down and my soon-to-be-ex-husband needs to stop drinking and be sober enough to see his son."

"Of course. All of these things take time. Sometimes, even when someone gets sober they need time to come to terms with what has happened."

"What do you mean?"

"Well, in the case we have, the mother has stopped

drinking but is crucified with guilt. Hopefully, soon she'll be feeling able to reconnect with her son and things can stabilise again. Like you, the couple are divorcing. Obviously, we've supported this boy as much as he needed and advised his father where appropriate. We're pleased with how things are going."

Patricia nodded and dabbed her eyes with the tissue again.

Outside Isobel could hear children shouting in the playground – school must be out.

"Perhaps we could see the classroom Luke would be in and maybe speak to his future teacher?" Isobel asked.

"Oh yes, that's a great idea," Patricia said. "That would give me a real feel for the school, a real feel for where Luke would be."

Mrs Winter frowned.

"We won't take long," Patricia said, "and obviously if the teacher is too busy that's fine."

Mrs Winter stood up. "Very well. I'll show you the classroom quickly."

Patricia smiled. "Thank you."

Conversation on the corridors was desultory. Mrs Winter stopped in front of a classroom and reached out to open the door. As she did, a young woman in high heels came marching along the corridor.

"Oh, here is Miss English now," said Mrs Winter.

The teacher had long auburn hair, a sprinkling of freckles and a ready smile. She seemed open and friendly and warm.

"Hello, headmistress!" she called out.

"Miss English, another week over." Mrs Winter smiled then gestured to Patricia. "This is Patricia King. She may be moving to the area very soon and her son, Luke, would be in your class. This is her friend Isobel. We were just discussing Luke and his needs. Patricia wanted to get a feel for our school so we came to look at the classroom. May I leave these ladies with you, Miss English?"

"We won't take up too much of your time," Patricia said apologetically.

Miss English smiled. "Come in, come in."

"Please let me know as soon as possible if you want a place for Luke, Mrs King," said Mrs Winter.

"I will – and thank you."

"Have a good weekend, Miss English – see you Monday." With a smile, the headmistress departed.

Inside the classroom, Patricia and Isobel wandered around, looking at the projects and artwork displayed on the walls. As Isobel perused the pictures she spotted one by a child called Tommy. It was a picture of a house, a big one, not unlike the one she had seen in Wimbledon through the gate, with a woman and a child in front of it. Isobel drew Patricia over to see the picture.

Patricia opened her eyes wide at the signature.

Turning to Miss English, she pointed at the picture and said, "That's the sort of family that my son is going to be in now. Just mother and child. I hope Luke will be all right."

"Oh, I'm sure he will, with time and support."

"Miss English, when I was talking to Mrs Winter I told her that a friend recommended this school. She didn't ask who but that friend is Anne Banks. The reason I'm considering this school for Luke is because she was happy with Tommy coming here and – because I'm in a similar situation to hers – I thought that would make it easier for Luke and of course maybe he and Tommy could be friends."

"Well, if you and Anne are friends no doubt the boys will be thrown together."

"Anne has had such a rough time recently," said Patricia. "To be honest, I haven't seen her much."

"Yes, she has. I was so surprised to hear about her circumstances."

"Yes. My soon-to-be-ex-husband is an alcoholic too."

"To be honest, I find it hard to believe," Miss English said. "I keep going over in my head all the times I spoke to her when she collected Tommy. There were so many times, and never once did I sense anything other than a very committed and attentive mum. No matter what it was that Tommy needed she did it – extra help with reading, a costume for a play – every sports day she was here, every parent-teacher meeting. To me she was a devoted mother. I never smelt drink on her breath, she was never inappropriate, never even late. Tommy's father does everything for him now but Tommy has become very withdrawn. He's missing his mum. I've told his dad that and Mrs Winter too. I don't know why they haven't arranged a meeting, any meeting, supervised access, whatever it takes. I'm really concerned. If you know Anne, please beg her to see Tommy. I find it hard to equate the woman I knew with what's happening now. To be honest, I think her drinking wasn't a problem for Tommy but not living with her, not seeing her, is."

Miss English had talked until her eyes filled up and she had to turn away. After a few moments she looked at Patricia again.

"Sorry, I shouldn't have said anything about any of this. Please forgive me."

Patricia reached out and gently touched her arm. "You obviously care about Tommy and Anne and that's a good thing. I do too. Hearing your concerns has just reinforced my desire to make sure things get resolved in the best way for Tommy." She withdrew her hand. "I can see how much you care for the children in your class and that gives me such reassurance when I think of Luke coming here. Thank you."

Miss English looked relieved. "It's been a long week."

When they left the school grounds Isobel hugged Patricia. "You were fantastic."

Patricia grinned back and looked at her watch. "It's nearly four thirty, by the time we get into the city it'll nearly be time for Peter to finish. We could have a coffee and then meet him for dinner."

"There is one more meeting I'm hoping to have today."

"Who with?"

"Anne's regular hairdresser, Aaron."

"What do you think he'll be able to tell you?"

"Maybe nothing, but it can't hurt."

"I keep changing hairdresser so I haven't got to know any of them."

"Well, you're missing out. A good haircut and a chat is great therapy. I'm going to stay around here and wait for Aaron to finish. I'll get dinner somewhere."

"Do you want me to eat with you?"

"No, you go and meet Peter and we'll catch up later."

"Are you sure?"

Isobel grinned. "Don't you want to have dinner with Peter?"

Patricia blushed.

"Go on. I'll see you both later and we can brainstorm."

Isobel smiled to herself. Maybe Anne and Thomas Banks' divorce would bring Patricia and Peter together.

Chapter 13

It was a quarter to eight when Isobel arrived back at Brushstrokes. Through the window she could see a man finishing a blow-dry. He was tall and slim with fair hair. From his body language it was clear that he was having an animated chat with his present customer. He certainly seemed the sort of person who was a great confidant. Isobel was encouraged – she just hoped she could get him to open up about Anne Banks.

The receptionist recognised Isobel from her visit earlier in the week. He showed her to a white couch and went to confer quietly with Aaron who glanced up at her briefly and then, giving a nod, went on with his work. Isobel picked up a magazine and browsed. Five minutes later, after showing his customer her hair from all angles and exchanging air kisses, he came over.

Up close Aaron had large, soft brown eyes and full lips that she could see were used mostly for smiling. He appeared to be a gentle person.

"Hello, how can I help?"

"Hi, Aaron. My name is Isobel and I know Anne Banks. I was hoping I could buy you a glass of wine and maybe talk to you privately. I'm a bit concerned about Anne and I thought you might be able to help me."

Aaron looked at her and pursed his lips. "OK – one drink because you've piqued my interest but I'm not promising to stay."

Isobel nodded. "That's fine."

Aaron collected his man-bag and led the way to a wine bar further down the street. Obviously he was a regular as the barman greeted him by name and asked if he wanted the usual. Aaron had a Hendrick's gin with cucumber and lots of ice and Isobel had a glass of cool Sauvignon Blanc. They found a quiet booth and faced each other across the table.

Isobel said, "Please just hear me out before you make a run for it."

Aaron sipped his drink and raised an eyebrow.

"I'm working as a consultant for Peter Wright, Anne Banks' solicitor in her divorce. Peter has been concerned that Anne's interests aren't being met in the divorce settlement. Before he speaks to her again about this, he's checking with some people in her world about how her life was and if there were problems that she may not have told him about which are working against her and weakening her position in the divorce. I had the idea of coming to you, because I know how I talk to my hairdresser and I thought if anyone knew how Anne really was, it might be you and, to be honest, she doesn't seem to have any close friends or be close to her family." She paused and then said, "We're concerned that things are not as they're being portrayed to us, but it's mostly a feeling and we're trying to see if there is indeed something to be concerned about." She cringed. "I'm sorry. I'm not explaining myself very well."

There was long silence, then Aaron leant forward and said, "I haven't heard from Anne in nearly four months. She always came to me every six weeks to get a cut and she never missed. Her last appointment was a no-show and she never rescheduled. I couldn't get her on her mobile. I was concerned so, in the end, I rang her house. I thought she might be sick. Her husband told me that she was in rehab and had moved to another part of London. When I asked for her new address he got really angry with me and told me that she had more important things on her mind than getting her hair done. I hung up. I've been worried about her."

"Do you know anything about her drinking?"

"Well, I know she liked a glass of wine or gin. We know each other a long time. She always got her hair done during the day when Tommy was at school and Thomas at work. A few years ago we started going for lunch after I'd done her hair. We'd have a couple of glasses of wine at the very most. I was working and she had to collect Tommy from school. It seems she didn't go out much. I invited her to come out with the staff from the salon a few times but she wouldn't come. She said she wanted to be with her family when they were home." Aaron paused. "She did call in on spec a few times to see if I could go to lunch with her, but I couldn't. Unless I plan something I just squeeze my lunch in, so I wasn't free."

"It seems that she was drinking during the day."

"Well, all I can say is that I'm shocked. I didn't think she had a problem with drink. I also find it hard to believe that Tommy isn't living with her. She loved him so much I just can't imagine her being happy to move away from him."

"What about Thomas, her husband, what was their

relationship like? Did Anne say much about him?"

"To be honest, Anne rarely mentioned him. Usually women either give out about their partner or else they're constantly saying 'we this', 'we that' and you know that things are good. With Anne it was neither of these. Mainly she talked about Tommy and the trips and things she'd planned for him. She never seemed to go on holiday, not even a short city break. I asked Anne once about that and she said that Thomas didn't like to be away from home. All her trips were daytrips with Tommy to London or Alton Towers."

"Aaron, one of our concerns, or one possibility, is that her husband is intimidating her and is forcing her to accept a deal in the divorce that is disadvantageous to her. Do you know anything about whether there was bullying or abuse in her relationship?

Aaron looked away and frowned.

Isobel bit her lip. It seemed there was something. "Please, Aaron, we're very concerned. If you know anything that might help us understand what's going on …"

"There was one thing years ago. Tommy was only three or four. Anne was in for her cut and as I was doing her hair I found this huge bump on her head. I was shocked at the size of it. Anne said that she slipped on the stairs and banged her head. That day she winced when she had to get out of the chair. I asked was that also from the fall and she said yes. I was really concerned. I wanted her to go to casualty and be checked out. She absolutely panicked when I said that. I had one of the other girls take over my next appointment and I took her into the back. She cried her eyes out. I didn't know what to do. I asked her what was wrong. She wouldn't say. I begged her to tell me. She looked terrified. In the end I asked if someone had hurt her. She just shut down. She assured me that it was a fall and that she was also worried about a family member who was sick and that everything was just overwhelming at the moment. I wasn't convinced but what could I do? I was always suspicious after that, but I never again found any bruises or bumps on her head. Anne always wore long sleeves and never anything revealing. As I said, she rarely went out but there was a benefit a few months ago. Anne got her hair done especially. I asked her to bring in a photo to show me her all dressed up and she called in a couple of days later. She just had one photo of Thomas and her taken at home before they went out. She looked beautiful. I wanted a copy to show our clients for hairdos we can do but Anne said no – she said that Thomas wouldn't like private photos being used like that. That was the last time I saw her."

Aaron wasn't looking at Isobel. He was looking out at the bar and seemed to be a million miles away. Isobel stayed silent.

After a protracted pause, he said, "Funny, though, about a fortnight later a woman came in with the same photo. I'd never seen her before. She asked if I could do her hair like the woman in the photo – you know, the same colour, the same cut. I said I knew Anne and asked how she'd got the photo, knowing that it was a private family picture. She said Anne had given her the picture. I thought that very odd, considering Anne had said that Thomas wouldn't like their photo being used like that. So . . . I did her hair . . . and when I'd finished she looked so like Anne it was as if she was a sister, even a twin. They say we all have a doppelganger, don't they? Well, I can tell you that this was Anne's."

Isobel could feel goosebumps rising on her arms and a cold shiver at her neck.

"Mind you, she may have looked like Anne but she didn't have one tenth of her personality. She was quiet, cold, unfriendly, not like Anne at all. Anne was always so warm and chatty, and she cared about people, you know?"

Reaching into her bag for her phone, Isobel brought up the photo of Anne and Thomas she'd got from the dress shop. "Is this the picture?"

"Jesus, for a supposedly private family photo the cat and his mother have a copy! But, yeah, that's it, the same shot."

"And what was the woman's name?"

"Sandra – Sandra Jones. I took special note of her name as it was all so odd. She was from Manchester."

"Address?"

"None given."

"Credit card?"

"No. Cash."

"Has she been in again?"

"No. She begged for details about the colour we used so she could get her own hairdresser to do it. I gave her those and I never saw her again."

"No tracing her then." Isobel grimaced. "So, when exactly did you last see Anne?"

"Let me see . . . the dance was on the Saturday before Valentine's." Aaron pulled out his phone. "That would have been the 10th of February. She popped in during the week to show me the photo. She had an appointment for a month later but, as I said, she didn't turn up." He paused and when Isobel didn't speak, asked, "Will you be seeing Anne?"

"Yes," Isobel said distractedly.

"Please tell her I said hello and that I hope life is going well with her. I would love to hear from her, so any time she feels up to a chat we could go for a coffee."

"Sure, Aaron, I'll pass on your message and when everything's sorted I'll let you know. It may be a phone call because I may be back in Ireland but I'll let you know."

The drinks were nearly finished and once they were Isobel said goodnight.

The minute she was outside she phoned Peter to arrange a meeting. Once again he suggested his apartment.

She sat on the Tube, counting off the stations on her route and mulling over all that she'd heard. She needed a map to help her figure out what was going on in the Banks' marriage.

Chapter 14

It was ten o'clock by the time Isobel arrived at Peter's. Patricia made tea and they sat in the sitting room.

Patricia had already described to Peter her experiences at the school with both Mrs Winter and Miss English. Isobel told them about Mr Byrne, Niamh, Brian and finally what Aaron had said.

"What I want to know is how Brian Poole got a photo of Anne that's a family picture if he wasn't in touch with her," Peter said.

"Good question – and the answer?" Isobel fixed her eyes on him as she waited.

"That Brian has been in touch with Anne and lied to you."

"Bingo. But why lie to me unless there's something to hide? And if so, what's he hiding?"

"An affair he's having with Anne?"

"Maybe," said Isobel. "He's certainly still in love with her or obsessed with her."

"We're no further forward," Patricia said. "There's this mixture of stories about bullying that turns out to be about drinking. It should all be clear but it still feels very mixed up."

"Yes, it does," Isobel said. "I had some mad dreams last night and then Aaron said something this evening that has got me thinking. May I have some sheets of paper, please?"

Peter went and took a few sheets of paper out of his printer at the back of the room.

Isobel drew a line down the centre and put bullying on one side of the line and drinking on the other. "Let's look at who we've talked to and what they've told us. Grace, the neighbour, said she had concerns that Anne was being abused – she mentioned bruises, changes in her behaviour, a sense of fear – so let's put Grace's name on the bullying side. Then Thomas came and told her about Anne's alcoholism. I'm going to put her name on the drinking side too but I'm going to put an arrow between the sides with Thomas's name on it because Grace never witnessed Anne's drinking, she was told about it. Next, Sharon from the nail shop had nothing to say about bullying but she found it hard to believe that Anne was an alcoholic. She was so vehement that I'm going to put her name down on the alcohol side but with a big question mark beside it. The most helpful thing that Sharon contributed is that she's so shocked that Anne is not in touch with Tommy. Then Donna, Anne's mother, early on in their relationship had concerns about Anne being bullied so she goes on that side. She believes now that Anne is an alcoholic but again because Thomas told her. She has no direct experience, so again an arrow with his name. Claire, Anne's sister, is definite that Thomas was a bully and was abusing Anne. She says Anne drank but she believes that the alcoholism is Anne's get-out plan, so she goes on both sides. Brian Poole claims ignorance of recent events but he dislikes Thomas and thinks he's controlling, so he goes on the bullying side. But, Brian Poole knows more than he's letting on and he is definitely lying to us, as we know from the photo. Mrs Winter is singing Thomas's praises as an attentive father. She's firmly in the camp of Anne being an alcoholic but again because Thomas told her. She goes on the alcohol side."

"Who else?" Peter asked.

"Miss English, Tommy's teacher, is surprised about Anne being an alcoholic. She used to see Anne regularly at the school when she collected Tommy and never thought Anne was drinking. So I'll put her on the alcohol side with a big question mark beside it. Bear in mind that she also says that Tommy has only changed his behaviour since his mum moved out."

Peter and Patricia nodded.

"Mr Byrne from rehab confirms that Anne is an alcoholic, so he goes on that side. And finally there's Aaron, who believes Anne was being bullied."

Patricia said, "So, things are no clearer. The only thing that everyone seems to agree on is that there was always a sense in the Banks' relationship that things were not as they were portraying them and that there was a problem."

Isobel smiled. "That's a very good point, Patricia. This is what is bothering me: the only person who has witnessed Anne's alcoholism is Thomas. Donna and Mrs Winter accept it but have never spoken to Anne about it. Sharon and Miss English don't believe it. Aaron and Claire know she drank socially but are surprised at the extent of it. Mr Byrne never knew Anne before. So all of the people who were in any way close to Anne find it hard to believe and also haven't spoken to Anne. Without Thomas telling everyone, they wouldn't know."

"Is that not normal in a situation like this – that the addiction is being covered up?" Peter said.

"Maybe. But bear in mind that without this recent conclusion a lot of people would still be thinking that Anne was the one who was in danger."

Patricia was nodding enthusiastically. "Exactly. It's like there was this one concern everyone had and now suddenly it's the complete opposite."

Isobel pointed her pen at Patricia. "Yes, exactly. It goes from people being worried about Anne to Anne being the problem. So . . . there are two different stories."

She fell silent as Peter and Patricia studied the chart, puzzled.

Isobel changed tack. "You know, there's a logic solution called Occam's razor. Basically it states that the simplest, least complicated solution to the facts is the right one. In a way what you do is strip away assumptions. So try this for a stripping away of assumptions. Anne is not an alcoholic."

"But she herself is saying that she is," said Peter.

As Patricia went to add something Isobel held up her hand and she reluctantly fell silent. Isobel rubbed her head as she tried to keep her woolly thoughts together and follow her idea.

"OK. Let's set aside the question of whether or not Anne really is an alcoholic and ask – why rehab?"

Peter opened his mouth to answer and Isobel shook her head. It was a rhetorical question.

"Rehab and her ongoing recovery and her move to a new area means that she's no longer in her own world. No one who previously knew her has seen her or spoken to her."

Patricia started. "My God, that's right!"

111

Isobel continued to think out loud. "Why would that be important? Why would someone want to isolate her like that?"

"To make her vulnerable to suggestions, so she has no support and just takes a bad deal?" Patricia suggested.

Isobel inclined her head. "Why can she not visit her child? Surely, seeing Tommy would make her more inclined to go along with anything?"

"What if she's being prevented from seeing Tommy until she signs the papers?" Peter said.

"Maybe. Thomas could be blackmailing her to take this deal. That's certainly a possibility. But . . . Aaron said something that's really bothering me and has got me thinking."

"What was it?" Patricia asked.

"He said a woman came in with a photo of Anne and asked to have her hair done exactly like hers, same colour, same cut."

"Where did she get the photo?" Patricia asked.

"She said Anne had given it to her."

"So? Loads of people copy other people's style," Peter said.

"Aaron said that when he'd done her hair this woman looked so like Anne."

"So he's a good hairdresser, the customer got what they wanted?" Peter said.

"No, she didn't just look like Anne – he said she was like her sister, her twin – her doppelganger."

Isobel paused and the others looked at her blankly.

"What if Anne isn't Anne?" she asked.

"What do you mean?" Patricia asked.

"What if someone is pretending to be Anne? They get

her all done up to look like her. Obviously then, they don't want her to meet people who know Anne. Who would see through an imposter, especially her son. What if a doppelganger is pretending to be Anne?"

"But why?" Patricia asked.

Isobel looked at Peter with a raised eyebrow. Peter returned her gaze but said nothing.

"What's to be gained by having someone impersonate Anne and sign the divorce papers?" Isobel prompted.

Initially, Peter looked at her blankly, then like a sunrise realisation dawned on him, "So that everything could be put in Thomas's name, the house, childcare, all signed to him."

"Thomas wants the assets, that's for sure," Patricia said. "But where's the real Anne, then?"

There was a silence. Isobel said nothing but glanced back and forth between the two.

"But Tommy – she wouldn't just run away and leave him, would she?" Patricia said and then flushed as he glanced towards Peter. Her voice sounded shaken as she continued, "I mean, that can happen but everyone is saying that Anne was particularly devoted to Tommy. That's one of our concerns – that she's not seeing him. He misses her . . ." She tailed off, now looking from Peter to Isobel.

Peter took a ragged breath. "What are you thinking, Isobel?"

She could hear the dread in his voice.

"We've always been concerned about how the Banks were with each other, that something felt off," she said. "Remember I said that I could feel no atmosphere between them, not even a bad one?"

"Yes, you did."

"Maybe Thomas and the Anne we met are not a couple,

113

just two people playing a role. We wondered if Anne was being treated fairly in the separation – well, this would explain that. We're concerned about Tommy and his mother – well, they have been kept apart – and rehab and recovery is a good explanation for time apart."

Peter face was slack with shock. "Jesus, Isobel, this is a bit farfetched."

"Yes, perhaps, but I am deeply worried."

Peter stood up and started pacing up and down. "What have I done? Why did I ever start this? You're going to ruin me with your crazy ideas."

Isobel's face tightened but she said nothing.

"This is madness. The jump you've made is into fiction. Maybe this is why you're on sabbatical."

Isobel's mouth dropped open in shock. Her eyes filled with tears.

Patricia stood and raised her hand to stop Peter. She took his arm and led him back to a chair.

"Go on, Isobel," she said. "What are you suggesting?"

Isobel looked at her and bit her lip, a tear running down her cheek.

Patricia sat and touched her hand. "Go on."

Isobel wiped her tears away with her hand. She swallowed and said, "I'm not going to be happy unless we check out this possibility."

Peter stayed silent.

"How can you do that?" Patricia asked.

Isobel chewed on her lip. "Look, let me think about this overnight and maybe tomorrow we can chat again."

Peter rubbed his face with his hands. "I'm sorry, Isobel. What I said was out of order. But I am worried. You aren't going to do anything rash, are you?"

Isobel stood up. "No. I'm going to think about things, you know, sleep on it." She turned to Patricia. "Why don't we head home?"

Patricia nodded and, looking at Peter, said, "Let's get some rest and we'll talk again tomorrow."

As they left, Peter was still sitting there, looking stricken.

Chapter 15

On the Tube trip home the two women said very little.

Isobel couldn't quell the idea that 'Anne Banks' was not Anne Banks. She knew herself well enough to know that she would have to research this idea. She pulled out her phone and did some googling. Having satisfied herself, she sent a quick text to Dave.

Work going well. On way to bed. Talk tomorrow.

She really wasn't up to talking to him tonight. She still had to talk to Patricia.

Patricia's flat was one bedroom, compact but very comfortable. The sitting room had a sofa bed and Patricia efficiently made it up. Despite the fact that it was almost midnight the two women settled down with cups of tea.

"What do you think about my idea?" Isobel asked.

"About the Banks?"

Isobel looked at her and raised her eyebrows.

Patricia frowned. "I think your point that no one has really witnessed Anne the drunk was good. Also, that no one has seen Anne – when you said that I got a bit of a shock, to be honest. I suppose the idea that Tommy cannot meet Anne because she is ..." She cringed.

"You think that was a bit of a jump?"

Patricia shrugged.

"What do you think is going on then?" Isobel asked.

"Any one of a number of things. Ann could be an alcoholic and Thomas could be sorting out the divorce to protect his son. Ann may want out of her life, out of being a mother and she may be happy to leave Tommy with Thomas – that's what happened with Peter. Maybe Anne is having an affair with Brian Poole and is going to make a fresh start."

"So you don't think my idea of the two Annes is credible?"

Patricia grimaced. "It's a possible explanation but . . . unless, of course, she's run away and Thomas is just using her disappearance to get all of the assets. For instance, if Brian Poole has taken her away . . ."

Isobel made a face. "The flaw in that theory is that Brian could get wind of what's going on, and then Anne could reappear and accuse Thomas of fraud."

"That's true. But, Isobel, you've met Thomas. He's very friendly, very personable. Do you really think he's doing all of this?"

"I don't know. But I have to say I found him a bit too smooth for my liking."

Patricia frowned. "So you think Thomas is a bully and has been bullying Anne. And now he has someone pretending to be Anne." Her voice faltered. "So where do you think Anne is?"

Isobel bit her lip.

Patricia frowned. "Isobel, we've no idea what's going on. There are so many possibilities."

"I'm worried enough to want to check something out."

"You have an idea?"

Isobel nodded.

"What are you going to do?"

"If I tell you, will you have to run and tell Peter?"

Patricia frowned. "Eventually I'll tell him but as long as you're not going to do him any harm professionally I won't say anything."

Isobel smiled. "OK. I'm going to ask Claire, Anne's sister, to come to London and have a look at Anne."

There was a shocked silence.

"You really do believe someone is impersonating Anne?"

"It's the only thing that makes any sense of all the facts to me. I know it sounds farfetched – that's why I'm going to this extreme. But I need to figure out a way for Claire to see Anne without Anne seeing her. Then if I'm wrong no harm done. Anne won't realise we're checking things out. Only Claire will know and she won't say anything."

"You came up with this on the train?"

"I'm not crazy, Patricia."

"I know. He shouldn't have said that."

"He shouldn't have." Isobel sighed. "Anyway, this explanation feels true to me so I'm going to either confirm it or prove it untrue."

Patricia nodded.

"I would ask Aaron but he'll be working tomorrow. It has to be someone who knows Anne really well and the only other person I can think of is Claire. She's her own boss so she should be able to take the day off and I think she'll do it. We just need to make sure that she isn't recognised."

"I know how we could do that."

"You do?"

"I have a Muslim friend, Yani, who wears a niqab – Claire could wear that and get close to Anne. As well as the head-and-face covering, there's a full-length black cover-all robe. Yani could lend her all of that. It would be impossible to suspect it's Claire."

"Patricia, that's a brilliant idea! But what about her eyes? I'm vague about the different styles but there's a slit, isn't there?"

"Well, she could make the opening very small or even wear sunglasses – Yani sometimes does."

"Perfect."

"Let's go see Yani then."

"Yes, let's." Isobel hesitated. "But, Patricia, are you sure I'm not putting you in a difficult position with Peter?"

"No. We need to find out if you're right or rule this out. Anyway, this is only going to help Peter."

Isobel hesitated and then asked, "Patricia, what's the story with you and him?"

Patricia shrugged. "Oh, Peter doesn't realise how I feel about him. Don't tell him. If he doesn't feel the same there's nothing I can do."

Isobel looked at her bowed head and shook her own. "Maybe he's been too focused on work to consider it, or maybe he's just being very professional – or maybe the man hasn't the sense he was born with."

Patricia's head snapped up. "If he felt the same he would know."

"Maybe . . . "

"Maybe what?"

"Maybe he doesn't realise how he feels, maybe he doesn't know that what he feels is more than a good working relationship and could be a good life relationship. At some point you have to take a risk and tell him – then you either date or you need to move on."

"I know."

"How long have you worked for Peter?"

"Five years."

"Soon then."

"Yes. I know. I just hate the thought of not seeing him."

"I know but what about what you might be missing?"

Patricia bit her lip. "Do you think I have a chance?"

"He thinks a lot of you, but you have to decide what you want. If Peter isn't interested then you need to move on. Five years is a long time. Have you dated anyone else while you've been working with Peter?"

Patricia looked at Isobel for a few seconds and then shook her head.

"You've got it bad, girl." Isobel reached out and touched her arm.

Patricia nodded.

"I'm going to have to go back to Petersfield tomorrow," Isobel said. "Claire is already worried and if I tell her what I suspect over the phone I can only imagine how she might overreact. So I think I'm going to have to go and see her."

"I'll come too."

"No."

Patricia looked her in the eye. "I'm coming because you can't take all of the stress of this yourself. You look really tired. I want to help."

Isobel bit her lip. "My sabbatical – it was because I was sick."

Patricia nodded.

"I had cancer."

"I know. I'm sorry."

"You guessed?"

"The wig, the sabbatical. Apart from that you wouldn't know. Is everything all right now?"

"I hope so."

"Me too." Patricia squeezed her hand. "You're doing us a huge favour looking into things and I want to help you with that. Plus, the niqab was my idea. I might actually be good at this investigating."

Isobel grinned at her. "True."

"What time do you want to leave tomorrow?"

"Early."

"Let's get some sleep then."

"I do appreciate the help, Patricia – thanks."

The sofa-bed was extremely comfortable. Despite that, Isobel didn't sleep well. Her dreams featured a child who was crying and searching for his mother. Isobel woke feeling sad. She was determined that, for Tommy's sake, they had to find out all they could.

Chapter 16

Saturday 26th May

Isobel and Patricia woke early and spent an hour trying to concoct a foolproof plan. They considered ways in which they might lure Anne from her flat – for instance, Isobel in her guise as Patricia's replacement making an appointment to meet her in the café across the road on some pretext. But, of course, she might insist on Isobel coming up to the flat instead which would defeat their purpose. Besides, Peter would get to know and would be enraged – that is, if they didn't succeed in proving that Anne Banks was a fraud. They were forced to conclude that a stakeout was the only option.

It was ten o'clock when they arrived at Claire's restaurant. When they enquired, they were relieved to find that she was there, and they were shown into her office.

"Hi, Isobel," she said, getting to her feet. "I didn't expect to see you again so soon. Do you have news?"

"May we sit down?"

"Sure, sure."

They sat. Claire was looking at them nervously.

"Claire, this is Patricia. She works for Peter, Anne's solicitor."

"Oh."

Patricia smiled at her. "Claire," she said gently, "we're concerned about Anne and we're trying to make very discreet enquiries to clarify what is going on. We don't want to alert anyone to our concerns until we know the lie of the land and so we're proceeding very carefully."

Claire nodded, looking sceptical.

"We're here because we need your help," said Isobel. "We need you to trust us and we want you to do something for us."

Claire tensed. "What's going on?"

Isobel leaned forward in her chair. "Claire, my background is as a psychotherapist. One of my concerns is that Anne seems very withdrawn. She seems resigned to not seeing her son. While on the one hand I can understand her shame, I am also concerned about this. I wonder if she is depressed, on medication. Since none of us have met Anne before, it's very hard to know. There is a limit to what, as a solicitor, is part of Peter's job but equally it would be wrong to facilitate Anne agreeing a settlement that is not in her best interests and the interests of her child."

"But Anne thinks this is the way to go."

Isobel chewed her lip. "Yes. I know. But we can all make decisions from a bad place that we later regret. Also we can have decisions forced on us."

"Do you think that might be happening here?"

Isobel shook her head. "We don't know, and we also don't know if Anne would be prepared to admit it if asked. We are in the dark here. What would help me to help Anne is your opinion of whether she is in a good place to make good decisions. Or is she depressed, withdrawn to the point where she might be doing ill-advised things? Or frightened? Any of the above would help us know how best to move forward."

Claire frowned.

"No one who knows Anne has seen her for months," Isobel went on. "All I want to know is how she seems to you after all that she has been through and is going through."

Claire tilted her head. "I suppose I can understand that. "But Anne has told me to stay away for now until she has things sorted."

Isobel straightened up. "I know. So what I was thinking of was more in the line of you observing Anne without her knowledge and just giving me your impressions of how you think she is."

"Without her knowledge? How could that be done?"

"We've thought of a way. I'll tell you in a moment."

"But, in any case, without talking to her, how would I know?"

"From how she walks, dresses, how she speaks. Most of communication is non-verbal." Isobel shifted in her seat. "You know how in the morning, when everyone arrives into work, you can tell who is in a good mood or a bad mood from how they arrive, how they come through the door, long before they ever open their mouths."

"True, especially when you know them a long time. With some of my staff I know from the tone of the hello."

"*Exactly*. And who better to give me a general impression of how she is?"

"Maybe."

"We were thinking that if you wore a niqab then she wouldn't see you observing her."

"A *what*? A niqab?" Claire raised her eyebrows. "This all seems a bit extreme."

Isobel rubbed her face with her hand. "I know, but I don't want to damage your relationship with her. This way you can help us help her but without her knowing. You can tell her when everything is over."

Claire frowned.

"You have to trust us though and do this exactly as we're asking." Isobel looked into Claire's eyes and could see myriad thoughts going through her mind. "Doing this will answer some questions and then we'll know better how to help Anne. Please help us. Do it for your sister. *Please*."

Isobel could almost see Claire swallowing the bitter pill she was giving her. Her look at Isobel was long and searching. After a long pause, she gave a stiff nod.

"Thank you, Claire. But we need you to do this as soon as possible – ideally now."

"*Now?*" Claire said, startled.

"Yes. It's urgent."

"But where? How is this supposed to work?"

Isobel grimaced. "We don't know that it will on first attempt. Essentially it's a stakeout situation. There's a small café across the street from her flat. You'll just sit, wearing your niqab, and watch her flat. It's coming up to lunchtime now, which means you can sit there for some considerable time, lingering over dessert and coffee, reading perhaps. Also, it being lunchtime, there is a chance that she may return home to eat if she is already out. If this doesn't work, you'll have to repeat the attempt later or tomorrow."

Claire drew a deep breath and considered. "Well, if I'm going to do it, I suppose it might as well be now. Let me sort things out here."

Patricia was looking intently at her phone. "There's a train in half an hour."

Claire nodded and hurried off.

"Good," said Isobel. "We've given her no hints. Whatever she says about Anne now will be what she really thinks."

Patricia sighed. "We're playing such a risky game. At the very least Peter will be furious."

"Only if we fail. And I have a really strong feeling that we won't."

Yani was delighted to see Patricia and her friends. Patricia quickly explained the help they needed. Yani was more than enthusiastic, producing the niqab and a full-length cover-all robe. She even produced shoes to wear that were in keeping with the outfit, black gloves and sunglasses. She also showed Claire how to walk with her head angled down. After her crash course it was time to find Anne Banks.

Isobel and Patricia accompanied Claire as far as a café a few streets away from Anne's flat. They would wait for her there.

Isobel gave Claire directions and Anne's address on a piece of paper.

"Claire," she said then, very seriously. "*Whatever* happens, do not betray your identity to Anne. It could have very serious consequences, believe me. Patricia losing her job would be the very least of it. Promise me you won't."

"I promise."

Isobel watched nervously as Claire set off down the street, a large black-leather bag slung over her shoulder.

In the café they ordered sandwiches, which they could

hardly eat from nervousness when they came, and then had two coffees with dessert, texting Claire every half hour. At three o'clock there was no answering text back and they were worried.

"She may be close to Anne at the moment and unable to reply," Patricia said.

Isobel exhaled noisily and nodded.

Ten agitated minutes later Isobel's phone pinged.

It was Claire: **On my way back.**

Isobel sat with her eyes on the door, clasping and unclasping her hands. It seemed hours before the door was pushed open and a niqab-wearing figure entered.

With a 'wait' gesture to Isobel and Patricia, Claire made straight for the toilets. A few minutes later she emerged, minus her niqab and robe.

Isobel's eyes were fixed on Claire as she sat down.

"Well?" Isobel said. "Tell us."

"*What the fuck is going on?*"

Isobel's heart pounded.

Claire's eyes blazed. "*That is not my sister!*"

Patricia gasped and grasped Isobel's arm. "*Oh my God!*"

Isobel said, "I knew it."

"What's going on, Isobel?" Claire began to cry.

Isobel reached across and took her hands. "I'm sorry, Claire."

"Who is that woman? Where's Anne?"

"Claire, please, I'm sorry. We don't know who that woman is or where Anne is. I'm sorry we had to subject you to that, but we couldn't prejudice you by giving any hints. We had to verify that the woman isn't Anne."

Claire wiped her eyes with a napkin. "But where *is* she? What have they done to her?"

Isobel looked at Patricia. "We need to talk to Peter, immediately. All of us." She nodded towards Claire.

In a few minutes they were hailing a taxi and travelling back to Peter's flat.

Chapter 17

When Peter opened the door, Isobel said, "Peter, you need to hear what's happened today."

He saw the two women behind Isobel and gestured for them all to come in.

"Peter, this is Claire Graham. Claire, this is Anne's divorce solicitor, Peter Wright.

Claire and Peter shook hands.

They all sat down in Peter's sitting room.

"All right, Claire – tell Peter what you did today," said Isobel.

Claire nodded and swallowed hard. She pulled the niqab from her shoulder bag.

"I sat in the café opposite Anne Banks' apartment, wearing this. As instructed."

"Oh Jesus!" Peter stood up and started pacing up and down.

Patricia got up and stood in front of him.

He stopped.

"You need to listen to all of this, Peter."

He stared at her and she held his gaze.

Then he nodded and sat down again.

Claire gestured to the niqab and, with a tearful laugh, said, "It's really difficult to eat and drink coffee with all of this on." She mimed sticking a forkful of food under the lower part of a niqab.

None of them laughed.

Claire wiped her eyes and continued. "I ordered a salad and had two coffees very slowly while pretending to read my book. The café was busy, and I felt that the waitresses were getting annoyed with me which made me more nervous than ever. Then, just at the point where I thought I would have to move, I saw Anne coming out of the building opposite. I left enough money on the table to cover my bill and rushed out. I could see her heading down the street. So I followed her and had almost caught up with her when she turned into a small shop. I followed her inside. She was looking at the magazines so I went and stood near her, pretending to look at the magazine selection too. But I was looking at her." She paused.

Peter gasped and sat forward in his chair.

"Suddenly a woman behind the counter called out, 'I have your regular magazine here, Mrs Banks!' and the woman beside me said, 'Thank you'. She stepped forward, took the magazine and paid. I followed her out and down the street. She went back into the flat."

"Are you sure she didn't recognise you?" Peter asked.

Claire gestured to the niqab. "Of course not. But . . ."

"Yes? But what?"

"But . . . I didn't recognise her either."

"What do you mean?"

"I mean that she looks like my sister, very like her, but she is not my sister."

Peter looked from Claire to Isobel to Patricia.

130

"She is so like Anne it's shocking. I can see why people are fooled but, I'm telling you, she is not my sister. That is another woman pretending to be Anne."

Claire had gone pale, as if all of the energy was draining out of her.

Isobel jumped up and touched her shoulder. "It's all right, Claire – relax now – you did well."

Patricia fetched a glass of water which Claire gratefully sipped.

Isobel raised her eyebrows at Patricia and then turned to Peter.

"Well, Peter?"

He opened and closed his mouth a few times. "I don't believe this."

"We need a DNA sample from Anne Banks," Isobel said.

"W-w-what?"

"Well, if someone is impersonating Anne with a view to stealing her assets then we need proof. Peter, you'll have to get Anne's DNA."

He looked shell-shocked.

"Claire is here so we can get a sample from her no problem. Then we need to get it analysed and prove that someone is impersonating Anne. At the very least this woman and Thomas are committing fraud."

"*And we need to find my sister!*" Claire cried.

Isobel nodded. "Yes, we do."

"Where is she? Why is she letting this happen?"

"I don't know," said Isobel.

"But maybe it's because you haven't seen her in a while that you didn't recognise her?" Peter said.

"*How dare you?*"

Peter recoiled.

Isobel reached out and touched Claire's hand gently. "That's why we need a DNA test. To prove what you're saying is true, that this woman is not your sister."

After a few moments Peter said, "I can't believe I'm going to say this but how are we going to get a DNA sample from Anne Banks and where are we going to get it tested?"

Isobel blew out through her lips. "The best I can come up with is that you call to her flat to clarify something about the contract, and go to the loo, and try to get some hair from her hairbrush, or take a glass she's used. The only other way is if she cut herself and we got a blood sample. Not likely."

Peter stood up and started pacing up and down. "None of those seem doable. Are we really seriously considering this?"

"Yes, Peter," Isobel said. "I believe Claire and, since you don't, I'm just trying to see how we can prove it to you."

"Are you sure that you didn't put this idea in Claire's head?"

"No, Peter," Patricia said. "Isobel never mentioned her suspicions to Claire at all. Isn't that right, Claire? All she did was ask Claire to see how Anne looked – to judge how she was."

Peter looked at Isobel. She shrugged.

"No, she didn't say a word," Claire said. "It was an awful shock."

Peter put his hands in his pockets, hunched his shoulders and lowered his head. After a moment he looked up at Isobel and said, "I'm sorry."

Isobel looked him in the eye and then nodded. Turning away, she rubbed her forehead. "A few years ago I met a woman on a psychotherapy course here in London. Her husband works at Scotland Yard, the missing persons division. I've met him a few times – you know, in the evening when we all went for a drink. Simon Jones. He's a helpful guy. His wife, Tracey, still emails me every few months. I could email her and see if I can meet them and persuade him to help us. Maybe he could get the police lab to do the analysis for us. If he won't we'll have to find a private lab."

"Money is no object," Claire said. "Whatever it takes to get to the bottom of what is going on, I'll pay."

"Maybe Simon could pull a few strings and rush it through," Isobel said.

Isobel used her phone to access her emails and send a query with an urgent plea for Tracey to make contact.

Peter stopped his pacing. "I've been thinking about this. I could meet Anne for coffee and get a sample that way."

Isobel jumped up and started pacing as well. "Maybe, but what about the other DNA on the cup – the waitress's?"

"How could we make sure that the cup is as clear as possible of other DNA?"

Isobel stopped. "I have an idea. Peter, has Anne Banks observed you eating or drinking anything?"

"No. Why is that important?"

"You could pretend to the waitress that you have an allergy to milk. Then you ask her to wear gloves as you're very allergic – and the cup should come straight out of the dishwasher. And in case the cups should somehow get mixed up, the lady's cup should be given the same treatment – dishwasher, gloves."

Peter shook his head. "You have an answer for everything."

"And, by the way, the real Anne Banks helped her manicurist when her son had that same allergy. If you want to be really sure, mention your allergy to Anne and

133

see if she shares her own experiences. Just see what she says. The real Anne Banks would tell you."

"Do you not think that this whole plan is a bit over the top?"

"Maybe. But, if it means we get a very clean sample without her suspecting, then so what?"

"OK, OK. I guess it's worth a try."

"Can you come up with a pretext for meeting her?" Isobel said. "You could use that café Claire was in today."

"But how am I going to get the cup?"

"Given how quickly the Banks move I am sure that Anne is not going to hang around. All you have to do is let her leave first then, stack the cups and saucers and slip one cup into your briefcase."

"You want me to *steal* a cup."

"People do break cups all the time in cafés. I know this isn't ideal but otherwise you will have to explain to the people in the café why you want the cup."

Peter put his head in his hands.

Patricia came in from the kitchen and held out some plastic sandwich bags. "Here, take these and put the cup into it."

Peter grimaced. "Are we really going to do this?"

Isobel stood in front of Peter with her hands on her hips. "Surely, with Claire telling you that someone is impersonating her sister and therefore you are party to fraud, you have to find out the truth."

Peter made a face. "True. God, I wish I had never started down this road."

"You mean you would be happier to let Anne Banks, your client, be defrauded at the very least? For goodness' sake!"

"No, of course not. That's not what I meant."

"Oh, spare me from people who want a quiet life! Something is happening here. You started this, so you need to see it through."

"All right, all right. But is this really the best way forward?"

"How are we going to prove that this woman isn't Anne Banks? Even you are questioning what Claire is saying."

Peter grabbed the sandwich bags. "Fine. I'll try to set up that meeting."

"It might be better if you rang her *from* the café," Isobel said.

"Why? She might not be home at the time?"

"Yes, there's that risk – but otherwise she's likely to tell you to drop up to the flat."

"You could tell her you're under pressure," said Patricia. "That you're grabbing a quick coffee before a meeting."

"I guess that's plausible," Peter said.

"Right," Isobel said. "I'm going to ring another friend and see if she has Tracey's number."

Peter nodded. "OK, talk to you later."

Isobel turned to Claire. "I get the feeling that your mum is very close to Thomas, so please don't tell her anything about what we're doing."

"I wouldn't dream of it. She never could see what Thomas was really like and she would probably ring and warn him."

"Exactly. Not a word to anyone until we find out what's going on here."

Claire nodded. "I'm going to stay in London until you know more. I'll find a hotel."

"I'll ring you later about where you need to go to give the DNA sample," Isobel said.

Claire nodded.

Isobel made some calls to get Tracey's number then phoned and left a message. Tracey returned Isobel's call within half an hour and they arranged to meet at a café near her house.

Chapter 18

It was five o'clock when Isobel barrelled into the café. Glancing quickly round she spotted Tracey's blond hair immediately. Then Tracey was on her feet and walking forward with a warm and welcoming hug.

"It's so good to see you, Isobel, after all this time. You look great. I know that you weren't well, but you look fantastic."

Isobel's eyes welled up. "It's good to see you too, Tracey. Thanks."

She looked past Tracey to the man rising to his feet. Of the two Tracey had worn the best since Isobel had last seen them. Simon was about five feet ten with blue eyes which were still bright but his brown hair, while just as prolific, was now very grey.

"Hi, Simon." Isobel gave him a hug too.

Tracey chattered on. "Great that you're in London – a holiday, is it?"

"No, some consultancy work for a solicitor and, actually, I need your help, Simon."

"Mine?"

"Yes."

Tracey said, "Oh." She looked at both of them. "If you need to talk shop why don't I leave you to it and I'll finish the shopping. Call me when you've everything sorted and we can all have dinner."

Isobel felt emotional again. "Tracey, thank you. What I need to discuss with Simon is to help a little boy and his mum."

Tracey smiled and, with another fierce hug for Isobel and a kiss for her husband, left.

Isobel and Simon ordered refreshments and then she told Simon her story from start to finish. He listened silently as she recounted everything, his face giving little away, until her story trickled to a close.

Simon took the lead. "So basically you want me to commit police resources to see if there's a crime, Isobel. That's not how things work. We can barely cope with the crimes we have, never mind spend money on imagined ones."

"Simon, I know that, but a woman is going to lose her home and her child. If we do the DNA test we will know for definite if something dodgy is going on."

"Maybe this sister made a mistake and there's nothing going on – maybe what's going on is exactly what they say, no big mystery, no big deal, just two people trying to sort out their fuck-up the best way they know how."

Isobel could feel her temper rising. "At the very least this could be fraud. Or, maybe we have a serial abuser who has murdered his wife and to get away with it he's having someone impersonate her so that he can claim all the assets. Then, his 'wife' will disappear or move or fall off the wagon and no one will ever know that the real Anne Banks was murdered!"

Simon looked at her askance. "That's madness. Isobel,

I can't just get some samples tested because I feel like it. There are procedures."

Isobel looked at him. "I know that I could research and find a lab that maybe on Monday would help me – but I was hoping that one of the lab men owed you a favour. I know DNA can be processed in 24 hours and I was hoping that with your influence we could get it done quickly and quietly. If it's Anne Banks, no harm done – if not, then there is a crime about to unfold and we might need your help."

Simon stared at her.

"Please, Simon, this is going to torment me otherwise. I'll pay to have it done. I just need it done right and as quickly as possible. The contracts are due to be signed on Wednesday, so the sooner we know the sooner we can do something." Seeing Simon's frown, she added, "If something needs to be done."

Simon looked mulish.

Isobel searched her mind for something to persuade him. "Simon, you must have a case that still bothers you, a case that you wonder about?" She glanced at him and saw his expression had shifted. "This is that case for me. I know in my heart that there's a problem here. Please do the test so that I can be sure and if I'm wrong I'll eat humble pie but at least I'll know that I did everything. I don't want to always regret this, always wonder. All my years working with people, with couples, tells me there is something here. Please put me out of my misery one way or the other."

Simon shifted in his seat. "OK, I have a friend in the lab, a workaholic, he has no life really. If I ask him and you donate a bottle of Irish whiskey he might do it, as a favour to me."

Isobel's shoulders relaxed in relief. "Great, can you ring him? Now. I need to check about collecting the samples."

Simon laughed. "You don't hang about, do you?"

In a few minutes he was handing her the phone. The lab guru was called Jeff. He explained that if Claire came to the lab he could collect her DNA sample. The sample that Peter was collecting would be fine in a plastic bag and the sooner he received it the better. Isobel took the address of the lab and called Claire to let her know. She then sent a text to Peter telling him where the lab was and wishing him luck.

Given the nature of the job, Jeff reckoned that the result would take not much more than 24 hours.

Isobel breathed a sigh of relief. "Thank you, Simon. I really appreciate this."

Simon nodded. "I'll phone you when Jeff gives me the results."

Tracey arrived back. Business out of the way, they all adjourned to the Indian for a meal and a decent catch-up.

Chapter 19

A good meal and a few glasses of wine later, Isobel made her way back to Peter's flat. It was almost ten o'clock. During the evening she had received a text from him saying 'sample collected' and she was keen to hear the details.

"Well, tell me everything. How did you manage it?"

Peter, sprawled on the couch beside Patricia, grinned. They were both sipping glasses of wine.

Patricia said, "He did great."

Isobel rolled her eyes at her.

Patricia laughed. "Wait till you hear!"

"Well, first I had to get the staff of the café to co-operate." Peter grinned. "The manager, a Mrs Marie Frost, was very helpful. In fact, when she heard about the allergies she couldn't do enough for me."

Isobel grinned.

"As luck would have it, it turns out that her nephew has a pretty serious dairy allergy too. Marie was great. I explained that I wanted her to be discreet and she completely understood. She had no problem about bringing both of us any cups, glasses and cutlery straight from the dishwasher and only handled by someone

141

wearing gloves. I offered to pay for the extra work and the inconvenience involved and the discretion of not mentioning it to the lady I hoped to meet. She wouldn't hear of it and said she was delighted to help. All she wanted to be sure of was that I wasn't going to have a reaction. I assured her that all I wanted was a coffee with a friend and no big deal made of the extra precautions. Marie told the other waitresses to leave me and she would serve me herself."

"So far so good," Isobel said.

Peter smiled. "Yes. Now I had to get Anne Banks to come. I told Marie that I just needed to let my friend know where to come and I went out into the street and phoned Anne, praying she would be home. Luckily she was. She picked up quickly and, needless to say, she wasn't happy. In fact she was very snappy, saying, 'Not another problem'. Initially I said that it was a case of dotting the i's and crossing the t's but she was annoyed and I realised I really had to lay it on thick. I said that I needed to meet to finalise some things with her personally, as she was my client not Thomas – that since Thomas has been with her each time I hadn't had a chance to ask a couple of simple but necessary things." Peter took a deep breath. "I was improvising like crazy."

Isobel laughed. "I'm sure in court you have to do that all the time."

Peter grinned. "Yeah, but this was different. I then suggested that we do it today to ensure that I didn't delay the signing. I told her that I was working a few streets away and I was squeezing in this quick meeting with her as I would be really busy next week. To be honest, I thought she wasn't going to bite. I had to really play up my busyness and the risk of delaying the signing if I couldn't clarify the couple of outstanding things. I said we would meet in the café – that I needed to grab a quick coffee before a meeting – as you suggested, Patricia. Then I emphasised that I needed to see her alone. She wasn't enthusiastic. In the end I said that if it didn't suit her today then we would probably have to postpone the signing. She asked me why I hadn't mentioned this before." He grimaced. "I had to tell her that it was only when I was going over the case for Wednesday that I realised that she and I had never talked alone. I sort of talked up how prepared and organised they were and how quickly things were moving in their case and that it had slipped my mind. I thought she wasn't going to come."

Isobel bit her lip. "What changed her mind?"

"She said something about checking her diary and ringing me back in a few minutes."

"She wanted to talk to Thomas," Isobel said.

Patricia nodded. "Definitely."

"I was getting impatient so I said that I had something on later and, if she couldn't let me know immediately, we would just leave it and I would reschedule the signing."

Isobel grinned and nodded.

Peter grinned back. "A bit of urgency, not so much time to think about things. She'd phoned back in two minutes to say that she would meet me. I was relieved. I went back to Marie and told her that my friend was coming and emphasised again that she must not say anything about my allergy."

"My God, it really was all touch and go!" said Isobel.

"You're telling me! The next problem was getting Anne Banks to drink something. I decided to order two black coffees immediately, just in case Anne wouldn't order anything. You know the old adage – you can bring a horse to water but you can't make it drink. I thought that if I had already ordered something, then out of politeness and because she would want to hurry, she might drink it."

"Good thinking," said Isobel.

"I ordered the coffee from Marie and she brought two black coffees wearing her gloves. I said to Anne when she sat down, 'Oh, I hope you don't mind but I took the liberty of ordering you a black coffee. It's really good here and I don't want to delay you.' She wasn't happy but she put up with it. I tried to chit-chat to get her to relax. You know, 'You'll be relieved when you have all the documents signed and sealed and can get on with the next phase of your life' and so on. It kinda made her relax but she wasn't inclined to drink. I started into my spiel again, 'Rather than slow down your schedule, I decided to sort things over the weekend. As I said on the phone, just a few quick, clarifying questions. To be honest, this will be the quickest case to resolve ever. I know our firm prides themselves on efficient service, but this is a record. I should advertise it as an inducement for other couples!' I was willing her to take a sip. She fiddled with her cup but didn't drink."

"Peter, you're stressing me out here," Isobel said.

"Well, it was stressful. I then said that the reason I needed to meet her was that firstly I wanted to be clear that she was happy with the deal. She didn't answer, she just fiddled with her spoon. I know that mimicking body language increases rapport – it's an old trick I sometimes use in court, so I started copying her body language by

144

fiddling with my spoon too. She seemed to relax a bit, you know, be less defensive, more chatty. So I laid on the part about my concern for her and then asked straight out if Thomas was coercing her in any way. I explained that I was asking this because she had never come alone, and I was worried about that. She laughed it off, but I think at this stage she really believed me about my being concerned. I was mirroring her movements but honestly I thought she wasn't going to drink anything. I sort of pushed it then by saying, 'Oh, you don't like the coffee – let me get you something else'. She refused and picked up her cup so I hoped we might have fingerprints at least. I took a sip of my coffee, hoping that she would mirror me, but no. She put her cup down again. Anyway I went on – pointing out that there was no guarantee for her in the agreement and I explained that if things with Thomas deteriorated then she would have no legal protection. These were my real concerns from the start, as you know. At this stage she touched my arm and smiled at me. She said, 'Oh, you're looking out for me, how sweet!'. I told her it was my job. She definitely didn't suspect anything. She said that she was very happy with the deal and that, though they were divorcing, it was amicable and that they both felt this was the best way to go forward."

"Peter! You're dragging this out – the suspense is killing me!" said Isobel.

"At this stage I was sipping my coffee and willing her to do the same. There was really only one more thing that I could talk to her about." He looked at Patricia and then Isobel and blushed a little. "I sort of took a risk and talked about my mum."

Isobel raised her eyebrows.

145

Peter looked at Isobel. "I apologised for getting personal and then said that as a boy who didn't see his own mother I wanted to beg her to reconsider and maybe prioritise resuming visits with Tommy."

Peter looked at Patricia who said nothing.

"Peter, that was brave," said Isobel.

Peter shrugged. "She thanked me for caring so much about Tommy. She said she was glad I was her solicitor and she promised that she and Thomas would sort out a meeting with Tommy very soon." He looked at Isobel. "Do you think I overstepped the mark?"

"Not at all. I think that was a very genuine thing to do and, to be honest, from her point of view, it was probably a very credible reason for wanting to talk to her."

Patricia reached out and touched his arm.

Peter smiled at her and gently rubbed her hand. "Well, back to the coffee. I took a sip and this time Anne also took a drink. Honestly, I had to stop myself from cheering."

Patricia and Isobel laughed.

"So, Isobel, there was just the dairy allergy thing to do now. I said, 'Oh, I love this café. I have an allergy to dairy products and here they're so good about being careful. The lady who owns it has a nephew who has the same problem so she understands that I have to be careful about what I eat and drink.' Anne said nothing so I laid it on with a trowel. 'When I was young it was a real problem and caused me a lot of serious digestive trouble but it's easier now and more widely understood. I suppose now nearly everyone knows someone who has this issue'."

"And?" Isobel said.

"Nothing. She just said, very off-hand, 'Yes, yes, I'm sure'. And then it was all about leaving."

Isobel nodded.

"I know I was a bit sceptical about your suggestion, Isobel, but she behaved exactly as you said."

"Not conclusive."

"But suggestive," Patricia said,

Isobel nodded. "Especially when she had such a good story about Sharon's son to tell. Anything else, Peter?"

"In the end she drained her coffee before leaving."

They all laughed.

"I was so relieved. I just had to get the cup then. I considered taking Marie into my confidence but since the café is so close to where Anne lives I decided against it. I stood up and, using my body as a shield between me and the staff, I opened my briefcase and put Anne's cup in the plastic bag along with the teaspoon. I stacked the remaining saucers and cup on the table, to try to disguise the fact that I'd taken one as you suggested and hoped that no one would notice. Obviously then the results of this test are outside of the law."

Isobel rolled her eyes at him. "Yes, we just need this sample to prove what's going on. If we need evidence we can get that later. I just need you to believe me."

"To be honest, I'm a bit more open now."

Isobel laughed. "Her non-reaction about the milk convinced you?"

"No. But evidence is mounting."

Isobel shook her head. "You'd think that Claire's statement would have been enough."

"It shook me up admittedly. It was so unexpected."

Isobel nodded.

"I thanked Marie and then I took the sample to the lab."

"What time did you get there?"

"It was about six. Jeff met me and said about twenty-four hours. He's going to call Simon when the results are in."

Patricia was quiet and seemed distracted.

Isobel said, "Let me check with Claire if she got her sample in before or after you – then we'll have a rough idea of when the results will be ready." She stood up and, pulling out her phone, walked into the kitchen. Behind her she heard a muffled conversation begin.

"Hi, Claire."

"Hi."

"Did you leave the DNA sample in?"

"Of course, but I don't see the point of doing all of that. Surely my statement is enough."

"It is for me, but I needed to convince Peter. Also, we may need more professional help on this case so we need a DNA sample and when we get the results things will be definite and we can move forward more confidently."

"OK."

"Did you do as I asked and not say anything to anyone about this?"

"Of course."

"Sorry. I just had to ask. I'm concerned about who we can trust, that's all."

"I think we're wasting time. We need to find Anne."

"I know, Claire, but I'm going to need help to do that and right now this is the best way to get everyone on our side. You've really helped. If you hadn't come up to London and managed to get a look at her we wouldn't even be this far on."

"I know, Isobel. Thanks."

"What time did you drop your sample in?"

"About half past five."

"So the results could be available any time from six tomorrow."

"Will you let me know as soon as possible what you decide to do when everyone believes me?"

"I promise I'll keep you informed. I know waiting is hard."

"Yes," then in a stronger voice, "Yes. Call me when you know more. I promise I'll do as you ask but please don't keep me in the dark."

Isobel could feel a lump in her throat. "I promise."

"Thank you all for caring about my sister."

"I have a sister too."

After the call, Isobel pressed another contact and sent a text.

Hi Sis, hope you are all enjoying the trip to America. Keep sending me photos. Catch-up when you get back.

Then she phoned her brother. "Hi, Dave."

"Hi, Isobel. Where are you? It's kind of late? Are you ringing from Patricia's?"

"No. We're still at Peter's. This case has taken a bit of an unexpected turn but we're getting closer to the truth, thank God."

"You sound tired."

"I am a bit, but it's been really good."

"Isobel, are you sure you're not doing too much? You were starting to get better and I don't want you wearing yourself out."

"Dave, I'm fine. I'm enjoying the challenge."

"Please take it easy. Get some sleep and ring me tomorrow. Everyone sends their love."

"Give them my love. Talk tomorrow."

Dave was right, she was tired.

Very soon she and Patricia were on the Tube home.

Isobel arched an eyebrow and smiled. "Did you and Peter have dinner together tonight?"

Patricia blushed. "Yes, as a matter of fact we did. And we talked about the case."

"Nothing else?"

Patricia shifted in her seat. "Well . . ."

"Spit it out, girl."

"Well, I made a sort of joke at one stage that my made-up son had started to seem almost real to me and that I really liked Miss English and if I had a child I would love them to have a teacher like her and before I knew it we were talking about whether either of us wanted kids and our ideas about their upbringing and education."

"Pretty serious talk for a first date."

"It wasn't a date. We had dinner together because we both had to eat and we were hanging around waiting for you!"

"So you didn't enjoy it then and there was no wine."

Patricia shot her a look. "There was wine, and I did enjoy it. I suppose the thing is we know so much about each other from working together that it's really certain areas of our lives that we have to catch up on. I know how he likes his coffee and what suit he'll wear on a given day but I don't know how he feels about certain things, or what he wants from life. And then later he talked about his mother. In a way I realised tonight how little I knew of the real man. I had made up things in my head but tonight I was talking to a real person and then hearing things about his life, painful things."

"And were you disappointed or disillusioned?"

"No – actually it was really good. It made me think about him more as a person. Tonight when you were in the other room talking to Claire he talked about how he missed his mother growing up. He said that he'd now started going to counselling. He actually said you made him." Patricia lowered her head and looked up from under her eyelashes at Isobel. "He said that it was helpful and that he was going to continue. He said that he realises now that he'd kept everyone out. He was really honest."

Patricia paused and Isobel waited.

"It's got me thinking about my own life more and what I want. These last few days, trying to find out things, interviewing people, I've really enjoyed it. Maybe I stayed in my job because I liked Peter and now it's time to find something I really want to do."

Isobel tilted her head in acknowledgement. "I think that's great, Patricia."

"Yes. This case seems to be changing us all."

"Yes, I think you're right."

Patricia said no more, and they lapsed into a companionable silence.

Isobel looked out at the darkness outside the carriage. She felt different too. Her instincts had proved correct. Uncovering this about Anne had given her a thrill, a sense of purpose, something important to think about and she liked it. She felt as if she was pitting her will against a puzzle and she was determined to solve it.

Isobel slept deeply that night. In her dreams a blonde woman appeared beside her. She kept her face covered with her hair and she whispered, "*Help me, help me!*"

Sometimes she walked ahead and reached back to pull Isobel forward and at other times she disappeared and there was the same disembodied voice whispering, *"Help me, help me!"*

Chapter 20

Sunday 27th May

Isobel woke early and sat looking out of Patricia's apartment window, reflecting on her dream. She couldn't shake the feeling that the dream had been about Anne begging her to find out what was happening and, with that in mind, she had a plan of what she wanted to do today while they waited for the DNA to come back. Patricia had half-heartedly suggested that she accompany her, but Isobel put her off. She guessed that Patricia wanted to see Peter and Isobel was looking forward to some time alone. While she'd been sick she'd spent a lot of time quietly resting on the couch and looking out at her flowers and plants and that contrasted sharply with being in the city and meeting lots of new people. It was a bit overwhelming.

Now she sat on the train looking out at the countryside passing by and felt relaxed, almost hypnotised. She was determined to talk to Brian Poole again and find out what he was lying about. She wanted to surprise him with her visit but there was always the risk that he wouldn't be there.

He wasn't. She rang the doorbell a few more times then turned and looked out towards the road, wondering what she should do. She was just about to leave when the door of the house adjacent opened.

A rotund woman with permed brown hair and hazel eyes stepped out. "Hello. You were here yesterday with Brian. Did you forget something?"

Isobel smiled. Clearly Neighbourhood Watch was alive and well. "Yes, that's right. Do you know where he is? Will he be long, do you think?"

"Oh, I wouldn't imagine so. Brian normally goes to Service and then he comes home and cooks his dinner. He shouldn't be too long. Would you like to have a cup of tea while you wait?"

"Oh yes, that would be lovely."

In a short time Isobel was sitting in Mrs Irene Smart's front room with a cup of tea and a scone. Irene loved to talk so Isobel figured she had nothing to lose by getting her impressions of Brian.

"Have you lived beside Brian for long?"

"He bought the house about six years ago, but I know him from when he was a little boy. He grew up near here. He's very quiet and such a good neighbour. He keeps an eye out and if there are any big jobs in the garden he does them for me."

"Yes, he is quiet and maybe a bit intense, perhaps too intense." Isobel smiled to soften her words.

"No, just quiet, and helpful."

Isobel tried another tack. "I'm surprised that he's still single. As you say he's helpful and quite good-looking – you'd imagine he would have a girlfriend."

"Oh, well," said Irene, leaning in towards Isobel, "he had a woman but unfortunately it didn't work out. I don't think he ever got over it."

Isobel leant forward too and lowered her voice, "Really. Did you know the woman?"

"Oh yes, one of the village girls. Very sad really. They met very young. I did wonder, though, when I saw her here one morning at about eleven o'clock a few months ago. I thought maybe they were getting back together but I haven't seen her since."

Isobel's smile was a mask, her mind whirring, "Are you sure it was the young woman he fell in love with?"

"Oh, yes, definitely – Anne Graham – she grew up here too. She's married in London now and has a child. She looked the same as ever. Brian was off work sick that day. He's never sick. I was going to ask him about Anne when I saw him next but when I mentioned the day he told me that he'd been asleep all day. I realised he didn't want to talk about Anne and, since she hasn't been back, I assumed that things were not on again between them. Anyway, it's none of my business but I was hoping for some happiness for Brian."

"Of course, of course."

Irene pointed out the back window. "Brian helped me with those roses. He really does have green fingers."

Isobel stepped to the window, admiring the roses enthusiastically.

Irene suggested that they go out to inspect the other flowers, which Isobel was delighted to do. Before long they could hear a car stopping close by.

"That's Brian home now."

Isobel slowly gathered her belongings and took her time saying goodbye, allowing Brian time to get into the house.

As Isobel went up the path to Brian's front door she realised that, while his intensity had made her nervous the last time, with this new information she felt much more

155

confident about tackling him.

He answered her sharp knock very quickly. When he saw her standing on the doorstep his face fell.

"I've nothing more to add to what I said the other day," he said, starting to swing the door closed again.

"I think you have, and I would prefer to discuss this inside or the whole neighbourhood will see and hear us talking," Isobel said, raising her voice.

He stared at her.

She met his gaze, maintaining a relaxed demeanour. Leaning close, she said, "Like her visit a few months ago."

His mouth fell open.

Isobel stepped back. "We can discuss it here or inside."

With a growl of impatience he swung the door wide open. "I still have nothing to add," he said as he led the way into the sitting room.

Isobel stood. "Things have changed since I was here last, Brian."

"Not for me."

"No, not for you but I know more now."

Brian said nothing.

"I know for a fact that you've seen Anne in the last few months."

"How can you know that?"

"I have witnesses."

He looked away.

"You also have her photo upstairs." Isobel pulled out her phone with her copy of the photo.

Mesmerised, Brian reached out for it. His eyes fastened on Anne's image.

"You really love her." It was a question but also a statement.

156

"I always have." He said it simply, clearly, unashamedly and with longing.

Isobel's eyes welled up with tears. She sat down on the sofa and a distracted Brian followed.

"You're worried about Anne," she said.

Brian nodded, his eyes still on Anne's image. Without looking up, almost as if he was talking to himself, he said, "So worried, I don't know what to do to help her, what to do for the best. I've been waiting for her to contact me again to send me some sign of how I can help now."

Isobel realised that Brian was responding to her as someone almost hypnotised. As she made statements that mirrored the thoughts that were circling in his head he was opening up. It was clearly almost a relief for him to voice them.

Not wanting to break the atmosphere, she searched her mind for what to say. "Things have changed and you're not sure what you can do to help."

"Yes," Brian breathed.

"Anne had a plan, now it seems different."

At this Brian looked up and the spell was broken.

"Please tell me what was happening with Anne," she said, "so that I also know better how to help her."

Brian shook his head. "You're on her solicitor's team – how can you not know how to help her?"

"Please, Brian, just tell me what you know and what's been happening so that I understand."

"Listen, when Anne came to me a few months ago she had no one to trust. I hadn't seen her in years, and I was still the person that seemed the safest for her to trust. Now, you want me to tell you things when she's your client. Get real. She'll tell you what she wants you to know. I don't know what her plan is now, so I don't want to mess it up for her and I'm saying nothing." He pulled a handkerchief from his pocket and rubbed his eyes with it.

"Please tell me her original plan."

"Look, if Anne has decided that divorce is the best option for her then I have to respect that. Yes, I'm surprised. Yes, it's a change of plan but it's her choice."

Isobel pinched her lips and shrugged her shoulders. "Maybe."

Brian's brow furrowed. "Maybe? What do you mean?"

Isobel again wondered what the right thing to do was. Could she trust this man? What was his part in all of this? He could be having an affair with Anne, hiding her, helping her to run away or implicated in a more sinister way. She didn't want to reveal anything she knew but she wanted more information from him.

"Look, Brian – yes, Peter is Anne's solicitor but the reason I'm on the case is that he is concerned that Anne might be under duress from Thomas to take a bad settlement agreement. She assures us that this isn't the case but at this stage we're very concerned that her interests are not protected. Our whole reason for talking to you was to make a better judgment about what's been going on so that we can see what, if anything, we can do. I've come back to you because we know that Anne must have given you that picture and we know that she visited you a few months ago. You've just told me that she had nowhere else to go and I'm begging you – fill in the gaps for us, so that we know better how to move forward." She paused then said, "For Anne's sake. We're trying to help." She waited.

158

Brian stood up, walked to the window and looked out. He rubbed his face with his hand as if somehow the wiping could make things clear for him. Clearly, internally a battle was raging.

The silence stretched. It was almost as if he had forgotten she was there.

Eventually, Isobel said gently, "Please, Brian, trust us. Peter could have just done the contract. We care. We're worried. We're trying our best. Please help us."

He looked over. His eyes were tormented.

In the end, it was a surrender, a laying down of a worry and stress he could carry no more. When he started to talk it was as if to himself, reliving what had happened.

Isobel just listened.

"I hadn't seen Anne for at least five years, then, a few months ago, out of the blue, on a Monday morning, I got a call that she needed to see me urgently. I was at work, I asked her to wait until the weekend. She said no, she was on her way down, it had to be now, today, she only had an hour. She asked me to go home sick from work and meet her at my cottage. I knew she was in a state, so I did what she asked. I couldn't believe it when she told me."

He looked up, unsure one last time, then taking a deep breath he pressed on.

"He, *Thomas*," he spat out the name, "he had nearly strangled her the night before." His voice broke and he buried his face in his hands. "She had a scarf on but she showed me her neck. Oh my God. She nearly died. She was terrified. He –" he stumbled in his narrative then taking a ragged breath said, "He'd warned her that if she went to the doctor he would beat Tommy. Anne was terrified that he would find out that she'd been to see me.

She'd been reading a book, *The Gift of Fear*. She knew that chances were this would happen again and she would maybe not survive the next time, so she wanted to leave, secretly." He looked at Isobel. "She didn't contact her sister because she knew Thomas would check there. In fact, we agreed that he might also guess she'd come to me. She was terrified. I contacted a friend of mine who works in the local woman's shelter and she talked to Anne. Fifteen minutes later she rang back with the number of a place in London where they help women get away and make a new start somewhere else. Anne contacted them and was planning to leave, just her and Tommy, to find a new life, in a new place. It meant starting again with nothing, but she was prepared to do that. She knew he would track her if he could, so I also was to know nothing. Anne, when she was settled, would eventually get in touch."

He gazed at Isobel, his eyes bleak.

"When I heard about the divorce I assumed that maybe she'd changed her plan. She didn't contact me again so I left it like that in case I made things worse. But worried, that's an understatement. From what Anne had been saying, Thomas wasn't going to let her go, so she would have to run – hence I was very surprised to hear about the divorce."

Isobel swallowed deeply. She could feel a horrible anxiety starting in her stomach but tried not to let it show. "Do you have the number of the person in London that your friend referred Anne to? I just want to see if maybe she knows why Anne changed her mind about what she was doing. I would feel more confident about the divorce if I could speak to this woman."

Brain looked at her in silence. Isobel could feel herself heating up under his gaze.

"I can see that," he said. "I shouldn't have kept the number, but I did – just in case."

Isobel nodded. Brain took a book on flowers from a drawer and flicked through until he found the page. The note was pressed between a page showing beautiful roses. He touched it with his fingertips. "Anne wrote the number down and then put it in her phone. She tore off the piece of paper and I kept it."

"You asked her for a picture too."

"Yes, I just wanted something of her. I wanted something to remember her."

Isobel could feel a lump in her throat: a photo and a piece of paper. Quickly she copied the number to her phone.

Brian looked at her. "I'm glad I told you. I think I can trust you. I feel relieved."

Isobel could feel tears on her eyelashes. "I promise we'll do everything we can for Anne. Please don't do anything until we see how things go."

"No, of course not. Let me know when things are sorted. I would just like to know that she's safe."

Isobel nodded. Speech was beyond her. In her heart she too hoped that Anne was safe.

Chapter 21

Isobel was thoughtful on the train back from Petersfield. Brian's revelation could be crucial in understanding what was going on, if it was the truth. He hadn't frightened her at all this time, but she could feel a part of her was still suspicious of him. He was just a bit too intense, too in love with Anne, too unable to let her go. When her carriage emptied she stayed seated and in the comparative quiet made a phone call.

The voice that answered her had a brisk, businesslike tone. "Yes?" Nothing else.

"Hello, my name is Isobel McKenzie, I was hoping to meet and talk to someone in person."

Nothing.

"I got your number from the shelter in Petersfield."

"Are you in trouble?" The voice was slightly more accommodating.

"I need help with something." Not quite a lie but not an honest answer to the question. "Please, can you meet me today?"

"All right. I'm in London."

"I know."

162

"Can you meet me in the café of the National Gallery? About an hour from now – can you make that?"

"Yes, I can be there in an hour, thank you."

"I'll be wearing a black jumper with a pink scarf. My name is Julia. What will you be wearing?"

Isobel glanced down at her top. "An emerald green blouse with a black cardigan. My hair is short and blond at the front."

"See you in an hour."

When Isobel arrived in the large refectory-type room that was the café of the National Gallery, it was busy. There was a pleasant din of people talking, exchanging ideas. There were a number of smaller tables and it was at one of these that Isobel saw a woman with a bright pink scarf. As she registered her the woman smiled and subtly nodded.

Isobel weaved her way through the tables.

"Julia?"

Julia smiled and put out her hand.

Isobel took it, saying, "I'm Isobel McKenzie. Let me get a coffee and a refill for you."

Julia nodded.

In the queue Isobel mused that Julia was probably attributing her jumpiness to the wrong reason. Starting with a misunderstanding or an untruth was never good for communication and getting Julia to trust her and maybe help was going to be an uphill challenge.

Isobel settled at the table and studied Julia surreptitiously. She was in her sixties with curly, grey hair quite untamed and a tanned face with lines which showed a great capacity to smile. Her eyes were blue, sharp, and full of life. She was calm and seemed strong, a rock, someone you could depend on. She was also undoubtedly a woman to be reckoned with – you would want her in your corner.

Isobel decided to take the initiative. "Julia, I got your number from Brian Poole." There was no response, just patient listening. "The reason I got it is because of Anne Banks." Julia really had a poker face, she thought. "I'm involved because Anne's solicitor recruited me as a consultant."

"Ms McKenzie, I cannot see that we have anything to talk about." As Julia spoke she used the table to push herself to her feet.

Isobel half rose too and gently touched her arm. "Please hear my story. I'm gravely worried about Anne's safety. Please listen to what I have to say and then decide."

"I'm a busy woman, Ms McKenzie!"

"I'm concerned about a woman's life."

"I deal with women whose lives are under threat every day. You're not under any threat so I can't help you. I'm not an information service, for obvious reasons."

"Of course, of course. But listen, someone is impersonating Anne Banks. We've only just found that out. We don't know where Anne is. I've just heard from Brian what her husband did to her. I'm afraid that Anne's husband is going to get away with God knows what. Please, I know you can't break confidentiality but just listen and then decide."

Julia sat back down but her face remained inscrutable.

Isobel took a deep breath. "We're waiting on the results of a DNA test. Anne's sister Claire says that the woman claiming to be Anne is not her sister. Thomas Banks has someone impersonating his wife so he can defraud her and get full custody of their son 'legitimately'." Isobel used air quotes. "To tell the truth, we have no idea what's happening but after talking to Anne's friend Brian, and if what he says is true, then I'm starting to wonder if Thomas has murdered his wife and is covering it up. I've only managed to get the police to do a DNA test because I know someone, and he called in a favour. Even when we prove it isn't Anne, I don't know if they will help us. We've talked to a number of people Anne knew and the story that's going round is that she's an alcoholic who is getting sober. As a result she's been staying away from contact with everyone who previously knew her, even her son. It was only yesterday that her sister Claire confirmed that the woman is an imposter and even so some people don't believe it, hence the DNA test, the results of which should be back tonight. We only have a few days before the divorce papers are due to be signed. We need to find out what's happening quickly and see what we can do."

Even to herself, Isobel could hear how upset she was and how personal this had become for her. She stopped and put her hand on her forehead, tears not far away. Running her fingers through her hair, buying time to compose herself, she looked up. Julia was regarding her with a soft look in her eyes. In that moment Isobel knew why women would come to this woman and trust her.

For a few seconds Julia regarded her as if looking into her soul and then she said, "So you're concerned for Anne's safety?"

"Yes. I'm concerned that something has happened to her and a cover-up is being perpetrated, and is working, let me tell you. Tonight hopefully we'll know unequivocally if someone is impersonating Anne. Even if we are believed, we'll still have no idea what's happened to her."

Isobel paused. "Initially we were just told the story about alcoholism. But there were a few people who had concerns about her relationship with Thomas. I've just spoken to Brian and under duress he told me about Thomas nearly strangling her. I need to know if he's telling me the truth or if this is something he's concocted for his own ends. I just thought, if you could corroborate Brian's story that would help me to understand what might be going on. I could then make a stronger case to Anne's solicitor and maybe the police. When the results come in tonight it will be make-or-break time. I have to get everyone to take this seriously. If what Brian says is true then Anne was in danger of her life. Someone is impersonating her now and no one close to her has seen her in months. I'm worried, very worried."

Julia looked pensive. "Obviously, there's only so much I can say. If Brian told you what Thomas did to Anne, here is what I can contribute. Firstly, my job is to help women in life-threatening situations to escape. Once strangulation happens in a relationship the risk to the woman escalates quickly. In such a situation we do a number of things. First, we help to get them to safety. That normally means a move to a new life, a new place, with only what they can carry. It takes us four to five days to get a situation ready for a woman and her child or children. In the meantime we offer temporary accommodation. We organise transport by multiple safe people so it's hard to trace the fleeing woman. And we organise a new home and help in developing a new identity. Some women want a day or two to get ready. If that's the case we set a date and time when the woman thinks there's a window to escape. Often that means in the morning so instead of the children going to school they head off and that means they might have a day before it's discovered they've gone. Usually we advise that no family or friends know of their plan as they're the first people an angry husband goes to."

"So Anne was getting ready to flee?"

"I didn't say that. I merely told you what we advise and what we can do. To be honest, many women don't want to do that or don't choose to do that. Others say they will, then go home and don't turn up at the agreed time – they've changed their mind. Our job is to support a woman, the choice is hers." Julia paused then said, "One other service we provide is to bring women to a doctor and document injuries and we get a solicitor to take a statement from them. Most women never use that documented evidence but, if they need it at any time, we have it for them with the solicitor."

Isobel could feel hope bubbling up. "So you would have evidence of what Thomas did to Anne, already documented?"

Julia deadpanned, "I didn't say that, nor would I. I'm merely telling you the procedures we follow in a given situation. Should the DNA come back as not Anne's, the police or a solicitor can apply for any information that we have. That would be judged on each case individually within the parameters of confidentiality and legality."

Isobel couldn't help smiling at this pompous statement.

Julia grinned as well then returning to a more personal note said, "Please contact me and let me know the results of the DNA test. I can then talk to our legal representative about our position on things."

This was as close to an admission as Julia was going to give. Isobel knew that she'd reached the end of the road, "I really appreciate you filling me in on the role you have.

I'm sorry about the initial subterfuge."

Julia looked at her. "I know you're fighting to help a woman and, of course, I will assist you where I can."

Isobel nodded, awed by the courage, dedication and wisdom of this woman and her cohorts.

Julia said, "We have to be so careful, protecting our own identity and the women who use our service."

Isobel felt humbled by that stark truth. "Thank you again. I'll phone you later and let you know the results." Standing up, she shook hands with Julia and left.

Isobel's emotions were all churned up. She decided to browse the artwork at the National Gallery. Maybe Monet could calm her worried mind.

Chapter 22

The tranquillity of Monet's garden only emphasised Isobel's disquiet and she found herself stressed and tearful. Despite the fact that Brian had scared her initially, after hearing what Julia had to say Isobel was leaning towards believing him. There was nothing else to do now except tell Peter and Patricia.

Isobel rang them and by five o'clock they were all together in Peter's flat.

"Today I went to see Brian Poole," Isobel said.

"Oh yes," said Patricia. "How did it go? Did he explain how he had the photo?"

Isobel looked at Peter. He was lounging on the couch, his arm on the side and gently resting against Patricia's who was sitting in the chair alongside him.

Isobel leant forward in her chair. "He eventually told me that Anne rang him up and insisted on seeing him a few months ago because Thomas had tried to strangle her."

Patricia gasped and her hand flew to her mouth.

Peter jumped forward on the couch. "*What?*"

Isobel sat back and looked from one to the other.

Peter said, "Do you believe him?"

169

Isobel pursed her lips. "I do."

Peter said, "Like you believe Claire?"

Isobel tightened her jaw and balled her fists. "Yes, like I believe Claire."

After a few seconds she exhaled noisily and leaned forward again.

"Peter, Brian gave me the number of a shelter in London where they help women get away and make a new start somewhere else. Anne contacted them. I knew you were going to react like this so I met with the lady from the women's shelter to see if I could get confirmation. Obviously, because of the need for confidentiality she wouldn't say anything, but she did ask me to let her know the results of the DNA test. Maybe then she will reconsider."

Peter had sat back in his chair.

"My God, then what has happened to Anne?" Patricia said.

"Any one of a number of scenarios," said Peter. "Yes, Thomas could have done this but equally Brian, the jilted lover, could be trying to cause trouble for them, or Anne could have run away or –"

"And left her child?" Isobel said.

"All I'm saying is let's not jump to conclusions. We first need to see if Anne is Anne or if Claire has just made a mistake or dreamed up a conspiracy plot. If the DNA is different then we can see what to do. Maybe this shelter woman has some more information she can share with us." He stood up. "But I'm warning you, this is not a game. My professional life is already in jeopardy –"

"And a woman's life may have been too and may still be." Isobel stood and faced him.

"We need to be very careful and only deal with facts, not wild and crazy suppositions and theories. Please, if we make any accusations that are unfounded we could jeopardise Tommy's future and also be open to charges of slander. All I'm asking is that you take time to establish what the truth is here."

Isobel sat down again and put her head in her hands. "I know you're right on one level but I have an awful feeling that something really bad is going on here."

Peter also sat. "Isobel, you might be right, but we can't just go by your feelings. We have to find proof. When we talked to all of Anne's friends and family what was clear was that no one really knew what was going on. We can't make the same mistake now. We have to move forward cautiously, establishing facts. Surely you can see this?" He turned to Patricia. "I'm not discounting Isobel's fears. I'm merely saying that we can't jump to conclusions."

Patricia reached out for his hand.

"Don't make me the bad guy here, Isobel," he went on. "I'm trying to move forward in a stepwise fashion. If what Brian says is true then we need to prove that."

Isobel nodded.

He stood again, came over and touched her shoulder. "I know you're working really hard on this. I'm not against you, just more cautious."

Isobel could feel tears on her eyelashes. She nodded again, reached up and touched his hand in appreciation.

He sat down again and said, "Let's see what the DNA results show and maybe you can talk to ... what's the lady's name?"

"Julia."

"Julia, again. I don't think we should tell Simon this

until we're sure that it's true. I don't think it would help."

Isobel nodded again. "OK. I'll talk to Julia again and then see. But if she won't tell me anything, I may still have to tell Simon what Brian said so that he can see if it needs to be checked out."

"OK."

At a quarter to seven Isobel's phone rang. She looked at her screen and could see that it was Simon. Taking a deep breath, she answered.

"Hello, Simon."

"Jeff and I want to meet you," he said abruptly. "Where would be good for you?"

"Where?" Isobel gestured with her fingers and Peter nodded. She said, "Can you come here?"

"Yes."

She gave him Peter's address.

"We'll be there in about half an hour."

There was a dialling tone.

"They're coming over."

Peter said, "Obviously the DNA samples showed something, or Simon and Jeff wouldn't be coming here. It must be serious."

By half past seven they were all ensconced in Peter's living room.

Jeff had brought his dinner with him and began to eat without announcing his findings.

Isobel was wound as tight as a spring but she and the others were doing their best to give him the space to reveal his findings in his own time and way. Eventually she could wait no longer.

"So what have you found?"

Jeff finished chewing his mouthful of food. "It turns out that Anne Banks is not a familial match to Claire Graham."

Isobel put her hand over her mouth. Even though she had been expecting this, it was shocking. The dark chasm of possibilities that she had been pondering all afternoon seemed more of a reality.

"Before you jump to conclusions, we need to confirm that there isn't another innocent explanation for this."

Isobel made a face. "Like what?"

"That Anne or Claire was adopted."

Isobel could feel her anger rising. "Of course they aren't. Claire would have told us." Her voice trembled.

"Isobel, I'm here because these results change everything. Yes, I was humouring you initially but now I'm not. And now we need to find out what's going on. This was important enough for me to give up my Sunday evening watching the sport round-up."

Isobel blushed. "Sorry."

"It's OK. I think all of us are shocked."

After a pause, Jeff said, "The first thing we have to do is ask Anne Bank's mother if any of her daughters are adopted."

Isobel, her head and heart back in the game, said, "But Anne and Claire are so alike, and so like their mother – they have to be blood relatives."

"Come on, Isobel," said Jeff. "The blood test shows that there's a woman walking round who is the image of Anne Banks and is not a blood relative so, of course, we have to know if Anne could be adopted. At the moment we have a sister who has been estranged claiming that this woman is not her sister and a blood test that shows they aren't sisters. You want us to believe that a crime is going on here but that may not be the case. I'm a scientist, my job is to eliminate all the other possibilities and arrive at the truth."

"We can't ask Donna Graham," said Isobel. "She's very biased towards Thomas. If we ask her she'll tell him immediately. If we want to keep him in the dark, then we have to find another way. She could already have aroused his suspicions with my story of being an old friend."

There was a silence.

Then Isobel said, "Surely hospital records would show that Mrs Graham gave birth to two daughters. Can we not find that out without Thomas or her mother knowing?"

Simon pursed his lips. "I'm not sure they hand out that information to the public. What about the sister? Could she check with her family doctor?"

"If he knows," said Peter. "They could have had any number of doctors over the years."

Isobel opened her mouth to speak again but Simon, pacing, clicked his fingers.

"You're proposing this theory of two Annes. If we had some old fingerprints from the younger Anne we could compare them with the set of present ones from the coffee cup. That would show if a substitution has occurred." Simon seemed to grow taller as he spoke and continued pacing up and down the room.

Isobel blinked. "You're right. That is brilliant."

Simon grinned. "I have done this before, you know."

Isobel smiled back.

"Can we talk to Claire now?" Simon asked.

Isobel nodded and pulled out her phone, knowing that Claire would also have been on tenterhooks.

"Claire, hi, this is Isobel."

"Well, what's the news?"

"The DNA supports what you said – the Anne Banks we've met is not your blood sister."

"I knew that."

"I know. Well, now the police are taking this seriously and they need a few things clarified."

"Like what? What's not clear? Someone is impersonating my sister and God knows what has happened to her and we need to find out what!"

Isobel moved over to the apartment window as she talked. "Claire, we're going to find out what's going on. I have a policeman friend here and he's helping us. We have to be calm and build a case, not rush in and mess things up. I know this is hard, but we have to be guided by Simon."

Simon smiled at Isobel with raised eyebrows. Isobel rolled her eyes at him.

"I'm impatient and annoyed too, Claire," she said. "I think what you're saying is true but the police –"

Simon gestured for the phone.

"Hold on, Claire, I'm putting you on speaker phone."

"Hello, Claire. My name is Simon Jones and I am a Detective Inspector with the Metropolitan Police."

"Hello."

"Claire, I need to build a picture, based on evidence, of what's going on here. To do that I need some more information."

"OK. What do you need to know?"

He gestured for Isobel to continue.

Isobel took a deep breath. "Claire, is there any possibility that you are adopted or that Anne is?"

"Don't be ridiculous. Look at the two of us – most people think that we're twins!"

"True," Isobel said, "but there is another woman walking around who looks very like your sister so, unless you're all related, that proves things like this can happen."

Simon lifted his eyebrows at her and grinned over at Jeff.

"Jesus! Are you sure the police want to help us? It sounds to me like they're just thinking up delay tactics. At this rate Thomas will get everything and nobody will be any the wiser."

Simon opened his mouth to speak but Isobel shook her head at him. "I know, I know. But the police are just eliminating all the other possibilities."

Simon nodded enthusiastically at her and Isobel turned away from him. She sat down, weary from all of the talk. "Please, Claire. I need the help of the police. We can't do all of this ourselves. Please jump through the hoops they need for them to stay on the case."

Claire clicked her tongue. Isobel waited.

"OK, Isobel. But for you and Patricia and the solicitor we wouldn't even have got this far. So for that reason I'll co-operate."

"Thanks, Claire. Right. How long have you had your doctor?"

"I've had the same doctor my whole life."

"Great. We just need to know if there's any possibility that you or Anne were adopted."

"I'll go and see him first thing tomorrow and ask him."

Simon said, "Get him to write a letter stating the facts clearly."

"OK."

Isobel said, "Now, the second thing is, it would be helpful if we had an old set of Anne fingerprints."

"We want something that Anne touched," said Simon. "Something only people we know touched as well so that we can eliminate them."

"God, I don't know. I haven't seen Anne for so long – I don't think I have anything."

Isobel said, "What about a card she sent you?"

Simon said, "No, that could have fingerprints from customers and people who work in the shop."

Isobel suddenly shouted out.

Claire called down the phone, "*What? What?*"

"Oh my God, Claire! You have a letter, what about that?"

Simon grinned. "Yes, that's more like it. We can get your fingerprints, Claire, and eliminate them and the others should be Anne's."

Claire was silent.

"What is it?" Isobel said.

"I burned the letter. Anne was so stressed about Thomas and I was really angry so I got rid of it once I'd read it."

Simon groaned and massaged his forehead.

Isobel paced up and down then stopped suddenly. "I know someone who has something Anne wrote on, that she touched."

"Who?"

"Brian Poole. He said that he saw Anne a few months ago. She wrote down a number on some paper and handed it to him."

Claire said, "Why did she go to him? Why didn't she come to me?"

Isobel chewed her lip. "I think she knew that Thomas would suspect you and maybe she thought he wouldn't think of Brian."

Claire was silent for some moments and then she said, "OK, Isobel. You've got us this far – I'll trust you another while but please . . ."

"I know, Claire. Just help with this step."

"OK, I'll get the letter from the doctor and hopefully the piece of paper from Brian tomorrow."

"Yes, bring it to Jeff in the lab," Simon said.

Jeff said, "Hi again, Claire. Please wear gloves when you're collecting the piece of paper and can you also collect a sample of Brian's fingerprints on a mirror so I can use them for comparison? Just wipe the mirror clear, wearing gloves yourself, and get Brian to put each finger and thumb on it – both hands. Keep the mirror in a bag then to protect it and the same with the piece of paper."

"OK, Jeff."

"I think I touched the paper too," Isobel said.

"OK, I'll get your prints now."

Patricia stood up. "I'll get a mirror."

"I'll process everything as quickly as I can," said Jeff, "but realistically it will probably be tomorrow afternoon. And, Claire, the sooner I get the prints, the better."

"No problem, Jeff. I'll be as fast as I can." She hung up.

Simon turned to Isobel. "What else did Brian tell you?"

Isobel looked at Peter. He subtly shook his head. "He said something that I need to get confirmation on. Hopefully I can do that tomorrow. The DNA results might swing it in terms of getting the information."

Simon frowned.

Isobel, searching for something to divert attention, said, "Peter, who is your client? Assuming there's no adoption, is your client the original Anne Banks or this imposter?"

Peter grimaced. "I've been thinking about that. It's not exactly a textbook case. I'll have to check out the legal issues. It could be a minefield so I'll have to be very circumspect about things. I might even have to get legal representation myself."

"OK, OK," Simon cut in. "You can talk about all of that yourselves. Let's meet at two o'clock tomorrow. Jeff will let us know if it's going to be later."

They all said goodnight.

Isobel and Patricia were quiet on the way home. Isobel felt too tired and stressed to talk to Dave. He knew her too well and would only worry. So she sent him a text.

Having an exciting time. Staying a few more days. Talk tomorrow.

Isobel went to bed with a heavy heart. She was exhausted. She felt tears coming. It had been a strain today with Brian and Julia, trying to get them to talk, and then later dealing with Simon and Claire. She felt worn out trying to move things forward and balance all of the different needs and wants and personalities.

Patricia came back into the sitting room and perched on a chair. "Are you all right?"

Isobel sat up, wiping her eyes. "It's just been a long day."

"It's hard to believe what's happening? How did you know?"

Isobel shook her head and shrugged, her eyes glistening. "I don't know." She swallowed the lump in her throat and brushed her hand over her eyes.

"I know you're tired and that meeting this evening was tough, but we're making progress."

"I know. It's just hard to be patient and wait for all the evidence Simon wants. I know he's doing his job, but I feel as if time is running out."

"I'll help as much as I can."

"Thanks. You've been great."

Patricia went to bed and Isobel lay on the sofa-bed, reflecting on Claire's revelation and the story that Brian had told her. Despite Julia's evasiveness, Isobel felt that Brian had been telling the truth. Where was Anne? That question disturbed her, but the possible answers disturbed her even more. She tossed and turned, trying to get comfortable and eventually fell into a fitful sleep.

She was standing in a bedroom. She stilled. Her heart hammered against her chest, the beat of it resounding in her ears. Her stomach flipped and danced and flipped again. She knew he was behind her. He had made no sound but she knew.

She could feel the threat in the air, emanating from him.

She turned slowly. His eyes locked into hers as if seeing into her soul. They were full of knowing and rage.

Panic filled her throat until she felt she couldn't take a breath. She swallowed and opened her mouth to speak. He twitched his lips, a fraction, barely perceptible, and her voice died in her throat.

With appalling certainty she realised the danger she was in. Any fight she had left in her trickled away. Time slowed. A sense of inevitability crept over her and strangely it brought a calmness, an absence of fear, almost relief.

He moved. As her eyes registered his advance she backed away until her legs were pressed against the bed.

He towered over her. His hands reached out towards her, big strong hands, cruel and punishing. They fastened onto her throat and tightened. His face contorted in rage and hatred and his hands kept step. She closed her eyes. From far away she could hear him screaming, "*Look at me!*" but she kept her eyes closed.

He shook her, her ears tuning out the torrent of words. His hands tightened in temper and frustration. She could feel the pressure building in her head. Her face felt red and flushed, her eyes straining. She had no breath left, her throat so constricted. As the darkness came she could feel herself surrender.

Isobel woke gasping and reaching to dislodge the invisible hands around her throat. Her heart hammered in her chest. She dragged in deep sustaining breaths. She was bathed in sweat, cowering in the corner of the sofa-bed. She wrapped her arms around herself and took some deep breaths. Gradually her heartbeat slowed and her breathing steadied. She swallowed hard and was surprised to find that her throat was not tender and constricted. Shakily she stood up and padded to the kitchen to get a drink of water. Looking out of the window into the darkened city, she shivered. This dream, this nightmare, this was what she believed had happened to Anne Banks. Silently tears bathed her cheeks.

Chapter 23

Monday 28th May

Shaken after her dreams, it was a relief for Isobel to stay in bed until ten o'clock the next morning. Once up, as daylight and normality dispelled the tension, she felt determined to talk to Julia as soon as possible. She contacted her and they arranged to meet at eleven o'clock.

On the way she received a text from Claire.

Doctor says we are both my mother's natural daughters. Paper at lab. Jeff says 2pm today. See you then.

Isobel wasn't surprised but was glad to have this further confirmation to tell Julia.

The venue was again the National Gallery café. Isobel spotted Julia immediately despite the less colourful clothing and she brought two Americanos as before.

Once seated, she immediately said, "The DNA for Anne Banks is not a familial match to her sister. This morning we got confirmation from their family doctor that the girls were naturally conceived and delivered, so at least maternally siblings. Someone is impersonating Anne Banks. We also have probable fingerprints of hers on the piece of paper she wrote your number on and it is being compared with those of the suspected imposter. We hope to have results by two o'clock today when we're meeting with the police again. My major concern now is getting the police to find Anne. Julia, do you know where she is? Can you confirm her whereabouts even if you cannot tell us where? *Please, can you give me any information that would help us find out if she's all right?*" Isobel realised her voice had risen and she blushed as she finished. This case was really getting to her.

Julia pursed her lips and looked speculatively at Isobel. "I need to speak to our solicitor. If there is anything we can share it would be best that we meet the police. Give me the address for the meeting. If we can do anything we'll be there."

Isobel gave her the address. "Hopefully I'll see you at two o'clock then."

By two o'clock Julia had arrived with a young woman with long brown hair. She was tall, dressed in a neat black power suit and carried a briefcase that was leather and heavy. The general impression was of someone who knew her job and was well able to fight her corner. Julia introduced her as Yvonne Dempsey.

Peter was also there with Patricia, both off work for the Bank Holiday.

Claire was introduced as Anne's sister and Simon and Yvonne clearly took particular notice of this.

Claire nervously sat beside Isobel who squeezed her hand.

Then, before anyone else could speak, Claire stood up and said, "I spoke to our doctor early this morning. He's given me a letter confirming that he tended my mother during both of her pregnancies and that Anne and I are her natural daughters. Needless to say, he couldn't understand why I wanted to know. He was worried that I was becoming paranoid, but I convinced him to give me confirmation."

She handed a letter to Simon who glanced at it quickly and nodded. He offered it to Jeff who shook his head.

Claire had paled. "So now we definitely know that someone is pretending to be my sister."

As before, it was what Jeff had to say that they were all waiting on.

"I've analysed the prints from the piece of paper Anne left with Brian," he said. "There were three sets of prints on it. Two of them were identified as Brian's and Isobel's. The third set was not a match for the ones on the cup which Peter took from the café. So what I can tell you is this – the Anne Banks who wrote the note and the Anne Banks who drank the coffee are not the same woman. There are two women calling themselves Anne Banks. Taken with the doctor's evidence that Anne and Claire were born naturally to the same mother, then the coffee cup Anne is not the Anne Banks who married Thomas and had Tommy, but an imposter."

Claire let out a strangled sound and buried her face in her hands.

Jeff concluded, "Simon, I'm telling you that a crime is being committed."

Simon nodded.

Yvonne cleared her throat and waited until she had everyone's attention. "Given that someone is pretending to be Anne Banks – choosing to act in what I deem to be Anne's best interests," here she glanced at Julia and received a nod of assent, "I feel we can make you privy to certain facts."

There was complete silence.

"Anne Banks got our number through Brian Poole and a woman's shelter in Petersfield. As I understand it, that's the number that was on the piece of paper you've been alluding to. She rang us on Monday 12th February at eleven thirty. She told us that she and her husband Thomas had had an altercation the night before and she was seeking help, support and guidance. She needed to pick her son up from school and, as she didn't want to raise Thomas's suspicions, it was the following day before Julia could meet her. She met Julia and told her what had happened."

Yvonne nodded at Julia who took up the story.

"On the Sunday evening after Tommy had gone to bed, Thomas got annoyed with Anne because she wasn't being affectionate enough to him. He punched her body a number of times, held her arms causing extensive bruising, shook her and in the end he put his hands around her throat and strangled her until she passed out."

Claire put her hand over her mouth and began to cry. Isobel put an arm around her. No one spoke, not wanting to break the thread of the story.

Once Claire's crying became quieter, Julia continued. "Anne woke up during the night lying on the bedroom floor. In the morning Thomas acted as if nothing had happened and, terrified, Anne went along with it. When she'd taken Tommy to school on Monday she drove to see Brian and he, through a contact he had, put her in touch with us." Julia looked around. "In a situation of this seriousness often the woman will end up murdered if she doesn't leave. When I told Anne this she agreed that this was a possibility and that she needed to leave. We followed our normal procedure in a case of this type. Firstly, we got the doctor."

Yvonne reached into her briefcase and produced an envelope which she handed to Simon. "Here is a medical record of her injuries, described and photographed." She reached again into her briefcase and pulled out a legal file which she also gave to him. "And here is the statement I took from her that morning of what had happened."

Simon nodded grimly.

Yvonne nodded at Julia to continue.

"I told Anne what I have to tell everyone, which is that it takes a little bit of time to arrange a safe house. We offered her a temporary place in the shelter until we had something more permanent for her to go to. She refused, saying that she needed the few days to get herself and Tommy sorted. We agreed that she would be ready to leave Thomas the following Monday, the 19th, at nine in the morning. She would leave the house as usual, as if taking Tommy to school, and we would pick her up. From the car she would ring the school and say Tommy was sick, so he wouldn't be missed. That would give us until at least half past three when school finished and maybe until five or six o'clock when Thomas got home from work before he realised she was gone. That's a very good head start. The women can take only what they can easily carry, and they must not contact close family and friends as that's the first place someone would look for them. Anne didn't turn up to the rendezvous on Monday the 19th."

Claire grasped Isobel's hand and squeezed it painfully. Mindful of her own vulnerabilities, Isobel gently freed her hand and put her arm around her.

"To be honest, that's not that uncommon," Julia said.

"It happens because the woman changes her mind. There's nothing we can do about it. But I was surprised that Anne didn't show as she was so frightened and understood the danger she was in, but we have to respect the woman's right to choose."

"Did you ring her?" Simon asked.

"No. If a woman changes her mind we wait for her to contact us again. We can only encourage the women – the choice has to be theirs."

"When did you last talk to Anne?"

"I last spoke to Anne on that Friday when she rang me to confirm the final details. She rang from a burner phone which she then got rid of so Thomas wouldn't find it."

Yvonne said, "That would be the 16th of February."

There was silence except for the stifled sounds of Claire crying. The silence lengthened.

Eventually Simon cleared his throat, but then lapsed back into silence.

Eventually, Isobel spoke. "So Thomas could have found out and killed her?"

Simon stirred to life. "That's a massive jump in deduction."

"But it is a possibility."

"It's a possibility but we have no evidence of that. At the moment he's calling this woman Mrs Banks. Yes, it's suspicious but they haven't committed a crime yet. On Wednesday when she signs the divorce, *then* she will have committed a crime and he will be an accessory. But there's no body, so murder is a bridge too far. Anne could have decided to run off herself, she could have got Brian to help her instead of going with Julia. Thomas may have no idea where she is and he could be doing this to sort out his financial situation. A crime yes, murder no. We don't even

187

know when she definitely disappeared. Maybe they talked that weekend, maybe she went to rehab to give them a breather. Maybe they decided to divorce and after that Anne fell off the wagon and rather than cancel everything he decided to see the process through. Who can say when Anne disappeared?"

Isobel was outraged. "Whose side are you on? That is like a defence for Thomas."

"I'm a policeman, Isobel. I follow the evidence, build a case and if I'm lucky the perpetrator is brought to justice. Sometimes I build a case and he still gets off on some technicality. I have to follow the evidence."

"You have to find the truth, protect the innocent!"

"Yes, and I need to make sure the guilty face the consequences."

"But once you find the truth surely it's not so hard to …" Her voice tapered off.

Simon looked at Yvonne and Peter and shrugged. "It is, Isobel. From the minute I start a case I have to think of the questions I'm going to be asked in court. I have to prove everything, every little thing." His tone was weary.

There was a long silence.

Isobel, knowing that she needed Simon's help and also as a part of her acknowledged that he was right, dialled it back a little. "Well, we need to decide on our next steps. What do we need to find out? To prove?"

Again, there was a resounding silence.

Isobel looked at Peter. He shrugged.

Simon said, "I can talk to a detective in the Fraud squad. We'll probably have to co-ordinate something for after the signing on Wednesday. I'll meet him today whenever he can fit me in."

"Julia, what do you think?" Isobel said. "Surely something can be done in a case where there has been this level of violence and he could have killed her?"

Julia looked at Yvonne who shook her head.

Julia looked back at Isobel. "Of course he could have killed her but, to be honest, anything is possible. The stress of what happened affects women in different ways. Many stay, but Anne may have run away herself, not able to cope. She could have started to drink heavily. Any of these scenarios is possible."

Isobel frowned. "But you said it yourself. With him strangling her, she was at huge risk."

"She was at risk, yes."

A thought struck Isobel. "A few people have told us how controlling he was. He wouldn't want Anne to leave. If he killed her because she was leaving, he would definitely want to keep her body at his home, to prove she could never leave."

Simon shook his head. "That is pure supposition but, even if it were true, as yet we have no grounds to search legally. But if we catch Thomas on the fraud claim we may be able to persuade a judge to allow us to search."

Isobel could hear the doubt in his voice, and she could feel her impatience rising.

"We have a special unit for that," Simon continued. "My friend Jason Watkins works with that unit. With cadaver dogs. When the time comes and we have a warrant, I will personally get Jason."

"Great," Isobel said.

"I should probably go," Simon said. "I need to start to run basic checks on Thomas. Jeff, will you check all the databases to see if 'Anne', the imposter, is in the system?"

"Sure, Simon, it's being done as we speak. I'll phone the minute we get anything."

Simon and Jeff left together.

Claire was very distressed. "I cannot believe this is happening. My sister was an abused wife, was nearly strangled, decided to run away. Now she's missing, at the very least, and at worst has been murdered, her husband is trying to pretend that nothing happened and none of you can do anything about it."

Isobel knelt in front of Claire's chair. "Look at me, Claire." She waited until Claire met her gaze. "I know this is terrible but we're all doing our best. We are going to find out what happened to Anne, I promise you that. But you have to stay calm and you need to think about Tommy. Ultimately we need to make sure that Tommy is with someone safe, who will love and support him."

Claire paled. "Oh God – Tommy! You're right. I have to stay calm. Sorry I lost it. I feel so guilty that I didn't know how bad things were for Anne. I should have been more there for her."

Isobel's face softened. "Claire, you have to be there for her now. Now, you need to make sure that what happens to Tommy is what Anne would have wanted."

Claire, with tears in her eyes, nodded determinedly.

"You have to hold it together, be smart. Look how many people were at the meeting. Everyone is on Anne's side. I promise you that we will find out what has happened to her."

Patricia came over and crouched down too.

Claire nodded slowly now. She took a deep breath. "I can do this, don't worry."

Patricia squeezed her hand.

Isobel said, "Claire, go back to work. Be as normal as you can. We'll ring if we need your help. Please bear with us and don't tell your mother anything yet until we know more."

Taking deep breaths, Claire got ready to leave. "Ring me any time, day or night, if you need my help or if you find anything."

"We will."

After Claire left, Yvonne and Peter conferred for a few minutes, arranging for him to have copies of all of the documents, then Isobel walked the two women down.

"Thank you both so much for coming. Without your help, well . . ."

"Isobel, I think you could be right," Julia said. "It's very possible that the reason that Anne wasn't there on the Monday was that Thomas stopped her. Despite all the other possibilities she could be dead."

Isobel nodded.

"What are you going to do?"

Isobel tilted her head. "I'm going to find out if the body is in the garden.

"How?" Julia asked, then as realization dawned she smiled. "You're going to find Jason Watkins."

Isobel nodded. "Now I need to persuade Jason to do an unauthorised check."

Julia reached out. "Any help I can give you about any of this, just ring. I want to know what happened to Anne."

Isobel gave her a quick hug and they parted ways.

Chapter 24

Since he was a solicitor, Isobel felt that it was better if Peter didn't know of her plans to find Jason, so she told him and Patricia that she was heading off for the rest of the day on her own. She decided the best thing to do was get online and do some research. She found a café nearby with Wi-Fi to speed up her connection, ordered a coffee and settled down to see what she could find out about Jason Watkins – more particularly, how to contact him.

To help her in her understanding of what cadaver dogs could do, Isobel looked up newspaper articles which discussed the use of dogs for finding bodies. There were a number of stories and Jason and his canine helper were even mentioned in a few centred in London. Isobel then did some general reading about the success of specially trained dogs in finding cadavers. Her last search was of the police website. It didn't take long to realise that finding Jason was not going to be easy.

Isobel had a huge sense of urgency. Perhaps her dream had something to do with it but it seemed to her vital to know if Anne's body was in the garden. If not, then she could rule that out and start looking at other possibilities, but for her this seemed the most likely possibility – in fact, she was sure of it. She needed to prove it or eliminate it and move on to an alternative. Maybe, she thought, it was her impatient nature, maybe she just hated not knowing and maybe she just was worried that somehow Thomas Banks was going to get away with murder. If the body wasn't in the garden then Isobel realised it could be anywhere. That was daunting. Maybe they would never find it. But for her this seemed the most likely and even if no one agreed with her she had to pursue it.

The one place Isobel could probably get Jason's number was from Tracey, but she had reservations about involving Tracey without Simon knowing. However, there seemed to be no other way. Feeling guilty but going ahead anyway, she gave Tracey a ring.

"Hi, Tracey."

"Isobel, how's it going? Your little favour seems to have morphed into a much bigger case for Simon. He's just called to tell me he had to have a dinner meeting with another officer."

Isobel was nonplussed. "Oh, I know he was hoping to speak to someone in Fraud. He thought he could persuade them to liaise with us. I'm ringing because at the meeting Simon mentioned another friend and colleague we might draw on, Jason Watkins. I meant to get his number from Simon but in the busyness of everything I forgot and I'm reluctant to bother him when he's obviously busy. So, I was wondering if you had Jason's number? He said Jason was great, that the work he does is amazing."

Tracey laughed. "You should hear the two of them when they get going. He's a lovely man, Jason, the one of Simon's friends that I most like."

Isobel cringed in guilt and realised that she couldn't do this. It wasn't fair to her friend who'd helped her when she reached out. "Tracey, it's not fair to put you in this position. I'll talk to Simon at the next meeting. I was just getting impatient, silly of me." They chatted for another few minutes about general things and Isobel rang off.

She breathed a sigh of relief. She couldn't repay her friend by betraying her. Turning to her computer she brought up the general article again and got on the phone. By assuming a number of guises – young person doing a project, dog-care enquirer, mother asking about a future career for her son – she gradually found out that the dog unit was a specialised unit and operated out of a certain police station. It was still not six o'clock and Isobel decided to go there and see if Jason was at work.

It was nearer six thirty when she got to the station. Going in, she asked the desk sergeant if she could speak to Jason Watkins, adding that she was a friend of Detective Inspector Simon Jones. She held her breath, hoping that he was at work. He was.

The man who arrived into the foyer of the police station had abundant grey hair and was very tall and broad – not fat, just brawny and strong, a man mountain, definitely not a man to mess with.

Isobel extended her hand. "My name is Isobel McKenzie. I'm an old acquaintance of Tracey and Simon Jones. Simon has kindly been helping me with a problem. I was wondering if I could talk to you as well. It's in relation to a crime."

Isobel often found that if you could engage someone's curiosity then they wouldn't say no immediately which allowed time to persuade them to say yes. Jason looked at her assessingly. After a moment he nodded and, without saying anything, turned and led the way through a security gate to an interview room.

From all the police shows she'd watched, Isobel thought it would be a bare room with a table and three chairs that smelt of urine and sweat and stale drink. It wasn't. It had four soft chairs and was furnished with curtains and a carpet.

When she'd chosen a chair and was seated, he picked one opposite her, dwarfing the chair. Crossing his legs casually, he said, "Shoot."

Isobel launched into a description of everything that had happened to date. Throughout her discourse he said nothing, his face neutral, giving nothing away. Isobel imagined that Jason would be a good poker player and no doubt he would be very good at interrogation and that was without saying anything.

She lapsed into silence, having reached the conclusion of all the facts.

"So why are you here?" Jason asked.

That was the million-dollar question, she knew. How she answered would determine what happened. Bullshitting this man was not an option.

"I'm here because I want you to let your dog 'escape' –" here she used finger quotes, "into Thomas Banks' garden and in the course of retrieving it I want you to see if there is any body buried in the garden. This will give us an idea of where the case could be going and also whether or not we need to start looking for Anne elsewhere." Isobel kept her voice steady, sounding confident, and met Jason's gaze.

"Simon doesn't agree."

"How do you know?"

"I'm a detective."

"No, so I've gone behind his back. I believe we need to do this sooner rather than later. Look, I was right about the imposter. Maybe I'm wrong about this but I have to know. I've met Thomas's neighbour. She, I'm sure, would let us visit and your dog could escape over the fence and you would then have to go over and get her. Thomas is at work all day so hopefully he'll never know this has happened. I was hoping we could do it tomorrow morning – then we would know as soon as possible and if I'm wrong I could start looking for Anne. You probably think like everyone else that I'm jumping to conclusions, but we have so little time. I feel as if no one believes me that this is, or could be, murder. They're all focused on fraud right now. I would feel more confident fighting for Anne if I knew the answer to this. To be honest, sometimes I feel as if they think I'm neurotic, but my intuition tells me I'm right and I would never forgive myself if I didn't see this through." She finished, having said more that she wanted to and now feeling vulnerable.

Jason tapped his hand on his knee. "Look, I think you and you solicitor friend have done fantastic work uncovering this. I can understand how you feel."

Isobel felt as if he was working up to letting her down gently. She felt deflated and tired as if she was pushing against the current and it was just too hard. Her shoulders sagged and she bowed her head.

Jason fell silent. After half a minute he suddenly sat up straight in the chair and waited for Isobel to look at him.

"OK, here's what we'll do. You need to phone this next-door neighbour and see if we can visit tomorrow. If she agrees I will introduce you to my old mentor in the unit, who is now retired – Malcolm Carr."

Isobel's face fell but Jason talked on.

"His dog Bella is also retired but is still one of the best in the business. Malcolm and Bella do a type of pet therapy where they visit homes for old people and sick children. Tomorrow they might go and see your friend as a surprise for this old lady, a kindness, and if Bella gets attracted over the fence, well, Malcolm may have to retrieve her."

Isobel almost whooped with joy.

"I'll meet you in the morning and introduce you to Malcolm and then you're on your own. How does that sound?"

"Great!"

"Get on the phone and see if it will work."

Isobel pulled out her mobile and called Grace.

Grace wanted to talk and ask questions, but Isobel quickly forestalled her.

"Grace, can I come and visit you tomorrow morning?"

"Yes, of course. I would love to see you again."

"Grace, I may want to look over the hedge into Thomas's and I don't want him to catch me. After he leaves Tommy to school does he come back home?" She guessed he didn't but there was no point wasting Malcolm's time.

"Oh no, he's gone by twenty past or half eight at the latest and usually he's not back until five or six in the evening."

Isobel smiled to herself. There was a lot to be said for Neighbourhood Watch.

"Grace, I'd like to bring a friend."

"Of course, of course, Isobel."

"He has a dog – would that be a problem for you?" Isobel asked, wanting to be fair to Grace.

"That's fine with me."

Isobel was really impressed with this septuagenarian.

"Tomorrow, in person, I can explain a bit better," she offered.

Grace laughed. "Leave it until tomorrow."

Jason was making finger drawings in the air: nine.

"We'll be there at around nine o'clock," Isobel said.

"Great, see you then, love. Goodnight."

Jason went out of the room. Isobel waited. She felt guilty that she'd betrayed Simon but what could she do? Finding Anne was her priority. In the final analysis she felt that Anne needed her help more than anyone.

Jason returned ten minutes later. "OK, I've contacted Malcolm and arranged things for tomorrow morning. I'll get the address from you now and text it on to Malcolm. We'll both park a few streets away and walk to Grace's."

"What about Simon? I don't want to create a problem between you."

Jason paused. "Isobel, Simon is a police officer. He made a judgment call to do a DNA test for you, as a favour, on minimal evidence. That's experience. I've just done the same. Simon is right about being careful not to mess up the case but I can feel that we need to see if Anne might, and I emphasise, *might*, be dead and buried in the garden. I think that's vital to know. I've listened to the facts, I see the fraud, but I feel there's a strong possibility of murder here and I'm going to do what I can about that. Having Malcolm and his dog Bella do the sweep is the best solution. Grace sounded clued in and is obviously supportive. I want to do this. Simon and I will be fine. We've known each other a long time." He looked at her speculatively. "You and Simon will probably be fine too. He knows you care, that's why you're doing what you're doing. Despite what you think, he cares too. He'll get it."

"Thank you. See you tomorrow morning."

Isobel sat on the train. The sound and action of it was soothing, rhythmic almost hypnotic. It seemed to help her brain make connections and something was surfacing in her mind. Thomas Banks was a mystery man – they knew very little about him. Having reached the level of violence he had with Anne, it was unlikely that this was the first time. Maybe it was time to do some digging into his past.

She called Patricia and arranged to meet her and Peter.

Chapter 25

They met again in Peter's flat which Isobel was beginning to think of as headquarters. The first order of business was tea and coffee. Patricia went to the kitchen to prepare the drinks while Peter tidied the living room.

Isobel followed Patricia and whispered, "Well, how are things going with Peter?"

Patricia smiled happily. "Very good. We had dinner earlier and a lovely chat. Peter is really upset about Anne Banks and we just talked a little bit about that and then we chatted about normal things."

Isobel smiled at this. "And?"

"And, mostly I'm mad about him because he cares and is such a great man."

Isobel laughed. "And very attractive."

Now Patricia laughed. "That too."

"I'm glad things are going well with you."

"Me too."

"You too, what?" asked Peter coming into the kitchen. Patricia blushed.

Isobel said, "Shocked about what we're finding out."

Peter leant against the kitchen units, folding his arms.

200

"I can hardly believe it. The things that Julia revealed are very distressing. I know I started all of this, but I didn't expect this . . ." His voice trailed off.

Patricia took his hand and led him back to the living room. Isobel followed, bringing their cups on a tray. Patricia sat beside Peter on the sofa, her hand on his arm.

After some minutes of silence Peter said, "What now? Just wait to see what Simon suggests?"

Isobel nodded. "Yes, but I think we have to find out more about Thomas Banks. I feel that based on how he's been with Anne there has to be more. He has to have done something violent before."

Patricia was nodding. "How can we find out?"

Isobel shrugged. "Well, I think we need to find someone else he's been in a relationship with, someone he worked with or maybe someone from his school. If he's this violent now, I'm sure he's been violent before."

Peter jumped up and collected a file from the dining-room table.

"You brought a file from work," Patricia said.

He grinned. "Correction, I brought a copied file from work," and he waggled his eyebrows at her. She laughed.

Isobel said, "Focus, people, focus!"

Patricia and Peter smiled at her.

"What do we know about him?" she said.

Peter riffled through the file. "Well, we have his father's name and profession, so we could research his father."

"He's dead, isn't he?" Isobel asked.

"Yes, both Thomas's parents are dead."

"If we knew where he grew up that would be a help."

"Remember I found that old work photo from ten years ago?" Patricia said.

201

"Perhaps we need Simon's help with this or should leave it to him," Peter suggested. "He can probably get lots of information very easily."

Isobel tapped her finger against her lip. "Simon is going to go do all the things policemen do but our talking to people is what uncovered the truth here, so I think that we should keep doing what we're doing. And," she continued, nodding now, "people find it easier to talk to ordinary people than to policemen."

"True," Patricia said, getting up and opening Peter's laptop. "OK. Let's find out what we can and see what it tells us."

Patricia's fingers danced across the computer keys as she searched, read and searched again.

Isobel, knowing that an expert was at work, went to make more tea. Peter followed her into the kitchen.

"God, Isobel, I can hardly believe that things are so bad."

Isobel looked at Peter. "I know. We couldn't have guessed how this was going to escalate but thank God you did realise there was something wrong, otherwise no one would know."

"Things seem to be spiralling out and getting bigger and bigger."

"I know. I can hardly believe that I flew in last Monday and a week later here we are facing God knows what."

"You suspect the worst, don't you?"

Isobel looked Peter in the eye for a few seconds before answering. "Yes, I think Thomas has killed Anne. I hope not, but to be honest, given what Julia has told us, it seems to me the most likely event."

Peter paled. "As bad as that?"

"Yes. I'm very worried and I'm afraid that we're running out of time. I want to get more information because it took a lot to persuade Simon to help us and if we want him to stay involved we need evidence. Maybe we can find some."

Peter nodded.

"Hang in there, Peter – finding out the truth has to be the most important thing."

Peter grimaced. "For Tommy, what sort of truths is he going to have to face? That his father is an abuser, a fraudster and maybe a murderer?"

Isobel could feel tears again not far away. "Maybe, but the truth is also that his mother loved him and was going to take him away. We're maybe not in time for her but we can still make sure that he's safe. Thomas is dangerous. I don't think Tommy is safe with him. As Anne's solicitor you need to start thinking about where Tommy will go, where he can live."

Peter rubbed his forehead. "I know."

"Like Claire, his aunt, maybe with her he could make a home."

There was a silence.

"Think about this, Peter, because it may all happen in the next few days. Anne Banks, your client, would have wanted you to make sure her son was OK. Please think about how to ensure his future because his dad can't look after him – he's violent, and he may be a murderer."

Peter nodded.

Suddenly there was a shout from the other room. They hurried in.

"What? What have you found?" Peter asked.

Patricia took a deep breath. "The only information that we have from the marriage certificate is Thomas's father's name and occupation." She grinned at them. "I googled how to search for people online and it has given me some interesting avenues to explore. I put in that photo of Thomas from the formal occasion and did a reverse images search. It worked. While Thomas has very little internet presence and no recent photos, I did find his last place of employment. There are some old photos of some of their nights out on the website of a man called Edward Small. When I checked his site it turns out that he's still with the same company. Maybe tomorrow we could visit him and talk to him."

"Great," Isobel said. "That's one avenue – anything else?"

"Yes. I found a search engine called Pipl that is great for finding people." She rolled her eyes. "I put in 'Thomas Banks, London' and some names did come up. I narrowed the search by looking for a train driver and streamlined it further by putting reasonable parameters on his father's age. I couldn't find one around the right age who had died and who had a son of Thomas's age."

"Oh, well," Peter said with a shrug.

"What I did find was a man who seemed the right age for Thomas's father who is alive – but his son is dead. It seems this man's son would have been the same age as Thomas but he died . . ." Patricia's voice tapered off.

Isobel looked at her shrewdly. "So the name is right, the occupation is right, there was a son Thomas's age but he's dead. What are you saying?"

"I think it's worth having a talk with this father." Patricia lifted her chin "It seems too much of a coincidence to me. Thomas Banks might not be a stranger to identity theft. If he found someone to impersonate his wife, maybe he thought of that because he's impersonating someone himself."

Isobel said, "It's a bit of a long shot. Thomas Banks is not that unusual a name."

Patricia looked crestfallen. "I still would like to check it out."

Isobel nodded. "We checked out my crazy idea so why not yours? It can't hurt. Who's going to talk to him?"

Patricia looked at Isobel. "I thought that you and I could go. It's a delicate situation."

"Have you an address for this Thomas Banks Senior?"

"Of course."

"Let's go and visit tomorrow then. I've something to do in the morning but I could meet up with you at around twelve at the Tube station nearest his house and we can visit together."

Patricia raised an eyebrow but said nothing.

Peter said, "I guess this tooth is still causing you trouble."

Patricia laughed. "I guess so, an infection. I just hope there's no karma."

Shortly afterwards they said goodnight and the girls headed back to Patricia's flat.

"Where are you off to tomorrow?"

"I knew you were going to ask."

"You're following another lead, aren't you? Why won't you tell me?"

"I'm sorry. What I'm doing is a long shot and Peter may not like it. I don't want to put you in a difficult position and at least now you can say you had no idea what I was up to. I promise when we meet at twelve I'll tell you everything."

"Immediately we meet I want to hear."

"Scout's honour."

Isobel slept badly. Her dreams were full of images of soil with fingers pushing through trying to dig their way out. Finally she woke from a nightmare where she could feel soil landing on her face. After that she lay awake resting and wondering if they would find Anne Banks tomorrow.

Chapter 26

Tuesday 29th May

Isobel was weary in the morning from lack of sleep but relieved that today might provide an answer to this dreadful suspicion that possessed her mind. She desperately hoped that her hunch would be proved wrong while at the same time she remained deeply convinced it would be proved right.

It was a beautiful morning, bright, sunny and warm. Isobel had a hasty breakfast with Patricia and then took the Tube again to Wimbledon. As she walked towards Grace's house she saw Jason standing and beside him an equally tall black man with white hair. On a lead at his side was a beautiful German Shepherd, Bella she presumed, whose coat was shiny and lush.

Isobel smiled as she arrived and reached out her hand to pet Bella.

Malcolm intercepted her hand. "No. Bella is working so it's best not to touch her."

"Sorry."

Jason laughed. "Everyone makes that mistake. Let me introduce you to Malcolm, the man who taught me everything I know."

"And that was a hard job, I can tell you," Malcolm

said, grinning at Jason. He reached out for her hand. "Jason filled me in on the case last night and I'm glad to help. Bella and I are looking forward to doing some real work today."

Isobel shook his hand, knowing already that she liked and trusted this man.

Jason said, "Right, I'll leave you to it. Let me know how things go. If you do find something I'll want to be involved."

Isobel caught her breath and shivered. "We'll let you know."

She turned to walk towards Grace's house and Malcolm and Bella fell into step beside her. The flowers in front looked bright and cheerful. Obviously Grace tended them well.

They had barely progressed through the gate when the front door opened. Grace's eyes took in Isobel with a smile and then Malcolm and his powerful dog. Her smile didn't waver as she welcomed them in.

She led them through to the kitchen. Isobel imagined that she would be bursting with questions, but Grace surprised her.

"I know that you've found out some things and I'm glad. When all of this is over I want you to come and tell me everything. But, even though I can guess some of it, I don't want you to tell me anything now. You're just friends visiting, that's what you said, that's the story I will tell and if I don't know anything more then I can't say anything." Grace sounded clearheaded and very determined.

Malcolm said, "I think that's very wise. Isobel, please introduce me to this lovely lady."

Isobel duly made the introductions.

Grace then fussed, making a pot of tea for herself and

Isobel and a cafetière of coffee for Malcolm.

"Why don't we have this in the garden?" Isobel said.

Grace nodded and, having placed everything on a tray, she opened the back door. Gesturing for Malcolm to carry the tray she led the way outside.

Despite the seriousness of what they were about to do, Isobel's love of plants took over and she found herself wondering at this beautiful garden. There were many herbs, lavender both French and English, rosemary and thyme and so plenty of bees buzzing from flower to flower.

Grace led the way to a central paved area where a table and four chairs were.

Isobel said, "I love your garden."

Grace smiled. "My haven."

Isobel looked to the right towards the Banks property and saw that there was a wall between four and five feet high separating the properties. She looked at Malcolm questioningly and he discreetly shook his head in dismissal – no problem, Isobel assumed. They seated themselves at the table and chit-chatted, laying the groundwork.

After about ten minutes Malcolm asked, "Grace, could I have a bowl of water for Bella, please?"

"Oh, Malcolm, I'm so sorry, you must think me a terrible hostess – and when you've been so kind as to bring your lovely dog to visit an old lady."

Malcolm smiled. "Of course not, Grace. Unless you're used to dogs you wouldn't know how thirsty they get, especially in this warm weather."

Grace hurried back to the house to comply.

When she emerged, Malcolm took the bowl. "I'm just going to move Bella over here and give her some room. She's not always the daintiest drinker."

He took the lead off Bella and carried the bowl of water towards the right-hand boundary, the dog trotting beside him. Malcolm crouched down and fussed with the bowl and Bella. Isobel knew he must be talking quietly to his dog because the next moment Bella ran, leapt up and scrambled over the wall into the next garden.

It all happened so fast that Isobel didn't have to act surprised – she was.

"Oh Grace, I'm so sorry about that!" Malcolm said. "I shouldn't have let her off the lead. She's usually so good and I wanted to give her a bit of freedom. Never for a moment did I think she would do that."

Grace, following his cue, said, "It's all right, Malcolm, you couldn't have known."

"Who are your neighbours? Will they be annoyed? I can go and ask to go in and get Bella and apologise for her escaping."

"Oh, the Banks live next door. But there'll be no one there. Thomas will be at work and Tommy at school. I'm sure they won't mind you fetching her. Can you not just nip over the wall?"

"Of course. And I'll check the whole lawn and make sure that Bella hasn't done her business there, especially if there's a child who might play in the garden. I always have poo bags in my pocket." Malcolm pulled a bag out of his pocket like a rabbit out of a hat.

He brought one of the garden chairs over to the wall and stood on it. It was no problem for him to get over the barricade and Isobel then took his place on the chair so that she could watch everything unfolding on the other side.

Bella sat waiting, not too far from the wall.

Malcolm crouched down and spoke into Bella's ear.

She listened, alert, and then she got up and started moving around the garden with him at her side.

The Banks garden consisted mostly of grass. In the middle there was one featured area. It was a cherry blossom tree, although the blooms were gone. Under that was a bench and in front of that a small flower bed with an assortment of flowering plants in shades of pink and blue. Malcolm and Bella were making quick progress up and down the garden. He kept his plastic bag out as if he were checking for dog poo.

From her vantage point Isobel took a quick look around to see if any windows were overlooking them. Most of the abutting gardens had trees for privacy. While the Banks' garden didn't, the other houses' trees meant Malcolm and Bella were probably unobserved.

Suddenly Isobel heard Bella whining. She was lying down under the garden seat. Isobel locked eyes with Malcolm and he gave a barely discernible nod. Did he mean yes, there was a body there? Her mind went blank. It was one thing thinking something, another thing when it might be proved.

Malcolm reached into his pocket, rewarded Bella with a treat and then led her towards the wall again. Giving her some room to run, he let her go and tapped the wall which she duly clambered over. Malcolm followed.

Isobel went to speak but Malcolm frowned at her, demanding silence.

To maintain the charade, he said ruefully to Grace, "I think we'd better go inside where I can keep a closer eye on Bella."

Grace laughed and agreed. Malcolm collected the tray, asking Isobel to bring the bowl, and they trooped inside.

Isobel sat at the kitchen table, her eyes locked on Malcolm. He knelt and made a fuss of Bella, telling her how wonderful she was. Grace busied herself making fresh tea and coffee.

It was Grace who spoke first. "You found something, didn't you?"

Malcolm looked at her and enquired gently, "I thought you said it was best for you not to know?"

"I know, I know but . . ." She lapsed into silence.

"Maybe I could just ask a few questions, gardening ones?" Malcolm said.

Grace nodded and he continued.

"Did Thomas do anything with the garden in the last few months?"

Grace paled but nodded. She took a minute to compose herself then, almost forcing herself to face it, she said, "Their garden used to be just lawn. Around February time, just after Valentine's Day – I thought it was romantic – he put in that cherry blossom tree. He had trouble deciding on where to put it. He dug a couple of holes ..." Her voice trailed off.

The silence was deafening. Isobel reached out and took Grace's hand, squeezing it gently.

"In the fine weather he sits there, most evenings in fact." Grace fell silent again.

Malcolm waited a moment and then gently asked, "Did Tommy ever have a cat or dog – a pet?"

"No, never. Thomas doesn't like animals."

Malcolm spoke gently. "Grace, obviously you're a clever woman. You've guessed what we've been doing."

"I might know but perhaps my first instinct was right – if you don't tell me then I can still claim innocence."

212

"Are you afraid of Thomas?" Isobel asked.

"Yes, I'm afraid of him. I never warmed to him but now, guessing what you're doing, I'm afraid. I'm not a good liar so the less I know the more convincing I can be."

Malcolm nodded. "I want you to promise me that you will stay away from Thomas."

"That's no problem. I never bump into him and he only came over that one time I told you about, Isobel, to tell me about Anne's alcoholism."

Isobel glanced at Malcolm. "If he calls again don't let him in. Tell him you have a cold. Keep a hanky on the hall table so that you can use it against your face if you have to talk to him. Do you have a chain on your door?"

"Yes, I have."

"Better you don't open the door at all," Malcolm said. "Just call out."

Grace nodded.

"You have my number," Isobel said. "Call me if you need me – or even if you're worried or fearful."

"Thank you, Isobel."

"By tomorrow things will be clearer. You stick to your story about not knowing anything. Today two friends called, one who had a dog. He does pet therapy, where they bring dogs to cheer people up and lower their blood pressure. Unfortunately, while in the garden, the dog escaped, and the owner had to go and get it. They assured you that they cleaned up. It's as simple as that. Plead ignorance of anything else, which is true – you don't know anything else."

"Tomorrow is an important day?"

"Yes, tomorrow is the day the divorce papers are due to be signed. If anything is going to happen, it is most likely to be after that."

Grace straightened her shoulders. "I'll keep my eyes open and my wits about me."

"Good," Malcolm said. "I'm sure you will."

"Thank you, Grace," said Isobel. "I'm sorry if I've caused you worry and upset."

Grace smiled at her. "I'm tougher than I look."

They hugged and Malcolm and Isobel left.

On the walk back to Malcolm's car they said nothing, not wanting anyone to overhear them. Malcolm stowed Bella in the back of his car behind the grill and he and Isobel sat into the front.

"Bella found something, didn't she?"

Malcolm said, "Yes, she did. There's obviously the possibility of an error but, to be honest, Bella has never been wrong."

"Is it likely to be a cat or dog?"

"It could be but, given Thomas's violence and the fact that Anne was leaving on the 19th of February, plus the holes dug for the new tree, two of them, it all seems to add up. And Grace says they had no animals."

"Oh God. This is real."

"Yes, I'm afraid so."

"What do we do now?"

"Now we make sure we catch this man and prove it. I want to come to the next meeting."

"That will probably be this evening. Simon is going to contact us today with the time."

Malcolm nodded. "You let me know then."

Isobel took his number.

He glanced at his watch. "I need to go."

"Of course."

Isobel got out of the car, waved Malcolm off and

walked slowly to the Tube. She felt bereft as the tragedy of Anne Banks' life got to her. She had nearly got away but sometime over that weekend it seemed she had met her end and then the charade of the drinking and rehab got peddled to cover it up.

Isobel caught the Tube to meet Patricia. She was dreading telling her what they'd discovered. But it was clear that it was time to find out more about Thomas Banks.

Chapter 27

Isobel was early for her midday rendezvous with Patricia and texted her to meet her in the café at the Tube station.

When Patricia sat down opposite her with her coffee, she said, "God, you look serious."

"I am."

"What's happened? Has this got to do with what you were doing this morning?"

Isobel nodded. "I got a retired police officer who has a cadaver dog to check Thomas Banks' garden this morning."

Patricia opened and closed her mouth but said nothing.

"And, the dog reacted to an area that Thomas Banks had dug holes in around late February. The neighbour said the Banks never had a cat or dog."

Patricia went pale.

"So it looks very likely that Anne is buried there." Isobel exhaled noisily.

Patricia put her head in her hands. "Have you told Simon?"

"No. You're the first person I've told. Simon's probably going to be annoyed but I just had to know what we were dealing with."

Patricia nodded. "What do we do now?"

"I don't think this is going to make any difference to how Simon goes about the next bit. What we did is not a legal search, so he'll probably have to pick Thomas up with regard to fraud and then apply for a search warrant as he was saying last night. At least that's what I think he'll do. What other grounds would he have for a search? And he is so careful."

"Should we just go ahead with checking on Thomas and then tell him when we see him later?"

"That's what I'm thinking. Maybe we can find out something more today that will strengthen the case and make it easier for him to arrest Thomas. What do you think?"

"That makes sense. He did hint that getting a search warrant might be tricky and we don't want to wreck his case." Patricia shook her head. "God, everyone is very upscuttled."

Isobel inclined her head. "What do you mean?"

"I've had Peter on the phone to me a few times this morning from work. I know that he initiated this whole investigation and got you involved but I don't think he thought for a minute we were going to end up dealing with all that we are. When he hears this about the dog and a body he's going to be worse." Patricia lapsed into silence, frowning.

"What did he say this morning?"

"He was saying that at the worst he had queried coercion and he thought your initial input would either support his concern or say it was groundless. He thought he might have to persuade Anne to admit it but that's it. He certainly didn't think it would get this sinister. He's been wrestling with his conscience about who he's contracted to work for. Legally, where does he stand? And he is really agonising over what he needs to do. He says he has never come across a case like this – you know, who is his client? I didn't know what to tell him so in the end I told him to ring Yvonne and chat it through with her. He thought that was a good idea."

Isobel smiled. "He's lucky to have you."

Patricia wrinkled her nose at her. "He rang me about an hour later to say that he'd had a great chat with Yvonne. They talked through everything. As far as I can gather, the papers he received, the woman whose birth certificate and marriage certificate he was given for the divorce, that woman is legally his client. That is Claire's sister, Tommy's mother. This doppelganger, even if she was the only person he has met, is, they agreed, not his client. This imposter is trying to defraud Anne Banks, so catching her is representing his true client. The fake Anne is committing a crime and hoping to use him to do it. In fact, now it seems she's covering up a more dark and sinister crime of murder. Anyway, he felt better after talking it through with another solicitor and Yvonne suggested that he might need to talk to the senior partner in the firm and let him know what's happening. He isn't going to do that yet until he knows what Simon is planning."

"That makes sense. So, shall we go ahead with our research to see what we can find out about Thomas Banks?"

Patricia lifted her handbag. "I'm on for that."

Chapter 28

Thomas Banks Senior, the train driver, lived only a few streets away from the station. Isobel and Patricia bought a half bottle of whiskey, a box of chocolates and some biscuits for their visit.

Isobel wasn't sure how they were going to do this. It might be a wild goose chase and this man might have nothing to do with the Thomas Banks they knew. In addition, getting someone talking was one thing but getting them talking about one of the biggest tragedies of their life was hard, not to mention morally challenging, and Isobel's conscience was troubling her.

The address was Number 21 Dame Street. It was a terraced house with a small garden in front. The garden had neat rows of purple, yellow and blue flowers along the path to the front door. Their tiny petalled faces turned towards the sun. Planters at each side of the door and on the windowsills had a profusion of violas and pansies with the same colour palette, their brightness a contrast with the grey walls of the house. Despite all that was going on Isobel could feel the beauty of the flowers comforting her and lifting her spirit.

The door knocker was a brass lion's head which Isobel rapped with medium force. Immediately they heard a voice shouting, "*Coming!*" and they waited. They could hear the intermittent sound of something being put down and so they weren't surprised to find the door opened by a man with a Zimmer frame.

He would have been a tall man in his day but now was hunched over the frame, leaning heavily on it. He was thin and had a bald head with a beard. He seemed weary, as if he'd had enough but this had not turned him bitter and impatient, more resigned, as if life had not lived up to his expectations. Despite this he retained an air of valiant gentlemanliness.

On seeing Isobel and Patricia with gifts in their arms he smiled and said with some warmth, "I'm not interested in religion."

Isobel burst out laughing. "Fair enough," she said. "I don't talk about football. So, now that we've both said what we won't discuss, can we still visit?"

"Of course, of course, I'm glad of the company. With my hip so bad I don't get out much." He waved them in, then led the way down the hall to the sitting room at the back of the house.

The room was pleasantly decorated but old-fashioned. It looked tidy but not well cared for and Isobel wondered if this man's wife was dead. She offered to make tea. Thomas Senior was appreciative and shouted in the location of everything to her. The kitchen was also tidy but a quick look revealed no personal information. Isobel assembled tea for three on a tray and carried it into the sitting room. While she worked she could hear the soft murmur of voices and knew that Patricia was chatting away to Thomas Senior. Having dispensed tea to everyone Isobel tuned into the conversation.

Patricia it seemed had been doing Trojan work establishing a rapport. Mr Banks was talking about his wife, now deceased.

"Do you have a husband?" he asked Patricia.

"No."

"But you have someone you like?"

Patricia blushed.

He smiled. "I hope you'll be as happy as my wife and I were."

"Did you have children?"

"One son but he died. His picture is on the dresser. He was a great lad, knocked down and killed by a drunk driver who fled the scene."

"May I?" Patricia asked, standing up and moving gently towards the dresser. She lifted a photo frame. She looked at it and passed it to Isobel. The picture was of a young dark-haired boy with brown eyes but where the Thomas Banks they knew had a hard face with cold eyes, this young man was smiling and open and friendly.

"He looks like a lovely lad," Patricia said. "I'm so sorry."

Thomas inclined his head in acknowledgement. "He was the apple of our eyes. It hit us real hard. The witnesses said the car just ploughed into him, so we assume drink or drugs. The driver fled the scene. A hit-and-run. The car was stolen and was found burnt out, so no forensics. The police tried but there was just nothing to go on. My wife, it broke her heart. Young Thomas died ten years ago and my wife two years later."

Isobel could feel her eyes welling up. "I'm sorry if we're awaking painful memories, Thomas."

He smiled at her. "No, talking about him helps, it's just all the thinking I do that gets me down. Crazy as it is, I keep hoping that somehow someone will confess to the accident – then I can go in peace."

Isobel reached out and touched Thomas's hand. He squeezed it and, laying his other hand over hers, patted it. She glanced at Patricia, wishing that they'd not troubled this elderly gentleman. However, having gone this far it would render it all vain if they backed away from their task. She nodded at Patricia and she nodded back. They both straightened imperceptibly, knowing now was the moment.

Isobel said, "We called to see you, Mr Banks, because we were looking for this man's father. As she spoke, on her phone she pulled up the photo of Thomas and Anne.

Thomas took it and looked in concentration, pursing his lips.

"This looks like Matt Cooper. He lived near us and was a sort of friend of Thomas's but not as bright or as popular. He even went to the same college and worked initially in the same company. I haven't seen him in years. His family sold up here shortly after Thomas died."

Thomas continued to regard the photo, lost in his reminiscence while Isobel and Patricia gazed at each other.

Isobel said, "So the man I'm showing you is not Thomas Banks but Matt Cooper?"

"Yes, Thomas's friend Matt. I probably have some old photos of them together. Would you like to see them?"

Isobel smiled and nodded emphatically. "Oh yes, we certainly would."

"It'll take me a while to find them. They should be in that cabinet. I haven't looked at them in ages," Thomas said, struggling to stand.

Patricia gently moved across. "If you don't mind me doing it, I'll find them for you."

Thomas looked relieved. "Go ahead." He settled back into his chair.

Patricia smiled. "Just tell me what I'm looking for."

Isobel rose. "I'll make more tea – this is thirsty work."

In the kitchen Isobel's mind was exploding with questions. Had Thomas Banks stolen his friend's identity? And, if so, why? Could he have run his friend down? Or was that a step too far? Maybe he just capitalised on a situation? Alongside the mental activity, Isobel boiled the kettle and arranged the tray.

By the time she returned to the sitting room with the replenished tea tray, Patricia was on the floor with a myriad of loose photos laid out around her and Thomas had a photo album open on his lap, turning the pages slowly.

"How are we doing?" Isobel asked.

Thomas answered first, adjusting the album in his lap so Isobel could see. "This is my Thomas at ten with Matt Cooper. My wife didn't like the lad, she thought him sneaky, but Thomas always insisted he be included with his other friends."

He flipped forward to near the end of the album.

"Here are the boys at sixteen," and he pointed out Thomas and Matt from a group photo of the same friends. "After that the only photos are from graduation and family Christmases. Those photos you have, Patricia, are Thomas's. He had them in his flat. Betty never got around to sorting them out and putting them in an album – her heart wasn't in it."

Patricia lifted a photo from one of the piles and passed it to Thomas.

He looked at it and said, "That's at university – there's Matt and there's Thomas."

Isobel reached for it and saw younger versions of the two men. The man she knew as Thomas Banks, Thomas clearly identified as Matt Cooper.

"Could we take some of these pictures? I promise we'll get them back to you."

Thomas nodded. "Something is bothering you?"

"Yes," Patricia said. "We're trying to find out about the man we showed you who we know as Thomas Banks. Coming here was a long shot really."

"You mean Matt. But why would Matt be using Thomas's name?"

"We don't know."

"Do you think this has anything to do with Thomas's death?"

Isobel could feel the yearning in him for answers and for justice for his son. She dreaded raising his hopes. Gently she replied, "Probably not, Thomas."

He returned her gaze. "You don't want me to be disappointed."

"No, I don't. More than likely this has nothing to do with your son's death." She sensed his deflation and in a way was glad of it. "If there is anything that pertains to it we will pursue it, I promise you that."

Patricia said, "Me too."

His eyes filled with tears. "Thank you, ladies." He reached out for both of their hands and squeezed. "I've enjoyed showing you Thomas, thank you."

Patricia started to gather the photos.

"Don't put them away," he said. "I want to look at them some more."

Patricia collected the box and the different piles and laid them on the coffee table in easy reach of Thomas. "Which school did they all go to?"

"St Colman's, the local school."

"Where did Matt live?"

"Two streets away – Sycamore Street – I'm not sure of the number." He stared off into the distance and then said, "For a while, Matt dated Ellen Murphy, until she moved to Scotland. Her mother lives here on Dame Street just down from me in number forty-seven. She might know more about Matt."

Patricia added her name to the list.

They each gave Thomas a warm hug and assured him they would visit in a few days.

As they walked down the path, Isobel muttered to Patricia, "I'm going to beg Simon to pull out the old file on that hit-and-run."

"Definitely," said Patricia.

They walked a few more steps in silence then Patricia stopped and waited for Isobel to do the same.

"What's going on, Isobel?"

Isobel shook her head. "I think you were right about Thomas Banks and identity theft."

"How bad do you think this is, or is going to get?"

Isobel's mind was running wild with suppositions and dark imaginings. "Honestly, Patricia?" She received a tentative nod in return. "Honestly, I think it's going to get very bad."

Hearing it seemed to steady Patricia. "You think there are more victims of Thomas Banks?"

"Yes. But now we need to go and see if we can generate enough credible leads to get the police to investigate."

"Yes," said Patricia. "The game is on." She grinned at her own Sherlock Holmes reference and they set off walking again. "Let's find Mrs Murphy and see what she can tell us."

There was a text from Simon saying he was liaising with the fraud squad and it would be later today before they could meet to discuss the plan for Wednesday.

Be careful, he added.

Chapter 29

Mrs Murphy's house was not unlike that of Thomas Banks Senior from the outside. They rang the doorbell and soon heard a shout, "*I'm coming!*"

Mrs Murphy had a heavily lined face topped by salt-and-pepper hair. She was a sprightly woman who looked as if she'd had a hard life but had borne it well and was fit for her years despite, or maybe because of, all the hard work.

"Yes?" she said. No anxiety, no over-pleasantness, just straight.

This, Isobel thought is a woman whose currency is the truth and who doesn't deal with anything less. "Mrs Murphy, we're here because a young woman we know may be in trouble and we hoped that you could give us some help – information really."

Mrs Murphy remained interested, assessing even, but said nothing.

"This young woman has got involved with a man who we believe may be Matt Cooper." Isobel noticed a minute tightening in the women's jaw.

Isobel brought up on her phone the photograph of Anne and Thomas Banks at the dance and extended it to

Mrs Murphy. She didn't reach for it immediately but continued to regard Isobel. Then, visibly steeling herself, she reached for the picture. Her gaze was long and steady then she looked up and her eyes had a modicum of dread in them.

"We fear for her safety. Please help us."

"How can I help you? What can I do to make her safe?"

Isobel was sure that internally there was a further part to that sentence – about someone else who she couldn't keep safe.

"We need information. We have a policeman who knows some of the case and is interested in helping us. We thought there may be old stories from the past that would substantiate what we're saying."

Mrs Murphy folded her arms. "I'm not giving you any information."

Isobel returned her gaze, then deciding she had nothing to lose said, "We don't need to know anyone's whereabouts. All we need are stories of things that have happened that show a pattern of violence."

Mrs Murphy uncrossed her arms and wrapped them around her body. After a moment she said, "I have those all right."

Isobel exchanged a glance with Patricia who said, "Please tell us so that we can do something about this man."

Mrs Murphy nodded and they followed her into the house and through to the kitchen. Isobel and Patricia sat while Mrs Murphy boiled the kettle and produced a pot of tea and some biscuits. Isobel left her to her tasks of hospitality. She obviously needed the comfort of it and was deep in thought.

When Mrs Murphy was seated, Patricia produced the

other photograph of Matt, Thomas and the boys. "Mrs Murphy –"

"Breda, please, call me Breda."

"Breda, just so that we're sure, can you point out Thomas Banks and Matt Cooper in this photo, please?"

Breda identified Thomas Banks, as they knew him, as Matt Cooper. Isobel then produced the photo from the formal occasion and nodded at Breda.

"That's Matt Cooper." Her voice was strong and clear. "Is this the woman who's in trouble?"

Patricia said, "Yes, his wife."

Breda paled.

Isobel leaned forward. "Tell us about him."

"He wanted to marry my daughter. God, I thought she would never get away. That's why she lives in Scotland now, far away and safe. For years I didn't even see her." It was like a dam had burst.

Isobel realised that now all the stress, all the secrecy, would come tumbling out.

"Tell us from the beginning."

"Matt dated my daughter Ellen when they were in their last year at school and for a year when they were in college." Standing up suddenly, she went out and returned with a photograph of a girl in school uniform, aged about seventeen.

Isobel smiled. "She's beautiful, she could be a model." She handed the photo to Patricia who nodded her agreement.

"Needless to say, Ellen was popular. I would have liked her to date Thomas Banks. He was always a lovely lad, like his dad, but my Ellen, she liked bad guys. She seemed enthralled with Matt and the more I objected, or criticised him, which I did, the more she stood up for him. At the start she was going out, staying later than the time I had set, the usual thing. Then I started to notice a change in her. She became quiet, she didn't want to see her friends, she didn't laugh or have fun. All she seemed to want to do was sit in or see Matt. She lost weight. I actually thought she was on drugs. I was beside myself. One day I tackled her." Breda looked up with tears in her eyes and pulled a tissue out of her sleeve. "Well, really, I just broke down and cried and asked her what had happened to her. I almost didn't hear her answer. 'I'm in hell,' she said – and the look in her eyes! I hugged her and she cried and cried. It took hours before she could even explain to me what was happening to her."

Breda paused and topped up all their cups though they had barely touched the tea.

"Ellen said that at first it was fine with Matt. She was mad about him. Then he started to get possessive and if she spoke to anyone else or spent time with them he had a fight with her about it. She stopped spending time with other people. Then, he told her she was fat and losing her looks and she started dieting and got so thin. Ellen said that he even kept her late getting home and said that I was impossible. Now I can see that he was manipulating her."

Isobel and Patricia exchanged meaningful looks.

"They'd got engaged when he went to college. He wasn't as bright as Thomas, but he managed to get in and do a similar course in accounting or banking or something to do with money. After they got engaged Ellen said it got worse. He started to hit her, always where I couldn't see it. The night we talked he had put his hands around her throat and squeezed until she almost passed out. My daughter was crying because she knew he was going to kill her."

The tears were pouring unchecked down Breda's face. She barely knew they were there – she was reliving a nightmare. Isobel and Patricia exchanged looks and Isobel moved her chair beside Breda and touched her back in comfort and support.

Taking a breath, Breda continued. "We talked about Ellen getting away. We knew it needed to be far and we knew it needed to be that night. We were also sure that he would come at me and expect me to give away where Ellen was so we agreed that I couldn't know. She packed a bag, left a note for me and one for Matt. I drove her to the bus station. She promised to get word to me and let me know that she was OK. She's happy now, with a good husband and two small kids. I'm not going to tell you where she is. He can never know."

"Of course not," Isobel said.

"Ellen got away because she knew if she didn't he would kill her. He's clever though. He believed I didn't know where she was. Like all psychos he knew the truth when he met it."

"He moved away from the area – when was that?" Patricia asked.

"It wasn't long after Thomas Banks got knocked down. Matt's mother decided to move to Scotland. You can imagine I nearly fainted when I heard that. I thought he might be going too. They sold the house and I haven't seen him since."

"Where in Scotland did his mother go?" Patricia asked.

"None of us knew. She just decided to have a new start up there. Matt took care of the sale of the house for her."

"Where did they live?"

"Two streets away. Sycamore Street, Number 42. A young couple bought it. They're very nice."

Isobel said, "Breda, we're going to tell our policeman about what happened to your daughter –"

Breda jerked back in her seat.

"Just to substantiate what we suspect. He probably won't even need to talk to you but all you have to do is tell him what you told us. You don't have to say where Ellen is."

Breda settled in her seat and nodded in comprehension.

"Thank you," said Isobel.

"I hope you get him."

"We're going to give it our best shot."

Leaving Breda's house, Patricia got out her phone and found directions for 42 Sycamore Street.

Chapter 30

Number 42 had been painted in the pale-grey colour so beloved of modern decorators. Isobel and Patricia opened the gate and walked up the short path to the front door, each side bordered with lavender. As Isobel passed, she rubbed one of the flower-heads and sniffed the soothing perfume from her fingers.

The front door was painted a glossy red and had shiny brass fittings. Isobel rapped the knocker. It was now three o'clock, still working hours, so she wasn't hopeful about finding anyone home. They were turning to leave when they heard the door opening.

In the half-open door stood a woman, very pale with the mussed hair of someone who had been asleep. She was also noticeably pregnant.

"Hello."

Isobel smiled warmly. "Hi, we were making enquiries about the people who used to live in the house before you, a Mrs Cooper and her son Matt?"

"Are you police? Is there a problem?"

Immediately Isobel could see the anxiety snaking up in the woman.

She smiled warmly. "Not at all. My name is Isobel, this is Patricia."

Patricia said, "We're trying to find him, Matt Cooper, who used to live here. We thought that during the sale of the house you might have heard something that would help us find him."

Both of the women smiled warmly and reassuringly.

The woman didn't respond.

Isobel said, "Perhaps we could speak to your husband just to clarify if he knows anything?"

"He's at work."

"Of course, and we're sorry we disturbed you."

"My husband will be home at six o'clock tonight. If you call back then you can talk to him."

They smiled and said they might call later.

They walked back along the street.

"Do you think it's worth coming back here?" Patricia asked.

"Probably, but for now let's go to the school. We might be able to talk to some of the teachers who knew Matt."

Patricia googled the directions for the school. It wasn't far and they set off at a fast pace to get there before everyone had left.

By the time they had reached the school gate teenagers filled the yard. They made a beeline for the main entrance and, stopping a conservative-looking teenager, asked the way to the headmistress's office which was in fact nearby.

An old retainer secretary sat on guard in the front office. She appraised them unsmilingly, clearly a sentry that they needed to get past.

Isobel squared her shoulders. "Hello, my name is Isobel McKenzie and this is –" she hesitated – what was

Patricia's second name? She couldn't remember. What a time for her chemo brain to kick in!

"And I'm Patricia King from the legal firm of Johnson, Collins and O'Brien. We would like to speak to the headmistress." Patricia spoke confidently, with authority, and stood tall.

"Have you an appointment? What is it in relation to?" the sentry said but her voice betrayed a waver of uncertainty.

Isobel smiled to herself. Patricia had won, she was sure. This stand-off was all over bar the shouting.

Patricia used a condescending tone. "You know we have no appointment. You must also know that I'm not at liberty to discuss legal matters with you, only with the headmistress. Please let her know that we're here."

The sentry rose and opened the door to her left. She entered, shutting the door.

When she emerged, she said, "Mrs Wood will see you now."

"Thank you." Patricia inclined her head regally.

Mrs Wood's office was bright with windows that overlooked the playing fields at the back. The woman who rose from her chair to meet them had dark hair cut in a bob. She looked to be around sixty, so her hair owed something to a bottle. Her eyes were brown and intense. She looked like she didn't miss much and had heard it all before anyway. Her manner was warm, welcoming almost. Isobel guessed that she came into teaching because she liked children and despite the time she'd served she still did.

"Erica Wood," she volunteered, extending her hand.

Isobel and Patricia shook hands and introduced themselves.

"I believe you're from a legal firm, ladies. What seems

to be the problem?" Her voice betrayed no anxiety, just interest. This was a woman who did not panic or imagine difficulties where none existed.

Patricia took the lead. "We're working on a legal case and we're looking for background information on an old student of yours. Have you been headmistress here for long?"

"Five years, but I've taught here for considerably longer."

Patricia smiled and gestured to Isobel to produce the photograph of the boys and she handed it to Erica Woods.

Isobel paid close attention but she didn't see any fear or tension on the headmistress's face. What she discerned was a deep sadness. There was a profound silence. Patricia and Isobel were loath to break it and waited patiently.

Eventually Erica Woods tore her gaze away from the picture. When she looked up there was a shine of tears in her eyes.

"Thomas is dead this long time, more's the pity, so it's not him you're enquiring after."

Patricia stood up and gestured towards the photo which Mrs Woods extended. Pointing to Matt, Patricia asked, "Can you tell me this boy's name?"

"That's Matt Cooper."

Patricia nodded at Isobel and she produced the picture of Thomas and Anne.

"Who is this man?" Isobel asked.

Erica took it and studied it a moment. "That looks like Matt Cooper only older. Is that his wife?"

"Yes," Patricia said. "She's our client."

"I see." Erica stood and walked to the window. Without turning, she asked, "Is she in trouble?"

"Yes." Patricia said. "How much we're not, as yet, sure."

Erica swung round. "Danger?"

"We believe so."

"What do you want from me?"

Patricia inclined her head. "The man you identified as Matt Cooper is calling himself Thomas Banks now and has been for nearly ten years."

Erica gasped. "What?"

"Anne Banks came to our firm to get a divorce. We were concerned and have been investigating covertly to determine what's going on. Our enquiries have led us to some facts that show Thomas Banks as we know him, Matt Cooper as you have identified him, to be a violent man. As yet the depth of his violence is unclear, but we are very concerned. Knowing that this level of abuse and violence usually follows a pattern of escalation, we wondered if there were any events in his school years that would add weight to our understanding of the case."

"You suspect a lot but have no proof."

"Yes," Patricia agreed. "We may need to produce evidence for a warrant, and we thought there may be things that you could tell us that would help."

"You know about confidentiality?" Erica asked.

"Yes."

"But?"

Patricia looked at her and frowned.

"But, her life may be in danger so I should help," Erica finished.

"She may already be dead and a nine-year-old boy's future is in the balance," Patricia said. "We need to help and protect this boy from his father."

Erica started and again turned to look out the window. She raised her hands to her face, withdrawing into her own world.

Isobel knew here was a woman tormented by something. Time had not faded or healed this and she needed to talk, to unburden herself, to confess. By doing this there might be some relief for her.

Isobel turned to Patricia. She gave her a thumbs-up and then put a finger on her lips. Patricia nodded back in understanding and agreement. They waited.

Eventually Erica turned slowly from the window. "Some years ago and against my better judgment, I was prevailed upon to be generous in my interpretation of a situation. I've worked nearly forty years and in the main know I've done my best for all concerned and sleep easily at night. But this one episode weighs on my conscience. For myself, for my peace of mind, to maybe right something I regret, I will tell you. You can judge my part and the consequences it has had."

For a moment she looked old and troubled then she shook herself, took her seat and began to talk.

"This all happened nearly fifteen years ago. I was a Maths teacher before I became a principal and an administrator. Matt and Thomas were in my classes all the way through school. Thomas was a wonderful child, one of those children who you know will go far," her voice caught at this, "could go far. He was very bright – not only that, he was one of those kids who everyone liked. Matt was a different kettle of fish altogether. To be honest, I never liked him." Here, she looked up at them. "I found him to be a sneaky child, crafty, and he would act and look so innocent. I often wondered if he and Thomas were friends because they lived near each other or if Thomas felt sorry for him. For A levels they were doing the same subjects, including Maths. It was a surprise to me when Thomas said that he was going into finance. The plan was that he and Matt were going to go to college together. I always thought that Thomas would have ended up going out with Ellen Murphy. They always seemed close but, no, it was Matt she started dating. It seemed to me that Matt had to win there to prove he was better than Thomas. Thomas didn't seem to mind – in fact, he seemed to be oblivious to Matt's faults. Academically, though, it was going to be hard for Matt to beat Thomas and he didn't. The night the results came out Thomas had done brilliantly, and Matt had done well enough. The next morning Thomas's dog was found hanging at the school gates. It had been tortured. God, Thomas was devastated. He just shrank into himself. Naturally, we called the police and they came and talked to everyone but nobody had seen anything."

Isobel said, "But . . ."

"But in my heart I knew that it was Matt. It was Thomas's punishment for doing so well, for doing so much better than him."

"But, you couldn't be sure that Matt did it," Patricia said. "You may have suspected, you may even have been right, but you couldn't be sure."

Erica smiled sadly. "Exactly. I couldn't be sure, but I suspected Matt and he knew it. He knew from the way I looked at him and he used to grin back at me. It was as if he was taunting me that he'd got away with it. After a few weeks it all died down. The lads were getting ready to go off to college and we were going back to school. I was in on the day before class started, tidying my room and getting lesson plans and books organised. Matt arrived, to thank me for all that I'd done for him, he said. He'd got me a little present. When I wouldn't open it in his presence he unwrapped it, because he wanted me to see it. It was a little ceramic dog that looked very like Thomas's dog. I gasped when I saw it. He smiled and said, 'So you don't forget, Mrs Wood, so you don't forget'. I was terrified even though I tried not to show it. When I looked up, he looked me in the eye and said, 'It doesn't matter what's true, only what you can prove.' And he grinned and then he left. To be honest, I had to go home I was so shaken. Many of the kids here have behavioural problems, even go on to commit crimes of theft and drug-dealing, but I've never encountered someone who frightened me as much as that." She shivered. "The next day I went to the principal and told her what had happened. She told me the boys were gone from the school, the incident was over and there was nothing more we could do. That was true but it felt as if we shirked our duty. All along Matt had done malicious things but we could never prove it so he got away with it. I couldn't sleep I was so concerned. After a week I went to the police station and spoke to one of the officers who'd come to the school to investigate. They said there was nothing they could do as there was no evidence. In the end I had counselling for a year and I also went on some extra courses on dealing with difficult children. All of which helped me in my career but I always felt that, because I wasn't on the ball enough, Matt got away scot-free and learned that so long as no one could prove you were guilty you were innocent."

The silence was deafening.

After a minute Isobel said, "We suspect that he's still living by that lesson and we're desperately looking for proof."

"I'm sorry, I don't think there's anything else I can do to help you. But let me say that I believe you're right and encourage you to do what I couldn't – find proof."

Patricia said, "We're doing everything we can."

There was little more left for anyone to say so they bid her goodbye.

Isobel and Patricia were slightly shellshocked as they walked through the now empty schoolyard and out onto the road.

Isobel took another few steps, and then stopped.

"There's the local shop which the kids probably use to get lunch. Let's get a sandwich and have a sit-down."

Patricia nodded. They were both pensive as they collected sandwiches and coffee and neither spoke until they were seated at the high counter in the shop.

Isobel said, "So it's likely that Anne is dead and buried in their garden."

"Yes."

"And . . ."

"There's more?" Patricia queried.

"Well then, today we hear that at school Thomas, as we know him, was killing animals."

"Allegedly."

"Allegedly, and sometime later he nearly strangled his girlfriend who ran away to stay alive, her mother says."

Patricia nodded.

"And then his mother disappeared to Scotland to a new life and he sold the family home." Isobel raised her eyebrows. "Does it not sound familiar?"

"What do you mean?"

"A very plausible reason why someone is not around."

Patricia shrugged.

"Like Anne."

"What?"

"I think his mother might be buried at number forty-two."

"Jesus," Patricia breathed, then standing up said more loudly, "*Jesus!*" She glared at Isobel then abruptly sat down. "What nightmare have we found our way into?"

Isobel massaged her forehead. "Maybe I'm wrong. Maybe I'm getting carried away."

"You don't think so, do you?"

"There's one easy way to find out."

"How?"

"Get Malcolm to bring Bella and check number forty-two's garden." Isobel frowned. "We really need to find out that couple's name."

Patricia rolled her eyes. "We have a pregnant woman who we found resting at home and we want to see if there's a dead body in her garden. Not conducive to a stress-free pregnancy."

Isobel nodded. "Yes, I think we need to speak to the husband alone just in case this is all pie in the sky. Maybe he could get his wife out of the house while we check the garden. If there's nothing there then she doesn't have to know."

"Oh my God, you're serious."

"Yes, and we're running out of time. We also need to talk to the work colleague you got from Facebook. Could you contact him and see if we can see him later today, maybe at eight o'clock? Hopefully we can have the planning meeting after that."

"Isobel, are you sure about this? Do we need to put these people through this? What if we're wrong?"

Isobel felt her eyes filling up with tears. "I don't want

to do this but I can't just walk away. What if he has done all of these things? I feel the same as I did about Anne, that I have to know for sure. Hopefully there's nothing but I need to be sure."

Patricia looked her in the eye and then nodded.

Isobel stood up and connected to Malcolm, quickly explaining everything to him. In a few minutes they were both back sitting at the counter.

"Malcolm thinks it's worth doing, especially because there's no risk of Thomas knowing. Malcolm can bring Bella for six o'clock-ish. Any luck with the guy from work?"

"Yes, he's working late. I have the address. When we finish here we can go straight there and then on to the meeting."

"Good." Isobel glanced at her watch. It was five o'clock, not long to wait. "Is there any way you can find the name of this couple?"

Patricia grinned. "I'm on it."

Isobel said, thinking out loud, "Maybe if we knew what he looked like we could stop him before he gets home and tell him all this and see what he thinks is best for his wife."

Patricia nodded in agreement.

Chapter 31

It only took Patricia ten minutes to find out that the couple at 42 Sycamore Street were Tim and Sarah Woodward. Another few minutes' work and she had found Facebook pictures of them. Having met Sarah, it was easy to confirm her husband's picture and Patricia saved it on her phone and sent it to Isobel so they would know him when they met him in the street.

By a quarter to six Isobel and Patricia were each stationed a number of doors down from Number 42 at opposite sides and out of the line of sight of the house.

It was just after six when Patricia stopped Tim in the street.

"Mr Woodward, my name is Patricia King. I work for a solicitor's office and I wonder if I could have a few words with you."

Tim Woodward, a brawny six foot with shoulders that would do justice to a rugby player, paused. "You're one of the women who called to my wife earlier. She said you were coming back this evening. I live near here, as you know – we can talk at the house."

Patricia persisted. "Mr Woodward, the subject matter

I need to discuss with you is distressing. I would prefer to discuss it with you and then let you talk to your wife."

Tim Woodward looked mystified and a bit distracted.

Isobel walked up to them. "Mr Woodward, neither you nor your wife have done anything wrong. However, you may be able to help us with a situation – not just us, the police as well."

Tim Woodward seemed to relax somewhat. "My wife is expecting me home. I don't want to worry her. She hasn't been well – high blood pressure with the pregnancy."

Patricia said, "We guessed that when we met her earlier and thought that talking to you first might be the wisest thing. We would like your help, Mr Woodward, but we don't want to stress your wife."

He nodded. "Tim, please. Let me ring her and let her know I'm delayed."

He pulled out his phone and walked away to speak quietly to his wife.

When he came back, he gestured down the street. "We can get a coffee and talk."

The local pub had retained the wood floors and bar of an old establishment, so rare nowadays. Behind the bar was a twenty-something blond woman who smiled a greeting when they came in. They collected coffees and took a table away from the bar.

"What's all this about?"

Isobel said, "We're looking into a case involving a man whose wife has disappeared."

"His mother also disappeared about ten years ago," Patricia said. "She used to live in your house. He sold it."

Isobel took up the baton again. "We don't want him to know yet what we're doing. So we were wondering if –"

"He killed his wife?" Tim cut in.

Isobel made a face. "We don't know that yet but it's a possibility."

"And you think he might have killed his mother too?"

"That's a theory we're exploring."

"So?" He waited for someone to reply.

"So, we were wondering if you would let us bring a cadaver dog into the garden to see if she can find anything."

Tim looked at her steadily.

Isobel continued, "All you have to do is give your permission. It will only take ten minutes."

"And if you find something?"

Isobel blew out air through her lips. "Honestly, Tim, we think this is a bad man and we're struggling to find ways to prove anything. If we found something here I'm not even sure what the next step would be. We would have to see what the police think is the best way to proceed. At the moment we're trying to make sure this guy doesn't know we're on to him."

Tim rubbed his face with his hands, "And my wife? If you find something in the garden, what's that going to do to her at this delicate time? Not to mention that this is our home?"

Isobel and Patricia exchanged a look.

Patricia said, "We know it's a lot to ask. But this man has a nine-year-old son and that's how all of this came to light, trying to find the best thing for him. If we don't get this straightened out he may end up living with a murderer. Maybe you and your wife could help us find the best outcome for this young boy."

"And justice for two women maybe," Isobel added.

Tim ran his fingers through his hair. "When?"

The women looked at each other and shifted in their seats.

"Now."

Tim raised his eyebrows. "You've already organised the dog?"

Isobel winced. "There's so little time. Tomorrow morning is the crucial day and we're trying to line up as many ducks as we can, so we know what has gone on. We didn't know if you would say yes, we just hoped you would. We've just made sure that it could be done tonight. We were praying that you would want to help." As she finished speaking her voice shook and she bowed her head.

Without a moment's hesitation, Tim reached out and stroked her hand. "There, there, love."

Isobel hastily wiped her eyes. "We've been fighting and fighting to get people to look at this case. He might get away with it."

Tim said, "OK, I'm going to ring my wife now and tell her to go round to my sister's. You do the dog thing. If you find something, we'll see what the police say is the best approach for you to take and I'll figure out how best to tell my wife. She's a good woman, she would want to help."

Tim got up to talk to his wife again on the phone.

Isobel called Malcolm and then they headed for 42 Sycamore Street.

When they arrived Sarah was gone, and Isobel wondered what Tim had said to her to persuade her to leave so quickly. She didn't ask. Tim offered more coffee but they declined, too tense now to take anything. They waited quietly in the sitting room. There were photos of Tim and Sarah on the wall and on the bureau. From the posed wedding photo to more relaxed and informal beach shots, they looked happy.

They heard a car stopping outside the gate, a door

banging then steps on the path. The doorbell rang.

Tim went to answer, and they heard Malcolm introducing himself in the hall.

Then the two men came into the living room.

Malcolm greeted Isobel and Patricia and explained that he wanted to be alone to do the sweep of the garden. He then went back to the car to get Bella while Tim went to open the back door for them.

Isobel and Patricia heard Malcom and Bella make their way down the hall to the kitchen and out into the garden. Then they joined Tim in the kitchen and lined up at the kitchen window to watch.

In a way there was very little to see. Malcolm and Bella walked up and down the garden. At one point Bella lay down and whined. Malcolm placed something from his pocket on the ground at that point and then continued on checking the remainder of the area. He didn't mark anywhere else. Having completed walking over all of the garden he petted Bella and talked to her, then called to the others that he wanted to bring Bella through and would they wait in the living room.

In a few minutes Malcolm returned.

"Well?" Tim asked. "You found something?"

"Yes, Bella has signed that there may be a cadaver in the place I marked but it isn't certain. I want to talk to the other police involved in the case. We're meeting later tonight. I can ring you then and let you know what's going to happen. To be honest, we probably don't have enough information for a warrant. We may be right but no judge is likely to sign off on this – they call them fishing expeditions – which is a shame because digging here wouldn't alert Thomas to what we're doing. If we found something here it would really help with the case against him."

"Can I do anything to help?" Tim said. "What if I dug there?"

"But why would you decide to dig there?" Malcolm said. "It would be suspicious."

Isobel made a face. "You could be digging a pond."

Tim nodded. "Yes, what if I was digging a pond and found something?"

"Now you want to really get involved?" Patricia asked. "What about Sarah?"

Tim drew himself up. "I'll be telling her everything the minute I see her, now that it seems possible that there is something there. There was no point distressing her over nothing but if there's a chance of it being something we will assist you in any way we can."

Malcolm nodded. "By all means talk to your wife but don't do anything until I've conferred with the police involved."

Tim nodded in acquiescence.

With murmured thanks Malcolm, Patricia and Isobel trooped outside.

"What time is this meeting?" Malcolm asked.

Isobel looked at Patricia. "I've no idea. Has Simon contacted you?"

"No."

"I need to take Bella home," Malcolm said, "so I won't be there until at least nine o'clock."

"We have someone else to talk to before the meeting," Patricia said. "We should be able to meet at ten."

"I'm a bit nervous about telling Simon all that we've done," said Isobel. "Perhaps I should tell him before he sees you."

Malcolm laughed. "You're afraid."

"A bit. Neither Peter the solicitor nor Simon the policeman know what we've been doing today and there could be ructions tonight."

"Well, I think we've found two bodies."

Isobel swallowed noisily. Patricia grasped her hand.

"I was a policeman. As a lay person and with my lay dog we haven't done anything wrong. Simon might be put out at your going off on your own but, to be honest, if he knew what you were planning he would probably have felt he had to stop you. This way you've found things out and he can genuinely say he had no knowledge of the actions you two members of the public took." He grinned and winked at them.

Isobel grinned back. "You're right."

Patricia texted Simon to say they would be at Peter's at ten o'clock. Isobel gave Malcolm the address and they parted company.

Chapter 32

Edward Small worked for one of the big banking giants in the financial district. By the time Isobel and Patricia had got the Tube over it was nearly eight o'clock. When they were close Patricia rang him and he suggested they meet in a local restaurant. It was an Italian with comfortable seats and Patricia and Isobel found a table which was in a corner, affording them some privacy, and waited for their last interviewee of the day.

Patricia saw him first, his image up on her phone screen to compare. He was short, five foot six, and slim with very pale skin from too much time indoors.

Patricia waved and gestured him over. "Edward Small?"

"Yes." His voice was tentative.

Patricia indicated the seat opposite them, but he didn't sit.

He glanced at each of them, unsure of what to make of the situation, then said in a rush, "What do you want to talk to me about? I'm telling you now that I can't talk about my clients and their financial dealings, not without speaking to our legal department."

Patricia and Isobel looked at each other, a little taken aback.

Isobel introduced them both and said, "We work for a solicitor involved in family law. This is a divorce and child-custody case."

Patricia smiled at him. "There's no need to worry, Edward. We want to talk about an old work colleague, not about any big deals you're making. Your client confidentiality is safe and so are your shady deals."

He started to protest then saw her smiling and grinned. "Fair enough." He sat down. "Do you mind if I order some pizza while we talk? I've been so busy today that I haven't had a chance to eat."

Patricia said, "Oh, the high-pressure world of big business!"

Edward laughed. He gestured to the waitress and ordered pizza and salad with a glass of red wine. He encouraged Isobel and Patricia to join him but they both declined and just had a soft drink.

With his glass of wine in hand and now visibly more relaxed, Edward said, "Who do you want to know about?"

Isobel once again opened her bag. The first image she showed him was of Thomas and Anne at the dance.

Edward Small picked it up and looked at it for a long time.

Eventually Isobel asked, "Do you know this man?"

"Knew," Edward said in an ominous tone. "I knew this man a long time ago."

Isobel and Patricia made eye contact.

"Can you tell us his name?" Isobel asked.

Edward looked up. "Surely you know him if you're asking about him?"

"Please, just confirm his name."

Edward waited another few seconds and then said, "Matt Cooper."

Isobel produced the photo of Thomas Banks that his father had given them. "What about this man – do you know him?"

Impatient now, Edward pulled the second image to him, another pause.

Isobel said, "Well?"

Edward gulped down some wine then said, "Thomas Banks."

"We have concerns about this man Matt Cooper and we wondered if you could help us understand what sort of man he was when you worked with him. This is very important."

Edward looked at her, his reluctance obvious.

Patricia added, "Please tell us what you know. We need the information to help a child and a woman – maybe two women."

Edward's forehead wrinkled in consternation at this. "Some of what happened involved other people. I don't know if they would like me telling it."

Isobel chewed her lip. "We're guessing that some people involved have been hurt. I promise we only ask with a view to preventing future pain to others. One of the problems we've had is that no one has said anything all along and so more people have been allowed to get hurt. Please break the silence and help us."

Isobel knew there was a moment in communication when the balance shifts and, in silence, agreement of the way forward is reached. This was that moment. Isobel held her breath and willed that this man be courageous enough. He didn't disappoint her.

His acquiescence came as a nod.

Just at that moment his pizza and salad arrived.

The waitress withdrew and Edward took a few hungry

bites. Then he said, "Thomas, Matt and I all joined the financial firm together, although they already knew each other. We were all starting out with money in our pockets at last after our student days and we thought we were the kings of London. That initial madness went on for roughly six months but by then you could see how things were. Basically Thomas was a financial genius and even I could see he was destined for great things. Matt and I, well, we were competent but not in the same class. It didn't bother me. However, as time went on and the bosses started to see Thomas's potential, they started to groom him for promotion. I could accept that but sometimes when Matt had a few drinks he would confess how unfair he thought it. But, honestly, he just wasn't as good as Thomas – the problem was he couldn't accept that."

Edward paused, took a deep breath and picked up his fork which he fiddled with.

"You can imagine, three young men, attractive enough, money in our pockets, hopefully careers ahead of us. Well, obviously, we were also interested in girls. Our firm had a lot of secretaries and they used to join us on some of the nights out. There was one girl in particular, Charlotte."

From the way he said her name Isobel knew that he had felt strongly for this girl.

He looked down.

Isobel could feel a knot of tension starting in her stomach.

Edward swallowed hard. Taking a shuddering breath, he continued.

"Charlotte was one of the pool secretaries – beautiful, sweet, kind." He looked up at them, "Obviously I liked her, but I didn't stand a chance, I knew that. I believe Thomas liked her, but he was the sort of guy to take things slow, a romantic really. I think she liked him too. Needless to say, Matt was also interested in her. I think he guessed that there might be something starting to develop between Charlotte and Thomas, and he was determined to get there first. He started wooing Charlotte. He did everything, flowers, chocolates, cards, perfume. It was a real charm and romance offensive. Everyone knew he was courting her and Thomas, being the guy he was, just left them to it. It took a while, but Matt eventually persuaded Charlotte to go for dinner with him and after that they were an item at work. Over the next few months Charlotte changed but it was subtle. And, yes, I was paying attention. Anyway, six months later *it* happened."

The atmosphere was charged with tension.

Suddenly he sat up straight and took a number of quick breaths.

"I've never told anyone this," he said then.

Isobel could feel how much he wanted to avoid talking about what had happened. What could she say? She bit her lip, wondering how she could prompt him. Then she thought of that old adage and, paraphrasing, said, "There's a time for silence and a time for telling."

Edward looked at her, distress written on his face. "I only know some of the facts from Angela – she was Charlotte's friend and another one of the group. She's my secretary now." He took a deep breath. "At this stage we were with the company a year and Charlotte and Matt had been going out together for six months. Thomas had decided to leave the company and had got a great job, a big promotion with White and Smith."

Isobel recognised the name of the company Thomas aka Matt now worked for.

"Angela told me that Matt took Charlotte out for this really flash meal in a very expensive restaurant. He proposed to her that night. Angela said that Charlotte had been talking to her about getting out of the relationship, but she was afraid. When Matt proposed Charlotte didn't say yes – she said she needed to think about it, and it was too soon. Needless to say, Matt wasn't happy. When he took Charlotte home that night he forced his way into her flat, raped her and almost strangled her to death."

"Oh my God!" Patricia's eyes were wide with dread.

Edward had almost forgotten about them, his eyes fixed on a distant point as he relived the past. "Charlotte rang Angela that night. She refused to go to the rape crisis centre, but Angela persuaded her to go to her own doctor the next day and I know he took pictures of her injuries. Charlotte refused to press charges. She ended up having panic attacks and giving up work but no one at the company knew why. Angela knew I liked Charlotte and cared about her but she told me nothing other than that Charlotte was sick. Eventually, a year later, around the anniversary of it happening, because Charlotte was so bad and Angela was finding it hard to cope, she confided in me but swore me to secrecy. She still tells me very little. She guards Charlotte's privacy – I know that Charlotte is doing better but that's all I know. I don't know where she is." Edward breathed out in relief. "Thomas also got sick and didn't work out his notice. Matt brought in his certificates from a doctor."

Isobel frowned and looked over at Patricia.

Edward continued. "Thomas started in his new company a few weeks later and I never saw him again. Matt gave in his notice as well and moved on, I don't know where. That was it. Everyone was gone within a month."

Isobel knew this was important. Charlotte was a possible witness, who could make a definite statement about what had happened to her and who maybe had some photographic evidence with her doctor. Yes, it was old, but combined with Anne Banks' own statement and the photographs which Yvonne had, it might be enough to trigger a police investigation. They needed Charlotte to be prepared to go on record about what had happened. Isobel glanced at Patricia and could see in her eyes that she was thinking along the same lines.

"Edward, we need to talk to Angela," Isobel said.

Edward threw his fork onto the table. "What? No, no. I've betrayed her confidence. You can't talk to her."

Patricia said, "Edward, the man you call Matt Cooper is now calling himself Thomas Banks. The man you call Thomas Banks is dead. He was hit by a drunk driver. Matt or Thomas as he calls himself now, is working for White and Smith."

Edward frowned at her and then glanced at Isobel. "What are you talking about?"

Isobel said, "We know that Matt Cooper is now using Thomas Banks' name and probably took his job. We suspect Matt of having killed two women. To get evidence we need someone to make a statement. If Charlotte did that, we might have a shot at proving some of this."

"And we might get some justice for Charlotte and for a few other women," Patricia added.

Edward's shoulders slumped. "I don't know. Angela would have to talk to Charlotte."

"Yes," agreed Isobel, "And we need to talk to Angela,

in person, so she understands the importance of what's happening. Please, Edward. There are so many victims here and something needs to be done."

Edward bit his lip. "OK, I'll talk to Angela tomorrow."

"Tomorrow is the day that Thomas is going to sign divorce papers," said Patricia. "We're meeting some police officers later tonight to see if we can persuade them to do something. It would be great if we could talk to Angela now, tell her everything and see if she can persuade Charlotte to make a statement."

Edward nodded. "Let me ring Angela and see if we can see her."

Isobel glanced at her watch. It was a quarter to nine. "We can get a taxi there," she said, checking her purse to make sure she had plenty of cash. "That will save time. Just ask her if we can come and talk to her."

Edward walked outside to speak into his phone. Isobel and Patricia could see him talking vehemently and then listening.

Isobel inhaled deeply. "Those sick notes that Matt brought in for Thomas."

"Yes."

"He did that to cover up Thomas's death."

"That is so cold and calculating."

"I can't help feeling that to be that organised, so together, so quick to come up with something, he might have planned it."

Patricia nodded. They sat in silence for a moment.

"Let's focus on Anne's case for tonight and Angela and Charlotte," Isobel said, "but when we get a chance we need to talk to Simon about the hit-and-run."

"Yes . . . here's Edward."

Reaching the table he said, "I haven't told her much, but she's agreed to listen to what you have to say. All I can add is that she's very protective of Charlotte and I'm not sure if you will persuade her."

"We have to try though," Isobel said.

They left the restaurant, went to a nearby taxi rank and Edward gave the address.

Isobel asked the driver how long it would take to get there.

"Half an hour, if you're lucky," was his reply.

It took thirty-five minutes.

On the way Isobel texted Malcolm and the others that they were delayed.

The journey passed in silence. What was going on had mushroomed out of all recognition.

The taxi disgorged them at the address. Isobel hastily settled up and included a tip for their speedy transfer. The door of the house opened as they approached it – obviously Angela had been waiting for them – and they hurried inside. The living room she showed them into was cream, with cream furniture. There was soft music on and candles were lit. It was beautiful and very restful. Isobel could see right away that Angela was one of those people who was great to have around in a crisis – strong, capable and calm.

Edward made hasty introductions and Angela cut to the chase. "Edward hasn't said much, but he has mentioned Matt Cooper's name. Why are you enquiring about him?"

Isobel looked Angela in the eye. "Edward told us what Matt did to Charlotte."

Angela whirled round towards Edward. "*What?* How *dare* you?"

Isobel said, "Under duress and for a very good reason. Angela, we know of two other women who Matt strangled, one like Charlotte who escaped and left the area and a second . . ." here she paused then continued, "who we suspect might actually have been murdered."

"*Murdered?*" In her shock her voice seemed unnaturally loud and she looked away towards the door at the back of the room.

Isobel was a bit taken aback at her tone and for a minute thought that she was going to bolt through the door. "Yes, we suspect that this woman may have been murdered but at the moment we have little evidence to force the police to get warrants."

Angela kept glancing towards the door at the back of the room.

Isobel realised why and raised her voice, "I suppose we're here because we're hoping that you can persuade Charlotte to come forward and make a statement. We know there are old photos of what happened. We know people who work with women, who have experience in dealing with these sorts of situations. They have their own solicitor and I'm sure they can provide someone to go with Charlotte to the police station, should that be necessary."

Angela said, "Charlotte was deeply traumatised by what happened to her. Maybe she just wants to forget about it, move on, not have to go through it again."

Isobel said, again speaking loudly and clearly, "If Charlotte's fear hasn't gone in the last number of years then forgetting about what happened isn't working. Maybe there's another way. Every woman who encountered this man has been too afraid to do something and the list of victims is getting longer. Maybe it's time for someone to stand up. Maybe Charlotte can stand up."

Angela looked ready to explode.

Isobel went on, her voice still raised. "We're talking here about a statement to the police that might give them grounds for a search warrant. She may never have to go to trial and give evidence. That would be up to a solicitor. Please, someone needs to break the silence."

"I'll tell Charlotte all of this and see what she says, that's all I can promise you."

Silence fell. No one moved. Isobel stared at the door at the back of the room.

Suddenly it opened. They all heard the noise and turned to face it.

A woman stepped through.

"*Charlotte!*" Edward gasped and stepped forward.

Charlotte shrank back.

Edward looked panicked. "Sorry," he whispered.

Charlotte looked at Isobel and Patricia. "Do you really think it would help me?"

Isobel said gently, "Are you still afraid?"

"All the time."

"I can't say what will happen. I just know that doing this may help you to stop feeling like a victim. We can talk to the police about protection. We can put you in touch with people who deal with these types of situations all the time. They can help you, support you. We just want to stop this happening to someone else." She waited a second and then said, "So must you or you wouldn't have revealed yourself."

Charlotte regarded her. "Maybe."

Angela stepped forward and took Charlotte's hand.

Isobel asked, "Do you want me to ring a contact I

have? Her name is Julia. She's great. You could speak to her on the phone."

Charlotte tilted her head to one side then said, "OK. Let me talk to her."

Angela gently hugged her.

Isobel got Julia on the line and explained the situation, then gave the phone to Charlotte. Charlotte and Angela sat down on the couch side by side as Charlotte listened attentively to Julia.

Edward, Isobel and Patricia stepped away to give them some space.

Patricia showed Isobel her watch. It was ten minutes to ten. "What should we do?"

"Text Simon that we'll be on our way in a few minutes and order a taxi for as soon as possible. I'll let Malcolm know that we were delayed."

Behind them, Charlotte was saying goodbye on the phone and they turned back to her.

Charlotte said in a surprisingly firm voice, "I'm going to meet Julia tomorrow at eight in the morning. Her solicitor will take my statement and we'll contact the police."

Angela hugged her friend. "Do you want me to come with you?"

"Yes, please."

Angela glanced across at Edward. She looked much happier than when they'd arrived.

He said, "No problem. I'll get a typing-pool secretary until you come back to work."

Angela's eyes spoke her gratitude. Edward smiled, relieved and pleased.

A horn blew outside – the taxi.

"We'll tell the police what's happening and see what

they can do now with this additional evidence," said Patricia. "Thank you so much."

With that they rushed out to the taxi.

Once seated in the back of the cab, they breathed sighs of relief. There was nothing more they could do. It was up to Simon and the police now.

Chapter 33

It was half past ten when Isobel and Patricia arrived at the entrance to Peter's apartment block and rang the bell. He buzzed them up.

As she went to enter the street door Isobel's phone rang. It was Dave. She had already ignored a number of earlier calls.

"I have to take this. I'll be up in a moment."

"OK."

"Hi, Dave."

"How come you couldn't talk earlier, Isobel?"

"Things have got a bit busy because the case finishes tomorrow." Isobel was holding the bottom door open with one foot and standing outside as she answered.

"How come you're still working on it? I thought your consultancy would be finished now?"

"Dave, I can't talk now. We have a last-minute meeting. Everyone is waiting for me. I have to go."

"Isobel, for goodness' sake! I think you're pushing it. You're doing too much. It's ten thirty at night and you're still running around London. This time last year you were finishing chemo."

Isobel straightened up. "I'm well aware of what I was doing this time last year. And, believe it or not, I'm doing a really good job now. I'll talk to you tomorrow. *Goodnight.*"

She exhaled noisily and rolled her shoulders.

"*That's telling him!*"

She spun around to find Malcolm grinning at her.

She grinned back. "Only Simon to deal with now."

"I didn't want to arrive before you because I didn't know how you wanted to do this."

They climbed the stairs together. Peter's apartment door had been left ajar and Isobel let him into the hallway.

"Can you give me a few minutes to talk to Simon and then I'll call you in?"

Isobel went into the sitting room, closing the door.

"About time, Isobel," Simon said. "We've so much to get through." He didn't make eye contact with her as he spoke. He gestured with his hand. "This is Rajesh, from the Fraud Squad.

"Simon, I need to talk to you about something."

"No, we need to tell you what we're planning for tomorrow."

"No, Simon, things have changed."

"What? It's been a long day and I'm really tired. Helping out my friend has turned into a huge case of overtime."

"Simon." She waited. He continued to fuss with some papers. "*Simon.*"

Eventually he looked up.

Isobel looked him in the eye. "I owe you an apology."

"For what?"

"I contacted Jason and he put me in touch with Malcolm."

"Jason? Malcolm? And?"

"I met Malcolm and told him about the case."

"*What have you done?* Have you jeopardised the investigation? Does Thomas know that we're investigating him? You have no idea what we do, how hard it is, how much work it takes – and one mistake and they get off."

"No, no. I'm sure Thomas has no idea what we've done."

"Get on with it then, what did you do? We've a lot to organise tonight and it's already very late."

Isobel opened the door and Malcolm walked in. He went straight up to Simon and offered his hand. "Malcolm, retired inspector, with the cadaver unit."

Simon reached out and shook his hand. "What's going on?"

Isobel said, "This morning I got Malcolm and his dog Bella to check Thomas's garden. I couldn't wait any longer. I had to know if Anne might be dead."

"Jesus, Isobel! What the hell do you think you're doing? You could have jeopardised this whole case. Malcolm, I'm surprised that as a retired inspector you got involved in this."

Malcolm inclined his head. "Bella found a suspicious area. Grace, the next-door neighbour said that around Valentine's Day two holes were dug in the garden and a new tree, a seat and flowerbed put in. It seems likely that Anne could be buried there."

There was a cacophony of responses.

Simon exclaimed, "*What?*"

Rajesh said, "If that's the case we have him."

"And poor Tommy, he'll never see his mother again."

Patricia's words halted everyone. As a pebble thrown into water sends out ripples, a wave passed over everyone.

As the silence lengthened people straightened up. There was a sea-change, a stillness descended, a calmness, a determination.

Simon took a deep breath. "Tell me everything."

Isobel nodded at Malcolm.

"A new friend asked me to visit an old lady she knew," he said. "While there Bella escaped and jumped into a neighbour's garden. When I went to retrieve her and make sure that she hadn't made any messes in their garden Bella reacted as she would to a body."

Simon said, "So that's your story."

Malcolm nodded. "And I'm sticking to it. I'm sorry, mate, if you feel I was out of line but when Isobel explained everything I just had to help her know if the original Mrs Banks was there. I'm not a policeman now but I have been mindful of not compromising your investigation. But let me be clear, I think Anne Banks is buried in the garden. Bella has never been wrong and she was only retired because I was."

Simon nodded at him. "I know, this case is getting under my skin too. I understand. I'm just trying to be careful legally and I suppose I was hoping that Anne Banks was still alive." He looked absolutely gutted. "At least we know now that the likelihood is that she isn't but we still have to get this bastard."

There was a sober silence.

Isobel spoke up. "That's not all. Patricia and I have had a very busy day and we need to fill you in on all the people we've talked to and what we've found out."

Between the two of them they described their day. At the end there was a stunned silence.

Simon said, "So, you're saying that Thomas Banks is really Matt Cooper. He killed a dog at school, nearly strangled his girlfriend who ran away, possibly killed his mother and got the money from her house sale, raped and tried to strangle another girlfriend, then changed his name and took his friend's job when he died. Have I left anything out?"

Nobody answered.

"So we have two reactions from Bella suggesting possible buried bodies and two women who escaped, one of whom will make a statement tomorrow."

The silence that ensued was bleak.

Peter said, "Is anyone in this case who they say they are?"

"The death of Thomas Banks needs to be looked at again, Simon," said Patricia. "It may not be a drunk driver. Maybe Matt Cooper killed Thomas Banks and took his job and identity. We promised his dad that we would try to get the case re-examined."

"For God's sake, Patricia, the police force is not your personal clean-up service. And, anyway, murder with a car is not, well, very easily accomplished." Simon winced. "It is only at speeds of about sixty miles per hour and above that the likelihood is that you would kill. That's why built-up areas have thirty-miles-per-hour limits. And I can't see Matt Cooper hitting Thomas with a car in their home area. That doesn't make sense to me."

"But surely it deserves another look, given that Matt took Thomas's identity?" Isobel said.

"Sorry, but it seems unlikely to me and it certainly is not a priority now."

Isobel shook her head at Patricia, hoping that she understood that she meant, 'Leave it for now'.

Patricia nodded back.

Simon rubbed his face and fidgeted. He was the chair of the meeting and everyone was waiting for him to take charge.

Peter spoke up. "The search that Malcolm did is not

official and not admissible. What we have is theory, suspicions. I'm not sure we have enough actual evidence to get a search warrant for the gardens yet."

"But with Charlotte's statement and the pictures of Anne that Yvonne gave us?"

Peter looked at Simon.

Simon said, "I think we need to let Anne the imposter and Thomas Banks sign the divorce papers. The minute that's done we can lift them. With Claire's testimony that this isn't her sister we can get official DNA tests and proceed from there. We'll be able to get a warrant for the garden when we show that Anne Banks has disappeared. We can use all of the other evidence that has come to light to nail him." Nodding at Isobel, he continued, "Once we've established the crime of fraud we can start to prove the other crimes and build the case."

Rajesh said, "How very Al Capone."

Patricia said, "What do you mean?"

"Al Capone, the big boss in Chicago," Peter said, "they could never get him for the murders he did but they sent him to prison for tax evasion."

Rajesh said, "When Simon contacted me last night I thought I was dealing with a minor fraud case."

Isobel looked at Rajesh. He had said very little through all that had gone on, just listening, his brown eyes observing. She guessed that he missed nothing.

Simon laughed, for the first time that evening seeming to relax a little. "Yeah, initially he told me that it was not major league enough for him to be involved, just a family isssue. Until I pointed out that Anne's share of a house in Wimbledon was worth between one and three million, not exactly minor-league fraud."

Rajesh smirked. "He did tell me that some of the team suspected more."

Simon glanced at Isobel who was shocked to hear herself and Patricia described as 'some of his team'.

Rajesh turned to Simon, "So, your team was right. You've stumbled into something much bigger." He looked at Isobel. "So this is your profiler?"

"I'm not a profiler."

Simon said, "She's a psychotherapist."

"That's a new one on me. Is this the new way things are going, the new type of case consultant and I haven't heard?"

Peter said, "I hired Isobel because I suspected that there was something off about this couple and that's how the whole fraud came to light, then the spousal abuse and so on."

Rajesh said, "Well, between you all you've uncovered a man who is dangerous and who needs to be stopped."

"So now, the plan," said Simon. "With Rajesh and me and maybe a few officers each we can do it."

Isobel wondered what plan they were talking about.

"Yeah, keep it tight, keep it safe," Rajesh said. "I have a few good men who can help us out."

Simon said, "Yes, a few of my officers are going to help too. And we need to remember that this guy has killed and thinks he's got away with it. He may be like a cornered rat. Everyone needs to be careful." He looked at Peter, Patricia and Isobel. "We're professionals and our idea of careful and yours may be very different."

Simon gestured to Rajesh and he took over.

"Tomorrow we need you, Peter, and you, Patricia, to stay calm and not arouse Thomas and Anne's suspicions. Get the signing done. We'll have officers in the building.

Once Thomas and Anne go into your office, Peter, then we can start to move in. We'll need some of the other solicitors to take the morning off and be replaced by police officers. You, Peter, are going to have to clear that with the boss. We don't want to tell any of the solicitors tonight because people talk. So first thing tomorrow you need to explain to the boss and get everyone to cooperate. The signing is scheduled for two o'clock so our men will need to be in place by noon. We'll have surveillance people on the street who will alert us when the Banks are on their way. That surveillance is going to be very discreet because I don't want them to become suspicious. Thankfully all of your investigating has been very careful and so Thomas has no idea we're on to him, which is good."

Isobel realised that they were taking this very seriously. "You're concerned something could go wrong tomorrow?"

Rajesh said, "Thomas Banks is a dangerous man and he's an experienced criminal, otherwise he wouldn't have been able to dream up this imposter scenario so quickly. His plan was quite elaborate and almost successful. And we now know he has a very violent past."

Simon said, "And Peter, if it hadn't been for you, Patricia and Isobel, he would have got away with it. He's very resourceful. Finding a doppelganger who can fool people isn't that easy."

Rajesh said, "You've done so well finding out all that you have but you need to leave it to us now. We need you to be very careful and stick to the plan. Don't take any risks. Peter, Patricia, once the form is signed and Anne and Thomas walk out into the reception area we'll be waiting. You two stay in the room, let them walk out ahead of you. Am I clear?"

271

"Yes."

"Yes."

"If you've been as careful as Simon tells me you have, Thomas and Anne shouldn't be suspicious and we'll have them. Easy." He smiled. "Any questions?"

Isobel looked at the others. Peter looked horrified. To distract him she asked, "Peter, do you foresee any problems with your boss?"

"I don't know. I'm sure he's not going to be thrilled."

Simon said, "He should be. Your intuition and actions are a credit to the firm. You're going to catch a fraudster and possible multiple murderer, pretty impressive. Why don't I go with you to talk to him and let him know how much we appreciate the firm's help?"

Peter grinned. "Well, since you put it like that, yes, I think that would help to get things sorted quickly and clearly. He's in by half past eight so that gives us time to explain."

Simon said, "Rajesh, you and one of your men can be solicitors tomorrow and monitor things in the office so dress appropriately. You and your team need to be ready to take your places at midday as I said. You'll be able to walk in and out to reception so you can let us know when the Banks are in with Peter signing. Be discreet, act solicitor-like. The rest of the policemen will be in the building and will converge when you tell us they are in the office. I have a briefing with them at 6am tomorrow. Anything else?"

He paused. There was silence.

"Rajesh, meet me at the early briefing and bring your men," he said. "I'll do the same." He looked at Isobel. "You don't have a role tomorrow, Isobel, so I don't want you to be anywhere near the office. I'm sure the others will call you as soon as it's all over. Malcolm, you won't be there either but we'll keep you informed and thanks for your help."

The two men shook hands.

After Malcolm and the policemen left, the enormity of the situation hit Isobel. Peter seemed really nervous. She wondered what she could do to focus his mind and help him.

"Peter, Simon is right. Your intuition has uncovered something really important and that's amazing. Anne Banks, Tommy's mother, is your client and you've looked after her interests so well."

Peter looked down. "Too late for her though."

Isobel swallowed. "Yes. But, you can get her justice and as her solicitor that's all you could ever do. More importantly, you can ensure that her son is looked after in the way she would have wanted."

Peter looked up.

"Not by an abuser and murderer," she continued, "but maybe by an aunt who is warm and strong and brave."

Peter nodded. "You're right. I can do that." He said it like it was a promise to Anne and Isobel knew in a way it was.

She got up, wished him luck too and left Patricia a few minutes alone with him to say her goodbyes. She felt sure that she and Peter would support each other through the meeting tomorrow and be fine.

The two women were exhausted. Before bed Isobel had one last call to make. She rang Tim Woodward, and he answered immediately.

"Tim, at the moment they're going to arrest the man we suspect tomorrow. I'm not sure how things will go or how quickly they will move but hopefully in the next few days they'll be able to get a search warrant to check the garden."

Tim said, "I spoke to Sarah. We both want to help. I also spoke to my solicitor."

Isobel cringed.

"He told me that if I found something like a body in my garden then the police would have to investigate."

"OK."

"What if in your visit you just asked me about who had previously owned the house and we told you what we knew, which is not that much. Maybe I go into the garden the next day and decide to dig that pond that my wife wants for fish and I find something."

Isobel bit her lip. "Well, it is your garden."

"That's what Sarah and I thought," Tim said in satisfaction and rang off.

Isobel got off the phone, wondering if she had just encouraged the Woodwards to force the police's hand. However, her bed beckoned and she did her best to put it out of her mind.

It was one thirty and she was exhausted. Despite this, she only slept intermittently. She dreamt of a man in black with a hat pulled over his face. He seemed sinister and Isobel ran away but he pursued her, gaining all the time until he was right behind her, reaching out to grab her. She escaped and tried to hide but he searched for her, drawing closer and closer to her.

She woke with her heart hammering and feeling terrified. Taking deep breaths she lay back and tried to calm down. She realised that she was afraid of Thomas Banks and what he was capable of.

Chapter 34

When the alarm went off at seven thirty Isobel woke with a pounding heart, feeling afraid. She could hear Patricia getting ready. Fifteen minutes later Patricia gave her a quick hug and, with promises to let her know when it was over, she was gone.

Isobel washed her face and teeth and made a cup of tea. At eight o'clock she knew there was no point putting it off – she needed to talk to Dave.

She had barely time to realise that he'd answered when he said, "Jesus, Isobel."

"What?"

"Don't play the innocent with me. I spoke to Peter at seven o'clock this morning and he told me what's going on. You're chasing a murderer all over London."

"I am not."

"Oh, he's singing your praises along with some woman called Patricia – apparently you're a right little Holmes and Watson team."

"Why are you so angry? We've uncovered something that could have stayed hidden forever."

There was a silence.

"I'm not angry, Isobel."

"Well, you sound angry."

"I'm terrified. What are you doing? You're just over a life-threatening illness and now here you are on the trail of a murderer. You could get killed. We don't want anything to happen to you."

Isobel could feel her eyes filling with tears. "It's not like that. I've only met this man once in Peter's office. Everything else we've done is background. There hasn't been any danger to me. It's more like solving a puzzle. Honestly, Dave, I'm fine. Today it's going to be over, the police are going to pick him up and hopefully he'll be going to jail for a long time based on the evidence we've uncovered."

"Really?"

"Yes. I care about what happens here. I want to find Anne. I want to find what happened to her. I don't want any more people to be hurt."

"You sound very involved."

"Well, I want Peter to find out what happened to his client."

"But you don't know this woman."

"I feel as if I do from talking to her family and friends. She matters to me. I want to do this. It's important to me." By the time she had finished talking the tears were rolling down her cheeks. "Please try to understand."

"OK. Just be safe. We love you."

"Love you too. I'll let you know tonight how it goes."

"OK, Sherlock."

Isobel was smiling when she got off the phone.

She had a bath and then a leisurely breakfast. Despite trying to force herself to relax she was obsessing about what was happening at the office. It was still only ten thirty. She realised that it was much easier to be in the thick of things, running around talking to suspects rather than sitting at home waiting and wondering. This was like torture. Eventually her curiosity got the better of her and she phoned Patricia for an update.

"Patricia, how are things progressing?"

Patricia's reply was murmured into the phone. "Peter spoke to the boss. Obviously he was a bit put out about things but when Simon told him what we suspected he was glad to help. Oh, Simon is here now, he wants to talk to you."

"Hi. Everything is progressing nicely. I know you want to keep abreast of what's happening but we all need to focus on playing our part here and not get distracted. I promise one of us will let you know the minute we've made the arrests. Please don't phone again. We'll call you."

"Sure, Simon. Good luck." Isobel had to be content with that. She needed a distraction and maybe some sightseeing would do the trick. Dave had mentioned Sherlock Holmes, her childhood hero. Maybe she would visit 221B Baker Street.

Isobel was putting on comfortable walking shoes when her mobile rang. Looking at it she saw that the call was from Tim Woodward.

"Tim, is everything all right?"

"Isobel, I went and started digging in the garden. We had to know. It was really bothering us. I rang in sick to work and then I started digging in the place where Bella reacted."

Isobel bit her lip. She could feel her stomach tightening.

"And, I've found some bones. I wanted to let you know. I've stopped digging and I've rung the local police station. They're going to send someone to check it out. The bones are fairly big. I only disturbed two of them. Sarah thinks they're ribs."

Isobel groaned. This was real. Her suspicions were starting to be confirmed.

"Is Sarah doing OK?"

"She's doing great." Tim sounded proud. "She wants us to help find out the truth, she thinks that's the least we can do. I'll let you know when they tell me anything else here."

"Thanks, Tim, take care of each other."

For a moment Isobel panicked. What was the best thing to do? Should she ring Simon? He was probably going to be annoyed and concerned about evidence and that might distract him. Maybe it would be better to let them go ahead with their plan? They needed to arrest Thomas, knowing this wasn't going to change what they were doing. Perhaps she would run it past Jeff from the lab. He knew Simon and would know what the best thing to do was.

Isobel phoned Jeff and quickly filled him in on all the new developments. She could hear him clicking his tongue.

"The local police will come and look at the bones in Tim's garden. When they see them, they'll request an opinion from a coroner as to whether the bones are human. If they are then the garden will become a crime scene."

"Should I ring and tell Simon?"

"Is there any way that Thomas could know about this excavation?"

"No, I don't think so. He left his old home behind over ten years ago. No, I can't see that he would."

There was silence for a few seconds then more tongue-clicking, "It's going to take a while for any useful info on the bones to come through. If they have Thomas in custody when it does, all the better, they can even hold onto him until that info is in, so no, I wouldn't tell Simon. They're picking him up anyway, so it won't change anything they're going to do. If Simon said leave him alone then let him focus on what they have to do today."

Isobel agreed with his logic and was satisfied.

Sitting on her bed now, she shivered. She also quailed when she thought of what her friends were attempting to do today.

Full of anxiety for Peter and Patricia, the civilians and also key players in this final piece, Isobel sent a text to Patricia's phone: **Please be careful. Love, Isobel.**

There was nothing more that she could do now so she gathered her bag and headed for Baker Street and some distraction.

The museum of Sherlock Holmes certainly was a distraction and Isobel found that after the journey and a little time browsing she actually felt calmer. Standing in the upstairs room, Isobel could picture Holmes and Watson as they paced and theorised, pursuing the truth. Which is what she had done. After not working for the last eighteen months because of her health crisis, Isobel experienced a near-forgotten feeling of having been useful, dynamic. After all the weakness and tiredness she'd been experiencing it felt good. Maybe she could find a way forward. It was certainly good to feel a new level of optimism and strength.

At twelve thirty her phone rang. Isobel rummaged in her bag, frustrated at how slow she was getting to it. It seemed a little early to hear from Simon and everyone. Looking at her screen she saw that it was Grace.

"Isobel?" Grace's voice was ragged.

"Grace, I can hardly hear you. Where are you? Are you all right?"

"I'm at home."

"Grace, I can hardly hear you. What's happened? Are you ill?"

"I'm frightened."

"What's happened?"

"Something's h-happening – n-next door," Grace said shakily.

"What? What's happening?"

"I don't know," Grace gasped.

"Grace, don't go outside and don't open your door." Isobel could hear the distress in her own voice now and took some deep breaths to calm herself down. She was going to be no good to Grace if she panicked. She found a corner in one of the rooms and turned towards the wall to create a natural barrier so she could focus on the information coming over the phone.

"I've locked the front and back door and I've locked myself in the bathroom."

Isobel breathed a small sigh of relief. "Good. Stay there. Now, what's going on next door?"

"All morning I was thinking about yesterday and just now I decided that I would look over the wall." There was a sob and some deep breaths. "And say a wee prayer in case Anne was buried there, as I know you suspect. So, I got the garden chair like yesterday and put it against the wall."

Isobel could feel her stomach knotting in tension. "What did you see, Grace?"

"The garden bench has been moved and there's one of those white tent-y things over where the bench was, where

280

Bella reacted yesterday. It has walls so I can't see inside but I think I can hear the sound of digging."

"*Shit, shit.*" Isobel was shaking now. "Have you seen Thomas? Is he there?"

"I only had a quick look. I don't know who it is."

"Grace, I'm going to come over to you. Stay inside. Don't open the door, except to me. I'll phone you when I'm outside your front door. Promise me. You have to stay safe."

"I promise. Hurry up though."

Isobel was already heading down the stairs and out onto Baker Street. "I'm on my way."

Isobel hailed a taxi and sat in.

To encourage the driver she said, "An old lady I know has just rung from this address. Something has happened. I'm worried about her, so can you please hurry?"

The taxi driver, seeing that she was genuinely distressed, promised haste.

Isobel debated what to do. This seemed like a significant development – should she ring Patricia? She decided yes and rang but there was no answer. She tried the number of the solicitor's office number.

This time Patricia answered.

"Patricia –"

"Isobel I can't talk now."

"Hold on, this is important –" but already Isobel was talking to a dialling tone.

She debated about ringing again and then decided that she would send Patricia a text.

Grace says someone is digging in Banks' garden. Going there now.

Having done this, she sat impatiently as the taxi driver tried to make good on his promise. It still took half an hour, longer than Google had said. Isobel asked the taxi driver to drive past the Banks' house. In the driveway was a white Ford transit van. She tried to see if there was a name on the van. There didn't appear to be.

The taxi driver dropped Isobel a little way down the street, puzzled by her changing instructions. Isobel paid and got out.

She walked back to Grace's house. As she turned in the gate she dialled Grace's number.

"I'm outside."

In a few minutes the door opened tentatively, the chain on. Through the small gap Grace peered out. Tears sprang to her eyes when she saw Isobel. She closed the door and reopened it then pulled Isobel to her in a strong hug.

"I'm so glad you're here."

Isobel bundled her inside and closed and locked the front door again.

Grace wrung a tissue in her hands. "Are they digging Anne up? What will we do?"

Isobel rubbed her face with her hand. "I don't know. I guess it seems like they might be." She sucked in her lip. "Have you seen Thomas?"

"He left with Tommy for school as usual. All I've seen is a workman but I don't know who he is. Maybe it's Thomas. I don't know. He's dressed like the guy back in February but all workmen look fairly similar."

Isobel nodded. "There's a transit van in the drive."

Silence fell.

"It has to be suspicious if he's digging now," Isobel said. "I'm afraid he's getting rid of the evidence. But what alerted him?"

She glanced at her watch and saw that it was one

fifteen. She needed to talk to Simon. She tried his mobile and got no answer. She phoned Patricia's mobile, it seemed to be off. Once again Isobel rang the number for the solicitor's office. Again Patricia answered.

Isobel jumped in immediately, her voice urgent. "Patricia, please listen, something important has happened."

Patricia spoke quickly. "I'm not even supposed to be answering the phone. Isobel, we've been speaking to Thomas this morning. He and Anne are on their way. Anne got delayed at the hairdresser's and so they're going to be slightly late. They're looking forward to getting the details completed. Simon says there's no reason for him to suspect that we are on to him."

"Patricia, listen —"

"I have to go."

Then the phone went dead.

Isobel was shocked. She put her phone away in the pocket of her fleece, her eyes smarting with tears. "I can't get hold of them. They are all at the office, thinking Thomas is on his way."

Grace clutched her arm. "What will we do?"

Isobel could see the confusion and fear in her eyes. Straightening her spine, she said, "I'm going to have a look over the wall."

Grace nodded her agreement.

They went through the hall into the kitchen and then the sunroom.

Grace turned the key in the lock and turned to Isobel. "I'll wait here and keep watch with the door ajar in case you have to run back."

"Good idea."

Grace opened the door and Isobel slipped out.

Grace already had the chair against the wall and Isobel experienced a sense of déjà vu. She quietly got on the chair and very slowly raised her head until she could see over the wall. It was as Grace had described. There was a small pop-up white gazebo in the garden. Listening, Isobel could hear the sound of a spade scraping and the heavy breath of someone working hard. Then, the scraping stopped and she heard someone making a noise in exertion. A few seconds later she saw some of the canopy moving on the side of the gazebo facing the Banks' house.

A man emerged and Isobel ducked down but not before she registered that he had a hat pulled low over his head and a big lumberjack shirt on, work gloves, black jeans and heavy work boots. He appeared to be the same height as Thomas Banks, around six feet, but in the outfit Isobel couldn't be sure if it was him or not. The man emerged from the gazebo and went up towards the house and round the front.

Then Isobel heard the van start up. He was leaving. This was her chance.

She looked back at the kitchen door and signalled that the man was leaving and that she was going to climb the wall. The door, which was slightly ajar, opened a little more and she could see Grace's finger shaking frantically. Isobel made an 'It's OK' hand gesture. She listened. She couldn't hear the van any more. He was gone.

She clambered over the fence and lowered herself onto the grass on the other side. She crouched down. Bent over, she ran quickly across the grass to the area where the man had exited the tent and slipped between the two pieces of material that formed the door.

Inside there was a fair bit of room. The grass, where

the garden seat had been, had been cut into divots and piled to one side. The soil underneath had been excavated and was in a heap. Isobel could not see the bottom of the hole. She crept forward slowly, a sense of dread building inside. Coming to the edge of the hole she peered in. She saw some hair and what looked like a black jumper. Kneeling on the edge of the hole, she reached down and gently moved the hair. What lay underneath was the remains of a face impossible to recognise. In her heart Isobel knew that this was Anne Banks. Her eyes filled with tears.

Chapter 35

For a moment Isobel did nothing. It was as if time froze. Coming back to the present, she thought of Simon. She pulled her phone out of her pocket and took a photo to prove what she'd been saying all along. Her next thought was: *I need to get out of here.* She got up from where she was kneeling and at the same time heard the metal gate at the side of the house bang. Her heart leapt. She looked through the door flap and she saw the man had come around the side of the house. He hadn't left after all. He was on his way back towards the gazebo. He was carrying a rolled-up bag for garden rubbish. Isobel's breath caught in her chest. She couldn't move. She was petrified. She thought she was going to faint.

Suddenly there was a crash from the direction of Grace's garden. To Isobel it sounded as if a garden pot had smashed. The man stood stock still. His head turned and he waited, eyes fixed on the wall between his garden and Grace's. Isobel lay on the ground and lifting the side of the tent as much as she could squeezed through the gap. She stayed flat on the ground, trying to control her breathing. She heard the man pull back the cover and enter the gazebo. A few seconds later there was the sound of a sharp expelling of breath as he exerted himself.

Isobel took a shallow breath and, heart pounding, crawled across the grass on her elbows to the boundary with Grace's. When she reached the wall, she paused and listened, her heart in her mouth. She could hear the sound of the spade and laboured breathing. Taking care not to make any noise, she slowly stood up. Isobel wondered if she would be able to get over the wall. Frantically she searched for any damage to the bricks that could act as a foothold. Sweating in fear, she found an indentation. Inserting her toes, she grasped the top of the wall and painfully pulled herself up while pushing with her foot. She managed to straddle the wall and struggled over. As she landed her legs weakened in relief and she nearly fell.

Shakily, she climbed onto the chair once again and raised her head enough to peer over the wall. As yet, the man had not come out of the gazebo. Ducking down, she took out her phone and set it to record. Time passed. At last the digging stopped. She remained crouched on the chair until she heard a different sound. The sound of something being dragged on the ground. Terrified, she raised her head again. The man had emerged from the gazebo and was dragging the garden bag with, she presumed, the body in it across the garden towards the house. She ducked down again and made sure that she was recording, then raised the lens above the level of the wall, angling the camera to film the man's journey across the garden to the side of the house.

Isobel jumped off the chair and stopped the recording. She ran to the back door which Grace flung open.

Closing the back door, Grace said angrily, "Why did

you take that risk? You nearly gave me a heart attack!"

"Sorry, Grace – I thought he had gone off in the van. But he must have been just moving it. I think he's about to leave now."

"Is Anne's body there?" Grace demanded.

Isobel steeled herself.

"It is," Grace said. "I can see it in your face." She put her hand to her mouth, as white as a sheet.

"I'm sorry." She paused then, gently holding both of Grace's arms and looking her in the eyes. "I need to follow the van. It contains the body. Do you have a car?"

Grace swallowed. "Of course, it's outside in front."

Still holding Grace, Isobel said, "I need to go now, or I might lose him."

Grace freed herself and reached for some keys. "I'm coming too."

Isobel ran to the car. Grace followed more slowly. At the driver's door, Isobel turned and put her hand out for the key.

Grace looked at her. "You must be joking. I'm driving."

Isobel looked at her doubtfully. "You won't drive fast enough."

Grace's lips formed a hard line. "You think with a dead body in the back he's going to be speeding and drawing attention to himself?"

"No, probably not. Good point but –"

Grace sat into the driver seat. Isobel conceded and ran round to the passenger side.

As Grace started up the car, she said, "And while we're at it, young'un, just remember only for the fact that I broke my beautiful flower pot you wouldn't have been able to get out of that gazebo and there might be two

288

bodies in the back of that van." She straightened her shoulders as she delivered this coup de grace. "You ring the police. Get us some help."

Isobel looked at her watch. It was only ten minutes to two. Simon and the others still thought Thomas was coming therefore they would be waiting and wouldn't take a call.

There was the sound of an engine starting from next door. In a few moments a white van passed the end of the drive.

"Give him a minute," Isobel said.

Grace tutted. "I know." Slowly she edged forward and watched the van move down the street. When it was almost out of view Grace pulled out and followed. In the distance they saw the van make a right turn and Grace sped after it. By the time they made the same right turn there were a couple of cars between them and the van.

Isobel said, "We need to get the registration number of that van."

"Right." Grace's voice was tense and she kept her gaze on the traffic as she went round a roundabout.

Ahead Isobel could still see the white van. She jittered in her seat. "We're going to lose him."

Grace flushed, her grip tightening on the steering wheel as she leaned forward.

Isobel glanced at her. "See if you can get directly behind them for a while."

Grace bit her lip. At the next roundabout the car directly in front of them turned left. Now there was only one car in the way.

Isobel could feel the tension in her neck. "*Come on, come on!*" she hissed at the car in front. "*Turn off, turn off!*"

At the next roundabout they stayed in convoy, then finally at the next junction the car in front took a left turn.

"Thank God," Grace said as she caught up with the van. She loosened her grip on the steering wheel. "We were lucky."

Isobel pulled up the notes page on her phone and typed in the number: **FUB 5456**. "Got it." She grinned across at Grace who risked a small glance at her, then studiously turned her eyes back to the road.

Isobel dialled **999**.

"What service do you require?" the dispatcher's calm voice intoned.

"Police. I've just seen a man put a dead body into a van."

Before she could explain anything the dispatcher said, "Stay on the line. I'm putting you through to the police station. Stay on the line."

Isobel tapped her foot.

"Hello. Police. What's the problem?"

"I saw a man dig up a body and put it in the back of a van."

"Where are you?"

"I'm in a car following the van. We were in Wimbledon. And now we're on . . ."

Isobel hesitated, unsure.

"I think it's Norwood Road." Grace said.

"I think it's Norwood Road," Isobel repeated. "I don't know where the van is going."

"Do you have the registration of the van?"

Isobel read off the number for him. "The van has just turned onto . . ."

"Village Way!" Grace called out and Isobel relayed it.

"Don't approach the van. I'll dispatch a car."

"How soon can it get here?"

"It's going to be ten or fifteen minutes. You need to update us about where you are. Stay calm. We have the registration. Do not approach the vehicle."

Isobel wondered where the driver was going. She wasn't sure how long it was since they'd left the house. "OK. I'll ring you back if we arrive somewhere."

"*Wait!*"

She hung up and dialled Malcolm's number. He answered after only five rings.

"Hello, Isobel."

When she heard his voice over the phone Isobel could feel relief welling up.

"Malcolm, someone, probably Thomas Banks, dug up the body in Wimbledon. I saw it, got a photo. He put it in a van and is taking it somewhere. Grace and I are following. I'm afraid we're going to lose him and the body, then what will we do?" She took a deep breath and tried to calm down.

"Where are you?"

Isobel was addled. The truth was she didn't know. "Grace, where are we? Where are we?"

Grace said, "Dulwich Road, I think."

"Dulwich Road, Malcolm. Hold on, I'll put you on speaker phone. Grace knows the area."

"I wonder if he's heading for the river," Grace said.

"Oh God! He's going to dump the body, Malcolm!

Malcolm said, "How long until you get to the river?"

"Maybe ten minutes," said Grace.

"That's all?"

Grace said firmly, "I would say so."

291

"*Shit*. That's not enough time for me to get there. Have you rung the police?"

"Yes, just now," said Isobel. "Realistically, are they likely to get here in time?"

Malcolm paused while he considered the question. "Realistically, probably not."

There was silence again and Isobel could almost hear Malcolm thinking.

Then he said, "Isobel, the most important thing is that you and Grace keep safe."

"I know – the policeman I spoke to told me not to approach the man."

"Exactly, don't approach him and don't let him see you. If you can take note of where he dumps the body do so but only if it's safe. Maybe we can retrieve the body later. Have you got that, Isobel? Are you clear that your safety is the most important thing?"

Isobel was nodding.

"*Have you got that, Isobel?*" Malcolm repeated.

"Yes, yes, I can do that." Even as she said it Isobel knew she was trying to convince herself.

"I'm on my way. I'll be there as soon as I can. Isobel, you're now a witness to the removal of the body. Don't let anything happen to you." Malcolm paused. "I'll contact the police and tell them that you think you are on your way to the river. See you soon. Ring me if anything happens." He hung up.

Reality was dawning on Isobel. She set the phone on her lap and rubbed her face with her hands. She took a few deep breaths, gradually trying to calm her panic.

Grace remained silent, her eyes locked on the white van in front.

There was something that Isobel knew she needed to do. She once again picked up her phone. She saw the time displayed on the screen. It was only two o'clock. She called Simon. He didn't answer. She left a voice message.

"A man has dug up the body in Wimbledon. I will send you a picture of the body. He's taking it somewhere, maybe the river. Grace and I are following him. The registration number of the van is FUB 5456." Isobel attached the photo to the text.

This done, she looked up at the road again. Ahead she saw the van indicate to turn right.

Grace didn't put on her indicator. She approached the junction slowly, keeping her distance. She turned the corner, hanging back, giving the van time to forge ahead. As they progressed along the road, keeping the van in view, Isobel could see that this was an industrial area along the river. There were a number of business yards and sheds, each with their own frontage to the water. The van was moving steadily. Traffic was light.

Suddenly the van stopped. Grace pulled up a long distance back and they watched. The man got out and went towards a big gate. He opened it, ran back to the van and drove in. The van stopped, he hurried to close the gate, got back in and continued out of sight.

Grace said, "What will I do?"

Isobel tugged at her lip. "Drive past slowly and we'll look in. If he sees us, just keep going. If not, drive on a bit and stop."

Grace said, "OK," and moved the car forward slowly. They craned their necks to look in the entrance. The white van was driving between two big warehouses, the river visible beyond them. There were no other signs of activity.

The place was deserted. Grace kept moving the car forward slowly. When they had travelled twenty-five metres past the gate, Grace stopped.

"What do you think?" she asked in a worried voice.

"I think I need to get out and see if I can get closer. You have to hide the car somewhere, Grace, out of sight. If this is Thomas, then he knows you and he knows your car, so we can't be seen. But, if possible, I want to get a video of what he's doing. Those warehouses mean I might be able to stay out of sight."

"Are you sure?"

"No, I'm not sure but I must try. Take the car somewhere and hide it and wait for me. When he leaves he mustn't see you or the car. Don't *dream* of getting out of the car. He could be dangerous. I'll come out about five minutes after him. Are we on the same page?"

Grace said in a small voice tight with worry, "I understand. I promise. Be careful. If you can't get a video, you can't get it."

Isobel ensured her phone was on silent. Taking a deep breath and giving Grace's hand a squeeze, she slipped out of the car, closing the door quietly. She gestured to indicate that Grace should go and hide, then ran back towards the gate.

The gate was a metal one, very wide but not so high and made up of metal bars. Afraid that opening it would make a noise, Isobel dredged up some old childhood memory and, doing her best to mimic it, climbed the gate and rolled over the top, landing on her feet on the other side.

Ahead were two corrugated-metal warehouses, side by side, like silver worms. There were cargo doors facing Isobel, but they were closed. The length of the warehouses stretched out towards the water behind. Whatever was stored here, there was plenty of room for it. The space between the warehouses was the width of a road and the white van had made its way as far as the river behind. Isobel ran wide to the left so she could approach the waterfront from the far side of the building.

Isobel was glad of the daily walks she had been taking on the beach at Ballycastle. At least her breathing was steady and slow and, more important in this case, quiet. Shaking her head to clear it of any distractions, she crept along the side of the warehouse towards the river, being careful not to trip over anything on the ground. As she came within a few feet of the end of the building, she crouched down well below eye level and cautiously peeped out.

The white van was now stopped fifty feet in front of the building and facing the water. With more luck than judgement she had approached from the direction that meant that the open side-door of the van was facing her. So, she had a good view of what was happening.

The man was reaching into the interior of the van and was pulling something out.

Isobel quickly set her phone to video and angled it so that it was recording what was happening.

The gardening bag loomed in the door and he bumped it down onto the ground. Suddenly he swung around, taking in the area around him. Isobel shrank back, terrified. When she dared to take a quick look again, he was moving in her direction. She scuttled back along the building, turned and got ready to run.

She waited but he didn't appear. She stood irresolute. Was he waiting for her to pop her head around the corner again? She remained very still, straining her ears for any sounds, her pulse pounding in her ears, deafening her.

Every second seemed like an eternity. Still he didn't appear. She moved forward again. She thought she heard a muttered oath, not anger, more impatience or irritation. She debated with herself. Despite her misgivings, she had no choice but to take another look.

She crept forward once more and peeked quickly round the corner again.

She was just in time to see the man who frustratingly she still couldn't identify because of his hat, placing a medium-size rock in the bag and then trekking back to a pile she'd failed to notice before. He lifted another stone and carried it, depositing it too into the bag. He gave the bag a trial lift and then, setting it back down, retrieved another stone. Once again Isobel used her phone to record his handiwork. After one more test lift, he seemed happy with the weight. Taking the two handles of the gardening bag, he tied them tightly together and dragged his package to the water's edge. He took a few deep breaths then, grabbing what was still available of the handles he lifted the bag and then heaved it into the water as far out as he could manage. There was the sound of a splash. He stretched his back a little, watching the sinking of the gardening bag. Then he rubbed his gloved hands together. Collecting himself, he broke into a light jog. He returned to the door of the van, reaching in to grab something which he then held against his body, then ran up the roadway between the two warehouses.

Isobel, almost mesmerized, recorded all of this until he disappeared from her sight. She made her own way back along the side of the warehouse. By the time she got to the end the man was clear of the buildings and was at the gate. He didn't open it – instead he reached up with his arms and swung his body clear of the gate, landing on the outside.

Once on the road he turned right and headed back along the road they'd driven into this commercial area. Only when he disappeared from view did Isobel exhale. She could feel her legs shaking from the adrenaline and she sagged against the wall of the warehouse that had given her cover.

A minute passed before she could rouse herself to any activity. The first thing she did was stop the video recording. Then, realising that action was needed, she rang Malcolm.

"Malcolm, he's just thrown the bag in the river and left on foot. I still don't know who he is, with that hat on." Isobel could feel her voice shake with strain and upset.

"Where are you, Isobel? Describe your location."

Isobel did her best, saying it was Deptford and describing the right turn they had made and the two warehouses.

"I'm on my way. Do your best to remember where he was when he jettisoned the bag so we can tell the harbour police."

Isobel cringed, realising how important this probably was. She made her way back along the length of the warehouse. Reaching the river, she visualised again what had happened and, keeping her eyes fixed where he had stood, made her way forward. She laid her phone down on the ground where the man had stood to dump the bag. Looking round, she spied the pile of stones and went and fetched a large one, placing it where her phone was, to mark the spot. She knew that was the best she could do. She picked up her phone and left. Shivering in reaction, she walked back to the gate.

She stood on a low bar of the gate and cautiously leaned over. She scanned the road but there was no sight of the man. Climbing over the gate, she began to walk up the road to find Grace.

Then Grace's head popped up from behind a wall further down. So, she had got out of the car after all. Grace waved and then disappeared.

Isobel kept walking and in a few minutes Grace pulled up in the car beside her.

"I told you not to get out of the car," Isobel said.

Grace ignored her. "What happened?" she asked.

"He threw it in the river."

"Did you record it?"

"I did," Isobel said and, despite how fearful she'd felt, or maybe because of it, she straightened her shoulders with pride.

She got into the car and they drove along to the gate and parked.

"We'd need to keep watch and take off quickly if we spot the guy again. He could come back, after all – though I doubt it," Isobel said.

A minute or two passed before she realised that she should ensure Malcolm knew where they were. Dialling him up again, she asked him to wait and then handed the phone to Grace. "Give Malcolm directions," she said by way of explanation and then she tuned out of the conversation.

It was probably fifteen more minutes before they saw Malcolm's green car approaching. Relief flooded Isobel. She couldn't think any more or decide what to do.

Malcolm stopped at the gate and approached them.

"All right, Grace?" he asked.

Grace dismissed his query with a wave of her hand.

He turned to Isobel. "You?"

She nodded.

"In here?"

"Yes."

Maybe it was police procedure, or maybe he knew that if she started talking about what she'd seen she would cry, but he didn't ask anything more. He just pulled down the sleeves of his jumper and opened the gate.

Isobel and Grace followed him.

"Show me," he said, no fuss, no questions, no talk.

Isobel led the way to the place where the van was and showed him where she had placed the stone.

He nodded then said, "Show me the photo of the body."

Isobel pulled up the image on her phone.

He looked at it for a few seconds. "Let me make some calls."

He stepped away and Isobel heard him contact at least three different people but was beyond following what he was organising. Grace came and stood beside Isobel and gently placed her arm around her back. They stood there together at the water's edge, silent and sad, almost in vigil. No prayers came to Isobel's mind – in fact, it was blank. Grace's lips moved but Isobel could hear no words.

An indeterminate length of time passed and then Malcolm came back to them. "I've let the police know. And I've contacted the Marine Policing Unit and they're on their way – they'll arrive by boat. Eventually, I managed to get Simon on the phone."

At this Isobel stirred. "What did he say?"

"He says that they've heard from Thomas Banks."

Shock registered on Isobel's face. "*What?*"

"Yes, he's rung them to say that he's been waiting for

his wife to call to let him know she was on her way. She hasn't called. It's getting very late and he thinks that she's balked at signing the divorce. He's going to go over to her flat to see what the problem is."

"*What?*" said Isobel again. "And where is he saying he has been all of this time? Just waiting for her?"

"According to him, he knew he wouldn't be able to concentrate today and so he didn't bother going to work. Instead, he went to a shopping centre to pass the time. Simon is allowing him to go to the flat to check for Anne but he's sending police to keep an eye on the situation discreetly."

Isobel felt as if she was living in a nightmare. "So now everyone believes him that he was in a shopping centre? He's getting away with this!" Her voice held disbelief but also the beginnings of rage.

Malcolm looked at her. "No, Isobel, he's not getting away with this. We just have to find evidence and at the moment we don't know that it was him here. So you need to stay calm and let everyone do their jobs and see how we can proceed with this."

Isobel could feel her anger rising to explosive level. "*But he moved a dead body and dumped it!*"

"Someone moved a body. We can't at this point be sure it was him. But we now have grounds to really investigate him."

"*It was him!*" Isobel snapped.

"Can you prove it?"

"I have the video."

"Does it show his face?"

"No, but –"

"So this isn't simple. Be patient and we will find proof."

Isobel turned in a sharp circle and faced him again.

Malcolm tried again. "All we have to do is retrieve the body and with your photographic evidence we can arrest him."

Isobel shook her head in disbelief. "I feel as if I'm in a chess game and he's always one step ahead."

"We will get him."

Isobel turned and wandered some distance away. Malcolm got back on the phone, but Isobel had lost interest in all the machinations. She felt hopeless. Grace said nothing but stayed near her, not intruding.

A police car arrived with two officers. Malcolm explained what had happened and had Isobel show the images from her phone. There were more conversations. They hung around like that for nearly an hour before Isobel observed Malcolm looking busily out onto the river.

An inflated boat was making its way towards them with a number of men in it. They pulled in close to the wall further down from where all the action had taken place. Malcolm reached down and helped pull a man up onto the cement dock and they walked over to where Isobel was standing.

"Isobel, this is Pat Smith, who is in charge of the river search. Pat, this is Isobel, the lady who witnessed the body being moved."

Pat's handshake was dry and firm but not crushing. Without further preamble he said, "Malcolm has filled me in on the phone about a lot of the story so no need to repeat it but I understand you also have some footage."

Isobel nodded.

"I'd like to see that, now, please, before we do anything."

Isobel pulled out her phone and firstly brought up the

photograph of the dead woman's face as she lay in the hole. She saw Malcolm and Pat exchange a look but no one commented.

She then showed the video of the man pulling the garden bag out of the gazebo and around the side of the house. And then the images of him taking the gardening bag out of the van, placing the stones in it, knotting it and then dumping it into the river.

"And the van?" Pat asked Malcolm.

"A forensic team is coming but, with no body, as yet this is not going to be a priority."

Pat nodded. "But you are preserving the scene."

"Yes, of course." Malcolm turned and pointed. "Isobel placed that stone where she thought the man stood to dump the bag."

Pat nodded, gestured as to whether he could have her phone and rewound and froze the picture. He measured things with his eye. "Isobel, I need you to send me all of these images so I can use them as reference."

"OK," Isobel replied.

With Pat's help that was quickly achieved.

Pat turned then to Isobel. "We're going to begin our search here. Obviously, it will be systematic and we will search a much bigger area than just the suspected spot if we don't immediately find the body. There's a current here so despite those stones the body may have travelled. I'm going to organise another team to go downriver a bit and search. My men can only stay underwater for a certain time. We'll see what we can find tonight, then review overnight and if need be plan tomorrow. Isobel, there are no guarantees with a river search. We know a lot about the likely currents and paths, but it is a river."

Isobel was dismayed. She had thought it would be a simple matter of bringing up the body from where she had seen it dumped.

As if sensing her depression, Pat said, "Your photograph shows clearly a dead and decaying body. There is someone there and we're going to do everything we can to find them."

"Yes, thank you."

"You did great to get so much footage. It was very brave of you."

Isobel acknowledged what he said with a small turn of her head and then he was gone, calling instructions to the waiting men in the boat in a technical language that was foreign to her. As he spoke the men started lifting face masks. Pat got back into the boat and within a few minutes she could see two men being helped into air tanks and another man take his place at the front of the boat with a clipboard and chart. Pat was on a phone speaking vehemently to someone else and giving instructions. Things were well in hand.

With the commencement of the search Isobel felt a measure of relief coming over her. She turned to Malcolm. "What should I do now?"

Malcolm tore his eyes away from the men in the water and looked at her, unsure. "Let me ring Simon and see what he wants done."

A muttered phone call followed.

He hung up and turned to her.

"Simon is following up with the police on where Anne is. He has the number of this van and is checking who owns it. He has a lot of information to gather. He's suggesting that you have something to eat, then make your way to Scotland Yard and give a statement to one of his officers. They'll be expecting you. Then, after that, hold on until he gets back and we can all have a meeting – he thinks that will be at about half past seven."

That sounded like a good plan and Isobel was glad to comply. Only now was she realising that she hadn't eaten since breakfast and, despite all that had happened, she was hungry.

"What about you, Malcolm? What are you going to do?"

"I'm going to hold on here for another while and then grab a quick bite on the way to the meeting. I'll see you there. Fingers crossed that we've found something by then."

Isobel crossed her fingers to show support then asked, "Does Grace need to make a statement too?"

"Yes, because she was the one who saw the gazebo and alerted you. Simon wants all the statements airtight, showing the development of the case. Then he'll have a better chance with the legal people of being able to get warrants when he needs them."

That made sense to Isobel. With a "See you later," for Malcolm and a wave for Pat, she hooked Grace's arm and they headed out to the road to retrieve the car.

Chapter 36

It was twenty to eight before the meeting started. At least ten people were gathered in a large conference room with whiteboards on the walls covered in writing. Isobel had rung Patricia earlier and asked her to come to the meeting, which only seemed fair, as it was their combined efforts that had uncovered the new information. Patricia had jumped at the chance. Now, they were sitting at the back of the room with Malcolm beside them.

While they were waiting for things to start, Isobel studied the information on the boards. There was the photograph she had taken of the woman's body and a picture of the front of Thomas Banks' house. Earlier, during her statement to a younger female officer called Stella, she had shown all the photos she had acquired during her interviews with the various people. The photograph of Anne and Thomas at the formal event was up on the board too, and one each of them individually. There was also a copy of some of Anne Banks' injuries that Yvonne Dempsey had supplied and a photograph of Charlotte. Beside that was a written list of questions with names beside each one.

Another whiteboard had photographs of some bones in the earth, also a photograph of an older woman and one of Thomas Banks with question marks beside them. Again there was a list of written questions and names assigned to each one. Spread out like this, Isobel could see the scope of this investigation and also all the areas where the police were pursuing active leads.

Simon stood at the front of the room and called the meeting to order.

"Before we begin, I want to introduce the civilians present. Many of you will know Malcolm. He's one of our own who just couldn't stay away."

There was widespread laughter and a few hecklers.

"How can you get bored playing golf?"

"Glutton for punishment!"

"Long hours, abuse, what's not to miss?"

Malcolm was clearly well used to the banter and was able to hold his own. "I had to come back to give you the benefit of my experience."

More laughter and teasing. Simon let it go a few moments and then got back to business.

"The other civilians are Isobel McKenzie and Patricia King who have been instrumental in alerting us to these bodies."

Everyone turned to look at them and Isobel blushed and shifted uncomfortably. Simon cleared his throat and everyone's attention turned back to him.

"I realise this is unusual but they're here because they've been active in uncovering information and if there are questions at this stage they can answer them quickly. We have a lot to get through and I don't want any needless delays. OK. First of all, I've just spoken to Pat Smith, the

MPU officer leading the search for the remains thrown into the Thames. As yet they haven't found them. This isn't good. Their best chance is tomorrow otherwise we may never find this body and with it the identity of the victim."

Isobel was devastated. They had come relatively soon after the bag was dumped. How could they not have found it already?

Simon continued, "Pat has called in their experts in tidal influences and current impact. Tomorrow they'll commence the search at daybreak wherever they suggest. Pat will call the minute they find anything." He paused. "Forensics have had a look at the van. A set of prints overlaying the others was lifted from the steering wheel. No match on file. There is also some liquid on the floor of the van. It's being analysed at the moment. It may be that some fluid leaked from the bag, maybe something from the body. That would be a break. We could identify the victim. We're waiting to find out what it is. If it's human, we can compare the DNA with that of Claire Graham, Anne Banks' sister. Jeff already has a sample." Another pause and Simon skipped to a new line of enquiry. "The van was a hire van. It was rented out to a Charlie Ellis. He's a handyman. Paul, where are you with that?"

A lanky officer with touselled brown hair made his way to the front of the room.

"Since no body has yet been found to tie the van to anything bigger, we've been taking the line that the van was abandoned at the Deptford wharf. One of the employees from the hire firm identified Charlie Ellis as the man who came in and hired the van. He signed for it and he paid with his bank card. We've questioned Charlie Ellis about hiring the van and he says that Thomas Banks phoned him and asked him to hire it and leave it at the Commercial Shopping Centre. Charlie Ellis is cooperating. He freely gave us his phone and there was a call at the time he said. That call was from a burner phone, not from Thomas Banks' phone. When we asked Charlie about this he said that Thomas explained that he had a problem with his own phone and had borrowed someone else's." Paul looked up to check that they were all keeping up and then continued. "We've pulled the CCTV coverage from the shopping-centre car park. Charlie Ellis does drive up in the van, place the car key behind the right front tyre and walk away in the direction of the shopping centre. Sometime later a man who has the same size and build as Charlie, with the same jeans, lumberjack shirt and boots, comes out with a cap and gloves on and carrying a B&Q bag. He takes the key and drives off in the van. Thomas Banks' car also shows up in this car park but in a completely different area. He arrives after the van and doesn't leave until around the time he phoned you, Simon. In fact he phones from the car park. We've pulled the CCTV from the centre and we're going through it to see if we can trace his movements for those hours. Also, tomorrow we're going to B&Q to see if they can tell us what was purchased."

Simon said, "Good. I want detailed accounts of both men's movements in the shopping centre. I'm not going to talk to Thomas Banks about this until I know the answers to most of the questions I will be asking him. What else does Charlie Ellis say?"

Paul flicked through the pages of his notebook. "Charlie Ellis says that Thomas Banks promised him a thousand pounds and told him to take the rest of the day off, which he says he did. He claims he went home and watched Sky Sports and had a few beers."

Simon asked, "How did he get home?"

"Tube, he says."

"Are you following that up?"

"Yes, we're collecting footage from the Tube stations that he says he used."

Simon said, "Thomas Banks called Peter the solicitor at half past two claiming that his soon-to-be-ex-wife had not rung to say she was on her way and that he no longer thought that she was going to come and sign papers. There is evidence in the form of a statement by Anne Banks' sister, and also DNA evidence that this woman was a doppelganger. Thomas Banks is of course claiming her as his wife. He says he was worried and called to Anne's flat but got no answer. Who followed up there?"

"I did, sir."

"OK, Frank, let's hear it."

"After we observed Thomas Banks leave his wife's flat, where he didn't gain entry, we checked with the shops below and nearby to see if anyone had seen her. We used the photo that you sent us, and we got something. The lady in the dress shop underneath saw Anne Banks putting a case into a taxi. Because the shop owner had ordered some dresses for Anne, thinking she might need them if she was going away, she followed her out. Mrs Banks said she didn't need the clothing that weekend and that she would call another time. The shop owner felt she was getting the brush off and she lingered and heard Anne Banks tell the taxi driver to take her to Euston Station."

There were murmurs around the room.

"And?" Simon prompted.

"We've been to Euston and have tracked Anne Banks going into the station and getting on the train to Manchester. I've been on to Manchester train station and they're sending me all the footage of the train arriving in Manchester. That information just arrived before the meeting so we haven't looked at it yet."

"What time did this all happen?" Simon asked.

"Between ten and eleven o'clock this morning."

Simon looked pensive. "So she wasn't delayed at the hairdresser's. She did a runner. How did she know to run? What made them suspect we were on to them? Thomas Banks is going to say his wife panicked but he was buying time." Looking at Frank, he said, "If we can prove his duplicity we would be in a stronger position, especially if we don't get the body. We really need to find that woman and establish who she is and show at least that he was colluding with her."

"I'll find her, sir."

Simon grinned. "Make sure you do."

He turned and looked at the whiteboard with the photographs of the bones. "Now to the corpse found in 42 Sycamore Street, which we have yet to confirm is part of this investigation. Ning?"

Ning stood up. "The bones have been examined by the pathologist and are definitely human. Seventy per cent of them have been exhumed and that process should be completed by tomorrow lunchtime. I'm pushing for an autopsy tomorrow afternoon. I've told the pathologist that it may be related to a possible multiple homicide and that we need results as soon as possible. The photograph up on the board here is Mrs Cooper, the previous owner of the house who allegedly moved to Scotland ten years ago. This is an old driving-licence photo of her. We've checked in Scotland and can find no trace of Mrs Cooper using her name or using her social security number."

Simon nodded. "Keep pushing for the autopsy to be done asap. I'll clear it with the Superintendent. Phone me the moment you have anything." Turning once again to the wider room, he said, "Obviously, because the divorce papers weren't signed we can't bring Thomas Banks in on suspicion of fraud yet. The more information I have the better so *push*, people, *push*! OK, everyone, pursue the lines you've been assigned and we'll meet again at midday. Hopefully the body will have been found by then. We really need it."

Everyone started to get up, some to go back to work and others to head home.

Isobel and Patricia waited with Malcolm. After most people had filtered out Simon came over to them.

"How soon can you bring Thomas Banks in for questioning?" Isobel asked.

Simon's brow furrowed. "It's tricky. Things would be so much easier if we had the body."

Isobel swallowed.

"Don't worry – we'll still get him – it's just going to be more difficult." Tomorrow will tell a lot. Hopefully the Thames will be kind to us and reveal her secrets."

Isobel nodded. Then, knowing that she had made a promise, she broached another subject. "Simon, the real Thomas Banks was knocked down by a drunk driver. His father is still really upset. I know you don't think there is anything there to pursue but could you please let me talk to the investigating officer? Just so I can tell Mr Banks we have had another look at things, to put his mind at rest? I know you're really busy but . . ."

Isobel knew she was pushing it and that Simon had a lot on his plate, but she was hoping that all she had uncovered already would count for something.

Simon pursed his lips then called out to one of the women officers still in the room. "Stella, find out who investigated this fatal road accident – Isobel will give you the details and then get them on the line for me."

"Thank you, Simon," Isobel said.

She gave the details to Stella and, with the help of the computer, the young officer soon had the name and phone number of the investigating officer. Simon arranged a meeting for Isobel with him at ten o'clock the next morning. There was little more to say and they all bid each other a weary goodnight. Isobel suspected that Simon would be working very late at the station.

Afraid that someone might overhear them, Isobel and Patricia waited until they got home to discuss the meeting.

"What do you think?" Patricia said.

Isobel was sitting on the couch. She leaned forward, putting her head in her hands. "I'm mad that I couldn't stop that body being thrown in the river. I should have done something."

"Jesus, Isobel, we think this man is a multiple murderer! So what could you have done?"

Isobel looked up at her. Patricia sat down beside her.

Isobel bit her lip. "OK, I couldn't have stopped him at that point – but the very fact that the body was moved, and potentially lost, is because of all the interfering that I have been doing in the case. Simon was right. He knows how to catch people. Maybe because of what I've done Thomas will get off."

Patricia opened her mouth to speak, then chewed her

lip. She took a deep breath. "Isobel, please stop this. Listen to me. No one would have known anything about Thomas Banks and what had happened to Anne if you hadn't figured it out. He would have been home free. You have to keep perspective here. It would have been impossible to find the truth if you hadn't talked to everyone as you did. We wouldn't even have realised he was moving the body if you hadn't met Grace and she trusted you." Patricia frowned. "I don't know how he figured out we were on to him, and maybe we never will, but at least we're on to him now. At least there's a chance we'll get him and I'm sure that, even if we don't, Simon is going to keep his eye on him. He's never again going to be able to do things like this. But in my heart I know we are going to get him. Don't give up. We've come so far against all the odds."

Isobel gave her a hug. "Thank you. I needed that pep talk." She smiled through some tears. "I guess we let the police do their job and just hope that they find the remains in the river."

"Exactly. Now what are you going to do tomorrow?"

Isobel took a deep breath. "Well, there is the investigating officer in the Thomas Banks hit-and-run at ten o'clock." She looked at Patricia with raised eyebrows.

"I must just give Peter a ring and fill him in. Maybe things will be very quiet at the office and I might take an annual leave day and maybe …"

Isobel grinned. "Fine by me if you want to come detecting." She took the opportunity to ring Dave.

"Well – all over. Are you flying home tomorrow?"

Isobel grimaced at the relief and cheerfulness in his voice. "All over bar the shouting but I'm going to stay another day or two."

"*What?*"

"You know, to celebrate, go for a meal, relax with my new friends here."

"Oh well, that sounds good. Thank God you're finished chasing after murderers."

Isobel cringed. If he only knew about today.

"Let me know when you're coming home. I want to hear all about it."

"Yeah. Talk soon."

Patricia grinned as she came back. "I'm good to go for tomorrow. Peter knows I really want to see this through."

Isobel had thought that tiredness and a measure of relief would have ensured a peaceful sleep that night but it was not to be. In her dreams she was standing by some water. As she looked in she could see a woman under the water reaching up towards the surface to her and she could hear a haunting voice saying '*Help me, help me!*'. Isobel ran up and down the bank but there was nothing she could use to help – no person, no flotation ring, no branch. She took off her shoes and socks and tried to get into the water but she couldn't get in. She tried again and again, getting more and more upset, but ended up on the bank unable to reach the woman. And all the time the voice called '*Help me, help me!*'.

Chapter 37

Thursday 31st May

Next morning, Isobel and Patricia made their way to meet the primary police officer in the hit-and-run case at his station. They gave their names to the duty sergeant who escorted them to an interview room. Within a few minutes they were joined by a man. He was six foot tall with dark curly hair touched with silver at the temples. His eyes were blue. He seemed confident and self-assured and got down to business immediately.

"My name is Adam Bryce."

Isobel and Patricia introduced themselves.

"Simon has been on to me this morning already giving me a more detailed insight into what you have uncovered and where the investigation is now. He tells me that you, Isobel, are consulting on the investigation, and that you, Patricia, are part of Anne Banks' legal team."

Isobel and Patricia turned to each other and smiled at their new, elevated status.

Adam went on, "It seems some new information has come to light, namely that Matt Cooper, Thomas Banks' friend, started using his name shortly after his death."

Patricia answered, "Yes."

Isobel added, "We're unsure if he impersonated Thomas and took the job that had been meant for Thomas or if he merely changed his name and got a new job with the same firm that Thomas was moving to. We haven't contacted that firm regarding who they employed or thought they employed."

Adam smiled. "No, but I did."

"Well, you're not hanging about! And?"

"And, I spoke to one of the people in Human Resources. Thomas Banks had an interview two weeks before his death and accepted the job when it was offered to him the next day. In actual fact, when Thomas did start with them his performance was, according to the firm, a bit of a disappointment. In their initial evaluations they broached this and he cited stress from some personal grief. Obviously, the firm was supportive and he still works for them but he never lived up to their initial expectations and what his previous work experience suggested. A competent but not inspiring worker is how they summed him up."

"So Matt took the job in Thomas's place," Isobel interpreted.

Adam nodded. "Yes."

Isobel frowned. "How did they not realise that it was a different guy?"

"Well, they obviously didn't. Maybe because it's a big company, maybe they had lots of interviews, maybe the people who were doing the interviews weren't so involved in the day-to-day contact with employees. And ten years ago this sort of thing was easier to do than it is now. Who knows?"

"And the hit-and-run?" Patricia asked.

"Also interesting. The accident took place near

Thomas Banks' father's house, ouside one of the popular local pubs."

Isobel shook her head. "We know nothing about the hit-and-run except the outcome. It was the man's father who told us about what happened. We were hardly going to press him for details."

"No, of course not. Let me explain then. I've been looking over the file this morning. Thomas was in the family local having a few drinks. He had three or four but was by no means very drunk. He left just before last orders to go home to his dad's house which is not far away. He was in great form that evening according to the landlord's statement back then. Shortly after he left a man ran in and said that someone had been knocked down. They rang an ambulance and some people ran out. They tried to resuscitate him, as did the ambulance crew when they arrived, but he was declared dead upon arrival at the hospital. The car involved was a black sedan which was found burned out the next morning. It belonged to a Jennifer Green who was a secretary and lived in Holborn. She reported it stolen that evening. A woman who lived near the pub witnessed the accident. Her statement is here. She said the car was driving very fast and seemed to head straight for Thomas. After the accident the driver stopped and got out and walked back to Thomas. He knelt down beside him for a few seconds then got up, went back to the car, and fled the scene. However, the driver couldn't be identified from the footage. We checked out the owner, but she had left her car at home and gone out for the evening – witnesses confirm that. We assumed that it was a joyrider or drunk driver."

Isobel asked, "Are joyriders not usually very young?""

Adam regarded her. "Yes, more frequently they are but

not always. The driver had jeans and a jacket and a baseball cap on. It was hard to say what age he was. We couldn't identify him and we had no other leads. How do you think Thomas's death relates to Simon's case?"

Isobel said, "It may not. In fact, Simon thinks we're wasting our time but we're interested in seeing if Matt Cooper could have done this."

"Based on what evidence?" he said coolly.

"Based on the fact that he assumed Thomas's identity and profited by his death," Isobel responded sharply. "And that he may have got away with a lot of things that no one knew about."

"Well, Simon told me that he is very dubious about what you are suggesting."

Isobel bit her lip. "Yes, he did say that a car would be an unlikely murder weapon because it is only at high speed that death would be inevitable."

"And he felt that Matt wouldn't have committed murder so close to where they lived," said Adam. "But it could have been at high speed." He frowned. "That pub is on a straight bit of road. To get a car to sixty miles an hour takes six to ten seconds." He tapped his finger on his lip. "Having a straight bit of road where you can see someone walking is a help."

"Are you saying it's possible?"

"That street has been used by joy riders because it is long and straight and only has local traffic which is light – that's why we jumped to the conclusion that it was a joyrider. But if you have an alternative theory, I think it's worth looking at." He held up his hands. "It might be pie in the sky but I think it's worth a look."

Patricia said, "And we promised Thomas Banks Senior

that we would try and look at things again, just to put his mind at ease. We know that you're busy but it would be great to review everything."

"Quite the tag team you got here, very persuasive."

Isobel bit her lip and Patricia shifted in her chair but they stayed silent.

Adam looked from one to the other. "Look, Simon has told me how you may have uncovered a number of different bodies so I would like to see if there's any chance of some new insights here. Matt Cooper didn't even feature in our investigation because he wasn't there that night – now maybe that's a significant fact and bears some scrutiny. What do you want to do?"

Isobel said, "I want to talk to the eyewitness and also to the woman who owned the car. Do you still have the footage from the pub camera?"

"Of course. Thomas died, so this is vehicular manslaughter – so, yes, we kept all of the evidence."

Isobel shuddered. "We'll probably want to look at that but let's talk to the witness first."

Patricia nodded her agreement.

Adam said, "I'll get one of the constables to copy the footage for you," and he left the room.

Isobel looked at Patricia. "What do you think?"

"Matt Cooper could have deliberately run Thomas down. Adam seems to be implying that it's at least possible."

They lapsed into silence.

Adam returned with a USB stick. "Here's the footage of the hit-and-run. The witness is called Mrs O'Dwyer. She lives a couple of streets away. We can walk."

"We have to be back to Scotland Yard for twelve o'clock for the update on the investigation," said Isobel.

They set out, walking briskly, and turned onto a long, straight street.

Patricia stopped. "Speed bumps."

Isobel stopped too. "Oh."

"They were put in a year after Thomas was killed," Adam said. "The community put together a petition about the danger to residents from drivers speeding along this road and eventually they persuaded the council to do something. I'm sure Thomas's death contributed to that."

Isobel swallowed a lump in her throat.

Mrs Dwyer, despite her advanced years, proved to be a sprightly lady with a twinkle in her eye. She recognised Adam immediately.

"I remember you. You came to see me after Thomas got knocked down and killed – so sad. It broke his mother's heart, killed her really, and his poor father has never got over it." She shook her head.

"We're just reviewing the case and I wondered if we could talk to you about it again," Adam said.

"Of course, of course, anything that I can do to help. It would give his father some peace if they got the person who did it. It would be some measure of justice at least."

They followed Mrs O'Dwyer into her front room. She offered them tea and Isobel went along to help her.

Whilst in the kitchen they chatted about Ireland and different types of tea and, by the time they returned with the refreshments, Mrs O'Dwyer was very relaxed and in a talkative mood.

Adam, perhaps sensing the informal rapport that Isobel had established, said nothing. After everyone chatted while having a cup of tea and a biscuit, Isobel stood up and went to the window of the sitting room. She looked out, contemplating the view of the street.

She turned from the window. "Is this where you were standing when you saw the accident?"

Mrs O'Dwyer got up and joined Isobel at the window. "Yes, yes, right here. I don't sleep very well and sometimes I get up and just watch people as they leave the pub in the evenings. To be honest, you would sometimes be amazed at who goes home with whom."

Isobel couldn't suppress a smile. Mrs O'Dwyer obviously loved to know all about what was going on.

"It's better than a soap opera." Her face became more serious as she continued. "Thomas was alone that night, walking on the footpath and not staggering. Suddenly I heard this spinning of tyres and then I saw a black car speeding towards him. It didn't waver, it just headed straight for him, mounted the kerb, hit him and knocked Thomas onto the road. The car drove on a bit and stopped a bit further up there." She pointed. "Thomas was lying on the road. The man got out, walked back and knelt down beside him to see how badly he was hurt. and then left when he saw how bad the accident was . . . but sometimes I think that man didn't stagger out of the car – he didn't look shocked and panicked. He seemed steady. It was almost like he stopped to check that he'd really killed him and then walked calmly back to his car and drove off. There was a deliberateness about him that actually gives me nightmares." She shivered.

Isobel asked softly, "Did you mention this to the police at the time?"

Mrs O'Dwyer looked uncomfortable. "Not really. I did say he seemed very steady and all."

Adam said, "What can you tell us about the driver?"

Mrs O'Dwyer shrugged. "I told you at the time. He was

wearing jeans and a loose jacket and a kind of baseball cap. I didn't see his face. I can't really be sure of what age he was. He seemed tall and slim as far as I could judge."

There seemed little more to say so they thanked her and left.

At the door she gave Adam a beaming smile. "Come back and see me again and don't leave it so long next time."

They were all smiling as they went down her path.

Adam led the way down the road and stood where Mrs O'Dwyer had been indicating. Isobel and Patricia followed him. They looked along the road in both directions. It was certainly a long straight street.

Adam pointed back along the street. "The car came from that direction. I reread the coroner's report and the crash report. They agreed that the injuries were consistent with being struck by a car that was travelling at sixty miles per hour or more. It's easy to find out on Google that sixty is a fatal speed."

Patricia pulled out her phone. Within a few seconds she was turning the phone to show Isobel a graph. A quick glance at the graph made it clear that very few people of any age survived being hit by a car travelling at sixty miles per hour.

Isobel nodded sadly.

Adam said, "If you feel up to it, I just want to get some idea of where the car would have started its acceleration from."

Patricia nodded.

Isobel shivered. It was strange. Despite the fact that Thomas had died here a long time ago she felt a connection to him.

Adam pulled out his own phone. "I checked the type

of car involved in the incident. It was a Ford Focus 1993 model. I've checked some car tables and if the driver was doing sixty miles per hour when he hit Thomas . . ." Adam pulled up some information on his phone. "It would have taken him maybe ten seconds to accelerate from standstill to that speed."

Isobel could feel her mind glazing over. She glanced at Patricia who was frowning in concentration.

"That means that the driver travelled about one eight of a mile from starting to impact."

Patricia swung around and looked back towards the pub. "So where would the car have started its acceleration from?"

Adam frowned. "How many steps do you think you take to walk a mile?"

Isobel smiled. "I know this. I monitored this when I was si –" She swallowed. "While I've been on sabbatical. A mile for me is 2000 steps."

Adam did some more computing. "So we are roughly talking about 250 steps." Adam looked up. "That seems a lot. Walk back that far, Isobel, to see where you would be accelerating the car from."

Isobel set off walking. She counted out the steps, then stopped and turned. From where she stood she could see Adam and Patricia, but she couldn't see their faces. At closing time at night it would be impossible to accurately identify anyone from this distance.

"*It's too far!*" she shouted. She wasn't sure if they heard her.

Adam beckoned to her to come back.

Isobel walked back. "It's too far, isn't it?" she said.

Adam nodded.

Patricia pivoted on her feet. "If Matt waited outside, hidden, when he saw Thomas coming out he could run back to the car, jump in and then accelerate after him."

Adam made a face.

"You don't think so?" Isobel said.

"I think you're making theories based on who you want to be guilty."

Isobel commented, "When we get to the police station we need to have a look at that footage."

They travelled in Adam's car to Scotland Yard for the midday meeting. They were a bit early so Adam spoke to Stella and the attractive athletic-looking young officer showed them to a side office where she left them to use the computer. They plugged in the USB stick and ran the footage.

Looking at it, all three of them could see that Mrs O'Dwyer was not faulty in her memory of the events. The man didn't appear very drunk or stoned or very shocked and distressed.

Adam said, "When the driver stands out of the car he does seem tall. From his shoulders I would guess definitely a man too but he has done well to keep the peak of his hat down and his head lowered."

Patricia said, "If this was Matt, he would know about the cameras outside the pub on the street. He would know that he needed to be careful."

Isobel nodded, "And Matt would know that the street was suitable for building speed."

Adam said, "Yes, but so would any of the joyriders from the area."

They looked at each other.

"Let's see if this secretary who owned the car knew Matt Cooper," said Patricia.

Chapter 38

Isobel, Patricia and Adam stood at the back of the conference room. The atmosphere was contagious, almost physical, like a tingle or a buzz. Something was happening.

Isobel saw Malcolm and he gave her the thumbs-up.

What? Did he mean they'd found the body? She had no time to find out anything more before Simon called the meeting to order.

"OK, people, settle down. First things first, I'm going to hand you over to Pat who is our Marine Policing Unit expert."

Pat moved to the front and centre of the room. "We recommended our search at first light today and searched in the area that our Thames expert suggested but we found nothing."

Isobel's heart sank.

There were murmurs and a general shifting around as people expressed their disappointment.

"Then we tracked along the riverbed from that point towards the dump site and . . ." He paused.

Isobel could feel a ray of hope igniting inside her.

"And an hour ago we found a bag snagged on a

protuberance on the bed of the river. The bag appeared to resemble the one videoed entering the water. The bag was moved to our examination area and a preliminary exam confirms that the bag contains . . ." He paused again, looked around the expectant faces and found Isobel's. "The bag contains the body of a woman."

A subdued rustle could be heard. No one wanted to celebrate a dead woman's body but everyone was hugely relieved that her remains had been recovered.

Isobel felt tears starting to her eyes and hastily tried to brush them away. Simon caught her eye and gave an acknowledging nod.

"The coroner is with the body now and we hope the autopsy will be done today," Pat finished.

"*Well done, mate, to you and your crew!*" shouted an anonymous voice and there was some backslapping.

Simon stepped forward now. "Thanks, Pat, to you and the lads. Orla, you need to make sure that the DNA from this is compared with that of Claire Graham. Any news on the fluid on the floor of the van?"

"Yes, initial analysis confirms that the fluid is human."

"Good, then we need a comparison between the fluid found on the floor of the van and the body from the river. The minute you know, contact me. Put a rush on things – but I suppose we're still talking at least twenty-four hours for DNA. If this is Anne Banks, which we suspect it is, then this case is coming together. If Thomas Banks did this, he's a slippery character. He's under surveillance at the moment and he's a very cool customer. I want the evidence so tight he can't breathe. When I pull him in for questioning I want to have everything we need to nail the bastard."

Isobel was no longer in any doubt about Simon's commitment.

"Next," Simon said, looking at the board. "Ning, where are we with the other body?"

Ning piped up from the midst of a group of men. "The autopsy is being done. Since we didn't want to alert Thomas Banks by getting a DNA sample, I've been on the phones all morning with dentists in the locality of the house. We eventually found Mrs Cooper's old dentist from ten years ago. We collected the old notes and X-rays and delivered them to the coroner. I had a call from him just before the meeting started and, using the dental records, he confirms that the body from 42 Sycamore Street is Mrs Joan Cooper's, Matt Cooper's mother – the man calling himself Thomas Banks' mother."

This time there was silence. Isobel was flooded with relief.

Simon said, "So we have one definite death associated with Thomas Banks and if the river body is Anne Banks that's two."

Ning spoke again. "The autopsy showed one more thing of note. Joan Cooper's hyoid bone was fractured. This is more indicative of manual strangulation than strangulation by ligature. The hyoid is not fractured in every case of manual strangulation but more frequently when the person is older. Given the fact that we know of Thomas Banks' attempted strangulation of his wife and also of an old girlfriend, it seems likely that he strangled and buried his mother, then sold the house which was in his name."

"Great work, Ning. Right. We need to find this doppelganger. She may be an accessory to murder. Where are you with that, Frank?"

"We looked at the footage from Manchester train station after the meeting last night. We had Anne Banks leaving the station and walking out onto the street. Manchester police were helping us and they tracked her on CCTV. I sent an officer to be our eyes up there. We had her going into a shopping centre. We lost her in there. However, Manchester police started interviewing shop assistants in the centre and they got something. She went to a hairdresser's and spent the day having a haircut and a new colour – brunette. We got a picture of this new look. She got a taxi from the centre. The Manchester lads again came through for us and that cab made a drop at the airport. They followed her on airport CCTV and so we have the name that she's travelling under now – Martina Bell – and she boarded a plane to Germany. At the moment we're researching that to see if it's an alias and we, on your say-so, Simon, contacted the German police. They'll let us know if they locate her and we can take it from there."

Simon nodded. "Good work. See what you can find out about this woman. Jeff has a sample of her prints and DNA."

Frank said, "Yes, nothing showed up with those, so she's not a known criminal."

Simon nodded. After a brief pause he roused himself from his thoughts. "Now, the man who rented the van – Paul, what's the story?"

"Charlie Ellis, well, we've taken his statement. His prints are on the van steering-wheel and door et cetera. As you know, he's always admitted that he left the van in the shopping centre. We requested the phone company to give coordinates of his phone to see if we could establish if he went home. In his statement he said he took a Tube home.

We looked through CCTV from the Tube stations and it looks like he did, in fact, go home."

Paul gestured to one of his associates and he wheeled in a large television. Simon moved away and everyone adjusted their seating so that they could see the television screen clearly.

"This is CCTV from the shopping centre," Paul stated and pressed a button. "This is Charlie Ellis walking from the van into the shopping centre. As you can see, he's wearing black trousers a loose lumberjack shirt, work boots and a black baseball-type hat. He goes into the centre and leaves, he says, by another exit."

Paul pressed a button again and more footage followed that seemed to support what he was saying.

"Now," he said, "here is Thomas Banks in his suit walking into the centre. We've requested his mobile-phone records too, but we think he left his phone in his car. Thomas Banks also is in and out of cameras in the centre. However, from footage and also from statements we've taken from sales assistants in B&Q, we know that a man who looks like him went into B&Q and bought work boots, a shirt, a Stanley fleece, black trousers, and gloves and a black baseball-type cap. We have a sale, in cash, and we have a witness who is fairly sure it was him. He gets his purchases put in a B&Q bag and we catch Thomas Banks in a suit walking with the bag here."

There was a brief image of Thomas walking, carrying a bag with a B&Q logo.

"We lose him then and we have a man dressed now like Charlie Ellis walking towards the white van, with the bag. Are you all with me?"

There was a murmur of affirmatives.

"We're surmising that Thomas Banks bought the clothes in B&Q and changed out of his suit in the toilets. He put the suit in the bag and then, wearing his new work-clothes and with the peak of the hat pulled down over his face, made his way to the van to collect the body and dump it. Physically the men have a similar build and with the hat it's impossible to do a facial recognition. One of the things that support this switch is – and we have Stella to thank for this – Charlie's boots are very dirty and this man's are very clean." Paul paused and there were murmurs of agreement. "This is our man in the hat later, with his B&Q bag, walking back into the shopping centre. Lastly, here about twenty minutes later, is Thomas Banks walking to his car. He then reaches in for his phone and makes a call, presumably the call to the solicitor. It seems to me that Thomas Banks has set Charlie up as the patsy. Charlie has no alibi at home and he's the one who rented the van and it looks like him, same build, same clothes. I think Thomas Banks is a very clever man and he knew once he'd disposed of this body, with the doppelganger in the wind, he would be really home and free. If Isobel hadn't got the photos of the body and if we hadn't found the body in the river, we would have very little." He paused. "We still have a way to go to make this case – eh, watertight." There were groans at the pun. "Obviously Stella's observation about the state of the boots is suggestive but not legally compelling."

Simon clicked his fingers. "What about forensic gait analysis?"

There were some puzzled faces and side-talking.

"What's that?" Paul said.

Simon raised his voice above the melee. "It's a new

area of recognition analysis. Basically, each of us has a unique gait or walk, like a fingerprint. Forensic gait analysts can examine footage of walks and determine who the individual is. We have footage of Thomas Banks walking and of Charlie Ellis walking and then we have footage of the man who dumped the body. Technically, the forensic gait analyst should be able to tell us which man walked to the van and drove off and then returned to the shopping centre. Isobel also captured some footage of him walking away from the van after dumping the body."

"So an analyst should be able to tell us which of these men dumped the body from his gait?"

Simon grinned. "Exactly."

"And where would we find such an expert?"

"I have a name. Paul, you need to get on to this guy, provide him with all the footage. Tell him it's an emergency, a multiple murder case and that we need an answer by tomorrow."

"How will that evidence stand up in court or with a jury?" Paul asked.

"I'm not sure how widely accepted it is but it might clarify for us what's happening."

There were more mutterings. Simon made no move to curtail it.

Patricia leant towards Isobel. "Thomas had no bag leaving the shopping centre."

Isobel said distractedly, "No."

Patricia looked at her significantly and said again, *"Thomas had no bag leaving the shopping centre."*

Isobel was mystified. "So?"

Simon called out, "Anything else, Paul?"

"Yes. Thomas Banks leaves the centre with no bag."

Patricia nodded at Isobel.

Paul said, "So that means that probably Thomas carried his suit in the bag and changed back into it in the shopping centre. When he leaves the centre he is carrying no bag."

Isobel nodded, still a bit behind the curve.

"*So he had to dump the bag and clothes somewhere in the centre!*" Patricia whispered.

Realisation dawned on Isobel.

"Those work-clothes, which must still be in the centre," Paul went on, "will have his victim's DNA if he moved the bodies."

There was a moment of silence where everyone digested this.

Isobel was looking at Patricia who was nodding energetically.

"Excellent!" Simon said. "Where are you with getting those clothes?"

"Stella has been helping me with this," Paul said.

Stella joined Paul at the front

She pulled a face. "Unfortunately, by the time we realised all of this, the rubbish had gone to the dump. We have a warrant sorted and what we need now are lots of willing searchers. This is a priority."

Simon called out, "I realise this is no one's idea of ideal working conditions but I need all the bodies I can get to do a rubbish sift!"

There were groans.

Isobel reached out and squeezed Patricia's hand.

"Well done, Patricia, for figuring that out."

Patricia blushed.

Isobel whispered to her, "Oh we almost have him! I can feel it."

"I've been on to the centre." Stella said. "The bins inside are emptied a number of times a day into big bins at the back. All this rubbish is collected at four in the morning and transferred to the dump. Unfortunately, we didn't realise until after four that we needed the rubbish. I contacted the dump and warned them that we were getting a warrant. They are doing their best to cooperate. The men in charge of the dump are already tracing where the shopping-centre stuff was dumped this morning. I've also contacted the company with the dump lorries and they're tracing where the loads from the centre were dumped from that end."

Simon breathed a sigh of relief. "Do we know yet how much stuff is taken to the dump daily from the shopping centre?"

"Ten trucks worth of rubbish."

Simon groaned.

"Some of that is recycling stuff, cardboard and plastics," Stella added. "They reckon there will be six or seven trucks with general waste."

Simon added, "He might have placed the different items of clothing in different bins so we'll have to go through them all meticulously. Still, with enough of us that shouldn't take too long. We'll need pictures of the clothes to distribute to all the searchers so they know what we are looking for."

"I have them." Stella lifted a hand holding a bunch of pages.

Simon nodded. "Brief everyone while I chat to Isobel, Patricia and Adam. All searchers at the dump asap." He gestured to Isobel and the others and they followed him to his office.

Simon turned to Adam. "I don't have much time but how are you getting on with the hit-and-run?"

"It's hard to say as yet. We intend to follow up with another witness now. We'll let you know how that goes."

"The evening meeting won't happen tonight as we'll probably still be rubbish-sifting. I'll text if anything changes, otherwise assume we'll meet here at midday tomorrow. The DNA should be back by then to make an identification of the body."

They nodded.

"Good luck with the rubbish search," Isobel said.

Simon grinned. "Just how I like to spend my time. See you tomorrow."

Isobel, Patricia and Adam made their way back to Adam's car. Adam contacted his own station and one of his team supplied him with the name of the owner of the car that had hit Thomas Banks – Jennifer Green – and where she was now working.

Adam drove off towards the financial district.

Chapter 39

By the time they left Scotland Yard it was four o'clock and traffic was heavy. Despite the excitement of the meeting no one said very much, each of them alone with their own thoughts.

Isobel thought back over the last week and a half. It had been so intense. She realised that it was Anne Banks and what had happened to her that had motivated her – the idea of giving her a voice. In a similar way, Thomas Banks Senior had got to her, really touched her heart, and she wanted to be able to give him some answers – however, she acknowledged it might not be possible to do so and that one of the answers could be a terrible thing to live with. Was that fair to this old man? Would it just rob him of more of his peace of mind? She thought of Tommy Banks too, even though she'd never met him. He'd lost his mother a few months ago and now maybe his father if things unfolded the way they thought. All she could console herself with was that at least once the truth was out there was the possibility of healing. She hoped there would be for Thomas Banks Senior and Tommy.

For herself, Isobel realised that tired and all as she was

she had also found some truth. She could see how Simon was motivated by evidence so that he could get justice in court. For her the motivation was different – it was about finding the truth and giving the victims a voice. Maybe she had a future somewhere. The last year and a half had knocked her for six and she knew her family had been worried. She had lost a sense of direction, any idea of what her life was about or where it was going. Now, for the first time in a long time she could feel herself looking forward with some hope, not fear.

Having got thus far in her musings, she gave herself a shake. Looking round, she saw that Adam seemed similarly thoughtful, while Patricia was engrossed on her phone.

"Everyone all right?" Isobel asked.

Patricia mumbled and Adam roused himself, saying, "Nearly there now. Jennifer Green is still working as a temp. She's been here with this firm for six months. Actually she's been with the same agency for ten years. She's one of their most trusted employees, very capable, very competent. She likes variety in her work, and flexibility to take time off. Apparently she regularly goes off for three-month periods of travelling."

They were now in the financial district and it was approaching five o'clock. Isobel was worried that Jennifer might have left work.

Adam, agreeing with her concerns, abandoned the car in a loading bay, putting up a sign saying that he was a police officer on duty.

They entered the ground floor of a multi-storey building. Checking the wall listing, they found that the office they were looking for was on the eighth floor. When the lift opened they were delivered to a small reception area with the name of the company on the wall. A young and glamorous receptionist was tidying her desk.

Adam stepped forward and Isobel and Patricia melted into the background. He put on a warm and charming smile which made him look very attractive.

"Hello," he said. "I'm an old friend of Jennifer Green, in town briefly. I thought she might be finishing work and I was hoping to arrange to meet her for a drink. Could I have a quick word with her?" He smiled again and the receptionist was putty in his hands.

"You're lucky to catch her. She normally leaves at half past five."

"Could I just set something up with her quickly?"

The young woman got up and led him through some glass doors to a bigger office where there were a number of desks. She approached one and said something. She lingered but Isobel could see Adam pointedly wait for her to leave. The receptionist walked slowly back to her post, her eyes trained on Adam and Jennifer.

Isobel could see Adam talking urgently for a few minutes, then Jennifer smiled and shook hands with him. He came walking out and stopped at reception,

"Thank you," he said, flashing his smile again. "I don't think she recognized me at first. I guess I've changed since we knew each other, lost some of my looks!"

The receptionist shook her head, laughing. "She was probably just surprised to see you."

Adam laughed too. "You're probably right."

He hurried over to Isobel and Patricia and they got into the lift.

When they were safely on their way down, he said, "I find it's always best to have any witnesses come up with explanations of the inconsistencies."

Isobel and Patricia burst out laughing.

"You're good," Isobel said.

He grinned, "We're meeting Jennifer a couple of streets away in a café."

They walked there, leaving the car where it was.

The café was busy with an afterwork crowd so there was plenty of sound around them. Adam went and ordered three coffees while Isobel and Patricia found a table in a corner. Jennifer must have left almost immediately because she arrived a few minutes later, waved to let them know that she had seen them and then collected a cappuccino.

She joined them at the table.

Jennifer had blonde hair in a bob and hazel eyes. Isobel guessed that she was forty-ish. She had a direct gaze and a firm manner, businesslike without being bossy.

"What's this about?" she asked. "And thanks for not saying you're police – that would have panicked the company no matter how innocent I am."

Adam smiled. "We don't want to cause you any trouble. We just wanted to chat, maybe get some information."

She nodded.

"We're looking into a hit-and-run that happened about ten years ago."

Jennifer frowned. "Yes, my car was stolen and then burnt out after a man was killed. I thought it was concluded that it was a joyrider?"

Adam said, "Yes, that was one of the theories at the time. Recently, however, there have been some queries about the incident and we're re-interviewing everyone."

"It was very upsetting to think that my car had killed someone."

"What time was it stolen exactly?" Adam asked.

"I'm not sure. I was out for dinner with some friends. I wanted to have a drink so I didn't take the car. It was parked at the house when I left at about seven thirty. When I returned by taxi, at just before midnight, it was gone. I reported it immediately but I think the accident had already happened at that stage. I don't know if any of my neighbours saw anything and I don't know if they were interviewed at the time. I guess that was your department."

"It was, yes."

Jennifer was silent a few moments then added, "What always kind of freaked me out was the fact that the man who was killed – well, I'd done some work in the same company he worked for a few months before. I didn't know him, I never met him, but it was a strange coincidence."

Adam tensed but asked as nonchalantly as he could, "Did you tell the police that at the time?"

"I didn't know at the time. They showed me a picture of the man who was killed, and I didn't recognise him at all. They told me his name and I didn't know him or the area he lived in. But when he was cremated a month or six weeks later, I read about him because my car was involved. In the little article about him in the paper it said where he worked. It was a strange coincidence but I didn't think it was worth going into a police station for . . ."

The others exchanged subtle glances.

Isobel reached into her bag and drew out a photograph of the true Thomas Banks. Jennifer looked at it but showed no signs of recognition.

"That's the man who was killed," Isobel said.

Jennifer looked distressed. "Sorry, I didn't recognize him after all these years."

Isobel drew out another photo. This one was a single shot of Matt Cooper from when he was in college. "What about his man?"

Jennifer took the photo and each of them could see the spark of recognition. "Yes, I knew this man. He worked for that same company. He wasn't in my section but I used to bump into him sometimes at lunchtime." She threw a quick glance at them and said, "To be honest, I kinda fancied him. I helped him out a few times with things."

Isobel asked, "What sort of things?"

Jennifer looked into the distance. "I typed a report for him when he was under pressure on one occasion. I also did some work on his CV another time. I thought he was interested in me so one weekend I even lent him my car so he could go and visit family." She shrugged. "Nothing came of it. I left the company and moved to a new firm and he never kept in touch."

"What was his name?" Isobel asked.

"Matthew – although everyone called him Matt. I think his surname was Cooper. I was disappointed, I thought he liked me." She blushed and looked down.

"So he had the keys to your car?" Adam asked.

"Just for that one weekend. What is this? Why are you asking me about Matt?"

"We're just establishing who knew who in the company at that time," Adam said. "Matt gave you back the keys, I presume?"

"Of course he did. Anyway, that was some time before the car was stolen."

"When you worked on Matt's report and his CV, did you do that at your place of employment?" Patricia asked.

Jennifer looked uncomfortable. "The report, yes, but

not the CV. It was to apply for another job so he came to my house."

"He knew where you lived then," Adam said.

"Well, yes," Jennifer acknowledged. "Do you think he was involved in this man's death? *Do you think he did it?*" Her voice was rising.

"We're just establishing some facts that we weren't aware of at the time," Adam said. "They may have no impact on the case whatsoever."

Jennifer listened but didn't seem one-hundred-per-cent convinced.

Adam spoke again. "Jennifer, we don't want anyone to know we've questioned you or what you've told us. Please keep our conversation totally confidential."

Jennifer breathed heavily. "You *do* think he's involved."

Adam, now the forceful policeman, said, "We're not prepared to speculate at this time," then more humanely added, "nor do we want any innocent parties unduly distressed."

Jennifer responded better to that. "Of course not. I won't say a word to anyone."

"Thank you, Jennifer."

She nodded her acknowledgement and rising they all left.

Jennifer walked away towards the Tube, her head down.

The others walked back to the car. There was no parking ticket on it, nor had it been clamped.

Isobel laughed. "I need to get one of those signs."

Adam laughed too. "No way. They'll have rung the police station to check that this is a registered police car, signed out to an on-duty policeman."

Isobel shrugged. "Oh, not so easy then."

They piled back into the car and Adam asked where they were going. Patricia gave Peter's address, saying, "Come on, Isobel, we need to go and fill Peter in on what's happened. He'll be dying to hear all the new developments. Why don't you come too, Adam?"

"Thanks, but no thanks. I need to write up my report on what we've done today. I'll drop you off though."

Patricia said, "So Matt Cooper took Thomas Banks' job. And now we know that he knew where Jennifer lived and quite possibly had a copied key for her car."

"Is there any way to find out if he did?" Isobel asked.

Adam winced. "It's a long time ago. Such places would have changed staff – that's if they haven't gone out of business. Maybe if we knew at the time we could have found something, but it's too long ago now. And they probably wouldn't have taken his name in the first place for a small quick job like that, probably done over the counter."

"So he had motive, the job, the means because he had access to the car, and opportunity," Isobel mused. "Well, we don't know where he was that night, but we do know that he wasn't in the pub with Thomas, so he could have done it." She continued thoughtfully, "If the forensic gait analyst looked at the video of the hit-and-run driver walking back to the body, would they be able to tell us if the man walking is Matt Cooper, even if that was ten years ago? Would age have changed his walk?"

Adam looked at her. "I don't know. But, I have to say, ladies, looking at the road, the pub, where the car would have to have started its acceleration from, it would be impossible for Matt. He would have to have been near the pub to see that it was Thomas leaving and then before he could get back to the car and accelerate forward Thomas would have been way down the street."

There was silence in the car as they drove on.

As the shop around the corner from Peter's flat came into view, Patricia said, "Just drop us here. We need to get a few things."

"No problem." Adam pulled in to the kerb outside the shop.

Isobel said, "Adam, could you get the forensic gait analyst to look at the footage of the driver walking and compare it with the guy who moved the body?"

"I guess."

"Just to rule Matt Cooper out, definitively, so we can tell Thomas Banks Senior we did everything and found nothing."

"OK, I'll ask him."

"Thanks, Adam. We do appreciate it."

He nodded. "See you tomorrow."

Chapter 40

Having recounted everything and also sated their appetite, they were now sipping tea and nibbling on chocolate.

Peter said in an awed voice, "Patricia, that was great that you figured about the clothes before Paul said anything."

Isobel nodded emphatically. "I know. It hadn't occurred to me at all."

Patricia blushed.

Isobel smiled. "You really love this investigative work, don't you, Patricia?"

"Yes, it's fascinating – finding things out, getting people to talk, figuring out what really happened – I love it," she enthused. Then, taking a deep breath, she said, "In fact, I love it so much I've had a look and there are actually approved courses that you can do and . . ." now she looked at Peter, "I'm thinking of going and doing one."

Her words were met with a shocked silence.

"You would be great at it," Isobel said then.

"Are you going to leave the firm?" Peter sounded crestfallen.

Isobel cringed, knowing that she was a gooseberry.

However, she knew that she needed to talk to Peter about something before she left tonight. Standing up, she lifted the empty cups and said, "I'm going to make some more tea."

Isobel adjourned to the kitchen, rinsed the cups and boiled the kettle again. She stood looking out of the kitchen window into the darkness of the city and the lights of houses and cars and streetlights illuminating it, shining light into the darkness. Her mind was miles away and she wasn't conscious of the murmured voices from the other room. Suddenly, like a light illuminating the darkness, she had an idea. She gripped the sink as she turned the idea over in her mind.

Pulling out her phone, she rang Thomas Banks Senior.

"Hi, Thomas, this is Isobel McKenzie. I hope it's not too late to be calling you."

"No, not at all, love. I sleep very little now. It happens as you get older."

"Those photos you gave us have been very helpful."

"That's good, love. The wife was a wild woman with the camera. After you left I spent ages looking at them and remembering the good times we had together."

Isobel bit her lip. She took a deep breath. "Did you ever get into videoing family occasions?"

"No. We didn't."

Isobel could feel her heart drop. Maybe she could contact Erica and see if the school had any video footage.

"That's why we bought that one."

"Sorry, Thomas, what did you say there? Bought what one?"

"I was just saying that because we had no video we bought the official video of the graduation at the university. I know Thomas is only on it for a few minutes, but we were so proud of him that the wife wanted to have all the speeches and the full ceremony. It was a great day. I watched it this afternoon. Thomas got a first, you know."

Isobel heard the catch in his voice and there were tears threatening in her own even as inside she could feel hope bubbling up again. "Are Thomas's friends on it too, like Matt Cooper?"

"Yes, they're all there. We were so happy that day, the wife and I," he said, choking a little.

Isobel gave him a few moments. "Thomas, I'm sorry if we're upsetting you all over again."

"Not at all, love. I can't explain it. It's as if Thomas is important to you too and, well, that's a good thing."

Isobel was nodding. "To help us to find out what happened to Thomas, we're going to need to borrow that recording of the graduation and copy it."

"I don't understand how it can, but if it helps in any way you can keep it."

Despite herself, Isobel's eyes filled with tears. "No, no, you'll get it back. The police officer who was on the case back then, Adam Bryce, is helping us look into things. Would it be all right if I get Adam to collect the video? If he called later tonight or early tomorrow, is that a problem?"

"Any time, love. I sleep in the chair here many nights."

Isobel couldn't stop herself. "Thomas, when I know more I'll come and tell you everything." Her conscience niggled her and she said, "But we may not actually find out anything."

"I know, love. I do understand. I'm just glad that you're looking into it. If there is something I know you'll find it. I won't get my hopes too high but I'll be waiting. Goodnight."

Isobel was crying by the time she hung up. Please God, this attempt on their part would yield some clarifying information.

The kitchen door opened and Patricia came in.

"Oh, Isobel, are you all right? Sorry – I didn't mean to upset you?"

Isobel shook her head. "It wasn't you."

"What was it then? Why are you crying?"

Isobel shrugged. "I was just talking to Thomas Banks Senior. He has a video of Thomas and Matt at graduation, hopefully walking up to get their certificates – which should help the forensic gait analyst, whoever he is." She made a face. "Even if it rules out Matt Cooper, I'll be happier that we explored everything."

Patricia nodded. "Yeah, me too. It is a plausible theory, but it would be good to have definitive proof."

"I just need to ring Adam and tell him. Maybe he can get the recording tonight."

"That would be good."

"How did things go with you and Peter?"

Patricia blushed. "Peter just panicked. He thought if I was leaving the firm that he wouldn't see me again. He admitted that the last two weeks have changed things between us."

Isobel frowned. "And?"

Patricia grabbed Isobel's arm and jumped up and down, singing in a whisper, "He wants us to see more of each other!"

Isobel started jumping too, her face beaming with happiness. "Fantastic!" She gave Patricia a huge hug.

Isobel laughed, "Probably not working together will help the dating."

"I know, I can hardly believe it. We're getting on so well. I'm so happy." Then she remembered herself and said, "You better ring Adam before it gets too late."

"Right."

Patricia went back to the sitting room.

Within a few seconds Adam was on the line. "You missed me," he joked.

Isobel ignored that. "I had an idea."

"Me too. I was just about to ring you."

"Oh."

"Ladies first."

"Thomas Banks Senior has a recording of Thomas and Matt at their graduation. Let's hope they had to walk across a decent-sized stage."

"Great. I spoke to Simon and to Dermot, the gait man. He says he could probably do it from the modern footage but, if there are any major injuries in between, that can screw it up. So, this could really help."

"You can collect it tonight. Thomas Senior says he'll be awake. I told him you might be calling. Just let him know if you're sending someone else."

"No, I'll get it tonight and send it on to this guy Dermot. It's the least I can do."

"Great. Now tell me your idea."

"I read back over the case file in detail after I left you."

"And?"

"And, we checked Thomas's phone at the time for anything unusual or suspicious. There wasn't anything that raised a red flag at the time. But, in light of what we saw today on the road near the pub and the time and distance involved, I was trying to see how Matt could have done it. He needed to know that Thomas had left the pub."

"Yes."

"And Thomas did make a call before he left the pub."

"*Oh my God!*" Isobel could feel her heart thundering in her chest and realized that she was biting one of the knuckles of her hand. "Was it to Matt?"

"No, no, it wasn't. It was to a burner phone."

"Oh."

"It was for less than a minute. The same phone had called Thomas earlier, again for less than a minute. It's virtually impossible to trace those burner phones and at the time it was put down to an initial wrong number and an accidental redial."

"And now?"

"Well, now I have to confess I'm wondering if Matt called Thomas and set it all up. I timed myself making a call. In fact, I borrowed another officer's phone and tried it on a friend of mine. All I'm saying is that it's possible but don't get your hopes up. It is a bit far-fetched and at the end of the day the two calls could be, as we originally thought, a wrong number and an accidental redial."

"OK, but it's definitely worth hearing what the gait analyst has to say."

"Definitely."

"Adam, thanks for going to all of this trouble."

"Not at all . . . listen, why don't we get together for coffee before the meeting in Scotland Yard tomorrow? I can fill you in then?"

"Sounds good. Name the place and we'll be there."

Adam mentioned a café and they arranged to meet at eleven o'clock.

"Any word from the dump search yet?"

"Yes, Simon said that they've found the boots and a shirt."

"Great!"

"They're at the lab being analysed as we speak. I think he's requested an all-nighter from the lab people. He feels we're getting close."

"Wait till I tell Patricia this. I'll see you tomorrow. Goodnight."

Isobel reboiled the kettle and wet the tea. She then carried the tray back into the sitting room.

Peter and Patricia were sitting side by side on the couch, holding hands and smiling.

Now that the personal stuff was sorted Isobel brought the discussion back to the case.

"Patricia, I've just been talking to Adam and he had some news." She relayed what she and Adam had discussed about the hit-and-run.

"So Matt may have run Thomas down!" said Patricia. "Hopefully, the gait man can say one way or the other."

"And there's more – they found some of the clothes – the boots and a shirt! No results yet from the lab but hopefully tomorrow." Turning to Peter, Isobel said, "I think it's likely that they may interview Thomas tomorrow and, depending on what the lab finds, they may be charging him with murder or even a number of murders. Can you sort something out for Tommy? Have you spoken to Claire? He could be without both his parents by tomorrow evening."

Peter frowned. "Yes, I've spoken to Claire. She's more than happy to have Tommy. However, she's worried that Thomas may oppose her caring for her nephew because they don't get on. I think our best bet is to get Thomas Banks' divorce solicitor to persuade Thomas to agree to Claire having Tommy. If not, we'll have to apply to the court. She is his closest living relative, after all. If Thomas is charged with murder a judge should be able to sanction it. Basically, we should be able to sort everything. Claire wants to be Tommy's guardian."

Isobel breathed a sigh of relief.

"I'll ring her in the morning and let her know that," Peter said.

There was nothing more that Isobel needed to discuss.

"I assume you're coming to the meeting at midday tomorrow, Patricia?" Isobel faltered, knowing that in a way her job was at the law firm.

Patricia smiled. "Definitely – that was part of my decision to think about a new career. There's no way that I want to miss out on that and well . . ."

Peter smiled at her and took up the slack. "So, Patricia is going to take some holidays which she is owed and I'm going to get a temp and then, when the Banks case is over, Patricia can sort things out."

Patricia added, "I need to find out when I can do my course, so we think this is the best thing to do for now."

Isobel laughed. "And all of that got sorted while I was making tea – you are two fast movers!"

Patricia blushed but said no more.

Peter laughed. "Slow starters but then we're sprinters."

It was a relief to get to bed later. Isobel felt tired and her body was aching from all of the running around. It had been a long two weeks. However, even in sleep Isobel was not finished dealing with Thomas Banks. He chased her on foot. She ran and managed to elude him. Then he was in a car chasing her and trying to run her over. She bobbed and weaved and tried to avoid him. Finally he chased her on foot again and this time he caught her, his hands closing around her throat. In the background a child cried out for his mother and a woman called out, *"Help me, help me!"*

Chapter 41

Friday 1st June

Isobel woke at nine o'clock. Her bedding was all wound up, bearing testament to her scary dreams. She felt tense, keyed-up. Today, in the dynamic of moves and countermoves that she felt she was playing with Thomas Banks, it would be checkmate or Thomas Banks would escape. Only this wasn't a game, the stakes were too high. People had already lost their lives and the cost of losing would be more lost lives because she knew he would do this again.

She had a leisurely bath and then went for a walk in the local park before she and Patricia caught the Tube over to meet Adam.

She'd been surprised that Adam had suggested this early meeting but assumed it was to discuss the hit-and-run information before presenting it to the main investigation at midday. They were a few minutes late and Adam was already there. They collected coffee and bagels and joined him in the booth.

"Hi, any news from the 'gait man'?" Isobel asked.

Adam laughed. "His name is Dermot and he sent me a text his morning. The video of the graduation helped, in so far as it legally gives his statements more weight, but he says he could already tell that it was definitely Matt Cooper walking back to Thomas Banks' body."

Isobel's mouth fell open and she just sat there.

Adam prompted, "So it is murder."

The starkness of this statement shocked Isobel into sound. "He's sure?"

"One hundred per cent."

"Jesus. How am I going to tell his father?"

Adam grimaced.

Isobel ran her hands through her hair. "I promised him I would tell him whatever I found out, so I will."

Adam lowered his head and spoke very quietly. "I feel so bad. I should have found this out at the time."

It took a moment for what Adam said to fully register with her. Now she understood the reason for the meeting. "You feel guilty."

"I should have looked at the video more closely," Adam said, his head down.

Isobel looked at Patricia. "The only reason that we've found any of this out is because we were already suspicious of Thomas Banks, so we've gone looking for evidence of murder because we know he's capable of it. Number one: there was no reason to even look at him at the time. He'd covered his tracks too well. And number two: doing things this way is the complete opposite of what you do as a police officer – innocent until proven guilty, remember – not let me make sure you're guilty." Isobel took a deep breath. "And, we may not be able to prove Thomas did it. A judge may not accept the gait analysis and that's the only thing we have."

"Yes," said Adam. "And even if they do accept the gait analysis, it could still be ruled accident or manslaughter."

Isobel straightened up. "Mr Banks Senior wants to know what happened to his son and we can tell him that. We can give him the truth – but justice, in this case, I'm not sure. Hopefully we will get Thomas Banks on the other murders. He nearly got away with everything because he managed to make it look like no murder had taken place – that's been his modus operandi. Only for Peter Wright none of these murders would have come to light."

Adam was listening but his face had not relaxed or shown any sign that what she was saying was helping.

"Adam, so many people feel guilty in this situation. Julia, the woman from the shelter that she couldn't get Anne away in time, Claire her sister who suspected Thomas of spousal abuse and couldn't do anything, Grace her neighbour who was concerned that there were problems but had nothing more to go on and only denials from Anne, Thomas's old schoolteacher who suspected Matt was violent but couldn't prove it. Me because maybe something I did tipped Thomas off and he dumped the body in the river and maybe I messed up some of the evidence tying him to the crime. Adam, when we wanted to relook at the case you facilitated it. You've worked with two members of the public in a collegial way. All of us are doing our best. But yes, it is too little too late for Anne and Tommy, but the answer isn't self-flagellation. The answer is a better support service for people in abusive situations, more understanding from the police, more cooperation, more awareness, more action against joyriders and traffic-slowing devices in known speedways before tragedy strikes. I don't know all the things that we need to do differently but there are people who do. And definitely we all have to listen more to what people say and also don't say, in the case of domestic violence."

"Isobel is right," Patricia said.

Isobel smiled at her. "Only because you helped me see straight again."

Adam had straightened his shoulders and was looking at her, contrite now.

Isobel said, "I'm sorry, this case has really upset me. I don't mean to preach." Changing tack, she went on, "What scares me most is that he made people disappear without anyone realising." She shivered then quoted from Nietzsche, "'Whoever fights monsters should see to it that in the process he does not become a monster. And if you gaze long into an abyss, the abyss also gazes into you.' Thomas Banks has really frightened me. He's got under my skin. I even dreamt about him last night. I just hope that today we have the evidence to catch him."

Adam had listened attentively to her words and now he said, "Isobel, I would like to go with you to tell Thomas Banks Senior the news."

Isobel looked at him. She saw strength and courage in his face now and a willingness to deal with the failure. She knew something about that feeling of failure, but truthfully she didn't know if she'd yet found the courage to face it herself head on. But that was for when she went home. What she did know was that she was going to support someone else facing theirs.

So she said, "Thank you, that would be great."

Silence fell between them, not uncomfortably but rather contemplatively, as they all thought about what had been said. Isobel glanced at her watch and with no words they rose together and made their way to the conference room to hear the progress of the investigation.

Chapter 42

As Isobel followed Adam into the conference room she heard someone shout her name. She looked up and before she could speak a word of welcome she was engulfed in an embrace. It was like being hugged by a bear.

When she stepped back, she said with a grin, "Hi, Jeff." Then noticing his dishevelled hair and bloodshot eyes, she asked, "Are you all right?" Simultaneously she noticed many of the police officers in the room listening in on this exchange.

Jeff took her two hands and shaking them warmly said, "We've got him, Isobel, you clever girl!"

Before she had time to reply, Simon swept into the room. Isobel gave Jeff's hands a squeeze and she and Patricia went to the back of the room.

Simon called the briefing to order.

"Good afternoon, everyone, especially all of you dump-divers."

There were groans and laughter with people holding their noses.

"Our intrepid searchers, marshalled by Stella and myself, did a sterling job and uncovered," he paused and turned away from them towards a screen behind him onto which flashed the image of a baseball cap. Enjoying the moment and acting like a conjurer, he said, "*A hat!*"

Then there was a succession of screen changes on the monitor and with each change Simon's voice announced: "*A top . . . a pair of trousers . . . boots . . . and a pair of gloves!*"

In her mind Isobel was adding a drum roll to each unveiling. She had never seen Simon so relaxed and she knew that, whatever she would hear now, in his mind he had facts and proof. She turned to Patricia and saw that she was delighted. They grinned at each other.

Simon continued, "Obviously there was lots of rubbish, including clothes, but no other items of clothing found matched the outfit of the man who drove the body in the van. Jeff and his team have worked all night and now I'm going to turn things over to him."

Immediately the room fell silent and was reminiscent of a primary classroom and Isobel realized that Jeff was immensely respected by all of these officers. No wonder they were so interested when he had greeted her with such familiarity. Jeff moved to the front of the room and flicked back through the photographs of the clothing.

"Of the items of clothing the easiest ones to get DNA from are the headband of a hat, where there is a certain amount of friction and also sweat and under the arms of a top where again there is sweat and friction from movement. Obviously this guy dug up a body and moved it, all of which would have taken a fair bit of pulling and dragging so we were able to collect very good samples for analysis. We've compared the DNA we got with that of Charlie Ellis and it's not a match. Our main suspect is

Thomas Banks. We don't have his DNA at present but we have the body identified as Mrs Cooper. Using a technique that is faster, called the integrated microfluidic system, and staying up all night my team and I have compared the DNA from the clothing with the DNA from Mrs Cooper's body and there is a familial match. The man who wore these clothes was her son."

Everyone was talking now.

"Well done, Jeff!"

"We've got him now!"

"Wish we could always get results that fast."

Simon left a few moments go by and then called them to order. "OK, folks! Jeff, anything else?"

Jeff said, "We analysed the fluid from the floor of the van and that's a match to the body taken from the river. The DNA from the body," he paused for effect here, "has been compared with a sample we had on file of the DNA of Claire Graham, Anne Banks' sister. The body taken from the river is definitely Anne Banks."

There was an outbreak of chatter which lasted a minute and then Simon began to speak and immediately silence fell.

"The autopsy results are back and there is no fractured hyoid on Anne Banks' body. There is no other obvious cause of death, no gunshot, no knife wounds, no blunt force trauma, so we cannot say one hundred per cent if she was strangled, although it seems likely." He paused. "We have Anne Banks' body turning up in her garden. She's been dead for three months. We have a man digging up this body and transporting it to the Thames and throwing it in. We have Anne Banks' DNA in the van. We have clothes that seem to be what he was wearing found in the shopping centre where Thomas Banks' car was parked. Those same clothes have his DNA on them. The weakest point is tying the clothes to the body, to prove that Thomas Banks actually was the one to move the body which implies knowledge and concealment of death."

Jeff said, "We're going over the clothes with a finetooth comb to see if any fluid from the body dropped on them but, to be honest, looking closely at the video and how he manoeuvred the body, it doesn't look hopeful."

"Thanks, Jeff," Simon said. "To add weight, we hope, to our case we have a forensic gait analyst here to help us. Everyone, this is Dermot Farrell."

Isobel craned to see. Dermot Farrell had red hair and was a very tall, pale man. He stood in front of everyone, slouched over. Despite this when he spoke his voice was clear and carried through the room. He seemed someone who was confident about what he did but not so confident in dealing with people. Everyone was very attentive, this new forensic approach being of interest to them. Isobel could see how complex building a case was and how methodical and meticulous Simon and his fellow officers had to be to prove things legally. Once again Isobel was aware of their differing perspectives. While she wanted to find the truth, Simon had to prove it. Both tasks were difficult but she acknowledged that finding the truth of Thomas's guilt if he managed to evade justice would really upset her. No wonder people plotted revenge and took matters into their own hands. If you knew someone was guilty and couldn't prove it, and they were living happily while the person you cared about wasn't, it must eat away at you. And probably it bothered the police involved just as much. No wonder Simon was so careful about the steps he took. She sent up a silent prayer.

Dermot used the visual aid as everyone had, flashing up the images of the different men walking as he explained. "I've analysed Thomas Banks walking into the shopping centre in his suit and compared it with this man in work-clothes walking out. From my analysis this man is the same person. This is Thomas Banks in different clothes." He flashed up another image of a man in working clothes. "This is Charlie Ellis walking away from the white van into the shopping centre. This man has a completely different gait to the man coming out to move the van."

He split the screen and put both images up simultaneously: on one side Charlie Ellis and beside it Thomas Banks, both dressed in work clothes. Dermott pointed, indicating the knee area on the man with older boots on. "You can see here this slightly rolling action on this side." When he highlighted it, it was actually clearly visible. "I've been in touch with Charlie Ellis and, with his permission, his doctor. This gait is consistent with someone who has had surgery on their knee. Charlie Ellis had knee surgery as a young man, for a football injury. You can clearly see that this other man does not have the same distinctive movement."

Simon said, "Yes, now that you point it out, I can see that."

Everyone was looking at the screen and there was a stunned silence.

Dermott waited a moment and then said, "I did notice something else. Thomas Banks is left-handed. Charlie Ellis is not. Charlie locks the van with his right hand and leaves the key. The man who opens the car door does so with his left hand as does Thomas Banks when he's in his suit."

Fran McDonnell

There was a cheer.

Simon looked as shocked and pleased as anyone. He went over to Dermot and slapped him on the back. Everyone was talking to those beside them and it was a full minute before Simon curtailed them.

"Thank you, Dermot," he said and Dermot got another cheer.

He grinned shyly. While the officers didn't know him and his work they were going to welcome him and his insights with open arms.

Simon said, "Just a few more areas to cover. Frank, you first."

Frank stood up and began. "The German police have been on the lookout for our blonde turned brunette and they found her. I've spoken to their officers and they've questioned her. She has made a statement. Basically she met Thomas Banks in a hotel in Manchester. He was there on business and he actually told her that she looked like his wife. She's an actress. She heard from him again three months ago. He met her in Manchester and explained that his wife had run off, that she was an alcoholic and dabbling in prostitution. He was worried about his son and he wanted this woman to sign divorce papers so that he could protect his son, if his wife came back. She thought he was a lovely man. She knew it was fraud but she thought she was helping. He paid her twenty thousand pounds. She's prepared to come home and testify about what happened."

Simon asked, "Why did she leave so abruptly? What happened?"

"Thomas Banks rang her and told her to leave. They'd agreed on that, in case his wife came back. She thought that was what had happened."

362

"Do we have her phone to prove that call?"

Frank again had a ready answer. "Thomas used a burner phone to ring her. He had given her a burner too. He told her it was for her own safety. When he called her on it she rang him to establish the story then ditched the phone and SIM card."

"Where did she throw it?" Simon asked.

"I'll find out."

"Do. Keep me informed about that. Now, we have one last piece of information that has only just come to light. Adam, will you do the honours?"

Adam made his way to the front of the room.

Speaking clearly, he said, "Thomas Banks was killed in a hit-and-run accident over ten years ago and at the time I put it down to a joyrider. The car was later found burned out. New evidence has been found, however. Firstly, the woman who owned the car worked for the company that Matt and Thomas worked for. She knew Matt Cooper. He knew where she lived and she'd loaned him her car one weekend, so he could have copied the key."

Adam played the video including the piece where the driver walked back to the body. There were murmurs but Adam raised his voice and talked on.

"Last night I obtained a video of Thomas and Matt graduating from college, which shows them being announced and then walking across the stage to receive their certificates. I gave that to Dermot to analyse." Adam indicated to Dermot that he should take the floor once more.

Dermot stood up and looked much more comfortable this time. "I looked at the two sets of footage and the man who knocked down Thomas and who walked back to the body is Matt Cooper."

More shouts.

Simon stepped forward. "So, three murders, his friend to get his new job, his mother to get the proceeds from the house and his wife because she was going to leave him."

There was a babble of talk and a lot of shushing as some shushed others.

He continued. "Since the aborted episode at the solicitor's which some of you were in on, I've had officers watching Thomas Banks. He seems to be going about his daily life secure in the knowledge that he's got away with everything. I'm going to bring him in today."

There was a cheer.

"When we interview him we're going to see if we can get him to incriminate himself. None of you are to attempt to see him when I bring him in. Knowing what you know, it's going to be hard to hide that but I want him lulled into a false sense of security. Do you understand?"

There was a general calling out of yes, sure and OK.

"Some uniform have been primed and are going to escort him here. Right, that's a wrap. Thank you, everyone."

As people stood up to filter out, Jeff headed down towards Isobel and Patricia.

"Well done," he said. "Both of you and Peter have uncovered a shocking tale of murder." He shook hands with each of them and left.

Adam moved back to stand near them.

For a moment they stood in silence.

Then Isobel mused, "So we still don't know. What tipped him off? Who warned him? Which thing did we do or say? Who did we speak to? What happened? What made Thomas realise there was a problem and call off the signing and move the body? Then he rings his imposter wife and tells her to run. He also calls Charlie Ellis to set him up. Neither of those calls show up on his phone because he used a burner." Isobel scrunched up her forehead. She knew there was something important here that was eluding her at the moment. She looked at Patricia, "There's something we're missing here. What is it?"

Patricia and Isobel looked at each other, both going over things in their minds.

Patricia asked, "What did he do that morning?"

Isobel shook her head from side to side as if she was shaking free an idea. "He took his son to school and then he went to the shopping centre?"

Patricia's face relaxed as realisation dawned. "He spoke to someone at the school who raised his suspicions."

Isobel followed her train of thought.

Patricia continued, her voice and confidence growing. "Probably Mrs Winter. Maybe she said something to him."

Isobel nodded. "That's certainly possible. But would that have been enough?"

Patricia continued their impromptu brainstorming. "Who else could or would have alerted him?"

"Anne's mum?"

"Could she have rung him?"

"I told her I was an old friend and wanted to surprise them but she might have. We could find out."

Patricia, now on a roll, asked, "What other risky things did we do?"

Isobel counted off on her fingers. "Aaron wouldn't have said anything, neither would Sharon, Claire wouldn't, nor Brian. I hardly think he checked the rehab place. What else?"

"What about when Peter met Anne on Saturday and got her DNA? What if that set something off? Not at the time obviously because he didn't do anything immediately but maybe after he saw Mrs Winter he started getting suspicious and putting two and two together and things started to add up."

"We need to find out if Mrs Winter spoke to Thomas that day."

Adam intervened. "Let's make sure Thomas is in custody before we contact anyone who might alert him. Let's talk to Simon."

They made their way over to Simon.

"Simon, can we have a word?" Adam said. "We want to track what alerted Thomas to the fact that we were on to him. Before we do that we want to be sure he's in custody."

Simon looked annoyed. "Is that really important? I have this vital interview ahead and, really, does this matter?"

Isobel bit her lip.

"All I'm asking is whether Thomas is in custody yet?" Adam asked.

Simon nodded impatiently then stepped away and used his phone. Within two minutes he was back to them, "I sent three units to pick this guy up. That was one of the back-up units. They have him in a squad car on his way here. He was shocked and is already asking for a solicitor."

Everyone heaved a sigh of relief.

Simon sighed wearily, "I can't see how any of that is relevant but go ahead if you want to." He heaved a sigh. "This guy is so slippery, and I don't want him to get off. This interview is going to be really long and really difficult."

Isobel said, "Simon, you're going to get him. He's so cocky that he's bound to slip up. He's probably going to get too clever."

Simon grimaced. "I certainly hope so." He walked off.

Isobel bit her lip. "*His* good humour seems to have evaporated very suddenly," she said.

"Don't worry about him," Adam said. "He's under ferocious pressure to have everything watertight."

Patricia said, "Of course."

Adam said, "Let's make some calls."

Chapter 43

They adjourned to Simon's office so they could use his speaker phone.

Isobel looked at Adam. "Would Mrs Graham know about us finding Anne's body yet? We can't really talk to her unless she's been informed."

"The police would have sent a local officer to deliver the news."

Isobel dialled Claire's number.

"Claire, this is Isobel. I'm so sorry about Anne."

"I know." Claire sobbed for a few minutes then recovered herself. "Thank God everything is coming to light now. Mum is here with me. We're devastated but we hope that you'll make sure that Thomas goes to prison for this."

"The police are doing everything they can to ensure that. In fact, I'm here with one of their officers, Adam, and we wondered if we could just ask Donna a few questions about when she last spoke to Thomas. Would that be all right? Patricia is here as well."

Claire acquiesced and they could hear the murmur of her speaking to someone else, then, on the line, a tentative, "Hello?"

"Hello, Donna, this is Isobel. I spoke to you last week. I'm so sorry about Anne."

Donna stifled a sob. "Claire has been putting my head on straight. I feel so bad that I didn't realise what was going on and just believed everything that man said instead of my own daughter."

"He was a professional liar. He's fooled many people over the years, not just you. But it's so important that we stop him now."

"It is," Donna sobbed.

"And that's why I'm phoning you. I want to know if you were talking to him after my visit."

Donna gulped and Isobel closed her eyes.

"Yes, I did tell him about your visit. I know you asked me not to, but I wanted to get on his good side, so that when he got custody he would let me see Tommy. He asked me to describe you and I did."

Isobel shrugged at the others.

Adam said, "When did you have this conversation?"

"Tuesday evening, at about ten o'clock."

"Was there anything else significant in the call?" Isobel asked.

"Not really . . . except . . ."

"What?"

"Well, when I said that you had an Irish accent we laughed about how common that was."

"Thank you for telling us, Donna."

Claire came back on the line. "What should I do about Tommy?"

"You'd better talk to Peter," Patricia said. "Things will have to follow a legal protocol and he'll help you."

Hanging up, Patricia mused, "So, on Tuesday night

369

Thomas might have heard something that made him uneasy."

Adam said, "But the doppelganger and Charlie Ellis both said they got calls at around ten o'clock on Wednesday morning. So it was only then that he reacted and set things in motion."

"So despite that call on Tuesday night Thomas didn't do anything that we know of," Patricia said. "At that point, it seems that he was still going ahead with the original plan. So something else must have happened."

Isobel nodded. "I agree."

"So we need to see if he chatted to anyone when he left Tommy off at school."

"Absolutely," Adam said.

Patricia had the name of the school and pulled up the number on her phone.

"Adam," said Isobel. "I think we're going to need your authority to get anywhere here."

Adam raised an eyebrow enquiringly and Patricia nodded.

Patricia dialled the number which was answered promptly.

Adam explained who he was.

Mrs Winter was courteous but cautious. They had to wait while she called Simon's office landline in order to verify that Adam was a policeman.

"How can I help you, officer?"

Adam put on the speaker phone and said, "Mrs Winter, we're at a very delicate point in an investigation and I need you to answer a number of questions about Wednesday morning."

"Wednesday morning? Why? Nothing out of the ordinary happened on Wednesday morning. I don't see –"

"Mrs Winter, we're in the middle of a murder

investigation." Adam had raised his voice and injected more authority into his tone.

"*A what?* A murder investigation? How can I possibly help you?"

"We need to know if you had a conversation with Thomas Banks that morning."

There was a pause.

"That's none of your business."

"Mrs Winter, you have two options here – you can either answer some simple questions over the phone now or I will send a squad car, with a blue light and sirens, to pick you up and bring you to the station."

"Are you threatening me, officer?"

"I am merely letting you know how important this information is and how serious I am about getting it."

Isobel smiled at Adam and Patricia grasped her arm and laughed silently. Adam grinned and shook his head at them.

There was a long silence. Isobel could almost feel the cogs of Mrs Winter's brain whirring as she calculated her response.

"Ask me your questions and I'll see if I can answer them."

Adam grinned at the others and Isobel bit her lip. Patricia pulled some paper towards her and lifted a pen off the desk, in case they needed to write down some prompts for Adam.

He said, "Thomas usually left Tommy to school at around half past eight before he went to work. Is that right?"

"Yes." The answer was clipped.

Adam read the piece of paper Patricia pushed towards him. "On the morning of his divorce, given what was happening, and maybe concerned for his son, he wanted to see you, Mrs Winter, didn't he?"

"That's not unusual, officer. When there's something going on at home parents often tell us, so that we can keep an extra-vigilant eye on the child and provide additional support. Thomas Banks called on that Wednesday to let me know that his son might be upset. He is that sort of father."

Patricia rolled her eyes and mimed being sick.

Adam said, "That may or may not be the case."

"That is the case. Thomas explained to me that Tommy knew about the divorce. He was sure that Tommy had noticed him being down and he wanted to let me know. He asked me to inform him about any changes I observed in Tommy. And to let him know if I had any suggestions of what more he could be doing to help his son. I reassured him that of course we would be extra vigilant. I said I would speak to Miss English, Tommy's teacher, immediately. Apart from that I told him not to worry. Tommy naturally would be upset and was missing his mum but he was coping nonetheless. These sorts of experiences are challenging for children but Tommy would be all right."

Isobel wondered how Tommy would cope with all of these new challenges he was going to be facing soon.

Patricia cut in, "Mrs Winter, this is Patricia King. Did you tell Thomas Banks that my son might be coming to the school?"

Mrs Winter asked imperiously, "What are you doing with the police, Mrs King? Are you in trouble?"

Patricia rolled her eyes.

Adam voice was steely, "Did you mention that another boy might be coming to the school with similar challenges?"

"As a matter of fact, I did. Obviously I never mentioned your name, Mrs King, but I thought it would reassure him that his son was not alone in what he had to deal with. I just said that there might even be another boy in his son's class soon who is in a similar situation. I said that I had been reassuring the mother of that boy recently. He was interested and he asked me if this boy had a mother who was an alcoholic? I explained that it was a prospective new family, with a little boy Tommy's age, but that in this case it was the father who was the alcoholic." She fell silent.

Patricia, realising that a change of tack was needed, said, "Of course, just as you reassured me."

"Exactly."

"Was he very interested in that fact?" Patricia asked. "I mean, did he ask more about it?"

There was a pause and then Mrs Winter spoke in a more conciliatory tone. "Well, yes, he asked if the enquiry was recent. And I told him that it had been on the previous Friday."

Isobel, sensing there was something more, said, "Did he ask anything else?"

"Yes, something odd actually. He said, 'They aren't Irish, are they?' and we laughed."

"So did you mention that I was Irish?"

Mrs Winter said defensively, "So many people are Irish, what difference did it make?"

"So you said no, but her friend was," Patricia said.

"Well, yes, I did. What did it matter? What's this all about?"

Adam cut in, "Did you discuss anything else?"

"Well no, he left fairly quickly after that."

"Thank you for your help, Mrs Winter," Adam said.

"How have I helped you?"

"Thank you again and goodbye."

The three of them stood looking at each other.

Isobel said speculatively, "So now he has an Irishwoman at Anne's solicitor's office, at his mother-in-law's and at the school. He wonders if there is something going on or if it's a coincidence or if he's being paranoid.'

Patricia took up the supposition. "There was one other thing that was a little unusual, the Saturday meeting with Peter in the café. It's still early, maybe only nine o'clock in the morning, he has lots of time so he decides to go over and check out the café and see if there was anything suspicious there. Maybe it was nothing, the proliferation of the Irish, nothing more or maybe someone was on to him."

Adam joined in, "So he goes to the coffee shop."

"Yes!" Isobel and Patricia chorused.

Isobel walked a little away to think and started pacing back and forth, going over things in her mind. "There's something still bothering me. When he decides there's a problem at around ten o'clock he then calls the imposter Anne on a burner phone and tells her to leave. Then he rings Peter saying that Anne is running late but they're coming."

Patricia said, "To buy him time to move the body."

Isobel says, "Because Charlie Ellis is the next person he calls, also on a burner, to get the van so the body can be moved."

"So in the café he learns something that makes him realise that we know that the woman is not the real Anne."

Isobel answers, "Exactly. He now has very little time. He puts in play the two things that are the most important pieces of evidence to hide, the body and the doppelganger. With those out of the way he can say that Anne fled or is on a bender and to all intents and purposes she has only just disappeared on Wednesday." Isobel paused. "Two calls from the burner phone and he has it all organised. He probably used the same burner to make the calls to imposter Anne and to Charlie. If only we could find that phone."

Adam said, "You're right. Those calls show that he's moving all the pieces on his board. But he probably got rid of it and that could be anywhere including the river."

Isobel said, "Maybe. But after making those calls he probably ditched it fairly quickly."

Adam said, " I could ask Stella if someone could look at CCTV from the street where the café is and see if we can track him and what he did with the phone."

Isobel said, "If they could track Thomas from the café they might get it."

Adam swallowed. "That's going to take a massive amount of time and people."

Patricia, galvanized into action, said, "Let's go to the café."

Isobel said, "Yes."

Adam called Stella, Patricia gave her the café location and then they left.

Adam drove under a blue light.

Chapter 44

Adam didn't bother parking the car. He just pulled it up on the footpath in front of the café with the blue light on the roof still flashing. The three of them entered the shop.

A young waitress came and Patricia asked if she could speak to Marie Frost, the manager.

Isobel said, "I think you should handle this, Patricia, as you're Peter's girlfriend."

Patricia grinned.

Marie Frost came out of the staff-only door. The young waitress nodded in their direction. Marie Frost approached them. She looked puzzled and impatient. Every few seconds she glanced at the police car pulled up outside.

Patricia said, "Hello, Mrs Frost, my boyfriend Peter told me how helpful you were to him when he was in here last weekend."

There was a slight thawing of the manager's attitude.

Patricia pulled out her phone, "Here's a picture of him to remind you."

Marie Frost glanced down and then smiled warmly, "Oh yes, I remember him. He has allergies like my nephew. You're the second person to come in asking about him . . ." Her voice trailed off and she looked very uncomfortable. "He's your boyfriend?"

"Yes, he's my boyfriend and a solicitor. I'm his secretary. He was meeting a client on Saturday, a woman, to check something about a case we're working on."

Marie visibly relaxed. "Yes, I'm sorry. I didn't think there was anything going on between him and the lady." She blushed.

Patricia indicated Adam. "This gentleman here is a policeman. We're all really concerned about this woman and we were hoping you could tell us about the other person who was enquiring. We're guessing it was on Wednesday morning and we were wondering what he wanted to know." She hurried on. "I promise we're trying to do some good here."

Marie looked at each of them individually and then back to Patricia. "Well, in fact, that other guy – he scared me a little bit."

Patricia said, "Tell us what happened."

"Well, he came in and had coffee and a scone and then asked to speak to the manager. He said that friends of his were in here on Saturday and that they'd left a jacket behind. He said that the man had an Irish accent," she smiled at Patricia, "and that he might have been in a suit as he was working. He described the lady as well as tall and blonde. Well, I wasn't sure because we have so many people in but he had a photograph of the woman and I recognised her immediately. I told him that I did remember them because of the man's allergies to milk and God knows what else and how careful we had to be with his order."

Patricia hadn't the heart to tell her that it was a fabrication.

"I told the man that I'd served them myself and he wanted to know what precautions I had to take. Well, I was surprised that as a friend he didn't know and I said as much. He told me that everything had been fine that day but that on other occasions there've been problems and he just wanted to be clear for future reference exactly the measures I'd taken. So, I told him how I'd worn gloves as your boyfriend had requested and made sure not to touch anything. I didn't trust it to any of the girls."

Isobel asked, "What did the man say when he heard all of this?"

"He asked about the gloves and I told him what I'd done – the plates and cups straight from the dishwasher only handled with the gloves. That's as clean as you could make things. To be honest he seemed more interested in all the precautions we'd taken than in the coat he'd come to locate. I had to remind him of it. I told him we hadn't found any jacket. But all he wanted to know was that it was definitely the woman in the photograph. I started feeling unsure then. I was wondering was he a stalker or something. Then, he sort of calmed himself down and showed me the photo of the two of them and they looked so lovely together. He said he just wanted to be sure that he had the right café when he told them he checked for the coat. He left after that.'" She looked at Patricia nervously. "Did I do something wrong?"

Patricia answered, "Not at all, Mrs Frost. You really helped Peter on that Saturday with something very important."

Isobel asked, "Did you see what direction he went in after he left here on Wednesday?"

Marie looked down and shifted in her seat.

They all held their breaths.

She fiddled with her ring and after a moment she looked up. "Well, as I said, he made me uncomfortable even a little bit afraid so when he left I went to the window and watched him."

Isobel nodded encouragingly.

"He went out and walked down the street a little and then he pulled out his phone and started talking. Then after a minute he took another phone out of his pocket and answered that."

Isobel said, "Just a minute, Mrs Frost, excuse me." She turned to Adam and Patricia. "So he rings to tell her to leave, using the burner phone. He also tells her to ring him so he has his story straight about the delay at the hairdresser's, so she does and he answers his own phone."

Patricia and Adam nodded.

Isobel said, "What did he do next, Mrs Frost?"

"Well, I wasn't exactly spying on him . . ."

Adam interrupted her disclaimer. "All of this is really helpful. We're in the middle of an important investigation and anything you tell us about what this man did is extremely helpful."

Suitably reassured, Marie Frost went on, "He then went back to the first phone and made another call. This one was longer and he talked a lot."

"That was probably him talking to Charlie Ellis." Patricia said to Isobel and Adam. "Now he has everything organized." She turned to Marie Frost. "What did he do then?"

"Well, when he finished the call he walked off."

Isobel said, "And the phone that he was using?"

"It was still in his hand when I lost sight of him."

Adam said to the others, "That phone could be

anywhere. That was two days ago. I can try Stella again and see if she has anyone looking into it but honestly I don't think we are ever going to find that phone."

"What's this all about, anyway?" Marie Frost asked.

Adam said, "We suspect the man who came here asking questions on Wednesday of some pretty horrible crimes. The phone might help us prove it."

Mrs Frost said, "I knew he was a bad one! I told you he scared me. Did he hurt someone?" She raised her hand to her mouth, her eyes wide. "That woman?"

Isobel said, "Yes, we think he hurt a woman but not the lady you met, someone else."

Marie frowned, "Well . . ."

Isobel said, "What?"

"There was something else that happened later that day . . ."

Isobel could feel her frustration threatening to erupt on Mrs Frost so she quickly took a deep breath and quelled it. "Tell us about what happened later."

Mrs Frost made a face. "It may be nothing but at about four o'clock Johnny, an old homeless guy that I often give some food to, you know a sandwich or a scone –"

"That's kind of you."

Mrs Frost smiled. "I'm very fond of him."

Isobel nodded encouragingly. She could feel Adam starting to fidget. "What happened with Johnny?"

"Well, he asked me first if a customer had had their phone taken and then asked if a man had been bothering me. At the time I thought he was imagining things and getting a bit confused."

Patricia said, "But now you wonder if Johnny saw the man with the phone."

Mrs Frost nodded. "Obviously, because I am good to him he is fond of me and –"

Isobel said, "And maybe he saw you watching the man and was concerned."

Patricia said, "And maybe Johnny saw what the man did next."

Mrs Frost said, "Well, I didn't notice Johnny that morning but he could have been standing in a doorway. I don't know. It's just strange that he mentioned a man and a phone."

Isobel said, "I agree. We've nothing to lose. Mrs Frost, where could we find this Johnny?"

Standing up, Mrs Frost said, "I'll help you. Johnny is normally in the park near here in the afternoons. I know him. He'll talk to me. Let me get a sandwich to take to him."

Patricia nodded. "We can find out if he knows anything."

Mrs Frost continued, "You said I helped on the Saturday. Then, when I said that I had told that other man about the gloves, I knew by your faces that that didn't help. So let me make up for it. I don't want him to get away with something. I don't want it on my conscience."

Mrs Frost went off to organise some food.

Patricia said, "What do you think?"

Isobel said, "It's a long shot but we have nothing to lose."

Mrs Frost came back carrying a paper bag.

Adam said, "How far away is the park?"

Mrs Frost looked out the window at the police car and said firmly, "Walking distance."

It was only a ten-minute walk to the park.

Before they entered Mrs Frost said to them, "Johnny doesn't like strangers so you'd better let me do the talking."

They nodded in consent. With Patricia and Marie Frost in front and Adam and Isobel a little way behind they progressed around the park. The day was warm and there were people sitting on benches reading papers and mothers pushing strollers with older children chasing each other on the grass. The flower beds had flowering shrubs and colourful flowers and insects buzzed.

Suddenly Marie peered and stopped. Ahead an older man sat on a bench underneath an oak tree with his legs stretched out in front of him crossed at the ankles. He had a bald pate with a circle of white hair. Beside him on the bench was an old overcoat folded up with a hat perched on top of it. He wore faded black trousers, a greyish-white shirt, a cardigan with holes at the elbows, mismatched socks and shoes that were battered-looking and would not last another winter.

Marie called, *"Johnny, is that you?"*

Perhaps unused to being hailed, it took Johnny a few seconds to sit up and turn towards them. He looked puzzled.

"Mrs Frost? What are you doing here?" He looked at Patricia beside her and Isobel and Adam behind them. "Are you out with your friends?"

Marie stepped closer and held out the paper bag. "I brought you something to eat."

Johnny touched his chin and eyed the others. "Well, I usually come to you. So if you're here with all these people I'm thinking that you're looking for something and I have nothing so it must be information."

Isobel put her hand over her mouth and smiled behind it. She liked this old man's style, not to mention his logic but then you didn't survive as Johnny did without having your wits about you. Marie stepped forward and Patricia followed.

Johnny took the proffered bag.

Marie said, "May I sit down?"

Johnny nodded. Marie sat down beside him and Patricia discreetly sat beside her.

Isobel and Adam stepped onto the grass so they were not in Johnny's line of vision but were still able to hear him talk.

"I'm very grateful for the food, Mrs Frost, but I'm wondering what these people want?"

"On Wednesday morning a man left my coffee shop. He was tall with dark hair. He went out and he made a few phone calls and then walked away."

Johnny said, "That man frightened you, Mrs Frost."

"How do you know?"

"I saw you peering out the shop window at him when he left."

Marie opened her mouth to speak but Johnny continued.

"I was thinking of calling for a bite to eat like," he straightened in the seat with dignity, "but then I saw your face and I kind of held back."

"I was afraid. He did scare me."

"*I knew it*. I knew he got to you and I didn't know what his game was."

Patricia said, "So you were worried about Marie – I mean, Mrs Frost, then?"

Johnny shifted his glance to Patricia. After surveying her for a few seconds he nodded. "Course I was. She's the only person who cares about old Johnny and here was this flash bloke doing, well, I don't know what."

Isobel could feel her eyes welling up. Oh God, here was this old man looking out for his friend. She bit her lip.

Patricia said, "What did you do then, Johnny?"

Johnny chewed on the inside of his mouth and turned and looked over at Isobel and Adam.

Adam was about to step forward but Marie stopped him with a subtle shake of her head.

She continued, "That man has done some bad things, hurt people, and I made a mistake on Wednesday and told him something that I wish now I hadn't. Please help me put that right."

Johnny looked back at her and his face softened, "Oh, Mrs Frost, don't you be upsetting yourself. You're a good, kind lady to old Johnny. I'll tell you what I know. He's a bad lot that guy and I don't mind daubing him in to the police." He gestured with his head towards Adam. "In fact, after he's upset you I'd be glad to."

Marie smiled. "Thank you."

He smiled back. "Sure aren't you always helping me with bits of food and stuff?"

Patricia said, "So what happened then?"

Johnny screwed up his face. "He made those calls using two phones, I ask you. Then he walked down the street and went into the corner shop. I saw him through the window. He was getting a scone and him only come out of your café. I knew that was strange. Anyway he came out of the shop with his wee bag and then he stood into a doorway and I see'd him slip one of those phones into that bag secret-like. Then he walked on down the street and threw the whole bag in the bin, scone and all."

Isobel bit her lip again to smother her smile. She couldn't help it – she was mad about this man.

Patricia said, "What happened then?"

Johnny rolled his eyes, "*What do you think happened? I went and got that scone. It was in a bag, clean as a whistle.*"

Marie said, "Of course you did."

Johnny said, "Wasting good food like that. It did me for breakfast. You know I loves a scone, Mrs Frost?"

"I do, Johnny, I do."

Patricia shifted on the seat. Her voice came out more strained than usual. "Where's the phone, Johnny?"

He frowned. "I'm getting to that. I thought he might be one of those protection people, you know, demanding money from people who have businesses and I was worried about you, Mrs Frost, so . . . in case anything happened . . . I was going to talk to you about it again when I had things straight in my mind . . ." Johnny looked at Marie.

She nodded at him.

"I have the phone here. I knew he was up to no good that man, throwing away a phone like that."

He reached into a big pocket in the inside of his coat and drew out the phone.

Adam stepped forward and pulled open a plastic evidence bag to receive the phone.

Johnny looked at him but then dropped it in the bag.

Johnny continued to eye Adam, "I suppose you'll be wanting me to come and make a statement?"

Adam smiled gently. "That would be a big help. We'll probably need your fingerprints as well to exclude them from the phone."

Obviously familiar with police procedure, Johnny nodded.

Mrs Frost said, "I'm sorry, Johnny, but I really want to help these people."

"It's all right, Mrs Frost. I reckon he must have been real bad if they sent all of these people to find the phone."

Isobel said, "And while you're helping the police I'm sure there'll be plenty of tea and food to keep you comfortable."

Johnny grinned.

Adam added, "And, you never know, we might find a pair of shoes in your size."

"I could do with a new pair."

Adam said, "Will I bring the car?"

Johnny snapped, "Don't be stupid. I don't want everyone here to see me getting into a police car. I'll walk back to Mrs Frost's."

Johnny got up and set off with Mrs Frost and Patricia while Adam pulled out his phone and called the police station. He spoke quickly to Simon who had not as yet interviewed Thomas, filling him in on what they had found. He also rang the lab to let Jeff know they had the phone. Fingerprints and phone history were a priority and Jeff had people standing by.

They walked back to the café. Mrs Frost was somewhat shocked to realise that she would have to make a statement too.

The car journey to the police station was cramped and rather pungent.

Chapter 45

Isobel thought that she and Patricia would be told to go home while the interview was taking place, but maybe in deference to all the work they'd done on the case, they were allowed to stay. More than that, they were being treated as part of the team. They followed Adam and Stella to a room which was crowded with faces she recognised from the meetings. Most people were standing along the walls. Stella ushered them to the few chairs in the room. They were all facing a wall where there was obviously a hidden window because they could see into an interview room where Thomas Banks was sitting with another man. Isobel assumed this man was his solicitor. There was a table and two more chairs.

Isobel leaned in and asked Stella in a whisper, "Has he admitted anything yet?"

"They haven't started to question him. We usually let the person stew for a bit. Mr Banks wanted a solicitor and that takes time to organise and they need time to confer. You haven't missed any of it."

"Are there usually this many people watching?"

Stella laughed. "No, but we usually have the body first

387

and then have to find the person who did it. This case has intrigued everyone because this guy has killed three people – he's a serial killer. The psychiatrists can argue over the type. And he almost got away with it. Patricia and you are here because only for you we wouldn't even have known what he'd done. Not only that but he has tried to implicate someone else in his wife's murder. Believe me, this is not a normal case and we all want to see the boss take him down."

Isobel shivered, partly with fear and partly with tension.

The door opened and Simon entered the interview room with Rajesh.

Immediately, the solicitor started talking. "I object to the way that my client has been dragged in here and doesn't even know why."

Simon ignored the solicitor and Rajesh went through a litany which Isobel recognized from watching television, giving the date and time, the location and then identifying everyone in the room. Thomas Banks' solicitor was Percy Fenwright.

Rajesh then read out the caution and asked if Thomas understood and asked him to answer for the benefit of the tape.

Then Rajesh started by asking some basic questions, name, address, then occupation.

Thomas answered to this, "I work for White and Smith."

"How long have you worked for them?"

"Almost ten years."

"They're a very prestigious firm. You must be a trusted employee."

"I like to think so."

Stella whispered in Isobel's ear, "Rajesh is just getting

Thomas to relax, asking some easy questions to get a rhythm going."

Percy Fenwright said, "I'm sure Mr Banks' job is fascinating but if it's not relevant to why we're here can we move on?"

Stella whispered again, "He wants to disrupt the flow of the interview so that Thomas doesn't get too relaxed – that's when people slip up."

Patricia was leaning in from where she was sitting on Stella's other side, as fascinated as Isobel was by the dynamics of the interview.

"Of course," Rajesh said with a smile. "Are you married, Mr Banks?"

"Yes."

"Does your wife live with you?"

Thomas Banks looked at his solicitor who nodded.

"No, she moved out about three months ago," Thomas said. "She was an alcoholic. She went to rehab and has been doing rather well. We were to be divorced this Wednesday. However, my wife didn't turn up as arranged. I tried her flat later that day and she wasn't there. I haven't heard from her since. This sort of thing is one of the reasons we are getting divorced. I just hope that she hasn't fallen off the wagon."

"Oh, I'm sorry to hear that, sir. Are you worried about her?"

Thomas shrugged. "Not yet. Maybe. A bit. I know from going to some of the sessions at the rehab centre that things like this can happen in the early days of recovery. Getting the divorce was to protect our son from the trauma of this type of occurrence."

"So you've no idea where your wife is, sir?"

"Not at present, no." Thomas Banks said this very clearly.

Percy Fenwright intervened again. "Is that why my client is here – to answer questions about his soon-to-be-ex-wife?"

Rajesh smiled. "Just establishing some facts. And your son, Mr Banks, where is he?"

"I had to ask an old neighbour to collect him from school. I had hoped to be home before it got too late."

Simon now spoke. "We want to show you some footage that a concerned citizen brought us."

Rajesh got up and opened the door and a constable brought in a laptop which Rajesh placed so that Thomas and his solicitor could see it. He played an extract of footage showing the man dumping the bag into the Thames.

Everyone was watching Thomas Banks like hawks. All that Isobel observed was a slight tightening at his jaw – otherwise he didn't move. Silence followed.

Simon asked, "Do you know this man?"

"No."

Percy Fenwright said, "What's the relevance of this?"

Simon ignored him. "Do you recognize the van, Mr Banks?"

"No."

"Obviously dumping rubbish in the Thames is something we frown on."

Percy Fenwright now vehement. "You brought my client here to talk about *illegal dumping*? This is ridiculous!"

Simon kept his gaze firmly on Thomas Banks and continued as if Percy hadn't spoken. "We've tracked this van through the city and it came from your house to this place by the river."

Thomas Banks paused a moment, seeming genuinely shocked, and then said, "*What?* What was this van doing at my house?"

Percy Fenwright said, "My client is clearly stating that he has no knowledge of this van."

Again Simon ignored this comment. "We have obviously run the van's plates and it's a rental."

No response from Thomas Banks.

"The van was rented in the name of Charlie Ellis."

"Oh, Charlie, my occasional gardener. I must say, I'm shocked that he would dump stuff in the Thames but surely I can't be responsible for what my gardener does with rubbish?"

"What was he doing at your house?" Simon continued.

"He did some work for me earlier in the year, digging some ground when I was planting trees and putting in a flower bed."

"Why would Charlie Ellis have gone to your house and then to the river?" Simon asked.

Thomas Banks paused a moment. "I don't know. When we did the garden there was talk of later putting in some special fertiliser to help the garden grow. He was to do that but we hadn't discussed any particular time for it. Maybe he had some time and was being helpful and forgot to tell me."

Simon asked, "Have you noticed any digging in your garden in the last few days?"

"No. But then I haven't been out in the garden. With Anne going off like that, and the divorce not happening, I've been spending a lot of time with Tommy, playing computer games, going to McDonald's, stuff like that."

Simon shifted the focus. "We tracked the van through

the city. It was collected from the rental place, driven to a shopping centre and then driven to your house. It was at your house for about two hours then driven through the city to Deptford."

Percy Fenwright said, "I have to object to this. Surely Charlie Ellis is the man to ask about all of this, not my client?"

Simon smiled an acknowledgment. "The Marine Policing Unit pulled a bag identical to this from the river yesterday."

Thomas Banks paled now but didn't shift in his seat.

Simon said, "The bag when opened contained the body of a woman."

Percy Fenwright looked flabbergasted. "What has this to do with my client?"

Thomas Banks said, "Charlie Ellis threw a body in the Thames?"

"It certainly appears like that, sir."

"I'm shocked."

"Needless to say we've brought Charlie Ellis in for questioning. He says that you rang him to rent the van, offered him a thousand pounds and told him to take the rest of the day off."

Thomas Banks now stood up suddenly. "This is ridiculous. Check my phone here, I never rang him." He sank back into his seat and put his head in his hands.

His solicitor, taking this cue, said, "This is a blatant attempt to incriminate my client."

Simon said, "You can appreciate, I'm sure, Mr Banks, why we had to bring you in and ask you some questions."

"Of course, of course."

"We just need to ask you where you were when this all happened."

Thomas nodded but said nothing.

"Where were you, Mr Banks?"

Thomas Banks looked at him. "You'd better tell me what time you want me to account for my movements. You haven't said when this took place."

Isobel could see the challenge in his eyes and the confidence. He really thought that he was too clever, that he was unassailable.

"Oh, haven't I, sir? My mistake. This would have been Wednesday before three o'clock."

Thomas Banks looked thoughtful. "That was the day of the divorce that never happened, so let me see. I dropped Tommy at school. I had a quick word with the principal to tell her what was happening and to ask her to keep an eye on Tommy. Then I went and had coffee in a little café." He paused. "And then I went . . . I was upset . . . I just wanted to wander around so I actually went to a shopping centre."

"Really, sir? Which shopping centre was it?"

"I'm not sure of the name."

Rajesh said, "Perhaps it was the Commercial Shopping Centre?"

"It could have been that one."

"*Could* have been?" Rajesh raised his eyebrows.

"It probably was."

Simon said, "There are a number of shops there, furniture shops, bed shops – what were you looking for?"

"Well, nothing specific but I was thinking of changing the bedroom, you know, after the divorce and that. Make a new start."

Isobel marvelled at how plausible that sounded.

"That's the same shopping centre where Charlie Ellis parked that van," Simon said.

"I never saw him there."

"He says he didn't see you either."

"Maybe he did. Maybe that's why he thought to implicate me."

"Who can say, sir? We'll check your phone. If you could just give us the authorisation we can confirm that you made no call to Charlie Ellis's phone."

Thomas looked at his solicitor who nodded, "Yes. This will prove that I'm innocent and he's lying."

Rajesh supplied a form and Thomas signed it. Rajesh opened the door of the interview room and handed it to a waiting constable.

"Is that everything, then?" Thomas asked. "Maybe I could get home to my son now." He started to stand up.

Simon forestalled him. "If you wouldn't mind, sir, there are a few more things that I want to clarify."

Thomas blew out impatiently.

Percy Fenwright said, "This seems like harassment."

Simon very calmly said, "On the contrary. Finding the body of a woman is very serious. I'm sure Mr Banks wants to assist us as much as he can."

There was no verbal response but Thomas Banks settled back into the chair.

"I'm sure you're familiar with the address, 42 Sycamore Street."

There was a long silence. Thomas Banks stayed very still, the only movement again a slight tightening of his jaw. Simon waited out the silence.

After a long pause Thomas Banks said, "That's the area where I grew up."

Everyone in the observation room was silent, watching intently.

Simon now appeared very relaxed. "You probably don't remember, sir, but a couple bought that house about ten years ago. Just this week the husband decided to dig a pond for his wife. She wants to get koi fish and to survive the winter here they need the water to be about five or six feet deep, about the depth of a grave."

Thomas Banks licked his lips. This was the first major sign of stress that he'd betrayed.

Simon continued with his tale, "The husband went out yesterday morning to dig the pond and what did he find?" He paused as if waiting for an answer. The silence lengthened. "He found some bones."

Thomas Banks had his eyes locked on Simon.

"Naturally he rang the police and they in turn rang the coroner. The coroner found the bones to be human and forensics took over the digging. The body is that of a fifty-year-old woman."

Another pause and again no one spoke.

Simon continued. "The coroner estimates that the bones have been in the ground for about ten years."

The stillness was intense in the interview room and also in the observation room.

Simon continued in his storyteller tone. "Ten years ago is the time when the house changed hands. Since the people who bought it contacted us about the body which would be stupid if they were trying to get away with murder, we tried to contact Mrs Cooper who lived there previously. There has been no activity on her national insurance number in all those years. Naturally we were concerned and so we wanted to find her son. There has been no activity on his number either. We were very worried, thinking that maybe they were both dead."

Thomas Banks seemed to twitch slightly at that, maybe in relief.

"In the course of our investigation with the neighbours it came to our attention that this missing Matt Cooper was very friendly with Thomas Banks. I suppose that would be you, sir."

Thomas Banks didn't say anything. He just looked steadfastly at Simon.

"Is that you, sir? Were you Matt Cooper's friend?"

Thomas Banks said nothing.

"Answer the question, sir."

There was another pause then Thomas Banks said, "I want to confer with my solicitor."

Percy Fenwright immediately piped up, "My client has that right."

Simon inclined his head and Rajesh told the tape the necessary things and stopped it.

Percy Fenwright said, "I want all sound to the observation room stopped also. This is confidential."

"Of course." Rajesh pressed a button on the wall and they could hear no more. Then he and Simon left the room.

Isobel expelled her breath and it was only then she realised that she'd been holding it.

"Come on, let's go and get a coffee," Stella said.

The three women left the room while Adam joined some of the other officers to talk.

Stella led them to one of the open offices and they helped themselves to coffee. Through a glass window they could see Simon and Rajesh in Simon's office, talking.

Stella said, nodding in their direction, "They won't really talk to anyone until this is over unless they need information from us. They'll already have developed a strategy."

"It seems to be going really well," Isobel said.

"Yes, already Thomas Banks knows he's in trouble and is going to try to minimize it."

There was not much else to say so they sipped their drinks until they saw someone tap on Simon's office door.

Stella said, "They're ready," and led the way back to the observation room.

Thomas Banks and Percy Fenwright were already seated. A few minutes later Rajesh and Simon entered. Rajesh flicked the switch so they could all hear again and then, starting the tape, stated again who was in the room.

Percy Fenwright spoke immediately Rajesh had finished. "My client has prepared a statement which I will now read to you."

"Go ahead," said Simon.

"'*When Thomas Banks was tragically killed by a drunk driver, realising that he had a new job lined up with White and Smith I changed my name and took his place in the company. I have been Thomas Banks ever since.*'" He paused. "Note that my client is merely admitting to capitalising on an unfolding situation."

Simon said, "He knowingly lied to his present employers and got this job under false pretenses."

"That may be true but that's all that he did."

"I'm sure White and Smith will not be happy to hear this. They may press charges."

Thomas Banks said, "Probably not – the publicity would do their company more harm than good."

"That may be true. Before you changed your name to Thomas Banks, who were you?"

Simon waited and Thomas Banks stared at him for a long while before answering.

"Matt Cooper."

Percy Fenwright didn't react or appear surprised so Thomas Banks must have confessed this.

Simon said, "I'm going to need a sample of your DNA to compare with the body found in the garden."

Percy said, "I must object –"

"We're getting his DNA now or later," said Simon.

Percy Fenwright nodded at Matt and he said, "OK."

Rajesh opened the door and a constable entered to do a mouth swab and quickly left.

"I want a sample of your fingerprints also," Simon said.

Again Matt Cooper acquiesced.

Once more, with everyone settled at the table, Simon said, "Thank you, Mr Cooper. Now, going back to the body at 42 Sycamore Street, we managed to find your mother's old dentist. Using her old dental records we can tell you that the body in the garden is definitely your mother."

Matt Cooper shook his head. "No, she told me she was moving to Scotland."

"I can further tell you that your mother was strangled."

"*What?*"

"Your mother was murdered."

"Oh my God! My poor mother! I thought she was having a new life in Scotland."

"Had she been in touch with you?"

"No, but she gave me the house and I thought she wanted to go off with her boyfriend and just live it up. She was a single parent and it had been hard for her. I thought she wanted to be irresponsible now, young, carefree."

"So you weren't surprised when she didn't get in touch?"

"Of course! Surprised and hurt. But I thought she'd

other things on her mind. You're going to try and pin this on me, aren't you? Well, I didn't do it. Maybe it was that old boyfriend of hers. I didn't do it. You can't prove that I did."

Simon said, "You can see my concern, sir. I have a body in your old house and then it seems that your gardener disposed of a body after leaving the garden of your present home. Just to put my mind at rest I contacted your wife's sister to get a DNA sample to compare with the body we pulled from the River Thames."

This time Matt Cooper paled very noticeably.

"DNA showed that the body dumped in the river was indeed your wife's."

Matt Cooper broke down, sobbing. "*Oh my God, Anne!*"

Isobel was shocked at how convincing he was. He cried for some moments and then said, "I need another moment with my solicitor."

Simon and Rajesh went through the same procedure and left the room. This time Isobel and the others remained. Even with no sound they could see that Percy Fenwright was angry.

Listening to the men around her, Isobel could hear some of what they quietly said.

"Jesus, Simon is playing a blinder."

"He has him."

The waiting this time was horrendous. Eventually the solicitor opened the door to signal that they were finished.

Once again after the preliminaries they resumed.

Matt Cooper said, "I had nothing to do with either of those bodies. I'm innocent."

Percy Fenwright intervened. "Once again I'm going to

make a statement. About three months ago Anne Banks left her husband. He came home from work and found her gone, leaving a note saying that she'd met someone else. Obviously my client was devastated and fearing that she and her new man would try to take Tommy's family home he concocted a divorce whereby someone pretended to be his wife in the hope of preventing any further battles about money. This was very ill advised but Mr Cooper was under considerable emotional stress at the time. He had no idea that his wife was dead. He now believes that Charlie Ellis may have been the other man, that there was a fight and that he is being set up to take the blame."

Simon said, "So once again Matt is admitting to fraud."

"Yes, he was silly, trying to capitalise on a situation but he didn't harm his wife."

Simon said, "When your mother went to Scotland, as you thought, you sold the house and kept all the money."

Matt said, "My mother had already signed the house over to me. She wanted a fresh start in Scotland. I offered her money but she refused. She said that she wanted to get me started in life."

Simon asked, "Have you got the note your wife left?"

"No, I was so upset about things that I tore it up."

"And you are suggesting that Charlie was going to run away with your wife?"

"Yes. About eight months ago, when Charlie was doing some other work for me, my wife said a few times that he made her uncomfortable. I was going to get rid of him but before I did my wife came to me and said that she was wrong and that he was a lovely man. I didn't pass any remarks at the time but maybe they started the affair then.

Maybe she wouldn't leave me and he killed her. I don't know what Charlie Ellis is doing but he's trying to frame me. You need to ask him what his game is. All I can tell you is that I certainly didn't harm my wife."

"Yet you are the common denominator in both cases."

"I'm innocent. You can't turn a coincidence into a fact."

Simon said, "Let me show you something." Using the laptop he brought up the images of Charlie walking and the other man in work clothes walking. Then, just as Dermot had, he displayed the images simultaneously. "Do you see the difference in these two men walking? This man has a shuffle because of an old knee injury and this man here doesn't."

Matt said, "I can't see much of a difference."

"We got a forensic gait analyst in. They give evidence in court. They can identify people by how they walk. He's looked at Charlie walking and this other man walking into the centre in workman's clothes and he says this man is you."

"*That's not true!* It's not me. You're trying to frame me."

Percy Fenwright said, "Forensic gait analysis! You're overreaching here."

"We don't think so."

A constable knocked and entered, handing Simon a piece of paper. He read it and passed it to Rajesh who nodded.

Simon calmly changed direction again. "We know that you had someone impersonating your wife and guess what?" He waited. "Not guessing? Well, I'll tell you then. We found her."

Matt said, "I've already admitted my duplicity there but that doesn't mean that I murdered my wife."

"She made a statement saying that you called her on the morning of the divorce to tell her to leave."

"I did not. You can check my phone. She rang me."

"She says you called her on a burner phone. Interestingly Charlie says you called him from a different phone number than your usual one."

Isobel could almost see Matt going over things in his mind, trying to think of what to say.

Simon continued, relentless now. "We have a witness who saw you on a phone outside a café."

Almost like a rabbit caught in the headlights, Matt's eyes were locked on Simon's, "You made the calls and then you got rid of it. A homeless man saw you do it and he retrieved the phone. We found him and I've just received word that it is the burner that you made the call to Charlie Ellis on."

A pause, everyone just waiting with bated breath.

"And, guess what, your fingerprints are on it and in a couple of hours we will show that your DNA is as well."

Matt just stared.

Simon continued, "Oh and we found the clothes that you dumped in the bins at the shopping area after you'd dug up and dumped your wife's body. There was DNA at the usual places – under the arms, the rim of a hat." He leaned back. "One more thing. We have photographs from an abuse centre of your wife's injuries from a few days before she was killed. She made a statement to a solicitor, saying that you tried to strangle her. She had made plans to leave you. Somehow you realised that and you killed her."

Matt screwed up his face and spat out, "*That stupid bitch! How dare she even think of leaving me? I suppose you found all of this out because of that Irish bitch? She needs someone to sort her out!"*

Isobel could feel herself cringing at the level of hatred. Patricia reached over and took her hand.

Simon said with satisfaction, "For the record we note your level of violence directed at this woman who challenges you."

Matt ground his teeth.

Simon continued, "Well, we're going to charge you with two murders. You won't be hurting any more women for a long time. Now, just one more thing . . ."

Simon whispered to Rajesh who got up and left.

A few moments later Rajesh appeared at the door of the observation room and said, "Adam, you're to partner Simon for this part of the interview."

Adam looked shocked. "I'm not prepped."

Rajesh smiled. "Simon is going to lead, just follow him."

Adam nodded and looked at Isobel as he was walking out.

Once again the ritual was adhered to with the tape.

Adam sat down at the table.

Simon commenced again. "Detective Adam Bryce works with road traffic incidents. We're going to show you footage of the hit-and-run where Thomas Banks was killed."

Again they employed the laptop and showed the car hitting Thomas and the man walking back.

Matt Cooper winced.

Simon went on, "Note the straight line the car took to hit Thomas. Also, note the man who walks back to the body doesn't show the usual agitated behaviour of someone in shock or fear." He paused. "The car that knocked down Thomas Banks belonged to Jennifer Green. Adam, you continue."

For a moment Adam looked shocked then he found his voice and spoke clearly. "You knew Jennifer from your work at the same company. In fact you knew her well. You often had lunch with her. You knew where she lived because you'd gone there to do work on your CV. Not only that but you borrowed her car for a weekend."

Simon cut in, "And copied the key and then a few months later when Thomas got the flash job and you were passed over you ran him down and killed him and took over his life."

Matt spat, "He always had it easy. Everyone liked him, he was clever and charming."

Simon said, "And he was going to be way more successful than you and leave you behind."

"No one leaves me behind."

"No, they don't, do they? Not your mother, not Thomas and certainly not Anne. We had the forensic gait analyst look at this footage and compare it to the one of you walking to receive your graduation certificate. He says it is you who ran Thomas Banks down. Matt Cooper, I'm charging you with three counts of murder, also fraud and conspiracy."

Simon stood and spoke to the officer standing by the door. "Take him and charge him."

Matt Cooper was escorted out. Simon sat back down in the interview chair. He looked exhausted.

Isobel had rivers of sweat running down her back.

Suddenly a cheer went up from the lads in the room. They started pushing out and Isobel could see Adam shaking Simon's hand.

Isobel could feel the tears coming to her eyes. It was just relief, she knew. It hardly seemed possible that this nightmare was over.

Patricia hugged her tightly. "I want to let Peter know that we got him."

Isobel nodded.

Stella led her out of the observation room into the big office.

Patricia joined them again, beaming.

Simon was being escorted into the room by a number of his colleagues. He came up to Isobel and Patricia. For a moment they looked at one another and then he hugged them both together.

"The first round of drinks is on me!" he announced.

He insisted that Isobel and Patricia came along to The Feathers.

Patricia and Isobel had one drink but their hearts weren't in it and soon, pleading tiredness, they left.

Isobel went up with Patricia to say hello to Peter. He listened spellbound to them telling him what had happened that day. He'd not been idle either. Claire was staying with Grace and Tommy. Peter had put in motion the relevant things for Claire to become Tommy's legal guardian as Anne would have wished.

Eventually Isobel left Peter and Patricia together and stepped into the kitchen.

"Hi, Dave."

"Hi, Isobel. How are things? Any word of you coming home?"

"Dave, we got him. He's just been charged with three counts of murder."

"Well done, Sherlock!"

Isobel laughed.

"You sound in better form despite all the murder and mayhem," he said.

"I am, Dave. It's really sad but this guy was so clever about covering his tracks. I'm glad you persuaded me to take this case."

"Good. And home?"

"Yeah, on Sunday probably."

"You can tell us all about it then, even the bits that you've left out in case I panicked."

Isobel laughed. "Deal. See you Sunday. I'll text my flight times."

Worn out, before long Isobel and Patricia headed back to her flat and to the relief of sleep. For the first time since this case started Isobel slept soundly with no disturbing dreams.

Chapter 46

Saturday 2nd June

Isobel woke at nine o'clock. She felt a sense of relief that everything was over and also a deep sadness. She lay there for a few minutes. There were a number of important things that she wanted to do before she went home.

Firstly, she used her phone and found a hardware store nearby where surely she could get what she needed. Secondly, she rang Julia and asked if they could meet. They agreed on their usual place at eleven.

Isobel heard Patricia moving around also.

Isobel asked, "How are you today?"

"I'm glad we got him but I also feel sad about Anne and about Tommy."

"Me too. I'm going to go round this afternoon and see Grace. Claire is there at the moment and Tommy. Do you want to come? I'm then going on to see Thomas Banks Senior to tell him everything."

Patricia said, "Yes, definitely."

"I'm probably going to go home tomorrow. Do you and Peter fancy having dinner with me tonight before I go?"

Patricia laughed. "Yes to that as well."

They arranged to meet at Grace's at two o'clock.

Isobel's last call was to Adam.

"Adam, Patricia and I are going to call on Thomas Banks Senior this afternoon. Do you still want to come?"

Adam answered very emphatically, "Yes."

Isobel said, "We'll be coming from Grace's so I'm not sure of the time yet."

"I'm working nearby anyway so just let me know when you're on your way and I'll meet you there."

Isobel then booked her flight home for Sunday afternoon. That done, she had a quick shower and went to the hardware store to forage for what she wanted.

Isobel arrived at the coffee shop in the National Gallery a few minutes after eleven, having taken a taxi and left her purchase at security. Julia rose and hugged Isobel and they settled down to talk. Isobel had thought that she would have to tell Julia all that had happened. However, she was surprised,

"Claire phoned me yesterday. She knew that Thomas had been taken in for questioning and she went up to Grace's to be with Tommy. She was worried about what to tell him and so she rang me. At our refuge we have a fulltime play therapist available to work with children and she gave Claire some advice about talking to Tommy. I think Claire might arrange for the play therapist to see him in the future."

"Oh that's great. So much has happened to him and now he has no mum or dad. I'm relieved that Claire is asking for help and support."

Julia nodded then rousing herself said, "Simon has been in touch. All of the officers are upset about how Thomas nearly got away with this and Simon wants to keep in touch and maybe refer people to us. We have an outreach programme so we can talk to women and men too in abusive situations and help and support them." She smiled. "I think they want to do more, so he and some of the lads are thinking of doing a mini marathon to raise funds for us."

"Goodness, they've all of that thought out already!"

Julia laughed. "Watch this space! They seem pretty determined."

Isobel smiled. "Thanks for your help, Julia. You and Yvonne were great."

"I just wish that we'd got Anne out in time."

Isobel said, "Me too."

There was nothing more they could say.

Isobel got to her feet and Julia got up to hug her.

"If you're ever back in London give me a call and we'll go for dinner."

"Sure will. Keep doing what you are doing, Julia."

Isobel stopped at the shop in the National and bought a couple of candles. Then she retrieved her package and took another taxi to Wimbledon.

She was early so on the spur of the moment she got dropped off at Brushstrokes. It was just over a week since she'd talked to Aaron yet it seemed like a lifetime. When she entered the shop he spotted her and after a few moments he was able to leave his lady. Isobel was unsure what was going to be in the papers but as it was Aaron who had given her the crucial idea she felt herself that she owed him an explanation.

He hugged her and said, "I only have a minute."

Isobel winced. "This is probably going to take longer than that."

Aaron, sensing her serious tone, said, "Can you give

me ten minutes to finish this cut and then I'll get someone else to do the blow-dry and we can go for a quick coffee?"

Isobel nodded. As she waited she thought about what she was going to say to him.

Aaron took her next door to a coffee shop.

He said immediately, "Something bad happened, didn't it?"

"Yes."

His eyes locked on hers, "What?"

Isobel exhaled. "She's dead. I'm sorry, Aaron."

His hand flew to his mouth and his head curled forward onto his chest.

Isobel waited a few moments then said, "I don't even know how much I can tell you and I'm begging you not to discuss it with anyone."

Aaron looked up. "I'm a hairdresser. I hear all manner of things and I never tell."

Isobel allowed a small smile. "Fair enough." Taking a deep breath, she said, "Anne was murdered."

Aaron inhaled sharply. *"Oh my God!"*

Isobel waited and then said, "Something you said to me really helped start the process of catching the person who did it. You told me about the lady whose hair you did who looked the image of Anne. That's how we figured out what was happening. She was posing as Anne. It may not seem like a lot but I hope it's some consolation."

Isobel found tears in her eyes as she spoke. Aaron grasped her hand as she sobbed.

Eventually she continued, "Her husband did it and he nearly got away with it."

Aaron's eyes welled up. *"Oh My God!* She was such a lovely lady. I can't believe it.

Isobel wondered if this was why she'd come here – to cry her heart out about what had happened and this was the only place she felt that she could. Maybe Aaron was a confessor, a lay one.

"I can't believe that he murdered her. Why would he do that?"

"Anne was going to leave him."

Aaron bowed his head and they sat there in silence.

After some time he said, "Thanks for coming to tell me. I do appreciate that."

Isobel nodded and said, "I'll tell Claire, Anne's sister, about you, how good you were to Anne and how much you helped in figuring things out."

"Thank you. Maybe she can let us know about any arrangements. I would like to go to the funeral and so would Tanya and probably Sharon from Ladies Made."

There was nothing more to say.

By the time she was approaching Grace's house, Isobel could see Patricia waiting for her at the gate. Patricia took the bag which had been getting increasingly heavy for her and they went up the drive. As she passed, Isobel couldn't help reaching out and touching Grace's little silver car that had served them so well.

When the door opened Grace stepped out and hugged Isobel. They had seen so little of each other since that intense day they'd shared.

There wasn't time for any discussion before a young voice said, "Who is it, Grace?"

Looking past Grace, Isobel saw, for the first time, Tommy. Somehow in her mind she had imagined he would look like his father but the opposite was true. He was all his mother. He had her fair hair, blue eyes and that beautiful bone structure. Age and puberty would modify it, but bone structure and colouring like that was timeless.

"Who are you?" he asked.

Isobel stepped out from behind Grace and said, "I'm Isobel and this is Patricia."

"You're the ladies who were finding my mum."

Isobel, unsure of what approach to take, followed Tommy's lead. "Yes, that's right."

Tommy cut to the heart of the matter, as only children can. "I knew it wasn't right that my mum wouldn't see me. She would never do that, no matter what happened."

Isobel thought her heart was going to shatter in her chest and she prayed for the strength to not just bawl her eyes out. Thank God for Aaron and the relief talking to him had given her.

She said, "No, you're right. Your mum loved you so much. She would always have wanted to see you."

Tommy, obviously coming to terms with many different things, said, "Auntie Claire says that I can come and live with her."

"How does that sound?"

"OK." He didn't say anything more.

All of this was going to take time.

Claire waved them in, and Grace made tea. They all sat around in the kitchen.

Patricia and Tommy started talking about Chelsea football.

Under cover of this Isobel said to Claire, "I bought a lantern." She gestured towards the bag in the corner. "I was going to light a candle and put it next door in the garden for Anne. What do you think?"

Claire looked at her and then at Tommy. "I would like that." Then she said, "Give me a minute."

She went over to Grace, who was watching everyone peacefully, and spoke quietly to her. Grace nodded. Gesturing to Isobel, Claire lifted the bag and they went outside. Isobel took the candles and matches from her handbag.

Once again she placed the garden chair over by the wall.

Isobel hopped up first and called back to Claire, "Forensics seem to have finished! They've left some of the garden taped off but we can put the lantern outside the cordon."

Claire nodded. First Isobel and then Claire clambered over the wall.

Taking the lantern from its bag, Isobel opened it and placed the candles inside. They positioned it outside but close to the police tape and then Isobel handed Claire the matches. Kneeling down, Claire paused a moment and then lit the candles. Closing the door of the lantern they stood back side by side and slipped their arms around each other. In mute agreement they said their own prayers or promises and then, turning, they climbed back over the wall. The others had barely noticed they were gone.

Shortly after, Patricia and Isobel said their goodbyes. As they left, Isobel texted Adam to say they were leaving Wimbledon.

Isobel knew she was saying goodbye to what had happened over the last week and a half. It was as if all of that had taken over her life, her mind, her emotions, even her dreams and now she was winning herself back before she went home. This promise to Thomas Banks Senior was one of the last she needed to keep.

Adam was sitting in the car near Thomas's house and he alighted as he saw them approach. They said very little. It was a very sombre party that advanced to deliver this news.

Thomas Banks Senior, when he opened the door, also said very little and they followed him in.

Once again Isobel made the tea while the others talked in a desultory way.

When they were all seated it was Thomas who spoke first.

"You found out what happened?"

Isobel was grateful for his direct approach.

"Yes, we did. The three of us have investigated and it was Matt Cooper who ran your son down, deliberately." She hoped she was doing the right thing.

"So, it wasn't an accident."

"No."

They waited, not sure what this knowledge would do to this man.

"I'm glad I know now. Maybe I've always known in my heart that it wasn't an accident. I'm sad, though, that it has turned out to be someone Thomas thought was a friend. I never liked Matt Cooper. I always thought there was something off about him. I was always trying to get Thomas to leave him behind, stick with his other friends. He argued with me a lot about it. He said that everyone deserved a chance." He stopped, swallowing hard, then finished, "That chance he gave cost him his life."

Isobel bit her lip.

Thomas continued, "I'm glad I know. At least I've found the truth for my boy."

Patricia said, "Matt Cooper did other bad things. Talking to you that day helped us find out about other people he hurt. We're so sorry about your son."

Adam added, "Matt has been arrested and charged with the death of your son and a number of other deaths."

Thomas looked up. "Yes, one of the neighbours told me there were lots of police cars outside one of the houses. Matt Cooper used to live there."

Adam said, "That's right. Mrs Joan Cooper's body was found in the garden."

"He killed his mother?"

"Yes."

Thomas was thoughtful. "Why did he kill my son?"

Isobel said, "Because he wanted to take the job that Thomas had got. When your son died he took his name and presented himself for the new job."

"He was always jealous of our Thomas. I always thought so anyway."

Adam said, "Mr Banks, Matt Cooper has fooled a lot of people for a very long time. Your son's only mistake was that he was too kind."

Thomas thought about that and nodded. "I'm glad you told me," he said again. "He mattered to me and I can see that my son mattered to you. Thank you."

They rose to leave, and Thomas struggled to his feet to say goodbye.

Isobel and Patricia hugged him, Adam shook his hand and they left.

Outside Adam said, "I'll call back and check on him again. I'll keep him informed about how the case goes and I can answer any further questions."

Isobel said, "Thanks, Adam."

Patricia meanwhile was on her phone.

Isobel said to Adam, "It's probably Peter."

Patricia cut in. "It is. Everyone is going around to his place."

Isobel laughed. "Who is everyone?"

Patricia grinned. "Oh Simon, Jeff, Jason, Malcolm, Rajesh. I think your friend Tracy is coming too and also Julia and Yvonne. We're going to order in some Indian food and have a few glasses of wine. Peter wants us all there like when we had our meetings."

Isobel laughed. "At Headquarters."

Patricia giggled. "Exactly. We're all going to Headquarters to celebrate the end, and a successful end at that, of a very difficult case. You must come too, Adam."

"I thought we celebrated last night. "

"This is the A team who were involved right at the start," said Patricia severely. "You really need to hear how little we had to go on."

Isobel laughed. "You do!"

"All right then," Adam said. "I suppose I'm giving you a lift."

Patricia and Isobel said in unison, "Yes."

THE END

Now that you're hooked,
why not try

BROKEN
SILENCE

Here's a sneak preview of
Chapter 1

BROKEN SILENCE
Chapter 1

Tuesday 18th June

Isobel McKenzie pulled up behind the row of parked cars. She could feel her stomach somersaulting and her heart fluttering in her chest. Was joining everyone for a walk really a good idea? She laid her head on her arms on the steering wheel and took a deep breath, held it and then exhaled for as long as she could. She pulled down the visor and looked in the mirror concealed there. Her wideset hazel eyes looked back at her, the frown between them testament to her anxiety. She rubbed her fingers through her short dark hair, rearranging the ash bit at the front. Despite the worries on her mind, she looked OK. Taking another deep breath, she cracked the door open. Ahead, she could hear the other women arriving and greeting each other, chattering about holidays and weather.

Isobel took another deep breath. She knew the walk would help calm her mind and burn off some of her stress. Meeting everyone, the normalcy of it, the friendship, would also help. One last deep breath and she felt ready. She climbed out of the car, lifted out her Nordic walking poles and moved forward to be absorbed into the chattering women.

The women were getting ready to leave on the four-and-a-half-kilometre walk along the banks of the River Shannon. She loved this walk on the outskirts of Limerick City. With the Shannon on one side and fields on the other, it felt like you were miles away in the heart of nature. The waterway was well populated, with ducks and swans shepherding their young up and down the river, and the hedgerows were abundantly leafy and fecund with birds and insects. Today the sky was blue with fluffy white clouds and, despite the fact that it was only ten thirty in the morning, it was warm. Isobel felt her heart lift.

The group set off on the walk, Isobel's poles marking each step.

Since everyone walked at different speeds, generally over the journey Isobel spent some time with a number of different women.

Today Marion settled into step beside her.

"I've missed you for a few weeks, Isobel – is everything alright?"

Isobel swallowed. She was struggling to give credence to her worries, never mind verbalise them to anyone else. She kept her head down as if concentrating on the synchronising of her feet and sticks. "Yes, I was in London meeting some friends and ended up staying longer than I initially planned." She flashed a quick smile and then returned her gaze to the path.

A cacophony of barks drew Isobel's attention. A woman was straining to draw her Golden Labrador away from a field gate on the right as he protested loudly.

Marion called out as they approached her. "Goodness, he's intent on getting into that field, isn't he?"

The woman grimaced. "I know. He's usually so well behaved."

The volley of barks increased as a terrier joined the choir.

Isobel kept her head down and her pace up. Marion hesitated but also continued walking.

As she swung her poles, Isobel could feel her tension unfurling. She inhaled deeply, her shoulders relaxed and her stride lengthened. Thank God for nature, movement and affable company.

Half an hour later, having looped over the river and back, Isobel and Marion were on the home straight, back to their starting point. Conversation between them had lapsed as they both kept up their speed. Isobel looked from side to side as she walked. The swans and ducks were still giving lessons, the hedgerow was alive with bees and birds chattered loudly.

As they neared a gateway, the strident sound of crows was much worse than usual. As they passed the gate, Isobel glanced in. In the overgrown grass she could see a group of crows flying up and descending again.

Marion said, "God, those crows are so noisy."

Isobel missed a beat in her walking and slowed considerably.

"Are you OK?" Marion slowed too, looking back in concern.

Isobel stopped. Marion took a few more steps and then halted and swung around.

Isobel's brain was firing: dogs barking, crows in the field, there was something wrong.

"Marion, will you wait here for me? I need to check something."

Marion looked puzzled. Isobel didn't give her a chance to ask anything. She handed Marion her two walking poles and climbed over the gate. Standing in the field, she saw a trail of trampled grass. She paused, then choosing an alternative route she walked to her left along the border of the field. The grass here was undisturbed. Now level with the crows, Isobel walked through the long grass towards where they were congregated. As she neared them the cawing reached a crescendo and many birds took flight. She could feel a dread building in her chest. She knew that feeling – when in your heart you know there is something dreadfully wrong but do not want to admit it. Wasn't that why she was stressed and out walking to begin with? She swallowed and emptied her mind. Her world had shrunk to the next two steps.

Isobel saw bright orange through the grass. She inhaled sharply and stepped slowly and deliberately. As her view shifted she could see two orange trainers. Her gaze shifted. Above that there was lightly tanned skin. She swallowed. Her gaze took in black rucked material then some white. The black was leggings, the white was underwear. Then, more tanned skin and knees. She took a deep breath, her hand coming to her mouth. Her gaze moved higher. A woman's naked torso, her top cut open, her arms still in the sleeves.

Isobel's breath caught. Her eyes moved on. The woman's neck, with red and purple marks. Glancing up to the face, she saw it masklike with damage that the crows had added. Spread out around it was blonde hair.

Isobel gasped. She knew the woman was dead. She wanted to step forward and cover her but a voice, informed by years of watching *CSI*, stopped her. It was too late – there was nothing she could do. She inhaled again through her fingers. She needed to get the gardaí but she had to move first. Her body felt frozen. This couldn't be happening. She rubbed her hands over her face, closing her eyes for a moment. When she opened them the scene was the same. She took a shaky breath. Her mind wanted to divorce from this reality, but it was real. She took another deep breath and straightened.

Turning, she retraced her route across the field.

"Marion, we need the gardaí."

"What's happened?"

"There's a body in the field."

Marion's eyes opened wide and she went pale.

"I know. It's hard to believe but it's true." Isobel injected some force into her voice. "There's a body in the field and we need to get the gardaí. Have you got your phone on you?"

There was no answer. Marion's eyes were locked on Isobel's and they were filled with rising panic. Somehow the shock and panic there made Isobel take charge of herself and the situation.

"*Marion, listen to me.*"

Marion shook her head.

Isobel heard another voice.

"Did you get caught short, Isobel?" Ann laughed gaily. Then seeing Marion's face, she said, "Is everything OK?"

Isobel shook her head. "No. It's not. There's a dead body in that field."

Ann gasped.

Isobel voice was clipped and forceful. "Ann, we need to call the gardaí. Can you ring them and tell them we have found a body?"

Ann nodded. She pulled her phone out of her waist pack.

Isobel said, "You'd better go to the start of the walk

and meet them. You can show them where to come when they arrive. I'll stay with the … with the body."

"Good idea." Ann nodded, then speaking into the phone ran down the path.

Isobel took a steadying breath. So far so good. What next?

"Marion," she said.

Marion's head snapped up.

"I need to go back to where the body is," Isobel said. "Can you stay here and make sure no one comes into this field except the gardaí?" She softened her voice. "Can you do that?"

Marion nodded. "Yes, yes, of course."

"Don't touch the gate or anything else."

Marion nodded again.

Isobel made her way back across the field, using the path she had already forged. Some crows had returned in her absence and she shouted and cleared them off. Her mind circled to one fact. A group of crows was called a murder of crows. Well, she was going to keep them away from this woman. She stood close to the body, in vigil. She thought of the woman and her family and said a prayer.

AVAILABLE ON AMAZON